FIFTH AVENUE
FLING

A Grumpy Boss Romantic Comedy

Rosa Lucas

ISBN-13: 9781739351311

The following story contains mature themes, strong language and explicit scenes, and is intended for mature readers.

Fifth Avenue Fling is a New York-based story, so its narrative uses American English in terms of grammar and spelling. However, Clodagh's dialogue and thoughts are heavily influenced by her Irish upbringing.

Photographer: Wander Aguiar
Ebook cover by Kari @ Kari March Designs
Paperback cover by Stacey @ ChampageBookDesign
Content edit by Heather Leigh @Heatherleighediting
Copy edit by Jenny Sims @ Editing4Indies
Proofreaders: Britt Tayler and Sarah Baker @ The Word Emporium

www.rosalucasauthor.com

ONE

Clodagh

KLO-Da. The *'gh'* is silent. Like Yoda with a *cl*.

New York, home to Broadway, bagels, and billionaires. Lots of billionaires. Everyone's on their A game here. Who wouldn't want a slice of that Big Apple pie?

I'm here for mine.

Back in my Irish seaside village, I dreamed of this slice. I knew what to expect.

Yoga in Central Park at dawn.

Breakfast at Magnolia Bakery.

Cocktails at the top of the Rockefeller Center.

Waking up in a penthouse suite at The Plaza hotel with a brooding six-foot-something gazillionaire's head between my legs who *insists* I soak in his hot tub, but only after he delivers multiple five-star orgasms.

"Clodagh."

"What?" I jerk my head up from wiping Guinness-marinated crisps off the hardwood bar top to see my best friend Orla's smug smile.

She stops sweeping for a moment. "It's your turn to do the men's."

Gah. "Yeah, yeah, I know," I bark.

Here's another fact about New York—it's also home to hundreds of Irish bars. You're never more than a block away from one. Irish bars with men who operate their dicks like heavy-duty fire hoses after a few pints.

I eyeball the three lads propped on stools along the bar. Their clothes are covered in dust from their construction jobs because the closest thing the pub has to a dress code is *no guns*.

Liam, Declan, and Aidan—regulars at The Auld Dog, the small Queens-based Irish bar Orla and I have worked in for three months. Nice guys in their late twenties. They smile back shamelessly. They're on their third pint each, and I know they've left a war zone for me to clean. They know it, and I know it.

Every evening, they sit on the same barstools. Never changing stools. Never changing drinks. Never changing Irish bars.

What's the point of moving to New York to spend every night in the same Irish bar, with the same Irish people, drinking the same Irish drinks?

I don't get it. I've wanted to live in New York for as long as I can remember.

Not on the outskirts, either. Right bang in the heart of the Big Apple, Manhattan, strutting around the streets in Manolo Blahniks and flashing a well-shaved leg to hail down a yellow cab.

In reality, since Orla and I moved to Queens from Ireland a few months ago, I've spent 95 percent of my time working at Orla's Uncle Sean's pub, arguing with Orla about whose turn it is to change the barrel or fumigate the men's toilets. I wear sports shoes since Manolos are beyond my budget, and even if I could afford them, I'd be waddling like a penguin.

But that 5 percent, when I see a glimpse of glitzy New York, the life I imagined back in Ireland?

Priceless.

Like the glitzy Manhattanite who has just walked into the bar. The guy looks in his mid-fifties, at a guess, and is wearing an expensive blue suit. People only visit the pub in suits if they've been to a funeral. An authentic, no-frills Irish experience is what Sean sells.

He's the kind of man Mam would lose her shit over. Granny Deirdre, too. Do handlebar mustaches and comb-overs become a turn-on at a certain age? Call me superficial, but those aren't things I want between my legs.

I see the exact moment the mild stench of stale beer and old-man smell wafts up his nostrils.

Orla stops sweeping, gawks at the newcomer in the doorway, then turns to me with wide eyes.

I roll my eyes as she hurries behind the bar to join me. While the guy screams tips, she couldn't have been any more obvious if she jumped onto the counter and did a victory dance.

He scans the pub, taking in the Irish football jerseys lining the walls, the flags, and the road signs telling you how many miles you are from Ireland. All part of Uncle Sean's interior design strategy to fill every inch of the pub with reminders of home.

He approaches the bar, making sure his sleeves don't brush the countertop.

I don my most professional smile. One wasted on Liam, Declan, and Aidan. "Hi, sir. How can I help?"

"What type of wine do you have?"

"Red,"—I pause—"or white."

He thinks I'm joking.

"We only have one type of each. The house red or white. It's not really a wine drinker's bar," I elaborate a tad defensively. I side-eye Orla for support. What does the guy expect? "Sorry."

"We have an extensive range of stouts and the best Guinness in New York," Orla pipes up with wildly unfounded claims. The small number of beer taps is the giveaway.

Mr. Suit exhales loudly, blowing air out his plump cheeks. "I'll have a... Guinness, please."

"Coming right up!"

I lift a pint glass from the shelf and tilt it to the pump as I sneak a glance at Mr. Suit. What's his deal? He must be having a bad day if he needs a drink so bad that he can't wait to get over the bridge to Manhattan and its selection of more appealing wines.

Not that bars in Queens don't stock good wine, but wine connoisseurs aren't Uncle Sean's target market. The Auld Dog sells stout to guys watching Gaelic football and Liverpool FC. You only drink The

Auld Dog's wine if you're drinking to forget.

I talk about Sean like he's my uncle because Orla and I have been friends since we were in nappies. Or *diapers,* as I'm used to saying now. After nearly three months in New York, I think I'm good at American lingo.

"Bad day?" I ask, sneaking another glance at him as I pull the tap handle forward.

He grunts in response.

I smile. I understand the bartender's code. *Don't fucking talk to me.*

No one speaks again as we wait for the Guinness to settle.

I lift the glass under the spout to fill the head to the rim, then place the pint in front of him. "There you are, sir. Served like in Dublin." It's not. I'm a mediocre bartender.

"Thanks." I'm rewarded with a dry smile as he passes over a platinum credit card *etched* with his name.

With his Guinness in his hand, Mr. Suit takes one look at the guys on the stools and walks to an empty table beside the window.

Orla pouts, disappointed. Anyone sitting at the bar is fair game, but if you interrupt someone trying to have a quiet pint alone, you're an ass.

"What do you think he's doing here?" she murmurs.

My gaze flickers back to Mr. Suit. One leg is crossed over the other, ankle over knee. His dark brows pull together as he scowls down at his phone resting on his thigh.

"Visiting relatives in Queens?" I whisper.

Orla hums, unconvinced. "Maybe he has a mistress in Queens."

I smirk. "Maybe he's *looking* for a mistress in Queens."

Liam clears his throat. "Another one, Clodagh. When you're ready." He uses an unnecessarily husky tone. His gaze catches mine, and he stares back unblinking.

This weird tension is all because I saw Liam's penis a few weeks after I moved to New York. About to ovulate, I was feeling horny, and it seemed like a good idea at the time. Now whenever I look at Liam, I see that wild glint in his eye that tells me he wants to wife me and make ten babies. And even though he vaguely resembles the new Superman when I squint, I know it'll mean a lifetime of missionary position.

Just no.

"Coming right up," I say, breaking Liam's heady gaze. I grab a glass and pull the pale ale pump, enjoying the quiet. In an hour, the pub will be packed.

"Glad to see you're staying," he says gruffly. Liam's from Belfast, so his accent is more guttural than mine. It made for the best sex grunts.

Panic rises in my chest as my heart does a little jig.

Am I staying?

Yesterday, my world came crashing down. ÉireAuPair4U told me that the Kennedys, a second-generation Irish family, won't need me after all. I was going to nanny their ten-year-old daughter to help bring her closer to her Irish heritage.

It turns out the Polish au pair agency was cheaper, and that's more important than their roots. The Kennedys were my ticket to staying in the States.

Luck of the Irish, my fat arse.

"I have a flight booked back to Belfast next week," I say mournfully.

Liam shifts in his barstool, making an abrasive screech with the legs. He looks as devastated as I feel.

Because in seven days, my American dream ends. I'll have overstayed my welcome.

Orla and I entered the States a few months back, intending to stay. I'm on a tourist visa, which bought me ninety days, and my egg timer has run out. We cheekily took cash-in-hand jobs in the pub to keep us afloat.

The au pair position was my only possibility of getting a visa to stay legally in New York.

He scowls at me. "Ack, sure, we're all in the same boat here. Ain't none of us legal. You'll be alright. You don't need to leave."

I don't want to be like you, Liam.

"Fuck's sake, Sean will give you a wee job here for as long as you need it," Aidan, also from Belfast, chimes in, looking at me like I'm being unreasonable. "And you have that wee stretching class you teach on Saturdays. Sure, what else do ye need?"

Belfast-ers use *wee* to refer to anything and

everything, regardless of size. *"He's bought a wee boat"* could be anything from a dinghy to a superyacht.

I don't want my only option to be cleaning the men's toilets of The Auld Dog. And yes, I enjoy teaching my wee yoga class in the park on Saturdays, but that's just a hobby with a few tips thrown in.

Yoga with Clodagh. Very clever, if I say so myself since it rhymes. Most people outside of Ireland try to pronounce the silent gh, though, so it's a marketing bust.

If I'm illegal, that's what I'll be restricted to.

But... I can't leave.

I *won't.*

I stare at the pretzel crumbs Aidan has all over his T-shirt and take a deep breath. Then I plaster a smile on my face. Smiling tricks your brain into feeling positive. "It's fine. I read an article that Ireland will be the best place to live in 2030 because of global warming."

"Stop that shitty chat. You're back on the waiting list for the au pair agency," Orla pipes up. "They'll sort you out with a job."

Orla is burying her head in the sand. If I'm honest, I am too. Immigration will have to take me to the airport in a straitjacket because I refuse to leave American soil.

Orla has gold-dust genes. Even though she grew up beside me in Ireland, she was made by *American* sperm, allowing her to stay in the States. Never in my life have I hated my deadbeat, absentee, Irish-born father so much.

"Unlikely." I sigh, refilling the lads' pretzel bowl. "They won't find another family in time. I've told them I'd nanny Satan's spawn for minimum wage if it means getting a job in the next seven days."

I am *fucked*, for want of a better word. I'm calling the agency so much that they'll get a restraining order against me. But it's my only chance of getting sponsored to stay.

"You'll be *grand*, Clodagh," Declan slurs, grinning at me. "You'll be grand. No need to worry."

Saying I'm grand is as useless as the *gh* in Clodagh. An overused filler word in Ireland. If I'm not on that flight on Monday, I'll be at risk of deportation and a life of hiding from immigration.

That's not *grand* in any way.

These guys don't get it. They've been illegal for years and have never been caught. But they're also in their own New York prison. It's one life or the other. Ireland or the States. If they ever board a flight home, it's game over.

Which makes sense why all they do is talk about what's happening in Ireland.

I don't want the American Dream that way.

"If you're that worried, do what everyone else who wants to be legal does," Declan says, stuffing pretzels into his mouth while he talks. "Find somebody to marry you. Good-looking girl like you should have no bother."

Declan's grin widens into something more sinister as he swivels one-eighty in his stool.

Mr. Suit catches his gaze and lifts a brow.

I stiffen. *No, Declan.* Don't play this game.

"Are ye looking for a nice young Irish wife?" Declan calls over to him loudly. "She's very bendy, so she is—"

"Declan!" I yank on his arm as Liam growls at him to quieten down.

Christ on a bike.

My gaze locks with Mr. Suit, and my cheeks heat. "Ignore him."

He looks pissed off at the attention. "If I were looking for a wife, this bar is the last place in New York I'd search." Rude. Texan accent or somewhere down South. Yup, Mam would have kittens.

"It's okay." I smile thinly, internally reeling. I wouldn't marry you either, buddy. "I don't want a visa that badly."

Mr. Suit returns a trace of a smile before focusing back on his phone.

"Let's call marrying a random guy plan C," Orla says with forced cheeriness. "We'll find another option."

Swallowing back the lump in my throat, I try not to let my eyes well up. It'll only set Orla off. I'm out of options. All my eggs were in the ÉireAuPair4U basket.

Brainstorming with Orla brought up no other viable solutions other than the following.

A) Claim a dead American guy was my father.

B) Take a dead person's identity.

Or C) get married to an American, obviously.

Ideally, not an old guy with a comb-over.

"Drink The Auld Dog's bad wine for the next seven days to forget I'm leaving," I say, trying to make light of my sticky situation.

"No!" she wails. "I hate that plan. The guys are right. You can stay here. Loads of people are illegal."

I give a tired sigh, averting my eyes from Orla. Annoyed from going around in circles with the same conversation. Staying illegally means I'd always be looking over my shoulder. And Nan is pushing eighty, even though she says she's forty-two. I couldn't live with myself if I couldn't go back... if I lost her.

"Another pint of Guinness, please." The dry voice from the corner catches me off guard.

"Right away, sir." I pull Mr. Suit's second Guinness as Orla comes out from behind the bar to move chairs around the tables. When there aren't many customers, she's like a bored child.

I take it over to him and set it down.

"Oh my God," Orla murmurs. "Clodagh!"

She kneels on the next seat over with her nose squashed against the window. "The FBI's outside!"

"The *FBI*?" Coming behind her, I look over her shoulder, my eyes adjusting to the sunlight streaming through the window.

Sure enough, an expensive car with tinted windows is parked outside. Two men wearing suits and earpieces lean against the car.

What does immigration look like? Do they do pub raids? Technically, I'm not supposed to be working on my holiday visa.

"Maybe Mafia!" Orla says excitedly.

"They're drivers," a low voice deadpans. "My drivers."

My gaze shoots back to the other table. Mr. Suit's lips curl in a hint of amusement.

"Oh." Why does someone need two drivers? In case one gets shot? "Uh, what is it that you do?"

"I work for Killian and Connor Quinn."

I stare back, confused.

One brow rises in amusement at my ignorance. "The Quinn brothers. They own the largest hotel chain in the States. The Quinn & Wolfe Hotel Group."

Oh. I nod, catching Orla's gaze. There's more chance of us vacationing on Mars than in one of those hotels. I used the hotel bathroom once in Times Square. The public bathrooms were so decadent I felt like I was in a spa.

"Perhaps you've been to one of their casinos," he adds.

"Gambling's not really my thing."

His brow arches again, but this time with something akin to interest. "Where are you from?"

"Ireland," Orla and I say simultaneously.

"Donegal," I elaborate. "The rainy bit on the northwest coast."

"And how long have you been in New York?" he asks.

"Nearly three months."

"Me too!" Orla adds beside me.

Now he's scanning me from top to bottom. "I

gather you're working illegally on a tourist visa."

"N-No," I stutter, folding my arms across my chest. "That was a joke."

"Relax. I don't care."

I release a breathy laugh. The guy heard us talking, so there's no point denying it.

"Do you have a boyfriend?"

Stiffening, I narrow my eyes at him. "I'm not looking for an American husband just to get a visa."

Or *am* I?

His lips flatten into a thin line. "I'm not interested in you, *sweetheart*." He pauses, giving me another once-over. "I might have a job offer for you. Chloe, is it?" He gestures to the chair in front of him. "I'm Marcus. Take a seat."

TWO

Clodagh

"Nice to meet you, Marcus." I take his extended hand, eyeing him guardedly, and plop my bum down on the seat opposite him. "*Cloh-dah.* Like Yoda with a cl." If only I had a dollar for every time I said it. "A job? What type of job?"

He reclines in his chair, smoothing out his tie before aiming a leisurely smile in my direction. "Good to meet you, Clodagh. Tell me a little about yourself."

My jaw hardens. I want him to cut to the chase. I sure as hell don't want to give out personal information, but if there's a sliver of a chance that he might have a job offer... I need to know more.

I glance over at the guys and Orla, who is now back behind the bar, pretending not to listen. Liam glares at me, face like thunder.

I turn my attention back to Mr. Suit. Marcus.

Well, Marcus, I'm nearly twenty-five and can list a failed business, a criminal record, and zero penetrative sex orgasms on my résumé.

"Uh, there's not that much to know." I never was

good at interviews, especially ones I didn't sign up for. "I'm working in the bar until I find my feet in New York. I'm actually a trained carpenter back home. I worked for a furniture store before moving to New York."

His brows lift in surprise. "Carpenter, huh? I would never have guessed."

I give him a strained smile. I may not be a doctor or a lawyer or have a job that requires a graduation cap, but I'm proud of my trade. And I have the best builder's bum. Or plumber's crack, as the Americans say. "No one's going to sponsor me to make furniture. You have enough carpenters in the country."

"But I overheard you talking about an au pair position here."

"That's right." I nod. "American families often get au pairs from Europe, particularly if the family have some European background. It's a way to get sponsored." I exhale a weary sigh. "I can't just pick any job I want here."

"You must be good with kids if you're applying to be an au pair?"

"I think so." I shrug. Not that the agency did much due diligence. "I have three younger brothers, and they were a handful growing up. My mum was always working, and my dad skipped town, so I helped raise them."

He likes this answer. "Can you cook?"

"I'm okay. I'm no Michelin-star chef, but I can boil an egg."

He doesn't like that answer as much.

"Do you take drugs?"

My eyes narrow. "No."

"How much do you drink a week?"

A huff escapes me. Is this guy fucking with me? "Enough with the questions. What's the job?"

My new friend Marcus smiles. "My employer needs a domestic assistant with some nannying duties thrown in."

My brows squish together. "What does that entail?"

"Looking after his daughter when he's not there. Cooking. Running errands. Cleaning. Doing his laundry. It's a temporary position for the next few months that we need to fill urgently."

That's got fuck all to do with making furniture. "Like a maid?" I ask. "A nanny maid?"

He gives a nonchalant shrug. "In a way."

I shake my head at him dubiously. "What makes you think I'm a good fit for this? You don't know anything about my experience."

His smile widens, undaunted by my resistance. "Because you'll take the job seriously. I have a feeling about you."

Translation: *I overheard that you're desperate. You'll do anything to stay in the country.*

I let out a skeptical hum.

"Besides, he has a soft spot for the Irish. He's Irish-American." He looks at me thoughtfully for a moment. "In fact, that might be his *only* soft spot."

Gee, great.

He glances at the lads. "And you seem to be able to keep people in line."

"Everything okay, Clodagh?" Liam calls gruffly from the bar.

"Yeah, Liam." I tilt my head around to appease him with a nod.

When I turn back, Marcus is taking out a small notepad from his jacket. He scribbles something on the pad and slides it toward me on the table.

I stare at the paper. Mild panic rises in me, as it always does when I have to read something under pressure. The joys of dyslexia. "What's this?"

"The salary per month."

My breath hitches as I do a double take. "Is the dot in the wrong place?"

He chuckles and takes a sip of his Guinness. "It's a live-in position in Manhattan, with unsocial hours. My employer wants to compensate for that."

"Absolutely not." I slide the paper back to him in disgust. "I'm not *servicing* some rich, old perv."

"You're right to be apprehensive, I understand. But there's nothing inappropriate about the position. You'll be a nanny..." He pauses. "An assistant in his house and nothing more."

"A naked nanny," I scoff. Visions of me cradling a man in diapers while he suckles my breasts flood my mind.

He fights a smile and repeats my words back to me. "Absolutely not. You're a cynical one, I see."

I narrow my eyes at him, unconvinced. Maybe his rich employer has an Irish fetish. My duties will include murmuring *'top o' the mornin' to ya'* as I rock some old fella to sleep.

My suited fairy godfather Marcus leans in, his hands interlocked on the table. "If you take this opportunity,"—he smirks at me—"and you'd be a fool not to, given your circumstances, you'd be working for the Quinn & Wolfe Group. You can ask the HR team any questions you need to feel reassured. Just be ready to go into the office to sign the contract and fill in the visa forms."

"Visa?" I repeat breathlessly. My new friend is playing a cruel joke on me.

"Yes, Clodagh," he says, tilting his head down to write something else on his pad. He knows he's got me, hook, line, and sinker. "HR will contact you to arrange a time tomorrow."

With my jaw hanging open, I watch him scribble down a phone number.

My brow furrows deeper as my heart races.

I so, so, *so* want to believe this story but...

"Let me get this straight," I say slowly. "You're telling me that you're willing to give a random barmaid in Queens a visa, accommodation in Manhattan, and an obscene amount of money to work as a fancy nanny maid for your rich boss?" I pause, searching his face. "All because you have a *feeling* about me?"

This earns me a chuckle. He relaxes back in his chair again. "It's not as glamorous as it sounds. My employer is paying someone to be at his beck and call in his home. Believe me, it's a tough job.

I need someone who can start right away and has no commitments." He gives me what I can only call a wolfish smile. "Frankly, I know you're desperate enough that you'll try to stick it out."

I swallow hard. "Why is it urgent now? What happened to the last nanny maid? Did he murder them?"

Another chuckle. "You're cute. He might like you. His full-time domestic assistant had to go out of state to look after her daughter. It was unexpected, and he needs a fill-in pronto. There were a few other nannies after, but..."

"But?" I raise my voice. They're in the attic. Dead.

He waves his hand as if the information is irrelevant.

Hmm.

I'm living in my own damn fairy tale. Except...

"My visa runs out in *seven days*." I blow out through my cheeks. "Even if this is legit, it's too late."

He dismisses that with another wave. "We'll expedite your visa."

My pulse spikes. Money skips the queue. Just as easy as that.

"We'll need to vet you, of course. Medical examinations, etc."

"Vet me?" I try to keep my expression neutral. "Vetting... like a criminal record check?"

"Yes." He scans my face. "Does that concern you?"

Fuck.

"Of course not."

Whether he believes me or not, he moves on,

tapping his finger against the notepad. "Write down your full name, email, and telephone number. Be ready to go to our headquarters tomorrow."

I nod slowly, my brain ticking over, searching for danger. He's not asking for my address. "Who's the employer?"

His lips twitch for reasons unknown to me. "Killian Quinn."

The dude who owns the hotels.

I take out my phone and do a search as Marcus watches me.

Killian Quinn is top of the results.

Oh.

The guy isn't in his eighties. He must be in his thirties and, unless the photos are filtered, cream-your-pants gorgeous. Dark hair. Arctic-blue eyes. Perhaps I would allow him to suckle on my breast.

But Ted Bundy, the serial killer, was an attractive guy, too. And I can't find a single picture of Killian Quinn smiling. It only takes one wrong decision to end up in an attic.

"Is it him, his wife, and his daughter?" I ask.

"No, he's a single father. Teagan's mom died when she was only two. She's twelve now, going on thirteen."

A new teenager. That makes things interesting. Teenagers are terrifying people.

No mother. That's sad. I wonder whether it was always just her and her father.

"It's an opportunity." Marcus breaks my thoughts. "Take it or leave it, Clodagh."

Take it or leave the country, more like.

But if they vet me, I'll fail, so what do I have to lose?

Right now, it's the only option I have.

Marcus knows it too, judging by the smirk on his face. He taps his fingers against the numbers on the pad.

This must be how people end up working for the Irish Mafia.

THREE

Clodagh

I can't believe I paid forty dollars to go up the Empire State Building. Now I'm staring straight at it from the fiftieth floor of Quinn & Wolfe headquarters while they complete my vetting.

I remember looking over at this building from the viewing platform. With its two spiked towers like horns, it looked more evil than the other skyscrapers. I think I'm in the right horn.

After my weird encounter with fairy godfather Marcus, I spent all last night researching Killian Quinn online.

At thirty-six, he's one of the wealthiest men in the United States. Self-made, too—the sexiest kind of money. He owns a chain of hotels and casinos across America with his brother and another business partner, ranging from upmarket hostels to luxurious seven-star hotels.

Yes.

Seven.

Doesn't that mean he wants a seven-star nanny

maid? My idea of cleaning is to move things to less obvious places.

Which is why the whole scenario stinks of something fishy. I'm likely about to be flogged on some billionaire black market. Why else would they need so many samples of body parts and fluids?

Blood. Hair. Pee. I half expected them to ask for a poo sample.

After much anxiety, I handed it all over, along with a signed twenty-page NDA.

I filled out a questionnaire so detailed I didn't know some of the answers about myself.

Blood type? I don't know my blood type.

Feeling self-conscious, I flick at invisible specks on my skirt. The HR lady left me in the waiting area for thirty minutes this time.

If buildings had personalities, this one would be a sociopath—cold and sterile, with monochrome walls and sharp edges. Negative energy swirls in the air every time someone strides by, talking into their wireless earbuds.

Like building, like owner.

"Clodagh." The HR lady pops her head out of the door and beckons me to follow. "One more form and you're free to go."

My heart thuds. Talking to the beautiful HR lady makes me nervous. Compared to her, I feel like a country mouse. I love New York, but sometimes it's so overwhelming.

I shuffle into the room and settle back in the same seat I've been in and out of all day.

Ugly words in a big black font stare up at me, and my stomach drops out of my ass and down all fifty floors.

Criminal record check

Looks like I'm getting on that flight back to Belfast.

***

"Let's get married!" Orla beams, taking a large gulp of her Manhattan. Since I'm leaving New York in six days, four hours and—whatever, I'm too tipsy to figure out the rest—I figured Manhattans would be a good choice.

Orla came to town from Queens to help me drown my sorrows. Now I'm treating us to expensive cocktails near Quinn's headquarters at three o'clock on a Thursday afternoon like we have money to burn. I thought it fitting to choose a Quinn Brother hotel bar.

Red velvet padding lines the walls, maybe to keep you from getting hurt if you get too drunk, like an adult playpen. Dim lights and fancy lampshades make it feel like eleven o'clock. Dangerous.

"I have an American passport, so we can get married," Orla suggests. She swings happily on her barstool as if she's figured out a solution to climate change.

"Shush." I nudge her knee. She's too loud for a bar like this.

After this drink, I'll take her home. For an Irish

woman, she's a lightweight with alcohol.

Though she has a point... marrying Orla doesn't seem so absurd anymore. We would be a married couple minus the sex, and there are plenty of those out there.

Jesus, I'm desperate.

"No." I sigh mournfully into my Manhattan, swirling the straw around the ice. "It's hardly a long-term solution. What happens when one of us meets a man?"

"They'd probably want a threesome."

The sophisticated older lady sitting a few feet away gives us a disapproving side-eye.

"I'm going to have to accept it, Orla," I murmur, staring into the V-shaped glass filled with red liquor. "I'm leaving. I tried, but let's face it..." My voice cracks. I can't cry in this fancy bar.

"No." She grabs both my hands, lifting them in the air like she's performing some ritual. "There *must* be a way. Maybe they won't find anything on your criminal record. Does it get wiped after a while?"

I give her a weak smile. "Not this soon, no. It'll still be a big dirty mark against my name."

She hums and squeezes my hands tighter. "Maybe they'll miss it?"

"They won't miss it."

"The au pair agency did."

"The agency are cowboys. They also tweaked my résumé so much I sounded like Nanny McPhee. Quinn took *blood* from me. He means business."

Her hands release mine as she sinks back into her

seat. We both go silent.

"Maybe they won't care what's on your record? You didn't go on a *murder* spree. It was just a... series of unfortunate events."

I smile to humor her. That's not how the police saw it and that's not what's on my record.

Drawing a slow breath through her nose, she places her fingertips over her eyelids. "Deep breaths. Positive thoughts. We have to have faith. One year from now, we'll be celebrating in this bar as legal citizens of New York. I'll be working for the NYPD, probably having earned a medal of honor, and you'll be a carpenter winning... Carpenter of the Year!"

She still has her eyes closed, so she can't see mine rolling. "Have you been reading *The Secret* again?"

She opens her eyes and grins. "If you *believe* it will happen, it will happen."

I exhale heavily and take a large gulp of my Manhattan, welcoming the burn on its way down. If my last hope is wishful thinking, it's a sad state of affairs.

"I'll be right back." Orla slides off her stool, causing her skirt to ride up. "Gotta go to the bathroom."

"I'll be here," I say cheerfully, swirling the last of my cocktail. "For now," I add quietly to myself.

I watch Orla walk away. My heart twinges. Soon, we won't be doing this together. We've been best friends since we were kids. We were neighbors, we went to school together, and we bunked off school together. The only time we spent apart was when she'd go on holiday to the United States to visit her relatives, and I was *so* jealous.

Now these past few months, we've living in each other's pockets, in the loft of Uncle Sean's house in Queens.

"He's *here*," the woman behind me says, interrupting my private pity party. Her excited tone makes me want to eavesdrop on their conversation. "I saw him coming out of the restrooms."

"You're kidding me," whoever is with her replies. "We have to find a way to bump into him accidentally."

I scan the bar, looking for signs of someone famous, mildly curious. Who's here? The guy in the corner looks vaguely like Al Pacino.

The woman says something in a lower voice to her friend, which is inaudible to me. Her friend laughs. I wish I could catch more of their chat.

I lean back slightly on my stool. This isn't a good plan, considering I'm a bit wobbly from the cocktails.

Bad timing.

The bartender zooms past me. I barely catch his arm as he reaches for my glass.

"Hang on!" I lunge forward and snatch it up, my fingers gripping the stem firmly. "I'm not finished."

He looks at the nearly empty glass and then at me, barely suppressing an eye roll.

I scowl in return. Waste not, want not. It's no more than a dribble, but I'm not wasting a drop.

I tilt the glass back, making sure I don't miss a

single drop, then place the empty glass in front of him.

"I've been thinking in the bathroom," Orla announces as she returns.

I wait for the grand revelation.

"We should have one more," she says, smiling at me with glazed eyes. "One more, and then we'll head home."

***

One becomes four. We drift around the hotel's ground level, surrounded by overpriced, high-end stores, in pursuit of the entrance.

Orla is going in and out of stores we have no business being in, and I wish I could put her on a leash.

It takes me a moment or two to realize what the buzzing noise is. The stolen cocktail glass clinks noisily against the toiletries from the hotel bathroom as I struggle to locate my phone under all the crap in my bag. I finally find it under the soaps and fish it out.

I press connect on the unknown number.

"Clodagh?" a deep American voice drawls down the line. "It's Marcus."

My heart goes from resting to racing. "Yes?"

"Good news," he booms. "You're good to go. You start Monday."

Abruptly, I stop still in the throngs of people, nearly dropping the phone. How much have I drunk? "I... passed the vetting?"

I look around for Orla, but she's wandered into another shop. Typical.

He chuckles softly down the line. "Weren't you expecting to?"

"Uh." I expel a strange gargle. I'm not even sure it came from my mouth.

"We'll need you to move in on Sunday." Marcus either chooses to ignore my shock or isn't fazed by it. He sounds like he's walking. "Mr. Quinn will meet you on Sunday afternoon."

"Right," I breathe, staring dazed into the window of a luxury lingerie store. I force a casual tone even though my heart does the bongo against my chest. "Send me the details. I'm delighted."

"Excellent. Don't mess this up, Clodagh. You won't be able to stay in New York if you do." The words hang in the air as an ominous warning. "Mr. Quinn's driver, Sam, will pick you up."

Something isn't right. Is it possible for the police to make mistakes? Doubtful. Is Quinn's vetting really lenient? Again, I doubt it.

My sixth sense says that something's wrong, but as Marcus ends the call, I bury that thought deep down under my delight. I can't stop the goofy grin from taking over my face.

I'm staying.

I'm staying in Manhattan.

I need to hug someone. Where the hell did Orla go? Shoppers and hotel guests mill around, but Orla is nowhere in sight.

My hands tremble as I dial her number. "Orla! Get

your ass back here."

She begins to speak, but I cut her off. "I'm staying, Orla. I'm actually staying! I passed vetting."

The screech down the line must be heard by everyone within ten meters. She says, "you're kidding," five times, and I repeat, "I'm not."

"On my way! I went to the loo when you were on your phone. I thought you were talking to your gran, and you know how she likes to chat."

The call goes dead. A long beat passes before I realize I'm frozen, holding my phone midair against my ear and grinning like a lunatic at a mannequin in the shop window. I think she smiles back.

I might be delirious.

She's wearing emerald-green underwear with embroidered lace that would complement my red hair perfectly. The matching choker around her neck makes it the sexiest damn lingerie I've ever seen.

Invisible cords pull me toward it. Maybe I'll save up and buy it now that I'm staying.

Orla comes up beside me and I grab her arm. "I'd look sexy as fuck in that. Don't ya think? I might buy it to celebrate."

Except when I turn, it's not Orla's arm.

It's muscular, hard, and wrapped in nice-feeling material.

A broad chest in a blue shirt and vest looms over me. I look up... up farther... and am met with an angry stare, as arctic eyes blaze into mine.

Wow.

"Holy shit!" I shriek. "I mean..."

He glares down at where I've grasped his forearm and detaches himself with a grunt.

My breath catches in my throat, and I look away, flustered.

I...

He's...

Just fuck.

Glass smashing snaps me out of my daze.

I hop back in surprise, away from the little shards of glass littered around me. My bag has slipped off my shoulder, spilling the contents across the floor, one of which was the fancy cocktail glass I had taken from the bar as a 'souvenir'. Now, it lies broken in a thousand pieces.

Ah, karma.

"Fuck," I hiss, staring in horror as the little soaps roll around the guy's feet in different directions before settling. "I'm so sorry. I thought you were my friend."

My cheeks feel like I've been sunbathing in Death Valley. I can't look at the man.

I asked him whether he thought I'd look sexy AF in underwear.

I need to get the soaps back in my bag before anyone notices I've depleted half the supplies in the hotel bathroom.

I squat down to grab them from among the broken glass, trying to decide how I will deal with the glass. My hands aren't communicating with my brain. I'm doing a juggling act with soaps and manage to shove some of them into my bag.

"Step away. You'll hurt yourself," the shadow above me says gruffly. It's a low, gravelly American baritone that sends unexpected shivers through me. It must take an enormous pair of balls to pump out that much testosterone.

Looking up, I see icy eyes flaring down at me with annoyance, and my stomach drops so low, I'm afraid it will fall out of my ass for the second time today.

He's quite a bit older than me. Strong masculine features. Thick, wavy, dark-brown hair. The icy blues, angular jaw, and prominent nose make him look ruthless. A vest and shirt combo that my vagina approves of.

Holy fucking potatoes. The guy is gorgeous.

His gaze sweeps over the disaster on the floor, and his eyebrows draw together. He couldn't look less impressed if I stormed in wearing a mask and robbed the reception desk.

Even through the glare, I can't stop gawking.

He looks down at me for a moment longer before nodding to someone behind me. I crane my neck to see a burly security guard walking toward us, speaking into an earpiece.

"It's only soap," I huff as our eyes lock again. Somehow, his stare manages to be hot and cold at the same time.

My gaze drops. I'm eye level with his cock. I bet it's as large and threatening as the rest of him.

"Get off your damn knees, girl," the guy growls.

Girl?

"Ma'am, do you need assistance?" another voice says from behind me. The security guard. His expression tells me that *assistance* is an escort out of the hotel.

Two cleaners scuttle over.

"I'm so sorry," I rasp to the cleaner bending down to sweep up the shattered glass.

Mortified, I steal a fleeting glance at the arrogant, god-like man. He's already striding off with a stunningly beautiful brunette dressed like the First Lady on his arm.

She's almost tall enough to look him in the eye, and he must be six-three or six-four. She makes gliding in stilettos and a tight dress look effortless. *She's* not penguin-waddling.

A perfect match for him.

I'm irrationally jealous for a fleeting second as he puts his hand on her lower back and leads her toward the entrance.

Then, unease grows in the pit of my stomach.

I've seen those eyes before.

Was that... Killian fucking Quinn?

FOUR

Killian

With a heavy exhale, I push open the door to my boardroom.

"Mr. Quinn." Alfred Marek leaps up from his seat, narrowly missing spilling his water. "I'm glad we can sort this out face-to-face."

Thirty minutes ago, I saw him at reception when I returned from lunch with Maria.

Paunchy short guy. Light-blue eyes, not dissimilar to mine. Something the Polish and Irish have in common. He's the type of guy who wears a suit regardless of whether he works in a coal mine or an office.

With steel in his eyes, he holds out his hand for me to shake. I might have been fooled if I didn't feel his clammy palm.

He's flanked by two guys, one of who must be his son. The son, who looks mid-thirties like me, has his jaw set tight, ready for a fight the old-fashioned way.

"Call me Killian." I remove my hand from his grasp.

Marek looks relieved. "Alfred." The older man smiles at me. "And this is my son, Alfred Jr."

Alfred Jr. mumbles a greeting.

Marek nods to the third guy farthest from me. "This is my lawyer, Mike Dempsey."

Dempsey looks like someone they found from the local phone book, operating out of a car wash in Brooklyn.

I take my place at the head of the boardroom table and gesture for them to sit. "I trust my team has introduced themselves." Sitting opposite the Marek family is Sarah, a senior lawyer, and a guy who looks fresh out of college.

"They have indeed," Alfred Sr. says as the Mareks simultaneously sit. "I'll admit, Killian, I'm surprised you agreed to the meeting. You're a busy man. I'm sure we can come to a resolution, like adults, so we don't take up too much of your time."

I relax into my leather chair, nodding in agreement. "You have my full attention."

He takes a sip of his water, then clears his throat. "Mr. Quinn... Killian." His lips curl into a tense smile as he knots his fingers on the table. "Do you know the history of our restaurant?"

I offer a friendly smile. "I assume you're going to enlighten me."

"I don't know how well you know our area in Brooklyn. Come out and visit us at the restaurant. You'll get to see the wonderful, proud Polish community..."

I try not to lose patience but find my attention

drifting out the window as he speaks. He's doing himself no favors by giving me a history lesson about Brooklyn.

"So you see, the restaurant is where our community comes together. My father handed it over to me, and I ran it for *fifty years* to pass it down to my son and daughter." He briefly looks with pride at his son before redirecting his attention back to me. "I want you to reconsider the development, Killian. Son. Think about—"

"Mr. Marek," Sarah cuts in briskly. "Our contract has already been communicated to your lawyer."

I lean back in my seat, letting out a frustrated grunt as I exhale. We should be finishing up the small details of this project by now.

"Please," Alfred's voice booms, but he fails to hide the slight rattle. "I'm talking business owner to business owner. Father to father. You have children too. Someday you'll want to pass your business to them." He pauses. "*Her.*"

He's done his research. Except handing over my business would require my beautiful daughter Teagan to say something other than "I hate you" to me. Anything beyond that seems like a pipe dream these days.

"I'm sorry, Alfred. This isn't personal, but the development is going ahead. It's already underway."

"We're aware of that," Alfred Jr. growls. "We can see the bulldozers from the restaurant window. The noise is driving our customers away."

"That's unfortunate."

Alfred Jr. hisses in response like the meathead I expected him to be. He slams his fist on the table, making the water glasses shake.

"Hold up, Son," his father cuts in, leveling him with a stern look. He places a hand over his son's before turning his attention back to me. "Killian. You're putting me out of business with your bulldozers."

"Which is why you should accept my generous offer."

Senior blanches. "So... what? You're going to ruin this community with a gaudy hotel and casino?"

"It's a prime plot of land near JFK," I point out calmly, drumming my fingers on the table with mild impatience. "Not a community center to drink tea in. Be sensible."

"Sit down, son," Senior snaps as Junior makes to stand. He grabs his son's arm and forces him back down into his seat. "So that's it? We have two options. Either sell our livelihood to you or watch you destroy it by building around us?"

"I would advise taking option one," I respond crisply. "I was expecting to have a sensible conversation with you today."

We've offered Marek a package that could give his family financial stability for life but he's too blinded by pride to take it.

Jr. growls something in Polish.

"Mr. Quinn," their lawyer pipes up from the corner, clutching papers that are probably props. Fucking useless. I forgot he was even in the room.

"You leave us no option but to seek an injunction from the courts under the Nuisance Law."

Feeling my phone vibrate in my pocket, I take it out. *Connor.* For a moment, the phone is the center of attention; a chance for the Mareks to regroup. Canceling Connor, I slide the phone back down on the table, out of arm's reach of the moronic son in case he fancies himself as a vandal.

"The hotel is going ahead on that land. We have your accounts; my offer is much more than the restaurant is worth," I remind them. "I was in a bidding war for the land with five other property developers. The others were willing to offer you half of what I did. See this as an opportunity, not a threat."

"Real fucking saint you are, Quinn," Alfred Jr. spits. I look in disgust at where droplets have landed on the table. "You sit in your glass box, thinking you're better than us. You think you can forget your roots? Your family came from nothing."

"Are you done?" I ask him coldly. "Because you've made life a whole lot more difficult for yourself."

I tap on my phone to alert security.

"Our community won't let this happen." Alfred Jr. rises to his feet. "It'll be burned to the ground with all your fucking high-rollers from the island in it. You don't have support in Queens, and now you don't have any in Brooklyn either."

I regard him coolly. Nothing new there. I grew up in Queens. Killian Quinn Sr., from whom I inherited my genes, was a lowlife, according to every Irishman within a ten-mile radius. A man who would show up to a dead man's send-off for the free food and then bed his widow. Unfortunately, his reputation extended to the wider family. Fortunately, he died before I hit my teens.

"Time's up," I say, my voice level. I slip my phone back into my pocket and stand, pushing my chair back as there's a knock on the door. A security guard opens it, raising his brow at me. He's danced this dance before. Two other guards linger behind him.

"Seek injunctions, protest, try to blow the place up. You won't win against me, Alfred." I address Sr. because Jr. is a fucking idiot. "I thought you were smarter than this. Now, if you'll excuse me, I have another meeting."

Alfred Sr. rises to his feet to join his son. "I almost feel sorry for you, Quinn. You don't understand what it means to be part of a community, do you?"

"After you." I gesture with my palms for them to get out as the two security guards come between the Mareks and me.

I turn to Sarah and the paralegal kiddo sweating buckets, now on their feet and anxious to leave. "Sarah, inform the team that we'll need to modify our construction phases since the Mareks' refuse to negotiate."

We'll build around them.

"I don't know why we expected anything different from a psychopath. Everyone in Queens knows what you did," Jr. sneers from behind me.

Everyone freezes.

The words trickle under my skin like parasites.

I slowly pivot to face him.

His eyes spark with smug satisfaction, pleased that his parting jab provoked a reaction.

I raise my hand to stop the security guards from dragging him down the hall, not taking my eyes off Junior. "And what exactly is that?"

He stiffens, his bravado faltering even though he's got the security guards between us.

"Leave it, Son," his father warns quietly beside him.

Junior narrows his eyes and stands tall. "You're the worst kind of scum. She was the mother of your kid."

"Get. The. Fuck. Out," I growl through clenched teeth, struggling to control the anger surging through me. I narrow my eyes, my knuckles white as I grip the edge of the table behind me.

At my signal, my security team escorts the Mareks away swiftly.

I watch as they disappear from view down the hallway.

I get no pleasure from knocking down his family or his restaurant. It's just business. But he made this personal. Now I want to tear down his damn restaurant and make sure my casino is the only view he ever sees from his house.

Mandy, my PA, approaches from where she's been watching. Perhaps I should be more concerned about how unfazed she is by the scene.

"Walk and talk, Mandy," I say in as calm a voice

as I can manage. I take the coffee from her and head toward my office.

She follows me in a slight jog as people scurry out of our way. "Your four o'clock is in boardroom two," she begins, referencing her notepad. "Then we have a car waiting for you for your five-ten meeting across town. Oh, and the *New York Times* called. They want a quote from you about the Dante Carlo hotel group going into liquidation."

I stop short in the hallway. "Why the fuck do they want a quote from me?"

Mandy looks at me strangely before responding. "Because you're Killian Quinn."

"Fine, get PR to put together a quote and run it past me. Cancel the five-ten. I want to be home when Teagan returns from school, since there's no nanny this week."

"But, Mr. Quinn—"

"No buts."

She bites her lip and nods as we walk until we reach my office. "I booked dinner for your daughter's birthday." She glances at the pad again. "Oh, and I sent Mrs. Dalton's daughter some flowers."

"Good. Has she been moved to the new clinic yet?"

She nods, smiling. "She's loving the VIP treatment. But Mrs. Dalton wants to stay with her in Boston for at least two months."

I take a deep breath, then push open the door to my office.

I get it. I have a daughter, and I would do anything for her too. I signed off on the checks to move Mrs.

Dalton's daughter to the best clinic in the country, not paying any attention to the cost. It's irrelevant.

But Mrs. Dalton's absence fills me with trepidation more than anything has in years, and I've been shot at twice. She's been with Teagan and me as my live-in nanny and domestic assistant for years. A sensible Irish woman in her early fifties whose children have all grown up. She has the integrity and discretion that I need for someone living with my daughter.

Since Teagan's nearly thirteen and at school, she only needs someone in the evenings until I get home. I don't care how grown-up Teagan thinks she is. My security team isn't good company for teenage girls. This is my dire attempt to have a more motherly figure in her life.

But finding a suitable replacement has been a fucking nightmare.

My younger brother, Connor, swaggers toward me. "How come you're the only one who comes back from your meetings and doesn't look like they want to jump out of the window?"

"Thanks, Mandy." I nod for her to leave, then turn to Connor. "Glad you were entertained."

He props himself against the wall. "So the old man won't sign?"

"They'll sign eventually. Just a pity they're wasting everyone's time."

"I don't know why you bothered to talk with him."

"What can I say? I'm a nice guy," I reply dryly,

taking a mouthful of coffee. I don't tell him that the prick of a son taunted me over Harlow's death. "Sometimes they feel better when they've been allowed to say their piece. I'd prefer they sign quietly."

"If you want them to sign quietly, put someone charming in front of them."

I stare at him, deadpan.

He chuckles as Marcus, our chief of staff, joins us, reeking of cigarette smoke. I might force him to quit.

Marcus' brows shoot up as he takes in Connor. "You shaved your head."

Connor chuckles. "Killian didn't even notice."

"Of course, I fucking noticed," I snap. "I've got better things to do than massage Connor's ego by telling him how much I love his new military hairstyle."

Connor lets out a laugh and pushes himself off the wall. "Christ, he's even grouchier than usual today. Good luck." He slaps Marcus on the back before walking away.

"I do have some actual good news for you," Marcus says. "I found Mrs. Dalton's perfect replacement."

My brow lifts. "Oh, yeah?"

"Thought a different strategy might work this time. I'm hoping someone so desperate won't run away."

"Let's hope so," I grunt. "Your current strategy is fucking abysmal."

He crosses his arms over his chest. "My job isn't

43

just to find a nanny for you, boss. The last one you made cry, and Teagan made the one before that burst into tears."

I shoot him a dark stare. He's lucky he's worked for me for ten years.

"You can meet the new one on Sunday. You'll like her; she's Irish. She'll be a great influence on Teagan. We've run the background checks. No drugs, illnesses, STDs. Scabies. No record of terrorism." His grin widens. "Cleaner than an Irish nun."

This sounds promising.

"Should I be concerned about your priority order?" I ask dryly. "Sounds like you've found me the Irish *Mary Poppins*."

"I couldn't have described her better myself. It's like you've already met her."

"Send me her résumé and vetting results." I'm not comfortable with someone moving in so quickly, but I've got very few options. Mrs. Dalton's absence was last minute. And my security team is prepared for any scenario—scabies, terrorism, or otherwise.

He pauses, swirling his coffee. "She's younger than Mrs. Dalton."

I give him a questioning look. "And?"

He shrugs. "And nothing. That's it. I'm just giving you all the facts."

I study him suspiciously.

FIVE

Clodagh

I gaze at the Fifth Avenue brownstone, counting six stories to the top. I have to crane my neck to take it all in. I bet they have a breathtaking view of Central Park from up there.

I left Orla brooding, with promises to return, and got in the car with Mr. Quinn's driver, Sam—a black SUV with blacked-out windows, reinforced with bulletproof glass, which Sam confirmed to my delight.

Thanks to Uncle Sean's dead wife, Kathy, I'm dressed in a long, floral skirt and white blouse covering my arm tattoos. I wipe a sweaty palm over my skirt. It's hideous, God rest poor Kathy's soul. I'm usually in yoga pants and a T-shirt, not dressed like *Nanny McPhee*.

It took all of ten minutes to shove my belongings in a backpack. Clothes, tweezers, razors, cold sore cream, hair products to tame my red frizz, and some adult toys I haven't been able to use knowing Uncle Sean and Aunt Kathy's ghost are in the house.

I scale the steps until I reach the double door. This must be what Alice felt like when she drank the shrinking potion.

Two stone lion statues with their mouths open stand guard on either side of the door.

My stomach lurches with nerves and excited energy. Am I really moving in here?

I give my armpits a quick sniff. I could fry an egg between my breasts. We Irish like to complain about the weather a *lot*.

It must be thirty-five degrees Celsius outside or, as the Americans say, a hundred degrees Fahrenheit. Something like that; maths was never my strong suit. Not like the owner of this tank of a mansion. You don't get to be a billionaire without being good at maths and other subjects.

I suck in a deep breath and press the doorbell.

"State your full name," a male voice says before I take my finger off the button.

That's unnerving. Is his butler waiting on the other side?

"Clodagh Kelly," I say each name slowly, unsure where to direct my voice.

"Look directly at the camera." There's a long pause. "Clodagh."

Wow. Impressive accuracy in pronunciation.

My eyes widen, and I search for the camera. There it is—a shiny round object above the doorbell. It moves until it's focusing directly on my face.

In the movies, this is when I'd get nuked.

With a tight-lipped smile, I stand rigidly facing

the camera, unsure if I'm speaking to a human or an electronic device. For a doorbell, it learned my name quickly. It could even be Killian Quinn himself; I don't know what he sounds like.

"Retinal scan initiated," the male monotone informs me.

I hold my forced smile, wondering if I'm being watched. This is worse than JFK passport control.

"Retina scan complete," the voice announces.

I wait. Now what?

My stomach tightens as footsteps come toward the door from the inside.

The double doors pull open and...

It's him.

Of course, it's fucking him.

Our eyes lock as his brows join in a deep frown. I see his brain ticking over... trying to remember... trying to place me.

I wait.

The moment recognition flares in those arctic eyes, my skin prickles like it's been jagged by a thousand icebergs, slowly freezing me to death.

He folds his arms across his chest as his scowl deepens.

God help me. I thought the Manhattans clouded my vision; that Killian Quinn couldn't be as unnerving as I remember. Jesus Christ, he's worse.

He's massive, excessively masculine, and absolutely fucking terrifying. Has he grown taller since I saw him at the hotel?

His heavy gaze roams over me, making his way

over every inch of my body. An inspection I'm flunking with a capital F. By the time he lands on my face, I feel like I've been stripped of Kathy's floral skirt and frilly blouse.

Yup, he remembers me.

I resist the urge to bolt back down the street.

"Mr. Quinn?" I swallow thickly. "I'm Clodagh Kelly."

"You," he says at last, his jaw visibly tensing.

"Me. Eh, sorry about that little incident at the hotel. I—"

"I was expecting you to be older," he cuts in, his voice as cold as his eyes.

"Oh." I blink, unsure of how to rectify that issue. "I apologize?"

I wipe my sweaty palm against my skirt before extending my hand. Marcus may not be so confident if he could see me now.

Another scan up and down of me, and his jaw tightens further. The man looks as though he's about to slam the door in my face.

He takes my hand in his.

I hide my nerves behind my brightest smile as his hand envelops mine. My pulse jumps a little from the contact with his skin. "I've never been vetted by a doorbell before."

His frown deepens as if even the sight of me displeases him, and he drops my hand.

I subtly unpick my skirt wedgie from my backside and shift uncomfortably from foot to foot. "Umm…"

Is he going to let me in? If I'm canned because of a

few missing soaps, then, for crying out loud, can't he put me out of my misery already?

"Come in," he says in a clipped voice. He sounds like he doesn't want me on the island of Manhattan, let alone in his house. He opens the door wider, and I force my feet into motion, skittering past him to step inside the foyer.

Holy fucking potatoes. Everything's huge. And white. I feel like an ant.

I want to spin and take in all the intricate details —the chandelier, the grand staircase with gleaming white stairs, the moldings, the door frames, and the marble floor that looks clean enough to lick.

Even the freaking door handles are like something out of the Museum of Modern Art. I know; I walked past it on my way here. The room looks like it's been plucked straight out of a New York-based movie.

Killian or Mr. Quinn, because he never told me what to call him, stalks toward a door to the left of the staircase. I assume I'm to follow.

Double doors open magically as he walks. So this is how billionaires live? No need to spend time on mundane tasks such as door opening.

"Your place is beautiful," I say breathlessly, wishing I could muster up something more eloquent.

"Thank you," he replies gruffly. "It's a Bosworth design."

I pretend I understand what he said and let out an "ooh" as he escorts me into a stunningly lavish lounge area with enormous white couches and a fireplace much taller than me.

I'm the scruffiest thing in the room.

He motions to one of the couches. "Take a seat."

I lower myself onto the couch, but my feet can't reach the floor. Trying to appear composed, I slide forward until I'm perched on the edge of the seat.

Quinn settles on the couch opposite me. He rests his forearms on either edge of the sofa and spreads his thick thighs wide while he scans me again critically.

Gone is the suit. Now he's in dark blue jeans, a black T-shirt, and trainers. I mean, *sneakers*.

I squirm in my skirt, which sticks to my skin thanks to the nylon fabric.

Marcus made this job seem like it was in the bag, but with how my potential boss looks at me, I'm not so sure anymore. My heart races in my chest, so palpable I think he can hear it.

"How old are you?"

"I thought you weren't allowed to ask that in an interview," I joke meekly.

He doesn't smile. "I have all your information, including your blood type, on file. It would be preferable for both of us if you save me time retrieving it and just answer the question."

I clear my throat and respond more seriously. "Nearly twenty-five."

"You look younger," he replies dryly.

"Oh, okay... um... thanks?" What does he have against younger people?

Another beat passes, and his scowl darkens. He rises abruptly, and I nearly follow suit until he waves me back down. "I need to make a call. Make yourself comfortable. I'll be back in ten minutes."

I watch him stride through the glass doors to another room and slam them shut. Unease settles in my stomach.

This is the difference between a plane ticket back home and a life in New York. It's obvious that I'm not what Quinn expected. I rub idle circles over the roses on Kathy's skirt. Maybe this is karma for borrowing a dead woman's skirt and calling it hideous.

Is this grumpy attitude because I stole soap and a glass from his hotel? Or did he find something in my pee test? Is it my accent? Most Americans love it. I've had a few drunken marriage proposals.

As he talks to someone on the phone, still scowling, I discreetly check him out.

He's too imposing, too intense, too severe. Taking up too much space.

He's too damn... *big*.

I bite a fingernail. When that one's chewed up, I move to the next. What's he doing in there? Is he calling fucking immigration or something?

He turns abruptly, looking sharply at me as if feeling the weight of my gaze. His lips move, but his focus remains solely on me.

I wish I could lipread, but the tic in his jaw is better than sign language.

I've fucked it.

Defeated, I sink into the leather couch, wishing it

would magically swallow me up.

Goodbye, New York. Hello, Belfast.

The doors swing open, and he reenters the room, sinking into the sofa in front of me with an irritated grunt. "The domestic assistant you're substituting has decades of experience. I expected the same from you. You're barely older than my daughter." He looks at me like I'm a two-headed beast that needs to be put down.

Bloody cheek of this guy.

I stare into his handsome face, wishing I could tell him to shove his job up his sexy ass. "With all due respect, sir, your daughter is barely a teenager. I'm a grown woman," I say bluntly. "My age doesn't make me incompetent."

Anger flares in his blue eyes. Quinn doesn't like being challenged. "I'm moving this person into my house, under the same roof *as my daughter.* It doesn't matter if they're doing chores. I need them to be a positive role model. Do you think I take that lightly?"

"No," I say succinctly. You don't take anything lightly, buddy.

"So why do you think *you're* qualified, Miss Kelly?"

We stare at each other, the tension flowing between us like a live wire.

I promised myself I wouldn't let another guy make me feel worthless.

"It's Clodagh," I correct him defiantly. "I may not be a billionaire, Mr. Quinn, or have a degree in childcare, but that doesn't mean I'm not a trustworthy hire."

"I'll be the one to decide that."

There's no point trying to bullshit the guy, so I'll stick with what I know. "Fine. Okay, as an au pair, I'll admit that I don't have much experience, but I did help raise three rowdy younger brothers." *Much experience* meaning *no experience* in this instance.

He grunts in response, making it clear my spiel isn't making an impact.

"I'm actually a trained carpenter." I stop briefly to check his reaction and work out how the hell I'm going to make this relevant. "It might not seem like a huge feat, but as a woman in a trade job, I think I'm a good role model." I pause to breathe. "And Marcus said you need someone, like, yesterday, and I can start today."

I remain still and hold my breath, not wanting to be the first to look away. I'm not going down without a fight.

"A *carpenter*?" he repeats in a clipped tone as if he hadn't heard me properly.

I stand my ground and look him straight in the eye. I've been here before with chauvinist dudes who think carpentry isn't for women. "Yeah, that's right."

Neither of us looks away. Neither of us blinks.

Bring it on, Quinn. I fucking dare you.

"Admirable."

He sounds, dare I say it... respectful? I'm floored.

"How did you become a carpenter?" he asks, looking genuinely curious.

"I left school when I was sixteen." I absentmindedly pull at a stray thread on my skirt, feeling anxious. "I wasn't very book smart, but I liked making things. It suited my brain better. After school, I got an admin job at a furniture store, and I watched the carpenters work. Then I started mucking around, making some basic furniture. I couldn't believe it when I got accepted to Belfast Met's carpentry course." I smile, remembering the day I got the email.

"Let's see your portfolio."

"My portfolio?" I ask slowly.

"Yes, some of the pieces you've created," he says less patiently, beckoning with his hands like I'm going to magic a portfolio out of thin air.

I wasn't prepared for this, but I pull out my phone to show him photos. I watch uneasily as he swipes through each picture, his expression indecipherable. I've no nails left to chew. Soon, I'll have to start on his.

"I want to set something more professional up soon, like an Etsy store," I say, feeling increasingly deflated as he shows no reaction.

He glances up from the screen. "Why haven't you tried starting your own business?"

"I did." I squirm in my seat. "It didn't work out."

Please drop it already. I'm applying to clean and look after your kid, not build you a new kitchen.

"Why not?"

For fuck's sake. "My business partner and I didn't see eye to eye."

My ex talked me into starting a business last year

—a business I never thought I'd have the nerve to start. I'd worked at a furniture store for a few years making bespoke cabinets, and he came to me with a plan. We'd be the dream team. I was the creative hands; he was the business brain. He'd take care of the money.

And boy, did he take care of my money.

I naively handed him over two thousand. He made up some rambling excuse about investing in marketing, then dumped me a few months later.

On behalf of female carpenters, I was a failure.

Now I'm so bloody jaded. It's part of what spurred me to leave for the States. At home, *everyone* knows about my failed business.

"I'm not your target audience, but they're good." He hands me back the phone, and I breathe a little easier. "Is there anything else I should know about you, Miss Kelly? Any unusual hobbies? Because things will go smoother if you're the one to tell me."

"No," I say, my pulse spiking at the thought of my ridiculous criminal record. "That's me. I'm a simple gal."

He scrutinizes me for a long, uncomfortable beat. "You're a trained carpenter, yet you've abandoned your trade to apply for a domestic assistant position," he says, matter-of-fact, one brow raised.

"I haven't abandoned it," I counter, annoyed. "My long-term plan is to make a life in New York doing what I love. I just need to figure out the steps from a to z."

"The job is demanding. You'll be a live-in

assistant, on-call all the time. If you think you'll have time to do woodwork, then walk out the door. I'm paying you to be at my beck and call."

"I can be at your beck and call, Mr. Quinn," I reply without missing a beat.

Our eyes lock. Has anyone ever managed to pull a smile from that mouth? Quinn needs to learn to chill. Do yoga. Face yoga.

"Marcus obviously sees something in you..."

My pulse goes wild as I try to cover my nervous energy with a cough. I'm as much in the dark as Quinn on that one.

"And I trust his judgment." Quinn sits and relaxes back into his seat, folding one leg over the other to rest on his knee. "You work five days a week, but you need to be flexible. I need my staff to be proactive, meticulous, and use their initiative. That includes my domestic staff. If I say you need to be somewhere at a certain time, you'll be there ten minutes before. If I ask you to do something, I ask once."

If he's telling me this, does it mean I'm still in the running?

"Yes, sir!" I smooth my palms down on my skirt. I feel like I'm being recruited for the army.

"You'll have your own living quarters, all-inclusive," he drawls. "Food and expenses are paid for on top of your wages."

I try not to react. Or pass out on his floor. That salary plus no bills... I'm going to be the richest nanny maid in the United States.

Quinn excels at unreadable expressions. With

that poker face, it's no wonder he owns casinos. His home security system showed me more emotion.

Me? I'm the opposite. I have a face that lets out all my secrets.

"You're on probation."

"Of course." I nod breathlessly. I've done it. I've bloody got the job. "For how long?"

"For as long as I deem necessary." He stands from the couch and moves to the large glass table near the window. After grabbing a large bound booklet and phone, he returns and hands them to me. "This is your instruction manual put together by my long-term help, Mrs. Dalton. You'll find all your tasks listed here."

I take the worryingly thick manual in my hands as he looms over me, hands in his pockets, watching my every move.

This is the second time I'm eye level with his dick.

"She's very detailed," I murmur, leafing through the pages without reading them. I hate when people ask me to read something in front of them.

"A quality I expect from my team. Bear that in mind."

"Yes, of course. Absolutely." My lips curve into a tight smile. "I'll digest this."

"Tonight, please, since you start tomorrow morning." His brow lifts. "Do you have a boyfriend? Girlfriend?"

I shake my head, blushing.

With his hands in his pockets, he strolls back to stand, staring out the window. "Anyone you date will be vetted. When you date, it will be outside this house. I don't let men stay, even in the staff quarters. That's a hard rule for my daughter's sake."

"Sure." I can deal with celibacy if it means living in an Upper East Side townhouse. Living under the same roof as Killian Quinn is terrifying enough.

He turns to face me again. "I put a lot of trust in my staff, but if you violate that trust, my security staff will be here in minutes. Cameras are all over the property."

"*Everywhere?*" I'm not taking a dump with Quinn's security team watching. "Even the bathrooms?"

"No, not the bathrooms. Your living quarters are exempt, too."

I glance anxiously around the room. "But I'll be watched all the time?"

"No." His lips quirk as he leans against the window ledge. It's the closest thing I've seen to a smile. "That's by exception. The security is as much for your benefit, Miss Kelly, as it is mine and Teagan's. Every room in the house has a panic button. My team will show you how to invoke an emergency. You'll also install an app on your phone to alert my team immediately if you're in danger."

"Panic buttons?" I echo, bewildered.

"I'm in the public eye. It comes with the territory," he says dryly. "I want you to feel safe here."

It's the first bout of compassion I've felt from him.

"I'm not planning to do anything to violate your trust, Mr. Quinn."

"Glad we understand each other." He nods to the

phone beside me. "That's yours. I expect you to always have it on you."

There's a knock behind me. I turn to see the double doors opening, and Sam, the nice Irish guy who drove me from Queens, enters. "Boss."

Quinn nods at him before turning back to me. "Sam will take you to your studio."

He pushes himself off the ledge, and I take it as my cue to stand.

"Teagan is at her grandmother's, so you can't meet her right now. Sam will show you your living quarters and set you up with access to the property. The rest of the evening is yours to settle in, Miss Kelly."

As much as I like the sound of my second name in his deep raspy voice...

"Please call me Clodagh. No one calls me Miss Kelly."

"Clodagh."

My neck hairs stand on end.

He runs a hand over his strong jawline. "Call me Mr. Quinn."

I start to laugh, then realize he's not amused. "Oh. Sorry, I thought you were joking."

"Do I look like a comedian?"

Does he want an answer to that? My nerves are shot.

"No. Mr. Quinn," I say hoarsely. "I look forward to working for you. Boss."

The corner of his mouth twitches slightly. "I'll see you at five o'clock tomorrow morning."

Wait, what?

For the umpteenth time during our exchange, I try not to react.

Who needs domestic assistance at five in the morning? I guess the answers are in the manual.

With a curt nod, Killian strides off.

"Ready?" Sam smiles at me sympathetically.

Too sympathetically.

SIX

Killian

I give the pint-sized redheaded soap thief with the emerald eyes until the end of the week.

SEVEN

Clodagh

Sam takes me to a secure room to program the security system at the entrance, enabling me access to the mansion. I press my thumb against a scanner and keep still while the device reads my retinal pattern.

I've never unlocked a house with my eyes before.

At least there's no chance of me losing my keys.

"Ready to see your new digs?" Sam grins. My skittishness seems to entertain him.

The foyer lights are on, but there's no sign of Killian or his daughter on the ground floor, and I'm relieved. Before I see him, I want to read this manual and understand what I'm dealing with.

I follow Sam past the double staircase, down the hall to another stairway to the lower ground floor.

"The dungeon," I half joke as I descend behind Sam.

He flips on a light and... holy shit.

Quinn hasn't skimped on the lower ground staff quarters. I follow Sam into a beautiful red-bricked lounge-kitchen area. This should be on ads for New York loft-style living.

He drops my bag on the couch.

"Wow," I say loudly, spinning around. Renting this apartment would cost *thousands* of dollars a month. "I get to live here... alone? As in... it's all mine?"

I turn to Sam, who leans against the fridge with a slight smirk.

"It's all yours, Clodagh."

"Fuck me," I breathe. Orla will lose her shit when she sees this place.

Swallowing hard, I take in every detail of the room. I always thought basement flats would feel dark and dingy. This one has soft furnishings and a fluffy white carpet that makes me want to curl up on the floor and never leave. The area is *perfect* for hosting my online yoga classes for my gran's friends back home.

And a nice place to hide from Quinn.

"Is my new boss always so serious?" I ask Sam as I wander around the lounge.

"Yes. He expects things to be done a certain way."

"His way."

"You're a fast learner." I glance over to see him smirking. "You're very different from Mrs. Dalton. She's a lot more,"—he pauses—"mumsy."

"Uh, Sam? I don't know if that's a compliment or an insult, given my new job title."

"Just an observation."

"He didn't choose me," I say quietly, plopping

down on the couch to try it out. "Marcus, the guy who works for him, did."

"Huh." Sam frowns, keeping his gaze on the floor.

I wait for an explanation and get nothing. "You're not filling me with confidence," I huff. "And I haven't even started the job yet."

He shakes his head and grins. "Sorry. I'm sure you'll find a way to charm him."

Charm Killian Quinn? I've more chance of charming Hannibal Lecter. Guys like him aren't interested in gals like me who don't have their shit together yet.

I don't say that.

"Are you from Dublin?" I ask, changing the subject. I've got a thing for the Dublin accent.

"Good guess." He smiles and crosses the room to come closer to me.

I take the opportunity to subtly inspect Sam. He's a looker; a stereotypical good-looking Irish man. Skin peppered with cute freckles and tousled brown hair to complement his bright blue eyes. Thirty, at a guess. He must do well with the American girls. Much more charming than his boss.

"Your Northern accent is too soft to be Belfast. I'd say you're from the country. Fermanagh?" he says.

I'm impressed. "Close enough." I grin. "Donegal. Any farther north and you're in the Atlantic."

He chuckles. "I've never gone that far north."

"Funny enough, we seem to get more American tourists than Dubliners," I say. "How long have you been in New York?"

"About six years."

So Sam's legal. Of course he's legal if he works for Quinn. "And how long have you worked for Killian Quinn?"

"Five years."

Oh. "You must know him well."

He chuckles softly again. "I'm not sure anyone truly knows Mr. Quinn. Except his brother, Connor."

"But you've survived five years with the guy." I search his expression. "Do you have any tips to help me not get sacked?"

"Just stay on the right side of him."

I groan, leaning back in my seat. "That's a tad fluffy. You got anything more tangible?"

He grins, giving me a quick glance. "Sorry, Clodagh. I guess if it were easy he wouldn't fire so many people."

So not what I needed to hear.

It's time to try out the bed. The lounge door opens into the bedroom.

"Do you live here in the house, too?" I ask curiously, turning to Sam, who has strolled into the bedroom behind me.

He shakes his head. "I live a few doors down. Mr. Quinn owns several houses on the street. Most of the security staff live nearby." Our eyes lock. "I'm close enough when you need me."

This does not fill me with comfort. There's safety in numbers. "Then why do I live here and not with the other staff members? Why am I the only one?" I sink onto the bed, testing the mattress. I'm going to sleep like the dead.

He watches me bounce, then averts his eyes sheepishly. "You're cleaning and cooking for him and Teagan. If Teagan wants something,"—he pauses—"*anything*, then you have to be close enough to jump."

I freeze mid-bounce. Teagan sounds spoiled. "She's a bit old for a nanny." When I think of what I was getting up to when I was twelve… *yikes.*

"Billionaires think differently." He nods toward the manual I had dropped on the bed, smirking. "I'm sure Mrs. Dalton has covered everything in that handbook. I better head off. Get a good night's sleep, Clodagh." A smile plays on his lips as he steps away from the wall. "You'll need it."

"No kidding." My fingers tighten around the manual. "Why does he get up so early?"

He shrugs. "You don't become a billionaire by sleeping in."

"I thought that was the whole point of becoming a billionaire," I mutter.

Sam leaves me to get settled in. By settling in, I mean spending five minutes emptying my small bag of clothes into a wardrobe.

Then I nose-dive onto the bed, thrashing my hands and legs about, and let out a deep throaty *Yee-haw.*

This can't be real. Living on Fifth Avenue isn't affordable without a million zeros in your bank account. It's a pipe dream.

Rolling onto my back, I let out a long, dreamy sigh as I stare at the ceiling. I can starfish in this bed and my feet and arms don't reach the sides. The mattress feels like I'm floating in a warm bath. Maybe this is why Quinn can get up so early.

Sure, I'm the hired help for three months, and then I'll be back in the same shitty visa-less scenario...

But I'm here now.

I could fall asleep fully clothed above the covers... except the light above me bounces off the laminated booklet.

First things first, business before pleasure. Propping myself up on the lush pillows, I turn the first page, and my stomach lurches.

The damn thing is the size of the Bible. This will take me all night. At least with digital text, I can use text-to-speech or my software, but with printed text, I can't process things as easily. I have to read something like three times before I'm comfortable understanding it.

The inter-word spacing is crowded. I hate the font. There is underlining and italics *everywhere*. That's why I *hate* reading printed copies. Most of them aren't dyslexia-friendly.

My reading pen is better with small amounts of text, not full-length novels like this beast. It'll read it out line by line, but it takes forever.

Flipping through, I see reams and reams of text interspaced with images. Did Quinn really make his housekeeper, Mrs. Dalton, create this ridiculously detailed manual for cleaning his house?

Maybe it's all lies. I'll walk past a graveyard near Central Park and spot a grave marked *Mrs. Dalton* who died two days before my arrival.

The manual is split into sections—workweek schedule, detailed house layout, dietary requirements, health and safety, security, and emergency contacts.

I flip back to the first section with the heading 'The Quinn family's weekly schedule'.

Monday. Quinn gets up at 5 a.m. expecting his protein smoothie and coffee waiting for him before he goes for a run. His high-protein breakfast needs to be prepared by 6 a.m. At 6:30, he leaves for work.

5 a.m. Fucking yuck.

I run the pen over it a few times, hoping it's faulty.

I only get up at 5 a.m. if I'm setting off on an early walk of shame or need to catch a flight. Mondays are hard enough without adding unnecessary torture. Billionaire brains must be wired differently than a normal working-class person's.

Teagan wakes up at 7 a.m., and I need to have breakfast ready at 7:20 so she can leave by 7:45. I prepare a healthy snack box for her to take to school.

So father and daughter don't even get to see each other in the mornings.

I slowly scan pages and pages of granular details with everything planned out for the Quinn family.

Everything is planned to a T. Every breakfast, dinner, evening, activity.

Teagan does so many after-school activities that

I hardly have to nanny her. I have to make sure she does her homework before dinner and check it when she's done. Blah. I wasn't great in school the first time around.

What about the days when Quinn's had too much to drink and his head's hanging out his asshole? Or when it's pouring rain outside, and he's not willing to brave a run?

Those days don't exist. Not on paper, anyway.

Teagan stays at her grandmother's some Tuesday nights when Mr. Quinn may have female guests stay over. Sounds transactional.

Discretion is expected when Mr. Quinn's guests are visiting.

"Jesus," I say aloud, blinking. Everything is laid out for Quinn, even sex. Is he ever spontaneous?

I wonder what his Tuesday lady friends are like. They're probably high-flying executives who only have time for sex once a week. Like the beautiful one he was with in the hotel.

The company credit card will be used for all purchases. Domestic staff have a personal allowance of $1500 per week for food, clothes, and entertainment. Any increase must be approved by Mr. Quinn.

I read it again.

And again.

Then flop about on the mattress, thrashing my legs about the bed like I'm doing a backstroke.

The sound that erupts from me is pure, raw hysteria.

The next section really has my eyes hanging out

of my head.

Off-limits areas.

The following areas are off-limits unless you have specific permission from Mr. Quinn. Off-limits areas are marked in red on the floor plan.

Sure enough, she has included a floor plan breakdown with red circles. I feel like I'm studying for a master's program in maidhood.

Cabinets in his office. His bedside cabinet. The attic.

She shouldn't have included this section. That's all I can think about now.

What's Quinn hiding in the attic? What a perfect horror movie. Nanny maid creates a manual with cryptic help messages. The new maid finds her dead body in the attic.

I blow out a long breath.

This is not conducive.

The wall clock chimes eleven o'clock, making me jump. My alarm goes off in five hours. I'm giving myself extra time tomorrow morning before Quinn wakes up. I've only plowed through a small part of the manual so far. People don't get that sometimes my brain has to work twice as hard and it's draining.

Staring at the clock, I get pangs of insecurity.

I'm living in a central New York townhouse with the most devastatingly handsome man I've ever clapped eyes on with all my food and bills paid for. Living in Manhattan, legally, is my dream.

But in Queens, I'm in my comfort zone. Working at the bar, living with Orla, teaching yoga in the park, bagels with the amazing crisp crust and lashings of cream cheese from Tony's. There's always "craic" there.

Quinn puts me on high alert, ready to pee my pants at any moment. Or cream them.

It's weird to think he's a few floors above me. His daughter must be in bed too.

I stare up at the ceiling, willing myself to go to sleep. I wonder if Quinn is in bed doing the same thing.

His bed looks massive on the floor plan. Not surprising, considering the size of the body it needs to house. As uncomfortable as I was meeting him, I couldn't help but notice how his T-shirt strained over his upper body.

He's probably sprawled out on his bed right now, naked. Does sleep come easy to a man like him? Maybe he rubs one out to knock himself out.

Maybe he's rubbing one out right now.

Why am I going *there*? Thoughts like that aren't conducive, either.

Except it's hard not to.

When I close my eyes, I can't unsee the image of Killian Quinn's disapproving gaze sweeping over me, the rough gravel in his distinctive voice, the icy steel in his eyes...

Miss Kelly.

My hands drift down under the lace rim of my underwear.

Does he ever thaw? I bet his orgasm face looks angry.

Nope, thinking about my scowling boss' face as he lies on top of me is *not* conducive.

EIGHT

Clodagh

This is *not* the city that never sleeps. The only two people awake are Quinn and me. The rest of Manhattan is asleep.

The manual didn't mention a dress code. I expected a control freak like Quinn to have uniform requirements, like a Victorian maid outfit with an apron.

Perhaps I'm being harsh, but it's hard not to curse the guy after wrestling a fancy coffee machine with thirty different settings for twenty minutes when it's still pitch-black outside.

"Motherfucker," I hiss at the stupid machine. It gurgles loudly back at me in defiance.

I let out a defeated breath. I might cry. I failed at the first task. Making coffee.

"Morning," a rough drawl comes from behind me. "I hope that wasn't directed at me."

"Mr. Quinn!" I squeak, nearly jumping out of my skin. I spin around to face him, feeling the blood rushing to my face. Why am I so damn skittish? I know he lives here, for God's sake.

It's just…

His frame fills the doorway, blocking off the oxygen supply in the kitchen.

Gray cotton sweatpants and a white T-shirt hug his hard lines and muscles. His hair is tousled with a fresh-out-of-bed look, and a slight crease marks his face from sleeping.

The sweatpants are *way* too low-hanging, and I'm not sure he realizes it, or maybe he doesn't give a fuck.

Sharing 5 a.m. is starting to feel very intimate.

"Good morning," I chirp, with a businesslike nod. Too forced.

His stern gaze cuts to me. The kitchen felt airy before he blocked the doorway. Now I feel weighed down by his heavy gaze as he examines my vest top and yoga leggings.

I should have covered up the tattoos. He hates them.

"Is there a problem?" he growls. An actual *growl.* Maybe his vocal cords haven't woken up.

I swallow thickly. "No. Coffee will be with you shortly. The manual didn't mention a dress code," I say, self-consciously. "I thought it would be best to wear comfy clothes to clean easily. You know, bend and get into the hard-to-reach areas." I laugh nervously. "I can wear a maid's outfit if you prefer."

That gets his attention. Something flashes across his otherwise unreadable face. "I don't need you to dress like a maid. Wear whatever's comfortable." His eyes move over me. "But cover your tattoos in front of my daughter. I don't want her getting any ideas."

"Sure." What a grump. "Sit down and make yourself comfortable."

It's probably not the best time to admit that one of my tattoos *might* be a Turkish mafia tattoo sported by certain inmates. The man in the beach booth told me it meant *loyalty* in Turkish. Turns out, it means loyalty to a specific Turkish criminal organization.

Quinn takes a seat on a barstool at the island. I set the green protein smoothie on the counter with unnecessary force and slide it over to him. I don't want to get too close in case he can smell fear.

"Slainté!"

I don't know why I said that. It means cheers in Gaelic. It's one of the only words I remember from school.

He ignores me and takes the glass. As he swallows, the prominent Adam's apple in the thick column of his throat bobs up and down. He chugs the smoothie in one go. Impressive, considering I liquidized a bag of spinach and almonds. Smacking his glass down on the counter, he turns his attention to his phone.

"Was it okay?" I ask.

I take his grunt as approval and turn back to the most complicated machine in the world.

Flustered, I read the instructions *again*, adding another portafilter with coffee beans and water. This is attempt number six, maybe seven, but I don't want to take out my reading pen in front of Quinn.

This coffee looks okay. Better than the last few

attempts. I'd sneak a taste if he wasn't sitting behind me. Instead, I turn around and place the cup in front of him.

He doesn't look up. His dark brows knit together as he reads something on his phone that makes him angry.

I watch as he lifts the coffee cup to his lips and takes a sip. Our eyes lock as he sets the cup down with a thud.

I smile. "How is it?"

"The worst coffee I've ever had in my life," he deadpans.

I wait for him to return the smile.

When he doesn't, my eyes widen in horror, and my smile dies.

He exhales noisily and slides off the barstool. "I don't care what you wear, but I need you to know how to make decent coffee."

"Sorry," I say, mortified, as he towers over me beside the machine. "I'm not used to this model."

"I noticed." He stands close enough so that our shoulders rub. It was safer when we had the marble island between us. The man exudes too much masculinity. My breath catches in my throat, and I hope to God he doesn't notice. "Watch."

Feeling acutely aware of my own breathing, I watch him as he adds water and fills the portafilter.

"The key is setting the grind consistency."

His warm forearm brushes against mine again, sending a jolt of tension through my body. Did he mean to do that? He has the forearms for cutting wood. Or aggressive fingering. Both are equally sexy.

I nod, trying not to feel the heat radiating from his body. I think I know where I'm messing up, but it's hard to concentrate when he makes the art of coffee-making sexual. Talking about grinding in that low husky voice while accidentally brushing his arm against mine.

I try to absorb his words. It's a coffee machine, for Christ's sake. I can handle this.

But his eyes, as blue and stormy as the Atlantic Ocean, distract me. So now I'm a poet.

"The grind determines the intensity. When you grind for too long, the beans become too finely ground, and the coffee becomes bitter."

This close, I see he has a scar running through one of his thick eyebrows.

"Are you listening?" He glares at me like I have the attention span of a fly.

Can he read my mind?

"Yes," I say hastily, nodding. "Get the grinding right. Got it."

His brow rises, unimpressed, as he turns to face me. I watch as he brings the coffee to his lips and takes a sip. Then he holds it under my nose. "Smell it."

I lean forward, taking a deep sniff. Mmm, the scent of a real man. He hasn't had a shower yet. My period is due. The last time I let my period hormones control the decisions, Liam happened.

"Now taste it."

He doesn't hand me the cup. Instead, he holds it to

my lips.

As I take a sip, his eyes drift to my lips, triggering my pulse to race. It's stronger than I usually drink. "Notes... of... nutty," I waffle as I wipe drops from my chin.

"That's what I need you to do every morning. Think you can handle it?"

"Got it, *sir*," I reply with an edge to my voice before I catch myself.

He glances at his watch, then chugs the coffee. With one swift motion, he pulls off his shirt and throws it onto the barstool, leaving him standing in just his low-hanging sweatpants.

I cough to stifle the choking noise in my throat and try to avert my gaze.

The guy has a massive cock. I just *know.* That distinctive V can't be pointing at a tiny penis. What would be the point?

Except I can't avert my gaze because I'm a warm-blooded woman and wild Irish horses couldn't force my eyes away right now.

Stiff Killian Quinn has a chest tattoo. A gray, sexy Celtic chest tattoo.

My ovaries come alive like beacons sending out an SOS. My blood is very fucking hot.

I can't... I just can't leave it alone. "You have a tattoo. I thought..."

He releases a long breath. "If my daughter sees an attractive young woman with tattoos, I'll be nagged for the next two years about why she can't get any."

Attractive young woman. My throat goes dry. "Oh."

"I'm going for a run now. See you in forty-five."

I nod robotically. Great idea. Get out, man, get out!

"Did you forget something?" He looks straight at me as he stretches his muscular arm above his head, providing me with a full view of his armpit hair. He alternates his arms, flexing each in turn. Now, that's what a real man's armpit looks like.

Yup, Aunt Flo is in control.

I blink, confused at the question being fired at me and the show in front of me. Are they related? "Umm...."

His hands come down onto his hips. "You need to check with me every morning if there are additional tasks to carry out."

"Oh!" Shit. Mrs. Dalton had put that in bold. "Sorry, of course. Are there any today?"

He frowns. "I need my tux dry-cleaned before the gala. Talk to my PA about getting two extra tickets." He pauses. "Oh, and check with security to see if Stephen's coming today. Make sure you're available if he needs you."

My eyes widen. Gala? When? Stephen, who are you, and what do you need from me?

I open my mouth, then close it when I realize his instructions aren't open for clarification. Thank God for Mrs. Dalton's attention to detail. "Sure."

Fixing his earbuds in his ears, Quinn stalks out of the kitchen, and I let out a strangled moan of relief. It's barely past five o'clock, and my nerves are shot.

I just realized the guy didn't smile. Not once.

This is bloody exhausting. How did Jane Eyre do

it?

***

True to the manual, Quinn returns from his run at five forty-five, and by some miracle, I have his high-protein breakfast of poached eggs, broccoli, and whole wheat toast ready. The man eats broccoli before six o'clock while the rest of us struggle to get our five a day.

I'm greeted by a freshly showered, suited Quinn wearing dark blue trousers and a white shirt, holding a laptop in one hand and a tie in the other. His hair is wet and tousled.

Damn.

"Hey." He takes a seat beside the island, discarding the tie on the counter.

"Hey," I echo softly. "Good run?"

He glances up briefly before opening his laptop. "Yeah." That's the end of that.

I hold my breath as he swallows the first few bites of breakfast, waiting for him to chastise me.

After a moment, he gruffly nods in my direction. "It's different from Mrs. Dalton's."

That's the closest I'll get to a compliment. I release my breath. Thank fuck. I knew I made good eggs.

He tucks into breakfast as he types. He pops earbuds into his ears, informing me our conversation has finished. Maybe he's doing critical billionaire things. Or maybe he's just an asshole.

I turn to load the dishwasher.

"Oliver," he growls loudly behind me, making me jump. "Where are we with the tender docs for the Vegas site?"

Six o'clock on a Monday morning, and the guy is talking shop already.

He barks demands behind me to Oliver as I fill the dishwasher as quietly as possible.

When I turn to collect his dirty plate, his gaze fixates on my lower half with a deep frown.

He is definitely checking out my butt.

I have a large ass for my size. I'd be adored if I were a female baboon. I've been told it's decent. It's not supermodel bootylicious, but it's round and full, and I've had no complaints.

When his eyes lift to mine, he glares at me like *I'm* the one in the wrong.

I turn back to the dishwasher, clenching my butt cheeks.

I wish he would leave so I could breathe properly. This weird tension is stifling.

Behind me, the laptop snaps shut, and he clears his throat. "I'm going to work now, so I won't be here to introduce you to Teagan." He pauses as I turn to face him.

"She's expecting you," he adds in a softer tone, suggesting that he's aware he's an asshole for not staying for the introductions. "I go to work early so I can get home to have dinner with her. Make sure she finishes all her homework. And keep her off her damn phone."

He doesn't wait for my response. I watch him

stride off, tie hanging undone around his neck, leaving me alone in the kitchen. A stranger moves in, and he can't rearrange his schedule for one morning to introduce his daughter?

***

My pulse quickens when I hear footsteps in the kitchen. I'm nervous about meeting his daughter. Turning thirteen is that weird age when crushes, puberty, and hating the world all collide to create an emotional roller coaster of angst.

The girl entering the kitchen inherited her father's genes. Unlike him, she has fiery-red hair, similar to mine. Did her mother have red hair?

She's wearing a red checkered skirt past her knees with a tie and knee-length socks. I would have raised hell on earth if I was made to wear that at her age.

The only hint of rebellion is the black eyeliner.

"Hi, Teagan." I beam at her. "I'm Clodagh. I'm really excited to meet you."

She eyes me guardedly. Another trait shared with her dad. "Hi."

Does she know who I am? "I'm the new nanny maid. I mean domestic assistant," I announce for clarity.

She rolls her eyes so far back in her head her pupils are in danger of disappearing around the back of her sockets. "I got that."

I put breakfast down in front of her. "I hope it's how you like it. Just tell me if not."

"Thanks."

Just as I'm about to talk, Teagan takes out her phone and scrolls through it with one hand as the other pushes her food around her plate.

I lean uneasily against the sink, wishing Mrs. Dalton had added instructions about engaging with a moody father-and-daughter duet. I'm supposed to keep her off her phone, but I don't think it would be wise to start our time together by scolding her.

"So you go to the Upper East Side Ladies' Academy?" Sounds posh.

Her gaze flickers up for a moment. "Yeah."

"Do you like it?"

"It's alright." She gives me a strained smile before turning her attention back to her phone.

This is messed up. How does she not want to have a conversation with a stranger who's moved into her home?

I persevere. Sooner or later, I'll hit common ground. "The manual says you do ballet. I've always wanted to try it. It sounds fun."

"I guess if the manual says it's fun, it must be," she sneers.

"It wasn't an option when I was in school," I add cheerfully, ignoring her snark. "Maybe you can show me some moves."

She gives me a strange look. "Sure."

"I teach yoga classes in my spare time," I continue. "It's supposed to be great for ballet dancers."

My new housemate doesn't respond.

I'm talking to myself. The Quinn family is as enthralled by their new lodger as they are by a spider on the wall.

While Teagan eats her breakfast glued to her phone, I go over my daily tasks.

In twenty minutes, she'll be taken to school by a driver and security guard. That sounds awful. When I was her age, gossiping with Orla on the school bus was the best part of my day.

This one is going to be a hard nut to crack.

NINE

Killian

"The Mareks have folded," Connor says from across the boardroom table, a triumphant gleam in his eye as he looks up from his laptop. "Their lawyer emailed five minutes ago."

I recline in my chair, admiring the New York City skyline through the window. Seventy stories up, my private boardroom is the only place I can enjoy the sun these days. "I'm glad they found common sense."

"I'll give the contractors the nod to start demolition. With a fair wind, we'll have the foundation of the casino built this side of Christmas."

I nod my agreement. "Are we done?"

"Yup." He rocks back in his chair as he rotates his shoulder. "Just in time for my massage. Are you sure you don't fancy one? Maybe she can help you relax a bit, you know, take the stick out of your backside. You need it before you schmooze the mayor."

Ignoring him, I open my laptop and click on the home security app.

My laptop screen lights up with a multi-screen view of all the rooms in my house. A soft Irish female lilt sounds through the laptop speakers. I search for which room she's in.

"Which reminds me... are we bringing dates to this schmoozing dinner?"

It takes me a minute to register his question. Dinner with the mayor about the Brooklyn casino development. I'm hosting it so we can discuss openly what the old guy needs to cut the red tape on the design restrictions imposed by the council.

"That depends." I glance up at Connor. "If you're bringing someone who models for *Playboy*, then no."

"You'd prefer me to bring someone in pearls and a cardigan?" he drawls.

"Someone who won't paw you at the dinner table would be nice. The mayor is bringing his wife."

"You're asking a lot from a lady there." He smirks and folds his arms over his chest. "And who are *you* bringing?"

"Maria Taylor."

Connor hums in approval.

Meeting Maria was a surprising turn of events. For the first time in a long time, I might have found someone who could hold my interest. Ivy League-educated, and an absolute head turner.

"Nice. She's a good match for you. Maybe you'll consider something serious."

"It's business rather than pleasure this time. She's friends with the mayor's wife." Although I have considered trying something serious with Maria.

It's been a long time since I had something more intimate than sex. Recently, I've been feeling like maybe it's time to try again.

"Good call." His brows draw together. "What's that sound?"

"I'm checking on the new Mrs. Dalton," I say grimly, maximizing the room with the movement.

My hand freezes over the mouse.

My bedroom.

Connor leans over and connects my laptop to the boardroom projector so Clodagh appears in full size on the screen.

I stiffen.

She's in my bedroom, her back facing the camera. She's in shorts so tiny they could pass for underwear and the same white tank top from this morning. Her red hair is tied up in a messy ponytail, and a sheen of sweat glistens on her back as she moves around my bed, adjusting the pillows.

Seeing her half-naked in my bedroom gets under my skin just as much as that feminine Irish brogue that makes every sentence sound musical.

"*That's* the new Mrs. Dalton?"

"Yes," I say, my voice low.

With her back to us, she flips through something on the bed, muttering to herself. Ah, the manual.

Connor leans forward to get a closer look. "Cute tattoos on her arm. Does she look as good from the front as behind?"

Yes. Better.

"You should pay for a streaming service. There's

plenty of premium nanny porn out there. Less chance of a lawsuit."

"Shut it. She's the hired help," I bite out, not taking my eyes off Clodagh. "I don't give a shit what she looks like. I'm paying her to look after my daughter and clean." My jaw tightens. "She's not right for the job."

He chuckles, grabbing the screen remote from me. "Why haven't you removed her then, like the last two? Oh wait, is it because it's nice to have a pretty Irish lady fluff your pillows for you?"

I swallow my irritation, never taking my eyes off the screen. That is what I call an ass for spanking. "She's not fired because Marcus convinced me to keep her while he looks for someone else." I should have fired her just for stealing products from my hotel's restroom.

Clodagh's guttural lilt fills the room as Connor turns up the volume.

My hands tighten around the laptop.

His brows lift. "Northern Irish?"

"Close. Donegal."

"Damn." His voice is a low groan. "They sound angry even when they're not. She can say whatever she wants. I might not understand it all, but I'll still listen."

My jaw locks tighter as she launches into a tirade of curses that would make a galley of sailors proud.

Connor's eyes widen as he chuckles. "Did she just call you a motherfucker?"

"Yes, I believe she did," I say through gritted teeth.

And as pissed off as I am, hearing the woman insult me in her thick accent rouses something in my chest that rarely surfaces anymore.

Adrenaline.

"Fantastic." Connor swings back in his chair, tipping on the two back legs. I hope he loses his balance. "Are you going to let her get away with that? I'm happy to help if she needs to be disciplined."

"Pipe down," I growl at the smart-ass, snatching the remote from him.

I'm about to kick him out of the boardroom when Clodagh turns with the manual in her hand and faces the camera, oblivious to the fact we're watching her.

Her cheeks are flushed. Her brows are pulled together in a frown as she wipes sweat off her forehead. Silver glistens on her button nose. I squint, zooming in with the remote... what is that?

A silver ring in the shape of a horseshoe pierces her septum. She must take it out whenever I'm around.

Ridiculous. If Teagan got one of those, I'd hit the fucking roof.

I stiffen as my eyes scan down all five-foot-nothing of her body.

She has the visible tan lines of a tourist who doesn't understand how strong the New York sun can get.

She's not wearing a bra. Her chest glistens as beads of sweat disappear into creamy curves. Peaked nipples poke through her flimsy vest top exposing small, firm breasts that my hands would engulf. Arousal stirs unhelpfully inside me.

She's tiny. A man like me would crush her.

I run my hand over my jaw agitatedly. I have two views of her now, one on the widescreen and one filling my laptop screen.

Connor lets out a low whistle, eyes fixed on the widescreen. "Nice. This is what she wears to clean your house?"

That wasn't in the fucking manual. When I said there was no dress code, I didn't mean it literally. I'll have to update it to say she needs to wear that hideous floral skirt.

My hands grip the remote tighter as Clodagh bends down to start the vacuum cleaner, giving us an eyeful of breasts.

Connor grins conspiratorially. "Funny how Marcus chose someone who would have been your type ten years ago. Pity she's too young for you."

"Hardly," I growl. "She looks like an overgrown teenager with a bullring through her nose. And by the sounds of how much she talks to herself, she's fucking crazy."

"Uh-huh." He smirks, pissing me off even further.

I might be getting aroused over the nanny, but attractive little redheads are a dime a dozen in Manhattan, and if I wanted one, I could pick one that was a tad more refined without shitting on my own doorstep.

"She's not even qualified as a nanny. And she

appears to have zero experience as a domestic assistant." I pause, letting my eyes roam all over her body. "She's a trained carpenter."

"A carpenter? That's cool. I don't know any female carpenters."

I have to agree with him; given a few more years and the proper guidance, Clodagh could have a decent little business.

We watch as she runs the vacuum back and forth across the carpet. It makes a grinding noise, like something is stuck in it.

No... no ...

I exhale sharply as the vacuum smashes into the bedside table, knocking over the picture of Teagan and me.

Connor barks out a laugh, apparently believing the situation is more humorous than it is. "Maybe keep your valuables up high."

Cursing loudly, she stops the vacuum with a kick and bends down to lift the picture, giving us a full view of her ass.

"Remind me why we're spying on your hot young cleaner? I could watch her all day, but even I have morals sometimes."

"I'm checking to ensure she can follow simple instructions and behave herself. I don't trust her yet." I clench my jaw.

As she puts the photo back, the nightstand drawer nudges open an inch. Indecision flickers across her face.

"Don't fucking do it," I snarl at the camera as her

hand hovers over it.

She does it. She brazenly opens my damn drawer. Just another few inches, but it's enough.

I swipe the speaker button. "Why are you looking in an off-limits area?"

Screaming pierces the boardroom's speakers.

Connor and I wince as she turns in all directions to identify the source of the voice. It's surround sound.

She shuts the drawer with such force the picture falls off the nightstand again, and this time, I hear the frame smash.

"What the hell?" she screeches, her panicked green eyes darting around the room.

Connor raises a brow, amused. "You have *off-limits* zones in your house?"

"It's good to set boundaries. As clearly demonstrated here, people can't be trusted."

Especially not a woman with an ass like that.

She runs to the door to check if anyone is on the other side, then comes back to the center of the room and inhales a deep breath. "It's the home security system," she says softly. "He's programmed it to trigger in an off-limits zone."

"No, Clodagh." My voice echoes through the bedroom. "It's your boss."

She freezes, looking like she's about to jump out of her skin. I'd laugh along with Connor if I wasn't so angry.

She turns to face the bedroom door again to see if I'm there. When I don't appear, she reverts to looking wildly in the air for cameras. She can't figure out where my voice is coming from because it's coming from all four corners of the ceiling.

"She's starting to look a little crazy now," Connor says.

"She can hear you. The speaker is on."

"Q-Quinn?" she whispers loudly in her distinctive lilt. "Mr. Quinn?"

"Day one on the job, and you're already ignoring my rules."

She draws in a sharp breath. "Are you watching me through cameras?"

"Yes." I do my best to ignore the way her chest heaves with every breath. "Explain why you feel the need to open my nightstand."

The crimson blush on her cheeks darkens. "I'm sorry. I was just making sure you weren't a serial killer."

"In my nightstand?"

"You can learn a lot about people by what they have in their bedside cabinets." She looks at the ceiling for approval, as if this is an acceptable reason for invading my privacy.

"I won't do it again," she adds, panic taking over her voice. She glances down as if suddenly realizing she's in little more than underwear and wipes sweat away from her chest.

Fuck, woman, stop that.

Connor chuckles beside me, looking inexplicably pleased with himself for no damn reason.

"Do you have somewhere you need to be?" I snap,

waving my hand at him to get out.

"No," Connor and Clodagh answer simultaneously.

"Not you, Clodagh," I say forcefully, turning my attention back to the screen. "Stay put."

She stands on the spot like an army cadet with her arms stiff by her sides. It looks like she's stopped breathing.

"Absolutely not," Connor drawls, slouching one arm over his chair. "I have nowhere better to be than here."

Sighing in frustration, I mute the security app. "Fine. If you insist on staying, this will be over in less than five."

I press the speakerphone again. "Security will be there in fifteen minutes. You have thirty to pack up your things."

She laughs shakily. "That was for the person in the room, right?"

"It's quite obvious that it was directed at you. *Clodagh.*"

"W-What?" Her hands rise to smack her mouth. "Mr. Quinn, *please.*" She flaps her arms around in the air. "Sir. *No.* I'll *never* do anything like this again. You vetted me. Don't you think I should do my own due diligence?" She pauses to catch her breath. "It would almost be irresponsible of me not to. That's all I was doing, but my vetting's complete now."

Her brazenness is almost admirable.

Connor snort-laughs, and I fire another glare at him.

"I can't have someone in my house who I don't trust," I say coolly. If Clodagh thinks this is the first time a pretty face has tried to win me over and been disappointed, she's in for a nasty surprise. "You're under the same roof as my daughter."

That's my bottom line.

Her face turns an unhealthy shade of white.

"You're being a bit harsh," Connor says casually.

"I agree with him," Clodagh pipes up, making Connor smile.

"Please," she begs. The emerald eyes hit the right spot to stare directly into the camera. "I need to trust you too. I binge-watched that Netflix series last week on serial killers, and I freaked myself out. For all I know, the last domestic assistant might be dead in the attic. I listen to a lot of true crime, so I wanted to do a few checks." She chews her bottom lip. "What with moving in with a strange man and all."

"Stop talking." I jab the mute button again. "Do I look like a fucking serial killer?" I mutter to Connor.

He shrugs. "C'mon, man. The girl's on the verge of tears. Cut her some slack. I get why a young woman would be scared of living with you." His lips twitch. "Like living with a homicidal maniac."

I roll my eyes in disgust.

On the screen, Clodagh adjusts her shorts self-consciously, her weight shifting from foot to foot.

"I'm the vulnerable one here." Her voice fills the boardroom. Apparently, now she knows where the camera is because those piercing green eyes stare unwaveringly at me. I've never seen a shade like it before. Are they contact lenses? The swallow action in her throat is visible on the screen. "Moving into a strange man's house."

I jab the speaker button again to tell her she's wasting my time when she should be packing, but Connor puts his hand over mine.

"Don't be rash."

"Fuck off. I don't need distractions or drama in my own home."

His brow arches. "What drama has she caused?"

"I thought you only checked the cameras by exception," Clodagh continues softly, dragging my gaze back to her. "I didn't realize you'd be *watching* me."

My lips press into a thin line. Is she telling me off?

"A new nanny is an exception," I bite back gruffly through the speaker.

She nods dramatically. "Okay, fair point. But please, give me one more chance. Please? I wasn't trying to steal anything." She pauses, pouting. "I just wanted to make sure you're a good guy."

Connor snorts. "She's in for a disappointment."

I turn my head, bemused.

"Are you still there?" Clodagh pipes up over the speaker. She nibbles on her lips like she's trying to chew them off. "Wherever you are." She waves both hands in the air, laughing nervously. "Am I looking in the right direction? This is really unnerving."

"Killian." Connor leans over and jabs the mute option, his expression turning serious. "Give the girl a second chance. What is she, like twenty?"

"Twenty-four," I correct, nostrils flaring. "Almost twenty-five."

"Come on, loosen up a little. Do you really think cleaners don't poke around in bedside cabinets? Get a lock if you're that concerned. Besides, you don't have any other options right now. You'd have to vet someone else." He shrugs, still holding the mute button. "What's the worst that can happen?"

I shift my focus from Connor back to Clodagh.

Swallowing thickly, I watch her rub the back of her neck. I watch her chest heave with shallow breaths. I watch her green eyes burn with the adrenaline and fear of knowing that my next words will decide her fate in America.

"Please, Mr. Quinn." Her soft lilt carries surprising steel.

Don't beg me. It didn't work for the Mareks, and it won't work for—

Damn.

Acting on impulse, I jab the speaker button. "No more fuckups. I don't do second chances, Miss Kelly."

The breath whooshes out of her. She collapses on my bed with such force it makes her small breasts jiggle. "Thank you, Mr. Quinn. I won't let you down. Again."

An irritating spark of emotion ignites inside me when I see that megawatt smile. It's a smile money can't buy, and surgery can't fake.

So now I'm a soft touch.

"Fantastic," Connor booms, clapping his hands together. "I can't wait to meet you, Clodagh."

"Me too," she calls out, confused.

"Show's over." Connor pushes to stand and slaps me on the back forcefully. "Try not to bury yourself inside the nanny."

"*Jesus,*" I hiss, glaring at his back as he leaves. He meant for her to hear that.

"Uh, Mr. Quinn?" Clodagh asks in a quiet voice after a long beat. "Do you need anything else? If not, I'll get back to work."

I realize I've been staring at her. "No. Did you read the instructions for Monday evenings?"

She nods. "I'll have dinner ready at seven o'clock for both of you. Is option four from the menu list okay this evening? Salmon and roasted vegetables?"

"Sure. Actually, no." Might as well make her sweat. "Teagan likes a nice huntsman pie. Here's your chance to redeem yourself. Mrs. Dalton makes a superb version."

"A huntsman... Great." Her smile falters for a moment, but she quickly recovers. "Consider it done."

She pushes her hair behind her ear and grabs the laundry basket. The idea of her handling my underwear seems too intimate.

"Mr. Quinn... will you be watching me any more today? Because it might make me feel a little paranoid."

"No." My jaw tightens. "It may surprise you that I have to work, considering I'm the CEO."

She laughs, holding the laundry basket. "Fair enough. Uh, anything else?"

"That's all for now." I pause. "There's A/C, you know? I'll show you how to use it when I get home."

Or maybe I won't.

I hit the mute button.

"Bye!" Clodagh shouts. Her eyes dart around the room guardedly, wondering if she's still being watched.

My finger hovers over the app button to close it just as my phone rings.

"Yes." I put Mandy on speaker.

"Alfred Marek was in reception, demanding to speak to you. Security escorted him outside, but he's hanging around the building." She pauses. "I thought you should know."

"The son?"

"Yes."

"How long?"

"About forty-five minutes. Should we call the police? Technically, he's not doing anything illegal. He's just watching the building."

"He's waiting for me." I sigh, scrubbing my face with my hand. I don't have time for this shit. It sounds like Junior didn't take his dad's decision well. "Call the police. I don't want him harassing any of the staff. I'll talk to them if you need me to."

"Right away, sir." She dials off, and I turn back to the screen to where Clodagh is cleaning.

I have somewhere to be... but...

I hit the zoom button, zooming... zooming... zooming until Clodagh's face covers the screen.

Heat courses through my veins. I shift

uncomfortably in my seat, wondering why I'm entertaining the thought of bending my disobedient nanny over my knee for not paying heed to the man of the house.

This is fucked up.

Mrs. Dalton's daughter needs to recover ASAP.

***

Go lasadh solas na bhFlaitheas ar d'uaigh.

May the light of heaven shine on your grave.

I stare at the Irish blessing and photo of Harlow on her tombstone, stuck in time.

Smiling, carefree and excited about what the world had to offer her. Excited that she was a mother.

Except I took all that from you, Harlow.

I took your hopes and dreams and your future.

You had so many dreams.

To be a mother to our beautiful daughter.

To prove that the kid from the wrong side of Queens was worthy of the New York Ballet.

To retire in a small village on the coast of Ireland, with your children around you.

I took it all from you.

I'm sorry I failed you.

I'm sorry I failed Teagan.

Time heals all wounds. Isn't that right, Harlow?

Wrong.

Teagan's nearly thirteen, Harlow. A teenager. I can't believe our little girl is growing up so quickly.

I don't know why I'm telling you, you'd never forget that. I'm taking her to see some pop star with floppy hair for her birthday, but knowing Teagan, she'll have gone off him and be madly in love with some other runt.

She's still wearing makeup, covering up her beautiful face, but when I say anything about it, we fight. I need you more than ever. It was easier when I was checking the closet for monsters. Now I need to check that she hasn't hidden her phone under the bedsheets so she doesn't spend all night on it.

We have another replacement for Mrs. Dalton. My nannies wouldn't run away if you were here. My nannies wouldn't be needed if you were here. Not that I'm allowed to call her a nanny. Teagan says she's too old.

I think you'd like this one, although she seems like a loose cannon. She's testing my patience. You were always more forgiving than I am.

I need you to talk back.

But of course, she doesn't, because the dead leave you alone with your own tortured thoughts.

I lay the fresh flowers on the grave. Visiting Harlow's grave is the only time I visit Queens. Sometimes with Teagan, often alone.

No one knows about my spontaneous midday trips here. I need to come, but it's too painful to stay.

"Bye, Harlow," I say quietly. I clench my jaw and

walk back to my driver.

TEN

Clodagh

What the hell is a huntsman pie? Is that like a chicken potpie but with Australian spiders instead of chicken?

Don't panic.

Do. Not. Panic.

He's testing me. He wants a reason to fire me. Another reason.

I stare at my phone in horror as the page loads. Pork... chicken... pulse the dough. Time to cook: three hours, thirty minutes, so I'm already late.

And I still have to take his tux to the dry cleaners. And clean the top floor of the house.

I open the fridge. Close the fridge. Open the fridge.

"Are you kidding me!" I shout into the fridge with no pork, chicken, or dough... stuff... whatever the hell dough is made from. The echo is mildly satisfying. God, he's a gobshite. Or a *jerk*, I should say, in the States.

This is all because I had an innocent peek at his condom drawer. I'll need counseling after getting caught in his *off-limits* zone.

When the bodiless Quinn told me off, I was more unnerved than when the police took me in for questioning after my series of unfortunate incidents, as Orla calls it.

My heart has only just slowed to a normal pace.

At least he didn't see me pick my nose directly before that.

Or *did* he?

"Siri, find me restaurants that do huntsman pies near Central Park." Thank God for delivery services.

"Sorry," says Siri. "I'm not sure I understand."

"I don't have time for your shit, Siri!" I snap back at her.

Taking a deep breath, I repeat the request in my poshest, slowest Queen's English accent.

She understands immediately and happily engages in conversation. The cheek.

On the other side of Central Park, Le Grand Cochon serves award-winning pies made from organic meat.

Done. Sold for one hundred dollars. I blow out a deep breath.

"Hey," a deep voice says from behind me, scaring the shit out of me.

I turn. "Sam!"

He leans against the wall, his eyes twinkling in amusement. "Someone's jumpy. First-day nerves?"

"Something like that. I got caught off-limits."

"Huh?"

"Never mind." I sigh. "Hey, I'm assuming that

Stephen, who *might* visit the house today, is Stephen, the drainage guy, and not Stephen, the dentist or Father Steve, the priest. I can't get ahold of any of them to check."

His lips twist. "Drainage guy. You're doing fine, Clodagh. It'll get easier."

"Here's hoping." I try not to ogle him, but it's hard when he's wearing his uniform of black trousers and black shirt with the top buttons undone. It's a hot look. "If you guys are undercover, shouldn't you wear something less man-in-black?"

"It's our job to be conspicuous. Mr. Quinn wants it to be obvious that a security team is present."

"I've only met you, Sam. Where's the rest of the team?"

"The rest are about watching and waiting." He grins and saunters closer. "I'm checking on my fellow countrywoman in case she needs anything."

"Thanks." I smile. "But... *watching*? Talk about making a girl feel paranoid."

He chuckles as he comes to stand right beside me. "Don't be. It's a boring job, waiting around. Mr. Quinn sometimes does spot tests on us with fake snipers, but most of the time, we're in the house working out to pass the time."

"Fake *snipers*? Are you freaking kidding me?" I manage to spit a little on Sam in my shock. This sounds very dramatic. "He won't put a fake sniper on me, will he?"

"Not unless you warrant it." He smirks. "Relax. Only the security team needs to know how to handle snipers. You're safe."

"Yeah, because living in a house at risk of sniper attacks feels safe." I suck in a groan. "Oh my God, that's why I've been recruited. They know no one will miss me in America."

The corner of his mouth twitches. "Oh, you'll be missed."

I rear back a little, blushing. Sam's flirting has upped a notch. I'm not complaining.

"I know he's a bazillionaire, but this seems extreme. Is he really in need of so much security? The house is already like Fort Knox."

"Yup."

That's all I get. There's a story there that he doesn't want to tell me. Maybe he *is* scared Quinn is listening. I'll get it out of him when we're away from the house.

I pretend to look serious. "So you big burly protector guys sit around working out in that house, huh?" Sounds like the perfect setup for a reverse harem. "Maybe I need to take a trip over and say hi."

"Damn, I should have kept my mouth shut. The house wouldn't be able to handle a beautiful lass like yourself." His grin widens, accentuating the dimple on his right cheek. "I'll act as the liaison between you and the rest of the team."

"Can you be the liaison between Mr. Quinn and me?" I whisper in case Quinn is watching through his cameras.

"Nah, don't worry." He shakes his head dismissively. "You're safe. He doesn't go after staff.

Or normal girls, for that matter."

"I didn't mean that... wait, what do you mean, *normal* girls?"

"He goes for a certain type of woman." Sam doesn't appear to be trying to offend me, which makes the jab even worse.

"Uh-huh." With my nose out of joint, I change the subject. "Listen, can you show me how to use the A/C properly? It goes from desert heat to arctic conditions when I turn it on."

My nipples are confused.

Just as he is about to respond, his phone buzzes. It's the fastest I've ever seen someone check a phone. They must be on high alert all the time.

"Damn," he mutters. His face relaxes, so I know there's not an emergency. "I'll be back in a while to show you, okay?"

I nod, smiling. Anyway, I have a pie collection to take care of.

He turns, but not before giving me a cheeky wink. "Oh, and for the record, Clodagh, I'm glad you're working here."

***

Dinner sorted, I finish cleaning the last level of the house, Teagan's floor. Up here, she has her own chill-out room with a massive TV and gaming equipment.

I walk down the hall to her bedroom. It's gigantic. Teddy bears and Disney cushions are juxtaposed with boxes and shelves of eyeliner, lipstick, hair products, and perfume. A girl becoming a young woman.

I survey the chaos strewn all over the room. It looks like it's been ransacked.

I move a million lipsticks off the dresser to clean it. Above it is a collage of photos of a baby and a female, with a few featuring Killian.

"Her mum," I murmur to myself.

She's beautiful. The blond curls are surprising; I thought she'd be a redhead like Teagan. She looks young. Maybe younger than me.

I gcuimhne grámhar Harlow Murphy, I read below one of the pictures.

In loving memory of Harlow Murphy.

American first name. Irish surname.

It's heartbreaking that she doesn't get to see Teagan grow up. Marcus said she died when Teagan was two. I have so many questions. Morbid ones like how did she die? But also, what was she like? What were *they* like together?

It's a pretty unique name.

I take out my phone and google *Harlow Murphy*. After a few clicks, I see Teagan's blue-eyed, smiling mother.

Man, 35, charged with murder of mother Harlow Murphy in Woodside, Queens.

She was *murdered*. God, I feel sick.

Miss Murphy was the partner of growing hotel entrepreneur Killian Quinn.

The article is vague. It happened at her home, but no motive is given. Did Killian and Harlow live in Queens for a while? I pictured Killian always living in Manhattan.

It feels wrong checking this out in Teagan's room. I clean quickly, feeling like there's a ghost here.

I need to keep my nose out; the Quinn family's personal life is none of my business.

***

"So? How was your first day?" Orla shouts down the line.

From the background noise, I can tell she's in The Auld Dog. Pangs of jealousy hit me as I stand in the kitchen of the lavish multimillion-dollar mansion.

Ridiculous.

"It's not over yet," I mutter, gripping my phone between my ear and shoulder as I strategically place vegetables around the freshly delivered huntsman pie. I'm relieved that I only cook dinner three nights a week, and his seven-star hotel delivers on the other nights. "And Tuesday's part of the manual is thick... if I make it to then."

"I can hardly hear ya," she shouts. "Speak up."

"I can't," I hiss in a loud whisper. "He might be listening."

"He's there now?"

"No." I pause and speak even lower. "But he might be watching me through the cameras. He was watching me early on. It was a bit of a disaster, actually."

"I really hope I misheard that last bit, Clodagh. The guys here say hello." There's a pause. "Especially Liam. He wants to talk to you."

Blah. Ever since I moved to Manhattan, he's upped the intensity. I need to nip that in the bud.

"Don't fucking put him on the phone, Orla. He's freaking me out. He must have sent *ten* messages today. If he doesn't calm down, I'll ghost him."

I hear her footsteps over the phone. "Okay, I've moved away from him. Come on, you know it's impossible to ghost an Irish guy in Queens. It's worse here than in Donegal. Besides, you'll see him this weekend when you come back."

Exhaling a groan, I flatten the pie with my knuckles to make it look less professional. She's right. "He's not listening. I tried to be as blunt as possible. I *want* to be his one-night stand. I don't want him to *court* me as he keeps threatening to do. Tell him I'm close to calling immigration."

"Ack, come on. Maybe you should give him a chance. Liam's a good-looking fella."

"Absolutely not." I shudder, hitting the pie with an exasperated grunt. "Every time my phone pings and his name flashes up, I want to hyperventilate into a brown bag."

"Fair enough. So... hurry up... tell me... what's Quinn like? Is he a psycho?"

I open the oven and place the plates on a warming tray. That's all I need to do for fifteen minutes, so I wander into the lounge. "I signed an NDA, so even if he is, I couldn't tell you." Stopping to look at some of the family photos on the walls, I stare into the icy-blue eyes of a younger Quinn. Are those psycho eyes?

"We tell each other everything," she huffs. "Do you think you could meet for drinks on Thursday night? We could go to that club in the Meatpacking District we talked about."

"Not this Thursday." I stare at a photo of Killian and Teagan on the wall. Teagan looks about six. Killian looks stony-faced even though he's smiling. "I have to get up too early on Friday. My afternoons tend to be free, so at least I can squeeze in some yoga and a walk. I'm free after I make their dinner, but the way I feel right now, I just want to collapse in bed by eight. We'll have to wait until the weekend."

There's an audible tut over the line. "It doesn't sound fun."

"No, not fun yet," I say dryly.

My hand trails over a picture of Killian and Teagan with an older woman, probably his mother. There's another photo of Quinn with a guy who looks like him, the same dark hair, the same handsome masculine features, and striking blue eyes. It has to be his brother. A few more of a much younger Killian with Harlow and Teagan. Harlow has the brightest smile of them all.

"Truth is," I whisper, "the guy is scary as fuck. There seems to be a stick lodged permanently up his ass. I honestly don't know how long I'll last."

"I give you another two days," a female voice sneers behind me.

I pivot in horror to find Teagan, the demon child, observing me with an expression of either indifference or disgust. Maybe both.

"Sorry, Orla," I stammer, ending the call.

"Teagan," I say shakily, plastering on a smile. What is it with this family spying on me? "Would you believe me if I said the stick thing is a term of endearment in Ireland?"

She rolls her eyes. She's less put together than this morning, but her thick black eyeliner looks fresh.

"You're supposed to be at music lessons," I say breathlessly, watching her toss her schoolbag on the table. I'm so screwed. When Teagan snitches, her dad will definitely fire me. Could I say she misheard me? Blaming the accent could work.

"I'm sick," she says, then has the audacity to add a blatantly sarcastic fake cough.

"What can I do to help? Are you nauseous?"

Ignoring me, she stomps into the kitchen through the double doors.

I follow her in. If I don't keep Daddy's dearest happy, I'll be off the runway tarmac faster than I can say *slan leat.* Irish for goodbye.

"Can I make you a drink or something?" I ask.

"It's fine." She opens cupboards and slams them shut as if looking for something. She doesn't seem that sick. Maybe she's bunking off music lessons.

I persevere. "How was school?"

She cuts me a glare. "You don't need to pretend you're interested. We don't need to talk."

Jeez. Mission failed. "Didn't you and Mrs. Dalton

chat?"

"*You're* not Maggie," she snaps. "She'll be back in a few months."

I try to remember what it was like to be a new teenager. Everything and everyone is the worst. "I get it. It's a pain having a stranger living in your house."

She shrugs defensively. "I'm used to the staff being around. I have security at school."

The staff.

My eyes widen. "Wow."

"I've had them since kindergarten." Teagan studies me strangely. "What I can't figure out is why he picked *you*. You're nothing like Maggie or the other two."

"The other two?"

"The nannies who got fired before you."

Great.

I turn off the oven, totally unnerved. "Your dad didn't pick me," I tell her, deflated. "And I don't think he would have either. Marcus, a guy who works for your father, did."

"Maybe it's because you're Irish." Her eyes narrow. "I bet you're only here to come on to my dad."

My eyes bulge out of my head. Where did *that* come from? "Excuse me?"

"Oh, please. He can't even go to the supermarket without women hitting on him. It's probably the only reason you applied."

"Firstly," I snap, putting my hand on my hips. "I doubt very much your dad goes to the supermarket, and *secondly*, I can barely *talk* to him." I snort indignantly. I'm not having a teenybopper make out that I'm a gold digger. "Coming on to your dad is the last thing on earth I'd do. I want to keep this job. That's very judgmental, considering you've just met me."

She eyes me skeptically for a long beat. "Whatever."

"Look," I say more calmly. "I want you to give me the chance I deserve. Let's get to know each other. When school breaks in a few weeks, we'll be spending more time together."

"Why are you bothering? You won't have to talk to me in a few months."

I frown. "How do you make friends with that attitude?"

She glares back at me. "I have enough friends."

"At twelve?" I put my hands on my hips. Now it's my turn to do a dramatic eye roll. "Listen, when you're my age, you won't be friends with half the people you are today. If you're lucky, you'll collect new people along the way."

Her upbringing seems so alien to mine. I'm starting to think growing up in a multimillion-dollar townhouse isn't all it's cracked up to be. Most of the rooms I cleaned today were guest bedrooms. Teagan's bedroom is on a separate floor from her father's. I get the impression I'm not the only one living like a stranger in the house.

"What if we end up getting on really well and staying in contact?" I ask, softening my tone.

"Doubtful." She comes up beside me and grabs a bottled water from the fridge.

She's not giving me an inch.

I let out a defeated sigh. "Is there *any* way I can convince you not to tell your dad what you heard me say? Or that I cursed?"

"I'm not *ten*. And Dad curses all the time." She smiles with an evil glint in her eye, accentuated by the eyeliner. "It'll be more fun to see what finally gets you fired."

"I haven't even been in this job a day, so I'm not sure where your lack of confidence comes from," I huff. "But you're right; I'm more than capable of getting the sack all by myself, so if you could not hurry it along, that would be great."

"Sorry, not sorry," she sneers.

"There's no need to be so snarky," I snap. "*Jesus.* Give me a break."

To my surprise, she looks mildly contrite. I groan, scanning the kitchen ceiling. "Your dad's probably listening right now."

"Probably."

At least I've got Teagan talking. It's a start.

"Truth, why are you really bunking off music?"

She snorts. "Why? Do you think you'll get points with my dad if you snitch?"

"I won't snitch if you don't." I grin. "Believe me, I'm in more trouble with your dad than you are."

She rolls her eyes, but the corners of her mouth twitch. "I play the cello. It's fucking wack."

Wack is a bad thing, I assume.

"Fair enough. I don't blame you. Oh, and language. Watch your language," I say halfheartedly. It feels hypocritical to tell her off when I cursed at her age. "I bet your dad wouldn't let you talk like that."

Another shrug. "He's so freaking salty all the time. It doesn't matter what I say."

Christ, I need a teenager translation guide at this rate.

"Did that hurt?" she asks, taking a step toward me. I frown for a second, not understanding what she's talking about.

My hand flies to the nose ring right through my septum. Damn, I thought I had taken it out. I covered the tattoos but forgot about the ring.

"Yes." I smile. "*Massively.* They use a needle rather than a gun. As soon as the needle went in, I screamed my head off."

"My dad would hit the roof if I got that done. What age did you get it?"

"Seventeen."

Her jaw drops slightly, then she quickly hides her surprise. I remember it's not cool to show a reaction other than indifference at her age. "Is your hair color real?"

"Yeah," I say with a smile. "Like yours."

Her face falls. "It's nothing like mine. Yours is smooth."

"Oh, I've been there." Finally, an in with Teagan. "I just learned to tame it after years of trying. I used to get teased relentlessly for having frizzy hair. I can help you with yours if you want? I have good hair products that will take the frizz out."

"Perhaps." She sniffs. "I hate mine. And Dad won't let me do anything about it."

"When I was younger, my mam didn't want me to dye my hair either, but I was so desperate to change it that I used food coloring. She went ballistic. But it worked! For about three days, my head was neon red. Not good." I laugh, remembering. "But different."

A trace of amusement crosses her face. "That's so stupid."

"What can I say? You live and learn."

I'm distracted by my phone buzzing in my bag. I take it out, and there's a message from an unknown number.

How are you settling in? Is Killian the ogre you thought he would be? Marcus.

Worse, actually, I refrain from texting back. *I'd prefer to lodge with the Addams family.*

Now I get why he needed someone desperate. It's not even the end of day one, and my nerves are shot.

ELEVEN

Killian

When I come home from work, astonishingly, the fire-engine redhead hasn't burned the house down. I hear voices as I head toward the kitchen. Laughter. Female laughter mixed in with the deeper tones of a male.

Sam and Clodagh rest against the island counter, their forearms almost touching. It's a nice surprise to see Teagan plopped on a barstool, engaging in conversation rather than retreating to her room.

Sam says something, and both girls laugh. Clodagh's laughter is loud, too loud; her warm abrasive tones dominate the kitchen, and I wonder what Sam said that's so amusing.

My hackles instantly rise. My security staff doesn't need distractions. This is how people get hurt.

"Hi," I call out, more as a warning than a greeting, walking to my daughter. "Princess." I pull Teagan in for a kiss on her forehead.

Clodagh's laughter dies in her throat. "Mr. Quinn."

"Boss," Sam says quickly, standing up straight. "I was checking if Clodagh needed anything. What with it being her first day."

"Get back to work, Sam," I say abruptly. "Last time I checked the schedule, you were on duty."

My sharp tone startles him, but he nods, giving me a quiet, "Yes, sir," as he leaves.

Not before Clodagh flashes that megawatt smile at him that pisses me off for no explicable reason. Thank fuck she's wearing more clothing than she was this afternoon. Now she's in jeans and a short tight T-shirt with a ridiculous cartoon bunny and sleeves in an attempt to hide her tattoos. On her stomach, a sliver of skin peeks out. Her auburn-red hair is in a messy bun on top of her head.

Her smile slips into something more measured as she moves toward the oven. "Dinner's ready."

"Right on time." My eyes dip to the distracting bunny. Is she aware that the bunny's eyeballs align with her breasts? She looks even younger than twenty-four. I need her to wear that big, old, floral skirt again, like she did when she first arrived.

Dropping my tie on the table, I ask my daughter, "How was school, princess?"

Teagan doesn't look up from her phone. "Fine."

"When I'm talking to you, Teagan, I expect you to look at me."

She drags her gaze up. Fuck's sake. We've gone around in circles about the black smudge she insists on smearing over her eyes. She's too young for all this shit on her face.

I don't have the patience for the fight tonight.

"The security team told me you didn't go to cello this afternoon. What's wrong?"

She shrugs. "I had a sore head." My daughter is a terrible liar.

I feel her head. "Is it still sore?"

She leans away from me. "I'm fine, Dad; stop fussing."

"Okay then. What did you learn today? Did anything fun happen?"

"The usual," she says without looking up.

I take the phone from her hand. She glares at me and tuts.

Another night of having a conversation with myself. "Where are your manners, Teagan?"

She wants to roll her eyes but knows better. "This morning, I did geography and learned that we're slowly killing ourselves and heading for extinction. This afternoon, we did an hour of religious studies. Is that enough, Dad?"

"Less of the attitude," I say sharply, trying to rein in my annoyance. "I'm taking an interest in your day."

"I hung out with Becky at break time. *Her* mom's letting her get highlights in her hair."

She gives me the stink-eye, and I sigh. Not this again. "Well, Becky's hair probably isn't as beautiful as yours."

She huffs out air. "Can I have my phone back, please?"

I resist the urge to fire the damn device across the room and ban her from using electronics until she's thirty. "No, princess. Thirty minutes a day, we agreed."

"How do you know I've used my minutes?" she wails.

Exhaling, I lean my forearms on the counter, rubbing my forehead.

"Uh… shall I serve?" Clodagh asks tentatively.

I give her a nod as I undo the first few buttons on my shirt. She looks away quickly.

"I'm having mine in my TV room." Teagan grabs her plate. "Thanks, Clodagh."

My jaw tenses. "I want us to eat dinner together, Teagan."

She lifts her chin defiantly and tries to brush past me. "I want to talk to Becky."

"Well, isn't that a fucking surprise," I snap, then immediately regret it. "Teagan," I call after her, but she's gone.

I let her walk off because I'm too tired for another fight tonight. Sadness washes over me. How is it that my employees skitter around me nervously, but my own daughter is brazen enough to turn her back on me?

When I turn, Clodagh looks like someone shoved a lemon in her mouth and demand she suck. I don't need judgment in my own home from a girl who's never been a parent. "Do you have something to say?" I snap.

Her eyes widen, and she looks mildly put out. "No,

Mr. Quinn. Uh, are you having your dinner in the dining room or…"

"Here's fine." I watch her awkwardly fumble with a knife and fork. "Before morning would be nice."

She forcefully sets the plate down in front of me and does a little bow. "Yes, *Sir*. You're a big guy, so I gave you an extra-large serving."

My eyes narrow on her. If I wanted a second snarky teenager, I would have adopted one.

She leans over the island counter so the bunny stares me right in the eyes. Is she trying to fuck with me?

I'm about to tell her she's already walking a fine line after her snooping act today when the contents of my plate catch my attention. Impressive.

But of course, it's impressive; I hire Michelin-star chefs in my restaurants.

"You're quite the chef."

Her face heats. "I try."

I don't know whether to put her across my knee for lying to me or give her a pay raise for having the balls to bluff me.

"Impressive woman." I smirk. "This must have taken you hours."

The pink in her cheeks stirs something unhelpful inside me.

"Uh-huh." She beams, all sweetness and light. "Yeah. It took a wee while, alright."

I lift a fork and trace along the faint remains of the restaurant pig logo imprinted on the pie. "Join me for dinner."

"No, I'll leave you in peace—"

"Sit." I gesture to the barstool opposite me.

She looks like she would rather swallow her own tongue than eat dinner with me, but in silence, she digs out a small piece of pie, places it on a plate, and tentatively lowers herself on the opposite stool.

Her eyes widen as I take a large bite. "You've really excelled yourself. I don't know how you found the time to cook up a storm between rifling through all my private belongings. And it's only day one."

She stiffens. "In my defense, the picture fell, and I was putting it back in place. I'm sorry for breaking your frame, though. Can we start over? Just tell me what you need from me."

Believe me, you don't want to know.

"Honesty, Clodagh." I raise a brow. "I need honesty."

"What if you don't like what I have to say?"

"It takes a lot to faze me."

"Okay." She nods. "If I'm allowed to be honest, why is your bedside table off-limits when all you have in there are condoms?"

"You must not have found the hidden compartment for my knives."

Her eyes widen. She sets her glass down.

"To reprimand disobedient nannies."

"*Oh.* You tried to crack a joke."

"I *tried.* Have you ever thought I might not want to subject my staff to my condoms?"

She smirks. "I know you have... lady friends. On Tuesdays."

"Christ, let me guess, Mrs. Dalton's instruction booklet?"

She laughs. "You haven't read it?"

"Fuck," I mutter, shoving another lump of pie into my mouth. "No, I haven't."

"She sure knows a lot about you." She grins. "And now, so do I."

"Good thing your lips are sealed by an NDA in that case."

"I'm not sure you have anything to worry about, even without an NDA."

My gaze drops to her lips as that distracting smile consumes her face. That smile is something else. "Why is that?"

"It wouldn't make for the best exposé. Billionaire Killian Quinn gets up at five o'clock, has his smoothie, then works all day."

"Are you calling me boring, Clodagh?"

"No!" Pastry flakes fall onto her fat bottom lip, and she self-consciously brushes them off. She seems torn between trying to eat daintily and devouring the pie. "You're just... not exactly a fly-by-the-seat-of-your-pants guy, according to the manual. There isn't anything in there that sounds like it's just for fun. Besides exercising. Like, what do you do to relax?"

"I fuck." The words slip out of my mouth before I can stop them. Probably because she's riling me up.

She chokes on a cough. "Tomorrow. Tuesday."

Christ. Can I set this manual on fire? "Look, I can't just do what I want whenever I want," I say gruffly, irrationally irritated that she thinks I'm a boring old man. "Some day, when you have responsibilities, you'll understand. Teagan is my priority."

She scowls. "I do have responsibilities."

I raise a brow, waiting for her to elaborate.

"*Me*. My manual might be shorter than yours, but it's still being written."

I chuckle at that and take a sip of water. I study her, recalling the image of her in the flimsy cotton T-shirt and shorts. "Where's the ring gone?"

She shifts uncomfortably in her seat. "My nose ring? I hide it when you're around. I didn't realize you'd watch me through the cameras this afternoon."

"I don't care what you have pierced." My eyes hold hers. "Just wear more clothes than you were wearing today when I'm around."

Or we'll both be in trouble.

Her cheeks flush red. "Most Irish houses don't have air-conditioning. No need. My room in Queens was in an attic, and it didn't have any. We got used to sweating. Stupidly, I forgot to turn on the A/C here. Now I know."

My eyes wander for a second to the oversized bunny eyes before finding her face again. I can still see the image of Clodagh in my bedroom from earlier and the air around us suddenly feels charged. My grip on the glass tightens. "Now you know."

We fall into silence as we eat. As she lifts the fork to her mouth and takes tiny bites, I find myself acutely aware of every movement she makes, wondering why I'm so riled.

Maybe it's because my daughter despises me so much that she can't bear the thought of eating dinner with me. Maybe it's because Clodagh's presence in my house gets under my skin in a way Mrs. Dalton's didn't. Maybe it's because despite getting paid a fortune for a job she's underqualified for, it's clear Clodagh doesn't want to dine with me.

Maybe a bit of all three.

I clear my throat. "Is all your family back in Ireland?"

Her fork pauses halfway to her mouth, as if she's surprised by the question. "Yup. My three younger brothers, Mam, and Granny Deirdre."

"Are you close to them?" My arm brushes hers as I reach for the pepper. It's an innocent contact, but with the look she gives me, you'd think I gave her third-degree burns.

"Yes." She nods. "I miss them. That's why I wanted to make sure I stayed here legally so I could visit home when I want."

Her sponsorship is based on this job. Marcus has been instructed to look for a replacement, but of course, Clodagh doesn't know that.

I exhale heavily.

She shifts in her seat uncomfortably, as if reading my mind, and sets her fork down. Her eyes lock with mine. "Look, I know you don't think very much of me, but I want you to give me a fair shot. I'm a hard worker. And... I really need this job."

I hesitate. I don't make promises I can't keep.

"This position was never going to be a permanent solution for you."

She nods, her face falling, and I feel a twinge of guilt.

"Why are you so determined to live in New York City? You're so far from your family."

She smiles. "The same reason the Irish have been immigrating to the States for years. We believe in the promise of the American dream." Her smile fades as quickly as it appeared as she looks down at her plate. "And sometimes we just need to get away."

"What is it that you're running from, Clodagh?"

"Nothing important." She shakes her head, closing down.

Her eyes lift to mine. "Tell me, what was it like growing up in Manhattan? I can't imagine what that must have been like as a child."

"I didn't. I grew up in Queens."

Her mouth forms a little *O*.

"My parents were Irish," I say, amused at her shock. "From Dublin. But I've been out of Queens for nearly two decades. I moved Mom, me, and my brother, Connor, to Manhattan years ago."

"Wow," she breathes. "I read you were self-made. Your mum must be so proud."

I give a slight shrug. I've been in this game so long that Mom barely bats an eyelash when another hotel appears.

Clodagh fidgets with a lock of her hair, wanting to ask me something else but stopping herself.

Whatever it is, she's not brave enough to ask.

I finish the pie while she asks me about my upbringing in Queens. I keep the details limited, avoiding the shit parts that no one needs to hear, like what a deadbeat dad I had.

She has a fresh-off-the-boat innocence about her that's endearing. Most people want to know how I earned my billionaire status. Clodagh's more interested to know what growing up in the city was like. I chuckle as she screeches when I tell her I took the subway by myself at age ten.

Her phone dings on the table, distracting us, as a message flashes. It's close enough for me to read.

You're driving me out of my fucking mind.

She slides the phone over beside her, pursing her lips as she reads.

"Is that a boyfriend in Queens?" I ask.

"No. Just a guy who's on a different wavelength than me." Annoyance flickers over her face as she studies the message again.

"Is there something you need help with?"

She turns the phone over to hide the screen. "Nothing I can't handle."

Her expression tells me she doesn't want to pursue the topic. She jumps up from her seat and starts busying herself at the sink.

I rise from my stool and come to stand close behind her, so close we're almost touching.

She freezes, plate in hand. I think she may have

stopped breathing.

My chest grazes her back as I lean over to open the bin. "Lie to me again, and I will personally put you on the next plane back to Ireland, sweetheart," I murmur into her ear as I lift the Le Grand Cochon container from the bin and set it on the worktop in front of her.

She goes perfectly still. If I put my fingers on her neck, I'd find her pulse racing.

"Okay," she croaks, tilting her head to look up at me. "I'll try better."

Up close, her emerald eyes sear into mine. I have a vivid thought of what it would look like to have her gazing up at me while she takes my cock into her mouth.

Her eyes widen as I let out a frustrated growl.

What the fuck am I doing?

I step back. "Clock off. You're done for the night."

TWELVE

Clodagh

I stare up at the ceiling. What about knowing you have to go to sleep makes your body do the opposite?

Day four of being a professional nanny maid. I won't win Domestic Assistant of the Year, but for some reason, he hasn't fired me despite his threats.

Yet.

I hate cleaning. It's fucking shite. Guest rooms get cleaned every other day. Killian's and Teagan's bedrooms are cleaned daily. It's a never-ending cycle of domesticated torture. Bathrooms must be clean enough to eat dinner from the sink. Mrs. Dalton didn't say that, but I got the message from all the underlined words.

Still, I can't complain. I'm cleaning Fifth Avenue toilets.

Then there are the blunt text messages from Quinn. Three yesterday and five today—with ambiguous instructions to run errands for him.

I feel like I'm constantly in trouble.

His voice repeats in my head from Monday night. *Lie to me again, and I will personally put you on the next plane back to Ireland, sweetheart.*

God, he was threatening deportation, but it sounded so sexual. I felt the heat radiating from his body. It was... terrifying.

Since then, the closest I get to communication is one-word answers or grunts, or he just ignores me entirely. I want to scream at him, *'can't you see I'm trying, mister!'* Every time Quinn enters the kitchen, every hair on my body stands on end.

Teagan gives me whiplash. Ninety percent of the time, she is sullen and snarky with me, and the other ten percent, she is delightful. But she thinks she can take me for a fool. Tonight, she tried to convince me that the video of baby goats was related to her homework.

I get more answers from the manual than those two.

I wonder if Quinn is asleep upstairs. What does he think about before he falls asleep? Probably his billions. I can't imagine him having actual *feelings* for anyone. Anyone other than Teagan, that is.

God, when he smiles at her like that, I'm at risk of melting into a puddle. I don't want kids yet, but I know that's how you want your guy to look at your babies.

I slide my hands down my stomach and into my pants. He doesn't deserve to be fantasized over, but thinking about my boss before bedtime has become my dirty pleasure.

I close my eyes and part my thighs wider, imagining his fingers circling my clit. Imagining his large hands controlling my pleasure, making me pulse and tingle as he sinks his fingers into me again and again.

Imagining his mouth hungrily replacing his fingers...

Imagining him staring up at me with hooded eyes, those icy-cold blue eyes full of fire... his deep hoarse voice rasping with emotion for me... the weight of his thick muscular thighs on top of me as his big, hard cock fills me up...

Imagining he's so turned on by my pleasure, he'll explode if he doesn't fuck me.

Yes... yes...

No. No.

It's no use.

I need something stronger than my imagination. With a frustrated breath, I reach over to open the bedside table.

If Quinn ever looks into *my* bedside table drawer, he'd be in for a shock when he finds a beast the size of a foot-long subway.

I pull out my vibrating friend and get to work. It's midnight, and efficiency is key. I need to release this sexual tension; otherwise, if Quinn returns from his run tomorrow morning, shirtless and sweaty, I might explode right there and then in front of him.

Oh. Yup, that's the spot.

Exactly. Right. There.

Sadly, this little helper will soon be retiring. Every few months, I have to buy a new sex toy. It's as if my body becomes immune to everything. Which is really shit because sex toys aren't recyclable, and obviously, you can't donate them to charity.

Even with toys, it takes me so long to come that it's embarrassing.

And coming with actual penises, tongues, or fingers involved?

Zero chance. I can't get out of my head.

Men expect orgasms. They expect you to go from zero to earth-shattering, yes, yes, yes O's with a finger twitch. The embarrassing truth is I've never come during sex.

My ex used his tongue with the same technique as painting a wall with a roller brush—long, broad strokes. After I told him that it wasn't about covering the whole surface but focusing on the right spot, it was game over for us.

The fact I couldn't come became this big thing in our relationship, and sex became a chore.

Would my boss upstairs be able to make me come? I've never been with a man like him. *God*, his bulge was so prominent in his running shorts this morning, I wondered if he wasn't a bit hard.

The familiar heat builds between my thighs.

Slowly... slowly.

I force myself out of my head, imagining Quinn's hard body on top of mine.

Yes... I'm getting there.

My breaths turn into moans with no one to hear.

My lass, don't leave me aloooooone.

I freeze mid-stroke. What the hell is that?

Singing. *Awful* singing on the street right outside my window.

The guy croons on, singing in a painful, mournful tone, like a male banshee. My bedroom is at the front of the house, but I rarely hear even the traffic, so this guy is singing *really* loud.

He hitches up to a higher note.

Fuck off, you idiot.

An annoying buzzing sound accompanies the bad singing. My phone.

Who's calling me at midnight? If it's someone from home forgetting the time zone, I'll kill them. Unless it's an emergency. Oh God. *Granny Deirdre.*

I grapple at the phone, cursing the fucker on the other end. They aren't giving up.

Sharp green light stings my eyes, and the caller flashes across the screen.

"Piss off, Liam," I hiss. Gobshite.

Groaning loudly, I press cancel on the phone, taking my anger out on the phone.

Uh. I'll never be able to come now that Liam has weaseled himself into my head. Now *there's* a guy who could come quickly. All I had to do was give the guy's willy a wee tug, and he was exploding faster than a gas tank with a lit match.

The lunatic outside sounds like he's drunk-crying.

"Answer the phone, Clodagh!"

Fuck.

Double fuck.

Please say this isn't happening.

I leap out of bed so quickly I feel dizzy. The vibrator falls to the ground with a thud. My pulse is pounding, but my limbs are frozen.

Stones hit the window. Not just at my window, but at the house in general.

This is not good. Not good at all.

The drunken ramblings grow louder.

Stalking toward the window, I rip up the blinds to see a disheveled Liam stumbling back and forward on the pavement.

He hasn't spotted me yet.

Please don't wake my boss.

Liam is singing Irish love songs. He's changing the words to suit my name, but it doesn't work. His feet hop as if the pavement's on fire.

"Cloooooodagh!" It's the desperate cry of an unhinged man, as if his soul is being ripped out of him. He closes his eyes and arches his back, rocking his hips back and forth as if in worship of the moon.

This fucker will get me fired.

I race through the studio to the front door, not bothering with socks, shoes, or a dressing gown. I don't care that I stumble up the stairs and graze my knee. I'm going to murder him.

If Quinn comes out, it's game over.

My heart hammers in my chest as I race out into the main hallway, the marble cold to my bare feet. I've never been so angry in my life.

The main door is heavy and hard to open. Finally,

I pull it open with force.

Mid-sentence, Liam stops singing and stares up at me as if I'm not real. Then he has the audacity to smile.

"What the absolute fuck, Liam?" I spit out, glowering at him.

His eyes are bloodshot and glazed. His hair is a mess. He's holding flowers that look like they've been stepped on.

"I've missed you, Clodagh," he slurs, taking a step forward. "I've come to see you." He stumbles up the first step of the townhouse. "I haven't had sex in eight weeks because of you."

"What do you want, a fucking medal? Stay away!" I yelp, looking for something in the hall to push him backward with. "You shouldn't be here."

"Clodagh!" It's another loud howl from the pit of his stomach.

"Shut up, man." I wave my hands to shoo him away. "You'll get me fired! Go away! Fucking hop it, dude. Go home." I use my fiercest Donegal growl. "*Now*."

There's movement upstairs.

"Liam, *please*," I whimper, begging him with every cell in my body. "*Please*. Just go before you get me in trouble."

He burps.

"Soz-sorry about that. No." He shakes his head furiously. "No. I can't do that." He takes one more step up, within punching distance. "That night, darlin'. God, that *night*. I can't think of anything else since."

Dropping to his knees, he thrusts the flowers out in front of him and begins crooning loudly again. He closes his eyes, and a vein in his forehead throbs as a painful rasp explodes out of him. It's safe to say he's not going to make Broadway.

I see red.

The cold stone slabs are like ice under my feet as I step out of the doorway, ripping the flowers from his hands.

Then I whack. I whack, and I whack, and I whack.

He's not expecting it. He stops mid-wail, replacing the singing with grunts.

There's no stopping me. Spewing curses at him, I bash him again and again over the head with the flowers. Petals are flying everywhere, and I don't care.

"You make me crazy, Cloooodagh! You're driving me out of my mind," Liam wails under the flowers. His breath smells like he's just given a pig a blow job.

I yank him by the arm and drag him down the steps with surprising strength.

"What the hell is going on?"

Dread hits me at the sound of the low, gravelly voice.

I turn, ass clenched in terror, to see a half-dazed, half-angry Quinn in low-hanging boxers glaring at me. He runs a hand through his dark hair.

Too close to the fantasy.

His eyes pierce through mine, fury building as he takes in the shit show on his doorstep.

"I'm so sorr—"

Arms wrap around my legs, and a drunken Liam lifts me off my feet before I finish.

I let out a piercing scream as he stumbles to his feet and hoists me over his shoulders until I'm fully airborne. Liam is strong. He works in construction. Even in his drunken state, he easily lifts me. With one arm, he pushes me into the fireman's lift. I flop down on his back until my face is against his butt.

What the fuck is happening?

My pj shorts eat my crack.

"I'm taking you back to Queens," Liam shouts as a deafening alarm sounds. The police?

No, it's Quinn's house alarm.

Kill me now.

I swing over Liam's shoulders like a rag doll, blood rushing to my head.

Quinn shouts something, but I can't make it out with my head banging against Liam's butt.

"Put me down!" I rasp, beating his back with my fists.

He's on the move. I feel every footstep he takes in my throat. He's going to drop me, and I'm going to land on my head. "Liam, put me the fuck down. *Now.*"

The house alarm drowns out my cries. Everyone on the street must have woken up now from the noise.

Liam's making good speed down the street as I hang upside down, watching the stones of the pavement move beneath me.

I'm past angry.

To make this ordeal worse, this must be the least flattering viewpoint of my ass.

I just want Liam to let me down so I can put some clothes on, pack my belongings, go to Orla, and put this terrible experience behind me.

I'm *freezing*.

He stops abruptly.

"Put her down," says a deep American voice above me. Quinn. He sounds close.

"She's my lass," Liam snaps, tightening his grip on my hips.

"She'll be the judge of that." Quinn sounds furious.

I see a second set of feet on the pavement. Hairy big toes. A warm arm slides under my belly, hoisting me off Liam's shoulders and onto even broader shoulders.

Quinn.

He's breathing heavily. His chest feels warm against my body, considering he's outside with no clothes on.

Now other feet are circling us.

Hanging upside down over Quinn's back, I grab the top of his boxers. Why isn't he putting me down?

"Sir," another voice says in an Irish accent. Oh God, I hope it's not Sam.

"Uh, Mr.—" I start.

"What took you so long?" Quinn growls, still holding me in a fireman's lift. "Deal with this guy."

"Yes, sir, right away," a second voice with an

American accent replies as Quinn gradually lowers me until my chest is in his line of sight.

I cling to his neck for stability, feeling his shoulder muscles tense beneath my grasp.

My body slides against his as he sets me down on the ground. I take in a deep breath, trying to calm my racing heart. My bullet nipples are hardened from the chilly air, lightly brushing against his chest through my thin tank top. His warm breath tickles my hair, and the heat of his hands radiates through my lower back, connecting me to him.

He feels like a hard, warm rock.

I'm *absolutely fucking boiling.*

His blue eyes flash down to mine like I've hit him with an electric bolt. Then he sharply releases me from his grip and steps back.

I see then who he's talking to.

About ten (I'm too distraught to count) men in black circle us. All are wearing the same black trousers, black shirts, and earpieces.

I feel like I'm watching a slow-motion movie. Two of them drag a belligerent Liam down the street by the armpits. He shouts my name as they haul him away.

I don't know where they're taking him, but it better be another state because if I see him again, I'm going to kill him with my bare hands.

As I watch Liam, my teeth chatter, and my whole body is like ice, but I don't care.

He just cost me my visa.

"Clodagh, you have no shoes on, for fuck's sake,"

Quinn growls.

I snap back to reality and turn to him, dazed. We're not touching, yet it feels like we are.

His glare intensifies.

I look down. He's standing in the street in his boxers. He's not wearing shoes, either.

One of the men in black clears their throat. "Sir, shall we—"

"No," Quinn cuts in. He lets out an agitated breath and stares at me as if I'm the biggest pain in his ass. "Clodagh can provide you with a statement in the morning."

My stomach lurches. A statement?

I look around at the guys. They all look as uneasy as me. I guess they fucked up too, by not being on the scene quicker.

There's Sam.

My weak wave is met with a sheepish smile from him before his attention drops to my chest.

Quinn's jaw tightens. "Go inside."

The neighbors probably don't see this kind of show very often. What do you get when you mix a drunken Irishman, a bad nanny maid, and an angry billionaire?

Deported.

As quickly as they arrive, the men disperse.

I stiffen as Quinn places his hand on my lower back and leads me toward the house. The touch of his hand burns my skin. It must be a combination of the cold night air and my embarrassment. Only minutes ago, I was fantasizing about those hands caressing me in bed.

I feel his breath against my neck when he speaks. "Mind your step. There's glass."

Quinn guides me into the house and shuts the door behind us. He lets out a heavy breath and then turns to me, arms crossed against his bare chest.

I stand frozen in the hallway, my teeth chattering and my heart hammering. "I'm fired this time, right?" The question comes out squeaky and weak.

I don't let him answer. "Don't. I don't want to leave New York."

Appealing to his emotional side isn't working, judging by the annoyed curl of his lip.

I smile weakly. "If you don't want to do it for me, do it for your immigrants."

Jokes aren't working either.

His jaw works as he glares at me. It's always working. "You're a fucking handful."

Hmm. It's not a term of endearment, but it's not "you're fired" either.

I attempt another weak smile. "At least there's not a dull moment with me. It's good to break from the schedule."

"Did you ask him to come here?"

"What?" I stammer. "No. Absolutely not."

"Is he your ex?"

I shake my head adamantly. "No! Just someone I... I made a mistake with, and he likes me."

"I gathered that," he mutters dryly. "Is that the guy who messaged you?"

I nod. "All I seem to do is apologize to you," I say in

a tiny voice.

The muscle in his jaw works overtime. "It appears so. And it's only been four days. Mrs. Dalton never had idiots showing up at my door like this. Then again, Mrs. Dalton doesn't look like you."

His eyes drop to my chest. I forgot I was semi-naked. Almost.

When they lock with mine again, they flash with something that looks a lot like desire. I must be delirious from the cold.

"Is that the last of the guys obsessed with you, or should I tell my men to be on alert for more?"

If he's joking, then I'm not fired yet.

Is he joking?

He's not smiling.

"I left the rest back in Ireland."

His scowl doesn't give way.

"Uh, what are they going to do with him?" I ask, feeling slightly anxious about Liam. The guy's an ass, but I don't want him to get into serious trouble for a drunken mistake.

"It's unlikely you'll be hearing from him again."

Jesus Christ.

"They're going to... kill him?"

My face must go white because he almost chuckles. *Almost.* "No, Clodagh, I'm not a murderer. They'll shove him in a taxi with a good stern warning."

"Oh," I breathe. "You made a joke." I sigh with relief. "I'm so sorry for waking you. Is Teagan awake?"

143

"She sleeps through everything. Apparently, it's a teenage skill."

I nod, feeling my shoulders jump with a chill. I glance down at my nipples, jutting up like coat hooks, and I brusquely fold my arms over my chest.

Killian stiffens.

Neither of us speaks.

My gaze drops down his delicious torso to the outline of his cock in his boxers. Is he half-hard? Heat floods me as I stare down. He's all fucking man.

I stop breathing.

When I look up again, he stares at me through hooded eyes ablaze with unashamed hunger.

He wants to fuck me. I think. No, I know. I know he does. Right here in the hallway, as hard as he can.

The man would tear me apart.

My lips involuntarily part. My thighs part slightly. My heart skips a beat.

He's going to kiss me.

Please.

"Go to bed," he says, his voice full of gravel.

He turns abruptly and takes a few steps toward the grand staircase to his bedroom before stopping. "Do you want a nightcap?"

"Sure," I whisper.

He nods curtly. "Put on a robe or something." His voice is extra gruff as his eyes slide over my body one last time, triggering another violent shiver.

I must have hypothermia.

THIRTEEN

Killian

I might have found the whole damn thing comical if I wasn't so irritated. God knows why I didn't fire her on the spot. Instead, here I am, against my better judgment, waiting for Clodagh to have a nightcap with me.

Soft footsteps pad toward the kitchen. I look up to see her wrapped in a nightgown. Thank fuck. I could do without the unwanted arousal.

"Hey," she says sheepishly, hovering at the doorway of the kitchen as if worried I'll bite her.

She glances at my outfit—gray sweatpants and a white T-shirt—and seems relieved that I'm no longer in just my underwear.

I get off the stool and go to the drinks cabinet, giving her a slight nod in greeting.

She comes to stand beside me, loitering awkwardly. Her robe is looser than I need it to be. I avert my eyes from the slit on her thigh to reveal soft, creamy skin.

"Do you want me to pour it?"

I direct my chin toward the barstool. "You're not on the clock now."

She smiles coyly, tilting her head up. "If I'm not on the clock, does that mean you're not my boss right now?"

I step closer to her, close enough to smell her scent and see every light freckle dotted on her nose.

Lust hits me at the worst possible time, and my cock thickens in my sweatpants. On a caveman level, I want to fuck her. To lay her body out on the kitchen table, push my angry throbbing cock deep inside her tight young pussy and feel it spasm around me.

But just because I want her physically doesn't mean I'm foolish enough to act on it. New York is overflowing with beautiful women, and I have no intention of crossing any boundaries with the little Irish troublemaker.

"I'm always your boss. Do as you're told and take a seat."

Her face flushes as she nervously laughs, trying to hide her obvious reaction to me. Is that little pussy getting wet for me right now?

She does as she's told and sits.

I pour two generous portions of whiskey on the rocks before making my way over to the kitchen island and taking a seat on the opposite stool. That way, I can't see the slit running up her thighs while she's seated.

I hand her the glass, our eyes meeting as she takes it from me. "The Irish don't do whisky as well as the Scots. This is one of the finest whiskys you'll ever taste, aged in the Highlands for over thirty years."

"Older than me." She places it under her nose and erupts into a coughing fit. "I'll take your word for it."

"Try it."

She takes a second sniff. "What if I hate whisky? Don't I get a choice?"

"You won't hate it."

Unconvinced, she brings the glass to her lips and tentatively takes a sip. Her face screws up as the liquid hits the back of her throat.

"Good?" I ask.

"Strong. I don't have much to compare it to." She attempts a second sip. "It burns on the way down."

She swivels gently on the stool, eyes crinkling in contentment. "I'm glad we're past the unfortunate incident this evening."

"We're not past anything. I'm still deciding whether to reprimand you."

"*Oh.*" Her mouth falls open as she tries to ascertain whether I'm being serious. She nervously bites her lower lip, her eyes conveying the thrill she's trying to conceal. "How... how would you reprimand me?"

Our eyes lock, the surged energy charging in the air between us.

My grip on the glass hardens. "You sure you want to go there?" I let my gaze linger, and her face turns bright pink.

She bottles it. She nervously twirls a lock of her deep red hair and looks down at her glass. "I don't understand how Liam got the address," she says softly, trying to defuse the tension in the air. "The only person who has it is my friend Orla, and she wouldn't give it to him."

"My address is on the internet."

"*See?*" She blows out a breath. "You can't blame me for that. In fact, I'm the victim in all of this." The glass comes to her lips again, and the sip is much larger this time.

Her robe is falling loose. Under it, she's still wearing the flimsy top. In another life, I would have stepped closer to her, gently pushing the robe off her shoulders to reveal her smooth skin. I'd start at her neck, slowly traveling down to her breasts where my tongue would caress each one until she begged me to fuck her. Dammit. I'm getting hard just thinking about it.

"Are you trying to tug on my heartstrings?" I ask, my voice full of gravel.

"Yes." Her eyes hold mine as I take a long gulp from my glass. "Is it working?"

"No." But I can't help the hint of a smirk. "Resilient little thing, aren't you? You really gave it to him with those flowers. I almost didn't have to step in."

She laughs, the tension leaving her shoulders. "I've had a lot of practice growing up with three crazy brothers. I get that you're concerned about Teagan, but Liam won't be setting foot near here again. I swear I'll kill him myself if I have to."

"One," I begin slowly, my fingers curling around

the tumbler. "I know your friend won't be back, I guarantee it. Two, he is zero threat to my daughter's welfare. And three, tonight, you gave me reason to be concerned about *your* welfare."

She looks surprised. "You don't have to be, but that's very kind."

"It's not kind. I have a duty as an employer. When my staff is kidnapped from my house, it's my business."

Her face falls. "Okay. Well... thank you anyway for coming to my rescue. You didn't have to."

"It shouldn't have been me." I sigh. "An inquiry will be launched to determine why the team was so slow to respond."

"What?" Her eyes grow wide in horror. "Don't fire anyone because of me!"

"It won't be over you. They know their scope."

"Well, I think they were quick. I swear they just appeared out of thin air."

My mouth twitches slightly in amusement. "The security system detected unusual activity and alerted them."

"I guess a drunken Irish man howling is a bit unusual on Fifth Avenue." She shifts uncomfortably, looking contrite. "I almost feel sorry for Liam. He wasn't expecting an army of bodyguards."

"Then he's a fool. I'm the thirteenth wealthiest man in the States. Of course I have security."

"But it seems so safe in this part of New York." Her brow furrows in confusion. "I didn't think you'd need such heavy security."

"Nowhere is safe. New York isn't a fairy tale." Harlow was like Clodagh—she believed the world was full of good people and didn't understand why anyone would need protection. My chest tightens at the thought of something happening to Clodagh under my watch.

Not like that Irish idiot. A *real* threat.

I swallow another sip of the whisky, studying her. "So that's the type of guy you're interested in?"

She looks affronted. "Now I feel the need to defend my taste in men. He's not always such a dumbass." She pauses, rimming her fingers over the glass. "He was sweet in the beginning. He just turned a bit territorial after we…"

My brows rise. "I just stopped a guy from kidnapping you and carrying you down the street like a sack of potatoes in the middle of the night. I don't think you're in a position to defend your taste in men."

She scowls. "I'd prefer not to be compared to a sack of potatoes, thanks very much. Was that supposed to be a racist joke? Believe me, I've heard all the potato jokes out there about the Irish."

I can't help but chuckle. "The Irish aren't a race, Clodagh."

"I do fit the stereotype, though," she says, grinning. "I love potatoes. They should be eaten for breakfast, lunch, and dinner. There's nothing better than butter flowing over all that creamy, fluffy heaven melting into your mouth. Everything else on the plate is just a side accessory." She actually licks her lips.

Jesus Christ, she makes eating potatoes sound erotic.

"There's not enough potatoes in your menu options."

"You can add some."

She gasps, feigning shock. "I'm allowed to make *amendments* to the manual?"

I'm beginning to begrudge Mrs. Dalton for being so thorough. "I'm not that stuck in my ways."

Her smirk implies that she thinks the opposite is true. "Am I the worst nanny maid you've ever had?"

"Probably, but the past two didn't last long enough for me to be sure."

She nods. "You scared them away."

"Must have." I pause. "Do I scare you, Clodagh?"

I watch her weigh the response in her mind. "I find you intimidating. You make me a bit nervous."

I don't attempt to appease her and let her words hang in the air. "You were thankful for me scaring people away this evening."

"Oh *God*," she groans. "I'm so embarrassed. I promise you won't have to scare anyone else off." She pushes her lower lip between her teeth to suppress a smile. "Although you must have your fair share of crazed admirers."

"Because I'm a billionaire?"

"No, because you're... hmm..." She looks away quickly. "It's obvious you have plenty of admirers. From the manual."

"Guess the manual has me all figured out."

She drains the last of the liquid from her glass, then gives me a coy grin that makes me want to bend her over my knee and show her exactly how I want to reprimand her for tonight. "I'm not sure anyone has you figured out, Mr. Quinn."

I run an agitated hand across my jaw. If she keeps looking at me like that, I'm liable to break my own rule about no fraternizing with staff.

Instead, I hear myself say, "You have the widest smile I've ever seen."

Her laughter rings out in the kitchen. "Is there a compliment in there somewhere?"

"You have a beautiful smile," I correct. Her smile is the first thing I noticed about her.

Her eyes widen in surprise. "People say it's too big for my face."

"Those people are idiots."

Stunned, she stammers out, "Thank you." She looks so floored that I've complimented her that I have to wonder if she thinks I'm a monster.

I'm closer to being a saint after how much she's tested me this week. In some ways, she's all over the place. In other ways, she seems to have her head screwed on.

But Teagan is warming up to her quicker than the other nannies, and my daughter comes first.

"Why are you looking at me like that?" she asks.

I must be frowning. "I can't figure you out."

"That's funny coming from you. I'm an open book. What do you want to know?"

"Why did you really come to New York? Why did you leave your life in Ireland?"

She takes a breath, then smiles. "Maybe my life in Ireland wasn't everything I wanted it to be."

My curiosity is piqued. "Elaborate."

Her gaze settles on the glass on the table. "I told you my business didn't work out," she finally starts. "I started it with my ex about a year ago. He had these grand plans about marketing strategies, renting a space, an online store... I got swept up in it, and I put my savings into it. Not billions, but enough to hurt me." She smiles sadly.

"He had me dreaming big without understanding any of the details." Her chest rises with a sigh.

"Then one day, the money was just... gone. Poof. Just like that. It just imploded in my face. Still, to this day, I don't know how he spent it." Her voice trails off into a bitter laugh. "I think he spent it on his new car."

Her expression stirs something protective in me. I'd kill any bastard who tried to screw over Teagan.

She looks up at me ruefully. "I quit my job to start the business. My dream was always to live in New York, so when everything imploded in my face like that, I figured it was the right time to go. Staying in Ireland just kept reminding me of how stupid I was."

"You're not stupid, Clodagh," I say softly. "You're just trusting. You deserve to be treated better than that. He sounds like a scumbag."

"I'm naïve, more like. I looked up to him because he was so smart. I never thought I could start my own business. In school, I came bottom of the class in the important subjects." She blanches. "I probably shouldn't tell you that. If I were your daughter, you'd be so disappointed in me. I'm bowled over by how much Teagan does, never mind her schoolwork."

"You're not my daughter." I stare hard at her, feeling my jaw tense up. "And that's not how being a father works. You love your daughter for everything about them, even their vulnerabilities."

She shrugs. "Anyway, it's not all doom and gloom. I've wanted to live in New York ever since I watched *Home Alone* when I was eight. And here I am."

"If only life in New York was a Disney fantasy."

"I don't need the fantasy. I'd be happy living in New York and sanding doors. That's it. I'm a simple gal. No big dreams." She looks at me curiously. "What's your dream? Have they all come true?"

"I don't dream."

She eyes me skeptically. "I don't believe that. Everyone dreams, even if they're scared to share them."

"If you say so."

"I do say so." Her grin suggests she's won some unspoken battle between us. Her fingertips trace around the rim of her glass, hinting at a refill. "I also think underneath the cool exterior, you're not as scary as you'd like people to believe."

My chest tightens as she stares at me, her eyes smoldering with a mixture of heat and hope. "Don't doubt it; I am."

She pouts slightly. "Do I really have to keep calling

you Mr. Quinn? Can I call you Killian? Killy?"

I drain my glass and stand. "Go to bed. We both have to be up at five."

Her emerald eyes widen in disappointment, but she nods.

Her robe slips off one shoulder as she stands, exposing the top of her perfect, small breasts. Definitely never getting to sleep now.

"And yes, you can call me Killian. Don't expect to keep your job if I hear you call me *Killy* even once."

***

I'm exhausted in the morning. After my run, I decided to go to work late. It'll be nice to have breakfast with my daughter for once. We don't get enough quality time together, and when we do, all I get these days are sullen looks and tantrums. Getting my baby girl to talk to me is like drawing blood from a stone.

"Heya," Clodagh chirps when I enter the kitchen. She hands me a coffee. "I made it to the end of the week."

My brow lifts. It's a little premature, considering the events of last night. "The week isn't over yet."

She scowls but knows to leave it.

The sound of Teagan's footsteps down the hall makes me smile. She doesn't know I'm here.

I turn to greet her. "Morning, hon—what the fuck?" This better be a joke. "Tell me that is a wig!"

My daughter's beautiful, naturally auburn hair

is a horrific neon red. Her forehead looks like it's breaking out in a rash.

Teagan winces, but stubbornly lifts her chin in defiance as she comes into the kitchen.

I slam my coffee down and push to standing. "What the hell have you done?" She looks like a mad fucking clown.

She takes the breakfast plate from Clodagh, avoiding my glare. "Thanks, Clodagh."

"Teagan," I growl, trying to temper my anger.

Finally, her eyes meet mine as she sets the plate down and takes a seat. "It's my hair. I can do what I want with it."

I narrow my eyes. "No, you damn well can't. Look at the state of your head! How the fuck do you expect to go to school like that?"

"Language, Dad."

I lean against the counter, pinching the bridge of my nose. Give me fucking strength. "You're twelve years old. You can't do things like this without my permission. No, scrap that; you can't do *anything* without my permission."

"You wouldn't have let me!" she cries, spearing her eggs with her fork. "And I'm nearly *thirteen!*"

"Damn right, I wouldn't," I yell.

She huffs as I take her chin in my hand to assess her forehead. "You look like you're having a goddamn allergic reaction."

I've had zero sleep. All I wanted was a nice breakfast with my daughter, yet here we are.

"You bought hair dye without my permission. I've

consistently told you that you're too young to dye your hair, yet you still went against my command." And the cheapest foulest shit on the market, judging by the horrific state of her head. "When?"

She pulls away from my touch. "I didn't buy any... it's... food coloring and some Jell-O."

I gape at her incredulously. "Are you insane?"

My chest tightens as I exhale. Is this normal behavior for young girls? Why would she want to do something so ridiculous and nasty?

"*Clodagh* did it when she was my age," Teagan says defiantly.

I turn to Clodagh. She's so quiet I'd forgotten she was in the kitchen.

She watches with her mouth open in horrified silence.

"Sorry, Clodagh," Teagan says meekly beside me.

Clodagh swallows a mouthful of air, the cheeriness drained from her face. "I just said I hated my hair when I was younger and..." Her voice trails off. "I didn't mean for Teagan to do it."

"That's what kids do, Clodagh," I say through clenched teeth. "They mirror adults. They repeat what we do."

Jesus Christ. This is my fault for accepting a young nanny with no experience.

"I'm nearly thirteen," Teagan whines behind me. "I can make up my own mind."

I whip my head around, giving my daughter a murderous look. "Teagan, if you say another word, I'm adding another week to your two-week grounding period."

Her lips quiver as she slams the knife and fork down on her plate. "But I'm meeting Becky tomorrow. I *hate* you. This isn't fair!"

"I know you hate me," I growl. "But you still need to show me some respect."

"A word, Clodagh," I say through gritted teeth, nodding to the back deck. Between my daughter and her nanny, I'll have stumps for teeth by lunchtime.

She follows me outside in silence.

"Do you have any idea how to be a responsible adult?" I snap at her as soon as she closes the sliding doors.

She frowns at me. "I don't know if you want a serious answer to that."

"What else did you do that I should know about? Is my daughter going to come home pregnant next?"

Her forehead creases into something angrier. "That's really out of line, Killian. I didn't lose my virginity until I was twenty-one if you must know. I was a late starter."

Three years ago.

I didn't need to know that.

I lean against the wall, towering over her. "Let me be clear for you. You do not influence my daughter in any way. Do you understand?"

She presses her lips together as hurt flashes across her face. "I think you're overreacting. She didn't harm herself or anyone else. You're acting like you caught her smoking *meth*."

"Don't tell me I'm overreacting," I snap, folding

my arms. "You know nothing about being a parent."

She stiffens and stands tall, attempting to meet my gaze. "No, but I was a teenage girl once."

As she rears up, she's close, so damn close that her scent of coconut and flowers floods my senses. So heady, sexy, fucking delicious. I almost forget why I'm angry for a moment. If I step forward just a little bit, I'll feel her soft lips against mine...

Instead, I let out a tense sigh. "Teagan can be easily influenced. I need you to be careful about what you say around her."

"Got it." She nods. "Look, if you really want her to heed your warnings, you need to explain why, not just fob her off with *'it's bad for you, because I say so.'*" Her voice deepens as she mimics my accent, and I glare at her. "She just wants to express herself, that's all. Do you even know why dyeing her hair is bad for her?"

My jaw clenches with frustration. "It's full of chemicals. Obviously, it's bad for her."

"But she sees adults use it, so that's not a good enough answer for her. I think it's because young people have thinner hair that's still d eveloping, so the dye is more harmful. But don't quote me. I'm not a doctor. Obviously." She lifts her shoulders in a shrug. "But you should look into it and explain it to Teagan in a way she understands."

I open my mouth to respond, then shut it again. Damn. Clodagh has a point. My answer isn't entirely based in fact, and she knows it. I'm repeating what I presume to be true.

I exhale heavily, the fight leaving me.

"For the record, I'm sorry I caused the argument," she says softly when I don't speak. "Here I was, thinking I had survived the first week. Famous last words, hey?"

FOURTEEN

Clodagh

Friday night, I figure if I stay away from the house, I can't get in trouble, and Killian can cool off. Thankfully, he orders food from one of his fancy restaurants so I can clock off as soon as he gets home from work.

Teagan roams around the house like an angry bull. I try to cheer her up, but nothing can break through the grouchiness brought on by her being grounded.

So when I cross the bridge back to Queens on Friday night, I'm actually mildly relieved.

Since Orla isn't bartending, we check out a comedy show and flirt with guys who attempt to mimic our accent (yawn) but are forgiven because they're pretty. I'm fickle.

Come Saturday morning, I teach my yoga class, then Orla and I go for a stroll in the park. I love New York parks on the weekends. Perfect for people-watching.

"Liam asked me to deliver a message since you're

ignoring him," Orla tells me. "He wants you to give him another chance."

I can't help but let out a snort. "Tell him message not delivered."

"He's gutted. I almost feel sorry for him." She grins at me sheepishly. "He…"

"He what? Spill."

"He told everyone in the pub that you're sleeping with your new boss."

I stop short, almost choking on my coffee. "What the fuck? Why the hell is he making shit up? Just because I don't fancy *him*? Ugh."

I didn't think I could be any more pissed off at Liam. I was wrong.

"I'm just the messenger." She shrugs. "He said he saw how Killian looked at you the other night."

"Like he wanted to kill me?"

"No, like he would take out Liam and anyone else who got in his way to get to you. I tried to tell him it was bollocks. Sleeping with Killian isn't on the cards." She side-eyes me. "Right?"

I roll my eyes and look away. *So even Liam noticed the charged atmosphere between Killian and me that night.* "Liam couldn't see in front of his own face. He was in no fit state to judge anything."

Did the security crew notice the weird tension as well? There's no way I can ask Sam about it.

My phone beeps, and I pull it out from my yoga pants pocket.

Killian: Where are you?

No niceties. No hint of tone.

Jeez, what is wrong with me? My heart is pounding. It's just a text message. And I'm not working today, so I don't owe him any answers.

"Liam?" Orla asks.

"No," I say, my eyes fixed on the phone as I wander. "Killian."

"What's his deal messaging you on a Saturday?" She scowls. "You're not even working today."

"He wants to know where I am," I murmur. *Why?*

"Dick. He better not be trying to rope you into some work stuff."

I message him back, telling him I'm in Queens with Orla.

Almost immediately, his typing dots show up.

Killian: One of the team will come to get you when you're ready to head back to Manhattan.

I show Orla the message. "I think he's trying to be nice?"

She reads it and frowns. "You don't need collecting. He's not your da."

I text back **I'm fine**, and the phone immediately rings in my hand.

"He's calling? God, he's so heavy-handed. Don't answer it."

"Killian," I say, bringing the phone to my ear.

"Clodagh," his gruff voice replies. "Why are you refusing the ride?" His almost accusatory tone sends my heart racing faster.

"I'm staying with my friend Orla tonight." I halt in my tracks, making the dog walkers and runners flow around me. Did I miss something in the manual

I was supposed to do today? "Is that a problem? I didn't think you needed me today."

I ignore Orla's glares and turn away from her. Why is he taking so long to respond?

"I don't need you," he finally says, his voice low and stern. "It's just that... you work for me. I want to make sure you're okay."

Heat rises to my face as I fight the urge to smile. "Do you call all your staff who work in that big glass skyscraper to check if they're okay?" I can't help myself.

I can hear the frustration in his voice as he responds, "No, I don't, but you live with me. I need to make sure you're looked after."

"Do you *miss* me?" The words fly from my mouth before I can think twice. Oh God, why did I ask that? "Ignore that. I'm fine, Killian. You don't need to worry about me."

"There's a tracker on your phone for safety. Call the team at any time if you need anything." He clears his throat awkwardly. "Or call me."

I notice he doesn't answer my question about missing me.

Why does he care so much about my safety? What the hell does he think will happen to me in a park in Queens at midday, surrounded by joggers and dog walkers?

To be fair, I almost got kidnapped last Thursday night.

"Thank you. What are you doing today?"

"Teagan's still grounded, but we're going to visit

her grandmother. My mom."

"That's nice for her." It shouldn't matter to me, but I'm glad Killian and Teagan are spending time together today. "Well, I'd better go," I say as Orla folds her arms across her chest, narrowing her eyes at me. "Have fun, Killian."

"Remember to use the credit card for anything you need."

I've been too afraid to use it for anything other than food and transport so far. "*Anything*?"

He laughs. He *laughs*. This might be the first time I've heard him laugh properly. "Anything. I don't care what you spend it on, but keep it legal. See you tomorrow. I gotta go."

The line goes dead.

"Orla." I smirk. "We've got some shopping to do."

***

When Monday comes, I regret splurging with my new shiny all-paid-for credit card. Yesterday, Orla and I went shopping to buy the sexy underwear I saw the first day I bumped into Killian.

Turns out that shopping in designer stores on Fifth Avenue isn't as fun as I expected. Some of the assistants were a bit snooty, and all one store seemed to sell was a single handbag.

That turned into a bottomless brunch, which turned into cocktail happy hour, followed by a nightcap at a late-night jazz bar, then shots o'clock.

This morning, I bounced out of bed at five o'clock, lured into a false pretense that I didn't have a hangover, likely fueled by the last of the alcohol leaving my body.

I cheerfully made Killian and Teagan's breakfast. I took Killian's suits to the dry cleaners. I cleaned all the ground-floor rooms.

Now, it's one o'clock, and I've spectacularly crashed and burned. My head is hanging out of my arsehole.

This is why when I find myself staring at the most beautiful bathtub I've ever laid my eyes on, I decide it would be a crime not to use it.

It's a freestanding white marble tub with a high, sloping back elevated up on two steps of blue tiles. I just need a good soak to ooze the rest of the alcohol out through my suffering pores. The bath in my apartment is good, but this is next level; a seven-star bath.

Killian never uses it. I know because I clean it every day. He only takes showers in the massive two-person shower.

I strip off my denim shorts and top, flinging them onto the chair along with my underwear.

Technically, I'm not breaking any of his rules. The manual doesn't explicitly say I *can't* use the bathroom on Killian's floor, just that I have to clean it. And I have hours before Killian will be home from work.

The water roars from the fancy wall-mounted bath taps.

I step in and sink into pure sweet heaven.

"*Yes*," I moan loudly as the water reaches my

shoulders. It's like bathing in the Icelandic Blue Lagoon. It's so deep I'm hidden by its sloping sides.

I tip my head back and close my eyes for a second. Cleaning a Fifth Avenue townhouse is no joke. Luckily for me, he doesn't check half the things I'm supposed to be doing, and he and Teagan only use a fraction of the house. Bit of a waste, really.

I toss some serenity salts into the bathwater, then play around with the hydro-jet settings. The jets are everywhere—on the four sides of the tub, as well as on its base.

Oh.

Oh.

That's nice. Very nice, indeed.

The pulsing water hits my exposed clit, causing wave-like sensations.

If I move a few inches...

Holy fucking potatoes.

I've never used Jacuzzi jets to get myself off before. Maybe this is an untapped kink.

I put my feet on the edge of either side of the tub and strategically raise my hips for a better angle over the jet, then I crank up the power.

Full speed ahead and hands-free.

My toes curl against the tub's sides, and my hands grab each side as I gyrate in a gentle, circular pattern around the jet centered underneath my pussy.

This is *intense.*

My pussy muscles contract in pleasure as the powerful pulsations pound me again and again.

Pure hydrotherapy horny bliss. Gyms should

include this in water aerobics classes.

I'm so swollen, so ready with need... and now I'm picturing my grumpy boss climbing into the bath. The thought sends tingling sensations through my body. Delicious shock waves make me buck and thrash about the tub.

What I wouldn't do to have his dick deep inside me right now. I want him to fuck me so hard the New York City Council would have to issue a noise pollution warning.

I really, really need to get laid.

Living under the same roof as Killian Quinn has me so wound up that I'm a horny mess. I have to find someone—not Liam—who can distract me.

The sound of the jets mingles with my breathy, desperate moans that echo around the bathroom. Nothing else matters except my overwhelming primal need to come hard with the help of a Jacuzzi jet.

I have no shame.

I let out a final cry and shudder as the climax overtakes me.

Well, that was interesting and unexpected.

***

Thirty minutes later, I'm a prune. I've turned the jets down to the lowest setting and reach up lazily to open the window above the bath to clear the steam.

I can't believe I just made myself come with a jet spray when my ex never managed to do it once. Unfucking-believable.

I could do with a post-coital glass of wine, but I have more chores to finish, so I need to force myself out of this tub. Magically, the water doesn't even go cold.

The steam has cleared, meaning it's my cue to get my shriveled ass out and back to work. I swing one leg over the tub. I can do this.

Except the sound of movement downstairs makes me go rigid in the bath.

Fuck.

What the hell was that noise?

My ass clenches in terror, and I worry it will swallow the plug.

Someone is coming up the stairs. Closer... closer. They're advancing too quickly for me to jump out and get my clothes on in time.

Who the hell is it?

Teagan's at school, and Killian's at work. Oh my God, what if it's an intruder? Or does his security team know I'm in the tub? Are there sensors in the bath or something?

I turn the Jacuzzi off so that the only sound is the mild sloshing of the water as I pull my leg back into the tub.

The bathroom door swings open. I duck down just in time, submerging everything but my face in the water.

It's him.

Killian.

I know just by his breathing.

"Connor, this asshole is showing up at the office every day," he growls from the doorway.

Dear God, are two of them in the bathroom?

I hear the distant sound of a male answering him. No... he's just on the phone.

He can't see me because the bathroom is the size of a one-bed apartment, and I'm hunkered down in the tub at the far end.

Now is the right time to wave a hand and communicate my presence.

Except I'm naked, and that's a tad inconvenient.

Slowly, I lift my head to peek out over the tub.

He's completely naked. He's growling something down the phone something about a casino in Brooklyn as he strides toward the shower.

I push my head back down again, my heart hammering.

I only saw his massive cock for a few seconds, but it will be forever ingrained in my memory. No wonder he's so arrogant. All those liquidized almonds are paying off for him.

What's my action plan?

What the hell am I doing? Why don't I speak up? Why don't I say I'm in the bath? Hmm. It feels like I'm one bad decision away from getting fired.

I hear the shower door slide open.

My action plan is just to breathe. Breathe, woman, breathe.

I'm past the point of no return now. Too much time has passed, and I can't just pipe up and say, "heya. Don't mind me!"

I brave another peek. He steps inside the shower and turns it on from above. Now I have a side view of that magnificent muscular ass and his heavy cock.

He spreads his large thighs wider as he directs his face against the stream of water from the ceiling. His eyes must be closed. He's in his own world.

Damn. His back muscles look even better with water running down them.

And those thighs. I love rugby player thighs.

He turns to face me, and I bite my lower lip to stop myself from squealing.

I'm playing with fire, not hiding. As panicked as I am, I can't look away. His eyes are closed as he lets the water run over his face, but he could open them at any moment.

I greedily take in every inch of his broad, toned body. The water runs down his V to his thick cock. That's definitely a two-hander. My pussy clenches as I imagine his cock driving into me.

He runs both hands through his hair, and dear God, I swear it might be the most arousing sight of my life. I'm melting in the bath water.

Any dick after this will be suboptimal.

The man has to have some physical flaw; he can't be perfect. He must have bunions or something. His toes looked a bit hairy the night Liam tried to kidnap me.

After a long moment, he lifts the shower gel and smears it across his chest.

Now is my cue to duck back into the water. If I'm quiet, I can get away with this. He'll never know I'm here.

Hurry up, man. You're clean!

My throat is tickly. I have the urge to cough, but I'm fighting it, swallowing hard to quell the sensation. My nerves rise as the itch refuses to go away.

A loud groan from the shower makes me jump out of my skin. Followed by another lower one.

No.

Please no.

Not here. Not now.

Sounds of movement come from the shower. Maybe he isn't doing what I think.

"Hi, guys!" says a chirpy female American voice. "I've missed you. It's super hot here in Cali, so I'm going to get more comfortable." There's a pause.

"Oh, that feels so much better," she coos in a low, breathy tone.

By the sound of Killian's heavy breathing, I can only presume she's taking off her clothes.

This is not good. He'll be furious if he knows I'm witnessing his personal library of fantasies firsthand.

The female stops talking, and there are more sounds of movement from Killian.

A second woman speaks up, her voice raspier and less cheerful. "You'll be feelin' the burn in your legs after ten minutes of this," she says.

For a second, I think I've spoken. It's the only explanation for why I can hear my own voice.

It's *me*.

It's one of my plié squat classes that I put on YouTube.

I have to look. I'll regret this for the rest of my life if I don't.

Killian groans louder, a fierce sound that sends heat racing through my body.

I poke my head up.

One palm rests against the shower wall above his head while the other aggressively fists up and down his length.

I can just about make out his phone through the steam, resting on the shower tray in front of him.

"It really works your inner thighs, so it does," I say on the video.

Killian Quinn is masturbating to a homemade Pilates video of *me*.

"*Clodagh.*" It's a low and drawn-out groan. It sounds like he's in pain. No man has said my name like that before. I feel it between my thighs. "*Yes.*"

He pumps his thick, angry cock harder and faster as I hear my voice instructing viewers to widen their legs into a nice deep squat. I watch his sexy forearm strain as he pumps.

Yes. I agree with him. Oh fuck, yes, yes, yes.

It's an enormous penis. A beast twice the size of anything I've ever experienced. That thing would rip me apart. Fact.

I wish I could see his face properly. I want to see what he looks like when he comes apart.

My hand slaps over my mouth to stop myself from screaming as another groan rumbles from him. Delicious female ear candy.

Is this like menstrual clocks? Does living with someone cause synchronization of masturbation?

The hand not fisting his cock fumbles with the phone, and the sound lowers, so my Irish accent disappears.

Should I be offended?

His breathing grows more aggressive and labored. He's no longer looking at the video. He's too far gone. His hips rock as I wonder if he's imagining thrusting into me right now.

His forehead leans against the shower wall as he stiffens, buttocks clenched.

His whole body tightens and shudders with a guttural growl that reverberates into my clit.

With a final jerk, every muscle in his body clenches and stiffens, and he comes *hard.*

Niagara Falls style.

I stop breathing. I can't cope with this.

His release seems to last an eternity. It streams down his thighs, being washed away by the water. His hands brace against the wall to steady himself.

Every muscle in my body clenches with him as if we're connected. I'm terrified, confused, and aroused, all rolled into one.

"*Fuck,*" he mutters through clenched teeth.

I duck my head down again and close my eyes. Show's over.

Shallow, quiet breaths and you'll get through this. Be brave.

The shower door slides open. He clears his throat

awkwardly as I hear him rubbing his skin with a towel.

Please don't come over here.

The bathroom door opens, filling the room with a gust of air. I'm safe. He's leaving. Thank God, because the tickle in my throat is back with a vengeance.

I shift slightly in the bath to relieve a cramp in my hip.

Bad plan.

Terrible idea.

Catastrophic mistake.

The luck of the Irish isn't with me today.

The plug is no longer in the hole. Houston, we have a problem.

My backside is firmly blocking the plug hole, trapping the draining water. The most annoying high-pitched whistle emanates from beneath me as the water drains slowly through the bottleneck that is my bum.

I can't stop it. I can't stop this train wreck. I can't move for fear that the water will drain faster.

If only there was a hairdryer nearby that I could electrocute myself with. It would be easier.

And there he stands.

Towering over the edge of the bath with his massive, angry cock, naked and glaring at me, eyes blazing in complete and utter disbelief.

My dignity flows down the drain with the water. This is worse than Killian discovering my criminal record.

"Hi," I croak, arms crossed over my chest like a

vampire in a coffin as the last of the water rushes away with a loud gurgle, followed by an undignified squeak.

FIFTEEN

Killian

My jaw hits the marble-tiled floor.

"Clodagh?"

I don't know why it's a fucking question. Maybe it's to check if my brain is short-circuiting or if Clodagh really is sprawled naked in the tub.

"What the hell are you doing?" I growl, breathing hard.

She stares up at me, her face flushed. "I'm having a bath."

My entire body stiffens in response. Half of me, the gentleman, is flustered, while the other half, the primitive caveman, is very fucking aroused at the sight of the pint-sized tattooed little vixen.

I try not to look at the water droplets trickling down her breasts. I try not to imagine biting and sucking on her hardening pink nipples as my hands run down her body to explore her sweet pussy.

What the fuck is she doing?

I would have noticed the bathroom door open, which means...

177

"You've been here this whole time?" I ask, trying to keep my gaze averted. "Let me get this straight. You were *having a bath* when I was taking a shower?"

"I couldn't find a good time to tell you I was here," she says in a strangled voice. "I planned to wait until you finished, then leave."

Jesus Christ. She saw me pleasuring myself in the shower.

Arousal surges through me as my eyes slide back to her. All I want to do is make a reckless mistake, climb into the bath on top of her, and lick those water droplets off her creamy skin.

She rises to a sitting position, making sure her legs remain close together, and quickly moves her red hair to cover her exposed chest. "In my defense, I was here first."

I glare at her in warning.

My cock swells again, heavy and thick from the naked nanny in my bathtub. In my shock at seeing her naked, I'd forgotten I'm naked myself.

"Put on your damn clothes," I growl through clenched teeth, still half convinced I'm dreaming. "I'm late. We'll have a meeting about this when I get home tonight."

"Yes, sir," she replies in a whisper.

I pinch the bridge of my nose and then storm out of the bathroom. It's only then that I realize I've left my phone on the shower rack.

I'm heading for a goddamn lawsuit.

***

"Clodagh?" I shout, sliding the patio door shut. She's nowhere on the first floor, and she's late for our meeting. If she's trying to provoke me further, it has the desired effect.

I came home early to deal with our little awkward situation before Teagan arrived home from school.

Now she's not even here at the time I specified. My jaw clenches.

This afternoon was a write-off. I had lunch with a beautiful, intelligent woman, and all I could think about was Clodagh in the bathtub. I had to tell Maria that I was distracted by work.

I head for the stairs leading down to her studio apartment.

My nostrils flare when I hear a man's voice from inside.

I knock hard on the door, and Clodagh answers.

"Killian." Her gaze shifts quickly to the wall clock, and she takes in a sharp breath. The T-shirt she's wearing slips off one of her shoulders. "Sorry. I lost track of time. I'll be right up."

My hackles instantly rise as I glance between Clodagh and Sam, who is casually propped against her refrigerator.

He straightens up, eyeing me sheepishly. "Boss."

"I told you no men in the house," I say frostily to Clodagh.

She stares up at me as if I'm deranged. "It's Sam."

"I know who he is."

"He's vetted. He's *your staff.*"

My jaw tightens. Just because Clodagh caught me in a compromising position doesn't mean she can talk back to me.

And maybe the idea of Sam being in her studio doesn't sit well with me. "I told you not to distract my security, Clodagh. What are you doing here, Sam?"

Hurt blazes across her features.

"I was just getting rid of a spider for Clodagh," Sam says, his intentions written all over his face.

"They're huge in New York," Clodagh adds defensively. "Gigantic spiders. They must be coming over from Central Park. I have a phobia because one time, in Ireland, I woke up to use the bathroom, and when I came back to bed, there was a spider on my pillow."

I give Sam a hard look, ignoring Clodagh. "I don't employ you to be an arachnid assailant for damsels in distress," I say sarcastically. "I employ you to be my daughter's security."

"Yes, boss," he mumbles.

"Teagan's at school." She glowers at me. "I think you're overreacting."

Is she deliberately trying to get a rise out of me?

"Go home, Sam," I grit out as I yank open the door a bit wider. "Clodagh. Upstairs. Now."

Her cheeks flush pink, but she nods and silently follows me up the stairs.

***

"What were you playing at?" I demand quietly as soon as she takes a seat in the lounge. Her legs cross at the ankles, her hands folded on her lap, and she sits up straight as if trying to find the most reverent position to appease me.

Her face falls in confusion. "What do you mean?"

"I don't expect to find my staff hiding in the bath while I'm taking a shower," I snap, picturing her small perky breasts in the bath. "If I wanted a voyeuristic nanny, I would have put it in the job listing."

Her eyes widen in horror. "*What*? Seriously? All I wanted was a relaxing bath."

"You have a bath in your own studio."

"It doesn't have all the different jet settings," she huffs, crossing her arms over her chest. "I wasn't planning on watching you! You shouldn't even have been home at that time."

"I can't come home and take a shower in my own house?"

She hums in annoyance. "I didn't expect you there. That's all I'm saying." She sinks farther into her seat. "I'm sorry I didn't speak up when you came in. I just froze."

"You should have told me you were there. You shouldn't have allowed me to..." I run a hand over my jaw, recalling how turned on I was. "To do what I did."

Her face turns bright red, and she looks away from me. The blatant reminder of what I did in front of her, of how hard I came in front of her. *Because* of her.

But it's the last time. This needs to end now. I heave a sigh. "Even if I thought I was alone, I shouldn't have acted on my impulses. It was undeniably wrong of me—I understand if you don't feel comfortable here anymore and want to resign. Just know that you are safe."

That would be the best course of action. If she quits, Marcus can hire a sensible replacement, one who won't make my blood run hot.

"Resign? I'm not resigning." She shakes her head so fiercely that her hair flies around her face. "Not a chance. I was just taken aback, that's all. I just never thought you'd see me like that."

"Like what?"

Her cheeks are now a flaming pink. "Hmm... a woman."

My frown deepens. I can see it all over her face. She's taking what happened and running with her version of events.

"This isn't a love story," I say more sharply than I intended. "Don't misconstrue it. You're an attractive young woman, and I am not immune to that fact." Me and every fucking man on my security team based on the other night's drama. "But you're my staff. That moment was a mistake, one I won't make again. It was inappropriate and foolish behavior on my part Something I'm not proud of."

Her green eyes blaze. She stays quiet for a few moments before responding. "Got it. Don't worry,

Killian. I know I'm not your type."

"I've no qualms about admitting that I find you attractive sexually. That's where it ends. You're my daughter's nanny and my temporary domestic assistant albeit not a very good one."

She tightens her lips. I may have overstated my point. "Understood, loud and clear. Sir."

I sigh and step back from her. How would things have gone if I was ten years younger and had no commitments? "I hope I don't need to remind you about your NDA. Anything that happens inside my house is not to be discussed outside."

"Of course," she says curtly.

"Good. I'm glad we understand each other."

We gaze at each other in tense silence for a long beat. Her lips form a flat line. I know I've offended her; it's written all over her face.

"Under my contract, I'm allowed to date," she says in a clipped tone, standing up. "I'm just not allowed to bring guys back, right?"

"Correct."

"And there's also nothing in my contract forbidding me from dating security personnel, am I right?"

Where is she going with this? "Technically, it's not against the terms."

"So Sam and I can go out when we're not working."

My eyes narrow. "You and Sam can do whatever you want off the clock. Just as long as it's not in my house."

"Fine." She juts her chin up. "I will."

A strange feeling grips my chest. "You want to date Sam?" I snap.

"Maybe."

My muscles tense. What the fuck is going on with me? "Don't distract him when he's working."

She looks like she wants to reply with something snarky, but she holds back. "No, of course not," she says with a slight edge in her voice.

She's silent again, and I'm about to walk away when she asks, "I have another question. Can I get deliveries to the house?"

"Of course," I say, relieved that Clodagh's love life isn't the topic of conversation any longer. "They'll go through explosive checks by the team."

Her mouth drops open. "I'm not a *terrorist*."

"Then you've nothing to worry about. What are you getting delivered? Clothes?"

"No. Wood. I want to start working on a few things in my bedroom."

"Fine." I shrug.

"Is there anything else you need from me, Killian?"

If only you knew.

I meet her eyes and wave her off. "No."

She walks off, leaving me with an unsavory image of a naked Clodagh doing woodwork in her bedroom.

SIXTEEN

Clodagh

Send a bouquet to Maria Taylor. Florist on Fifth.

I stare at the text message from Killian with a strange pang of annoyance, practically hearing his gravelly voice say the words in my head.

He was especially distant this morning, talking to me in a businesslike way. Like he wanted me to understand that yesterday's bathroom interlude meant nothing. It's not like I expected us to ride off into the sunset together in a horse-drawn carriage through Central Park.

What should I write? I message back.

I'm certain that Maria Taylor was the woman I saw him with in the hotel. She was dark-haired, maybe Latino, and had legs for days. An absolute stunner. A perfect match looks-wise for him.

I bet she's touched his massive cock.

I get a mental image of the woman from the hotel chirpily saying, *"It's super hot here, so I'm going to get more comfortable,"* while he masturbates.

Ugh.

Am I jealous?

Why am I torturing myself? I feel a cold sore coming on from the stress.

My phone buzzes with a notification.

Killian: My name? Use your initiative.

Jerk. He could have given me some context. Is it her birthday? Is he apologizing for something? I didn't take him for a romantic. Then again, it's not very romantic when you get a bouquet from your love interest's nanny maid. I wonder how many rich guys actually send their own gifts.

I've never even gotten flowers from a guy before.

I dial Sam's number. I was only half bluffing when I said Sam and I should date. He's a great guy. A part of me wanted to see if Killian would be jealous. That way, I would know if this weird sexual tension between us is real or imagined.

My attempt failed miserably.

Sam answers on the third ring. "Clodagh," he says warmly. There's traffic in the background, so he must be outside.

"Hey, Sam. I need some help. I'm sending Maria Taylor flowers from Killian. Can you message me her address?"

"Sure thing, I'll do it after the call." He sounds a little out of breath, like he's walking.

"Did I catch you at a bad time?"

"No, I'm just leaving Teagan's school after my shift." A siren goes off in the background.

"You have to wait outside the school?"

He laughs a little. "When you say it like that, it

sounds worse than it is. But yeah, a few of us take shifts while Teagan is in school."

Jeez. What a strange life.

"Er, so Killian didn't give me any context, so I don't know what to write on the card. Are they in a relationship?" I ask casually.

"They've been out a few times." Sam pauses for a moment. "Mr. Quinn isn't really the type for serious relationships. Although he does seem to be quite taken with Miss Taylor, so who knows. Just keep it vague."

The irritating jealousy in my chest sharpens.

"Yeah, he doesn't seem like the hearts-and-flowers type of guy." I laugh lightly. I wonder if Maria gets to experience Killian's softer side. "Thanks, Sam. Call in when you drop Teagan off from ballet." Seeing Sam will be a nice distraction. Compared to Killian, he's like a ray of sunshine.

"Sure thing," he drawls. "Remember, we'll be thirty minutes late this evening. She has the monthly showcase."

"The what?"

"Once a month, there's a showcase; the parents and others get to sit in and watch."

"Oh." Teagan never mentioned it this morning, but she's not exactly a morning person. "Is it a big deal?"

"Not sure, sorry, Clodagh. That's as far as my knowledge goes. I wait outside and make sure no one tries to assassinate her."

I chuckle a little, thinking he's joking, then realize

he isn't. "Wow. Another day at the office, huh? Is the threat of danger really that high?"

The line grows silent for a few moments. "He won't take another risk."

I ponder whether or not it's a good idea to enter this conversation but plunge onward anyway. "This is about Teagan's mum, right?"

"Yeah. It's known about... but Mr. Quinn doesn't like to talk about it." Sam sounds wary. "I gotta go. I'll chat to you later, Clodagh."

"Hey, Sam?" I say quickly. "Wait up. Does Killian, I mean Mr. Quinn, go to the showcase?" Seriously, is Sam not allowed to call him Killian after five years? "You said parents attend?"

"No, he doesn't."

"Why not?"

"I don't know," he says slowly, sounding surprised at the question. "You'd have to ask him." He clears his throat. "But I wouldn't advise you to."

"Do the other parents go?"

"I see others go in. I'm mainly checking for threats, so I don't keep tabs."

So no one turns up for Teagan.

The more time I spend with Teagan, the harder my heart aches for her. Underneath the moodiness is a vulnerable little girl. She has an amazing education, she lives in a luxurious mansion in the poshest part of New York, from the pictures on the walls, she's traveled all over the world with her father, and she has more electronics than Japan.

But I wouldn't want her life at her age. She seems

to spend more time with security guards than with her own family.

I know Killian tries. He gets home every night and looks exhausted but still tries to spend time with Teagan.

"I'm going to come with you to ballet," I tell Sam. "Can you collect me on the way?"

Maybe I'm not doing the right thing. Who knows how Teagan will react when I turn up, but I'll feel guilty if I don't at least try.

"Of course." Sam sounds chuffed. "I'd love the company."

I hang up and call the florist and ask them to send their most pretentious bouquet to Maria Taylor.

Use your initiative.

I'll show him initiative.

"What's the message?" she asks me.

I grin. "To my babe," I say slowly. "From your dreamboat, Killian. Then add ten kisses and ten hugs."

Technically, I'm doing as he told me.

***

Sam heads back outside to sit in the car while I'm led into the viewing gallery of the ballet studio.

I'm nervous as hell. Is this a stupid idea? What if Teagan doesn't want me here? I didn't tell her I was coming.

I expect a school gym like the one where I used to play netball but find myself in a large intimidating studio with mirrors on all the walls and bright lights reflecting off them. The viewing gallery above the stage is packed.

It takes me a moment to register which dancer Teagan is. They all look alike with their blue leotards and soft satin shoes as they point and flex on their tiptoes, warming up. With the mirrors around the studio walls, it looks like there are twice as many of them.

At least the food coloring has faded to a dull red.

Some chatter, looking relaxed. Others stand in statuesque poses, deep in concentration.

Teagan looks nervous. She's alone as she stretches, arching her body and reaching her arms to the ceiling. She doesn't even look up at the viewing gallery.

From the crowd in the viewing gallery, it seems everyone's parents are here except for Teagan's. There are even some kids.

I squeeze into the only vacant seat left in the second row behind all the parents chatting.

This seems like a bigger deal than Sam thought. Does Killian realize?

"Places, ladies!" the teacher barks. All the girls fall into line.

Just as the music begins, Teagan looks up and sees me. Her eyes widen in surprise, then her mouth forms a confused frown. Oh no, she doesn't look pleased.

I wave down nervously.

Then slowly, she nods and smiles. Her lips quirk

up into a crooked smile, her face torn between two emotions.

It's a start.

She takes a deep breath and steps forward as the music changes. From my limited knowledge, I think it's from *Swan Lake*, although I've never seen a ballet before.

Their feet fly across the floor in a continuous flurry of twirls and leaps. I feel absurdly proud.

And sad. Killian should be here to watch his daughter.

"Teagan Quinn!" the teacher says sharply. "Please try to keep up. Less ego, more focus."

Less ego? That was unnecessary. She didn't need to call her out so abrasively. Would she treat her the same if Killian were here?

Teagan's face burns with shame as she stumbles, falling slightly out of sync with the other dancers.

She tries to regain her composure, but the bitchy teacher barks another passive-aggressive command, and she struggles to find her footing.

Some of the other girls get reprimanded, but it's in a much softer tone. With Teagan, there's an undercurrent of something stronger.

What is this woman's problem? She's watching Teagan, ready to pounce on any mistake.

The teacher snaps at her again, and I resist the urge to yell for her to stop. This is really uncomfortable to watch. It's like she doesn't *want* Teagan to do well.

Flustered, Teagan nods and tries to follow her

instruction, but the bitch isn't helping her; she's putting her on edge.

I glance up at some of the other parents, wondering if I'm being paranoid. They're smiling, in their own bubble, captivated solely by their kid's performances.

But the more I watch Teagan's face, the more I know I'm not imagining this.

She winces a little as she does a single spin and lands awkwardly. She's lost her mojo.

My heart aches for her. I want to run down and hug her. It takes me back to a teacher who made me feel like that. She thought I was being obstructive, but she never took the time to figure out that I wasn't lazy; I just found reading difficult.

As the last notes of the music fade away and the girls return to their starting positions, I let out a huge whoop. Way too loudly. There's a civilized round of applause from the rest of the crowd. From the disapproving looks I get from parents, whooping like I'm at a concert is not the done thing here.

The slight smile from Teagan is worth it.

***

"I can't believe Dad's making the nannies come to watch the ballet now," she grumbles when she sees me in the studio reception waiting for her.

"He's not." I take one of her gym bags from her. "Sam told me about it."

"Oh." Her brow furrows, and I fear I may have

made a mistake.

I open the double doors to the street where Sam and the other security guy are waiting in the not-at-all-obvious SUV with blacked-out windows across the street.

"Do you mind me coming to watch you?" I ask hesitantly as we stand at the pedestrian crossing. "I heard spectators were allowed today, and I wanted to see you perform."

Her frown deepens. "Not spectators. Family."

Damn. I have messed up.

I slow my pace as we cross the street so I can look at her. "I'm sorry if I stepped out of line."

"No, it's fine." She gives a slight shrug, her voice quiet. "You just caught me by surprise, that's all. You didn't need to come."

"I wanted to." I smile. "You were great! Your dad must be so proud of you."

The way she defensively shrugs crushes me inside. Has Killian *ever* gone to one of these? He would have noticed the weird vibe between her and her teacher if he had.

I don't understand the man.

"Is your teacher always like that?" I ask, wondering how I should word this. "She seemed a bit hard on you. Maybe she was having an off day?"

"No, she's always like that." She scowls as we weave through the crowd of people. "She's a bitch. She hates me."

"Have you told your dad?"

"He just brushes it off. He says we don't always get

along with everyone in life." She smiles sarcastically. "She's the best in New York, so why would he send me to anyone else?"

"Because if she's making you unhappy, then it doesn't matter if she's the best in the world. Has he ever met her?"

"No."

I hesitate, unsure what to say. "He hasn't come to watch you?"

"Nope. He'll never watch me."

"Why not?" I press cautiously.

Her face tightens. "Because Mom was a professional ballet dancer. He wants me to keep up the tradition but says it hurts him too much to watch."

We arrive at the car, so I can't press her any further. "Sorry about your mum. I saw the picture on your bedroom wall of her."

"It's okay. I don't remember her."

"Wait." I put my hand over hers to stop her from opening the door.

Her eyes narrow at me suspiciously.

"Look, I know I'm not as motherly as Mrs. Dalton, but if you need to talk, I'm here." I smile, trying to lighten the mood. "And I can definitely take that teacher down in a fight if you need me to."

"It's okay." She rolls her eyes dramatically, but at least she's smiling. "I'll be thirteen next week, and then, hopefully, I'll move into a different class."

"You're a Gemini, just like me!"

"Do you actually believe in that stupid shit?"

"Only the good parts," I say as I climb into the back seat next to her.

The guys in front nod at us.

"What are you going to do for your birthday?" I ask.

"Dad's taking me to see Cayden Aguilar. We're going to the concert, then we get to meet him afterward."

I pause my fight with the seat belt and look at her, astonished. "*The* Cayden Aguilar? The singer? Are you freaking serious?"

He's the biggest pop star in the world right now. Every teen has posters of him plastered all over their walls.

A smirk tugs at the corner of her mouth. "Yeah. Him."

The guys chuckle in the front seat, clearly accustomed to this lifestyle.

"What about you?" Teagan asks. "What are your birthday plans?"

I blink, still in shock, as Sam pulls out. "There's no way I can top that. I'll probably just hang out at the pub."

Sam's eyes meet mine in the rearview mirror, and he winks.

Teagan's face says she thinks that's a crap plan, but she quietly says, "You should ask Dad to give you the day off."

I grin at her. "Listen, lady, I don't care if I'm scrubbing your toilet bowls on my birthday. I'm just happy to be in New York."

***

The moment Killian steps through the door from work, I can tell he's in no mood for talking. He grunts in acknowledgment before taking off his tie and undoing a few buttons.

"I need to talk to you," I say quickly. "I went to Teagan's ballet show tonight."

His brow lifts. "Why?"

Why? What is it with this family questioning me? "To support her. A lot of the other parents go." I forge on while I'm still feeling brave. "You should go sometime."

The angry flash in his eyes is my warning that I should shut up. But I have to say this, or I won't feel settled, and now is as good a time as any with Teagan upstairs in her room.

"Do you know she isn't getting along with her teacher?" I ask.

"Her teacher is the best in New York," he says curtly, opening the fridge. "She pushes her hard. Teagan's going to complain."

"No, I think it's more than that. The teacher seems irrationally sharp with her. Much more than the other kids. I think you should do something. Maybe even move her to another class."

He slams the fridge door shut. "Teagan's nearly thirteen; she needs to learn to respect authority."

"I think you should ask Teagan what she wants. Right now, she's not enjoying ballet. She seems to only be doing it because you want her to."

He steps closer, his gaze darkening with each step as he corners me against the sink. My throat tightens as if a lump is lodged there. I'm on very shaky ground here.

We're dangerously close; it feels like #huntsmanpiegate all over again. His eyes never leave my face as he lowers his head to mine.

"Did I ask for your opinion on parenting my daughter?" His voice is low. I would almost prefer it if he shouted at me. "You've been living here for a week, and now you're telling me how to raise my child?"

"You weren't there," I say quietly. "You can't possibly know if what I'm saying is correct."

Ignoring his glare, I take my phone out of my pocket and scroll to where I've taken pictures of Teagan at ballet.

By the way he looks at the phone, you'd think I showed him pictures of animal cruelty.

"Mind your own damn business, Clodagh," he growls through clenched teeth, jerking away from me.

To my horror, tears prick my eyes. I won't eat with this arrogant man tonight. I grab my plate and skitter past him, out of the kitchen and down the stairs to my studio.

He doesn't come after me.

***

Just as I slip into my pajama shorts and vest top, there's a knock on the studio door.

Bracing myself for round two, I open the door to Killian.

He looks me up and down warily. "Can you be here at eight o'clock next Tuesday night?" He pauses. "I need you to stay with Teagan. I'm going into the ballet school to talk to the teacher."

"Sure," I reply, suppressing a smile.

He gives me a slight nod before walking away.

It's the closest I'll get to an apology.

***

It's midnight before I realize I don't have my phone. I have to set my alarm, but I left it upstairs when I ran off in a rush.

I creep upstairs without turning the lights on to find a large figure on the sofa.

Killian.

Naked except for shorts.

His thick bicep spills over the side of the couch, and the other rests on his bare, toned stomach. His legs are spread apart, one extended over the edge of the couch. There's no question he's a beautiful man. Sleeping, he looks almost vulnerable. Boyish.

Is he dreaming?

He lets out a loud, grunty snore, and I clap my hand over my mouth to stifle my giggle.

What if he sleeps here all night and doesn't get up in time in the morning? Should I wake him?

Probably not; he'll only yell at me.

Ever so gently, I pull the blanket bunched up at his feet up over his legs and stomach.

When I look up, he's awake and staring right at me.

I freeze. "Sorry, I—"

Abruptly, his hand comes up to my cheek, almost as if forgetting himself.

The heat from his touch radiates into my skin, and I forget how to breathe.

He goes entirely still, neither of us saying a word. An inner battle plays out on his face as he contemplates what to do next.

Kiss me.

Then he drops his hand from my cheek. "Go to bed, Clodagh."

SEVENTEEN

Killian

Anyone who said "just wait until she's a teenager" to me over the years, was right on the money.

I thought the "period talk" would be the hardest conversation to navigate, but that was only the beginning. With no blueprint to follow, every day is a wild ride of teenage emotions as I try to blindly fumble my way through the highs and lows.

Today's emotion of the day is rage, and it's directed at me, Daddy dearest.

Teagan eyes me with a glare that could cut through steel as I enter the kitchen after my workout. I try not to be too offended; being a father to a teenage daughter has thickened my hide much more than running a billion-dollar corporation.

Her hair is thankfully back to its natural color.

"Morning, beautiful." I lean in to kiss her forehead, but she swivels in her stool away from me. I'm surprised to see her even out of her room at this time on a Saturday morning.

"Don't talk to me. I still hate you."

I exhale heavily in response. "I know, princess." I wonder if this'll last until she's eighteen.

"Don't call me princess."

If she rolls her eyes any further back in her head, I'll have to summon a priest for an exorcism.

"Don't roll your eyes at me. They'll get stuck like that."

I place a cup beneath the coffee machine and make my morning espresso. "Since you're grounded, why not use the day to practice the piece your cello teacher gave you? I'd love to hear it. The music competition is only three weeks away."

"I'm *supposed* to be hanging with Becky today," she fires back in contempt.

"And you would be if you hadn't dyed your hair," I point out calmly, knowing that for a twelve-year-old girl, having to be away from friends is the worst punishment imaginable. "You knew the rules and the consequences, yet you took the risk. You're grounded for three more days."

She skewers me with a look of wrath that the Mareks would be proud of. "It doesn't even make sense! Why don't you just end it now? Why do I have to be grounded for three more days?"

I down the shot of espresso. "Because I say so."

I already explained to her why hair dye wasn't suitable for anyone under sixteen. We sat down together and read articles about it. Though she wasn't happy about it, she was smart enough not to want to damage her hair.

Now on to the next argument.

"But why *three*? Why does it have to be three?"

I've got nothing rational. "Because I decide the numbers."

"That's so unfair," she wails, throwing her hands in the air.

"Life's not always fair. Next time, you'll think more carefully about the consequences."

I join Teagan on a barstool at the island. We sit in one-sided angry silence as she stares down at her phone.

What would Harlow say if she were here? Would we be having these fights?

Have I been going at this all wrong? She's still a child. I don't want her dyeing her hair or wearing makeup. No daughter of mine is going to sexualize herself at twelve. When she turns thirty, then she can use cosmetics.

What would Clodagh say?

I clear my throat. "What are you looking at?"

Her eyes snap up to mine. "Why are you even asking since you probably already know? You have my passcode."

I sigh. "I don't look at your phone. I have it for security reasons, Teagan. You know there are risks inherent with growing up wealthy."

"Sometimes I wish they *would* take me away," she huffs.

"Less of the attitude. Listen, I know you're mad about not meeting Becky, but how about I take you out for lunch?" I give her chin a playful flick and smile, offering my white flag of surrender. "It'll be a reprieve from your grounding for the afternoon. We haven't had a daddy-daughter date in a long time."

"You can't call it that anymore. I'm too old."

"Princess, I'll still be calling it that when you're thirty."

Her frown softens, and I can tell she wants to accept my offer but is too stubborn to say yes. "No," she eventually replies. "It's fine. I'd rather stay here."

I can't say the rejection doesn't sting.

Footsteps sound from the hall.

Another reminder of how I'm fucking up. I jerked off in front of the nanny. I nearly kissed her the other night. What the hell was I thinking?

I look up to see Clodagh standing in the kitchen doorway. To say I'm not prepared for the sight of her is an understatement.

She's wearing pale-blue yoga bottoms, a top that I'm not sure is a sports bra or a top, and a sleeveless hoodie over it. Her bottoms fit tightly around her gorgeous ass, making them look painted on. Her hair is tied in a high ponytail, making her already sharp cheekbones stand out even more. She looks so fresh and relaxed—the opposite of me.

It's sexier than if she had walked in wearing lace lingerie and completely fucking distracting.

"Good morning," she chirps enthusiastically, her eyes twinkling. She's likely glad that Saturday has arrived so she can escape my presence for a while.

"Morning," I reply, my throat tight.

Teagan huffs a *"morning"* without looking up.

My eyes lock with Clodagh's, and a pink flush of

heat travels across her cheeks. Under the bravado, she's flustered.

That night, I almost lost it. I almost pulled her down on top of me on the couch and showed her exactly what I wanted to do to her.

Ever since the disastrous incident in the bathroom, I've been fighting to keep my arousal under control. Just thinking about it has my adrenaline spiked again.

I need to fuck soon. Having sex with someone else is the only way to quell my strange fantasies about my bad nanny.

Clodagh breaks eye contact first, turning to Teagan instead. "Oh, it looks like your hair is back to normal!"

"About fucking time," I grumble, ruffling a strand of my daughter's hair.

"See?" Teagan glares at me before turning back to Clodagh. "Doesn't that mean I shouldn't be grounded anymore?"

"I'm Switzerland in this argument." Clodagh shakes her head, smirking. "I'm not that dumb. Killian, I just wanted to check that you don't need me today?"

I raise a brow at her question. "You don't work Saturdays."

"Great." Her wide smile hits me right in the stomach. "I have to go teach my yoga class in Queens. Have a great day."

"Do I pay you that little you need to work a side job?"

"No." She smirks. "I can definitely handle myself on your salary."

"So why do you do it?"

She looks at me quizzically, then her lips turn into a mocking half smile. "Isn't it obvious, Killian? I *like* it. They just throw me some tips. I put a sign up at the bar, and it got a bit of interest." She looks between Teagan and me. "What are you two up to today?"

"I'm stuck inside this prison because I'm not allowed to decide anything in my life," Teagan pipes up.

Clodagh smiles sympathetically in return. "At least it's a nice prison."

"One of the team will drive you to Queens and pick you up again," I tell her.

"Oh no, it's fine." She waves a hand dismissively. "I'll take the subway."

"Nonsense." I reach for my phone, annoyed that she's refusing my offer of a ride. "I'll call one of the team." Although the way I catch Sam and the others eyeing up Clodagh, I feel like I want to drive her myself.

"It's fine, really," she says more firmly. "I like the subway."

"You *like* the subway?" Teagan looks up, disgusted. "But it's supposed to be dirty and crowded. I would never go on the subway."

Clodagh's mouth falls open. "What? You mean you've never been on the subway?"

Teagan's face scrunches up. "Nope."

"Seriously?" Clodagh laughs. "Oh my God, it's the only way I get around. I consider it a tourist attraction. It was top of my New York bucket list."

"Eww." Teagan wrinkles her nose. "You can be so weird sometimes, Clodagh."

"Manners." I shoot Teagan a warning look. "Just because you don't use the subway doesn't mean you can make rude comments about people who do."

Clodagh's hands come up to pull her hair into a tighter ponytail. "We don't have subway systems where I'm from in Ireland. I'd be lucky if the bus came on time. I like riding the New York subway and being surrounded by so many strangers. It makes me feel like I'm a part of something bigger." She shrugs. "Anything new is exciting in my book."

"Anything?" I raise a brow skeptically. "I'm not sure that theory holds up."

She rolls her eyes and swings the backpack onto her shoulders, pushing out her chest as she does so. I try not to notice. "Well, you won't know if you don't try. You sound just like the grumpy footballers in my yoga class. They always thought yoga was a waste of time." She smiles. "Now the whole team comes every Saturday religiously."

"The whole football team?" Teagan asks with a hint of interest.

"Yup." Clodagh nods. "It's funny how it started out as an activity for a few ladies, but now consists of mostly young Irish footballers."

"Oh." Teagan looks even more intrigued.

Clodagh pauses to glance at me before addressing

my daughter. "Do you want to come, Teagan?"

"No," I answer for her. "She's grounded."

"*Ugh*," Teagan shrieks, slamming her phone on the table. "You're not letting me work out? That is so wack."

I narrow my eyes on my daughter. Work out? Bullshit. If the yoga class wasn't full of football players, we wouldn't be having this conversation.

Clodagh barely hides a smirk.

"Besides," I say to my scowling daughter. "You're not imposing on Clodagh's day. She doesn't want to see us on the weekends."

"Not at all," Clodagh says warmly. "I don't mind."

"I've always wanted to try yoga." Teagan pouts. "And I need to get out of the house. I'm going insane."

"I'm not stupid, Teagan," I warn her. "It's got more to do with the fact that football players will be there. I already said I'd take you out to lunch."

"But I would rather do yoga," she sniffs, giving me her best doe-eyed look. "Pleaaaase, Daddy? I'll have the security guys with me."

I know when I'm being played. "If you think you're talking to any football players, you have another thing coming."

She rolls her eyes. "Fat chance with Sam and co. watching."

Clodagh laughs. "You know this is just a small Gaelic football team in Queens, right? It's not NFL. And our version of football isn't the same as yours."

"I know. I went to a match with Dad and Uncle

Connor once."

I look at Clodagh. It's not fair to put this on her.

Her eyes meet mine. "You can also come if you want, Killian," she says softly.

"Great," Teagan mutters. "Dad will call me princess in front of everyone."

I'm about to respond, but then, against my better judgment, I find myself nodding. Despite Teagan's protests.

Harlow would go.

If watching a yoga session is how I get to spend time with my daughter, then so be it. Even if she's reluctant to spend it with me. And perhaps it would be nice to have a reason to visit Queens other than visiting Harlow's grave.

"All right," I reply.

Clodagh looks so shocked I worry she's going to faint.

"Under one condition," I say. "I'll drive."

Clodagh frowns. "But the subway is faster."

"You've never been in a Ferrari, have you?"

"Okay, I have a condition of my own."

My brows lift. "Go on."

"It's Saturday, so everything is off the record, and nothing I do will get me sacked."

"I'm going to regret this, but you have a deal."

***

We park just outside the entrance to the park in Queens.

"That was amazing!" Clodagh laughs as I open the

car door for her and Teagan. "I suppose a Ferrari is sometimes better than the subway."

"I'm starting to think you've never been in a car before, from how you were screaming," I grumble.

The three of us head to the park, where a group of older ladies and a girl Clodagh's age are milling around. They're all wearing sportswear.

"Morning, ladies," Clodagh greets them and runs over to hug the girl in her twenties.

What the fuck am I doing here?

The girl whispers something to Clodagh, and they both look my way.

Teagan fidgets next to me nervously; I place my hand on her lower back in reassurance.

"Hello, Mr. Quinn," Clodagh's friend says reverently. "I'm Orla, Clodagh's best friend."

The sound of her Irish brogue does nothing for me compared to Clodagh's; thank fuck. If all Irish women had that effect on me, I'd never set foot in an Irish pub again. I'm convinced Clodagh uses hypnotism on me with hers.

"Killian," I reply.

"And this is Teagan," Clodagh says, drawing her into the group of women.

We exchange pleasantries with Orla and the ladies. More women in their sixties come over until a circle of about ten are around me.

"Where are the football players?" Teagan mutters beside me.

I shoot her a stern glance.

"Who is this strapping young man?" one of the

women asks, unabashedly undressing me with her eyes. Her American accent holds the slightest trace of an Irish lilt.

I chuckle a little. It's been a while since anyone called me young.

"This is my boss, Killian, and his daughter Teagan," Clodagh tells them. Now I have the attention of all the ladies. More join them. Their accents are a mixture of American, Irish, and a few others.

Clodagh grins. "Our new boy, Killian, is a little shy, so make him feel welcome, girls."

The women swarm around Teagan, asking her questions and telling her how pretty she is.

As for me, I'm being pawed and stroked. A hand on my back drifts dangerously close to my rear end.

"It's Clodagh's rich boss from Manhattan," one of them whispers loudly.

Another hand reaches out to stroke my arm. "He's very muscly."

Someone runs their fingers through my hair, and I hear a gentle purr at my back.

"He's not wearing a ring."

Another hand nudges me on my lower back.

For fuck's sake, is this how women feel in a strip club? I didn't think *Yoga with Clodagh* would be so depraved.

Clodagh can barely contain her smirk.

"Is he single, Clodagh?" one of them asks her without even looking at me. "If you don't want him, my Kelly's getting divorced."

"Is he in the military?" asks another throaty voice behind me.

"Oh God." Teagan groans beside me. "This is gross."

Jesus Christ. I'm being attacked by a gaggle of insatiable sex-hungry women.

"I'm right here," I grumble. "I've got working ears."

"Leave him be, ladies." Clodagh smirks at me. "Mr. Quinn scares easily. Ah, here come the guys."

I turn to see a group of brawny men stroll over, wearing Irish football jerseys. They look like they're in their twenties.

I feel the excitement ooze from Teagan.

"I'm watching you," I warn her.

She rolls her eyes in disgust and scuttles away from me, ashamed of being seen with her embarrassing dad in public.

"Hi, guys," Clodagh says to the group of men.

Looks like Clodagh has a lot of guys under her spell. They surround her, asking her how she is and telling her she looks great.

"How's the new gig, Clodagh?" one of them asks in a thick Irish accent. "Orla was saying your man's a right anal—"

"La, la, la!" Clodagh shrills. "This is my boss, Killian!"

The younger guys glance at me warily.

Clodagh clears her throat and claps her hands together. "Alrighty then, let's get started."

I stand to the side as the rest of the group unrolls

their mats on the grass. Clodagh places her pink mat at the front.

"Teagan, this one is yours." She hands her a mat. "Put it down beside Marg there."

To my daughter's delight, some of the guys peel their tops off. God, give me strength.

"This mat is yours, Killian." Clodagh holds out a mat, smiling at me.

My brows lift. "I'm not participating." I jut my chin to a bench. "I'll watch from over there."

"Nonsense," a woman barks beside me.

The rest of them voice their objections loudly.

Clodagh walks to a patch of grass beside one of the women and sets the mat down. When she bends down, I have a perfect view of her chest disappearing into the tiny sports top.

"You need the benefits of yoga more than anyone." She smiles innocently. "*Sir.*"

I clench my jaw. "No chance."

"It's only yoga, Killian. I'm not asking you to stick your head in a fire. Break from the manual for a change."

I grunt back at her. Her comments piss me off. I look at my daughter rolling her eyes at me and the football players eyeing me smugly, and for some inexplicable reason, I want to prove to Clodagh that I'm not the uptight guy she thinks.

The women cheer and Teagan groans as I make my way to the yoga mat and take off my T-shirt in an unashamed act of peacocking. My body was built strong even if I didn't lift weights; I got my well-built frame from my useless father's genes.

Clodagh's eyes go wide as she stares at my chest. "Great! Hop on your mat, and let's get started."

I smirk at how flustered she is.

She flops down on her ass in a cross-legged pose, her knees touching the grass. I don't know what the technical term is, but damn, it's sexy.

My thighs are tight from running, and my knees are nowhere near touching the grass. Maybe I have an inflexible Dad bod.

"Is this your first time at yoga, sweetheart?" queries the woman next to me, who looks to be in her seventies.

Sweetheart? I quirk my lips at her. "It is."

"You have a *wonderful* teacher." She beams and gives me a wink.

"Today, we're going to give you a really deep stretch," Clodagh says in a loud, soothing voice. "I know you guys had a match last night, and some of you work in high-stress environments." She catches my gaze and smiles. "I want all your worries and stress to melt away."

She takes us into stretches. We're supposed to have our eyes closed. I watch her chest hitch up and down as she takes long, deep breaths, ordering us to do the same. Her lips form a perfect O as she breathes in and out.

Without warning, her eyes open and catch me watching her.

Blushing, she continues, "Okay, let's do a nice deep straddle stretch."

She opens her legs until they're almost in a complete split.

Fuck.

"Open your thighs as far as you feel comfortable. Place your hands in front of you and give me a nice circle with your hips."

She glances around the group as she circles her hips.

I'm entering dangerous territory. I wasn't expecting yoga to be so sexual.

"Keep your back flat. Open your chest," she instructs us. "Ugh. I am so tight today. How are you guys?"

Fuck.

You're killing me, Clodagh.

Blood flows south without my permission to my thickening dick.

Jesus, not here.

Not in front of my daughter.

Some of the group answers her with seemingly innocent responses.

I didn't realize *Yoga with Clodagh* would provide the perfect conditions for unwanted public arousal. Which makes me a fool, considering I've been jerking off to her online videos.

Thank God Teagan chose to stay far away from me. She already thinks of me as an embarrassing dad. This would make her disown me, and I wouldn't blame her.

We begin the first position, standing in a close-legged pose with our feet touching.

"Keep your back straight and go down into a chair pose."

I blink. Where the fuck do I put my balls? Am I supposed to tuck them between my legs? They're already starting to ache from my depraved thoughts.

I let out an involuntary groan, and Clodagh glances at me.

"Killian, you can separate your legs a few inches if you feel discomfort."

She smiles at me, all sweet and innocent. "Good," she purrs. "Well done, Killian."

No one fucking tells me well done.

The sorceress contorts her body into positions that make it impossible for me not to become aroused.

Did she plan this?

Clenching my jaw, I swallow hard to keep control. Is yoga supposed to make your fucking balls ache like this? They've enough fuel in them to fly a plane.

"Now we'll go into the bridge pose," she says, the picture of tranquility. The opposite of me.

As Clodagh demonstrates the pose by lying on her back and thrusting her groin in the air, I realize that the bridge pose isn't the best for hiding my massive erection.

Dammit. At least with *down dog* or whatever it's called, I could hide it.

"This is a great Kegel exercise," the woman beside me helpfully explains with a wink.

I mutter expletives under my breath. I'm conditioned to think of sex in these scenarios.

215

I glance at the men, but the women are in the way. I can't be the only pervert here.

Clodagh lowers herself to the ground and then leaps up.

"Keep going," she calls out as she circles the group.

She stops to adjust one of the footballer's feet. He grins back, delighted with the attention.

I attempt to hide my rock-solid erection.

Why is she on the move?

"I'm going to sit this one out." I glare at her as she approaches me. It's her fault for getting me all worked up.

"Are you sure?" She arches an eyebrow at me. "You look pretty tense, Mr. Quinn. This stretch is perfect for stiff men."

My jaw clenches. "I'm sure."

"Relax, sir," she whispers in my ear before returning to her position at the front.

"All right, now it's time for the cat-cow stretch," she explains as she slips down into a four-legged position on the floor.

Oh, fuck me.

***

At the end of the session, I watch from a distance from the bench. Trying to pry Clodagh out from her harem of athletes and seniors will be challenging. She has them all eating out of the palm of her hand. I swear I saw one of them sniff her hair when she whipped it from the ponytail.

I can just about hear their conversations. Clodagh has her arm around Teagan, and both of them are being bombarded with incessant questions by the women.

Clodagh's laughter carries across the park, loud and contagious. Three women have tried to marry her off to their sons or grandsons so far. Mischief and happiness shine in her eyes.

It makes me feel like a moody old bastard.

The sight of Teagan so happy is almost bittersweet.

Queens has a real community feel away from the Manhattan skyscraper jungle, especially among the Irish. Teagan deserves this life, but I failed to provide it for her. Would she have been better off if I had been a tradesman living in Queens?

Community.

This is what Marek talked about. This is what Harlow wanted for Teagan. What I've failed to give her.

When Clodagh spots me waiting at the bench, she excuses herself and comes over.

I stand. "You ready to go?"

The wind ruffles her red hair, and she swipes it from her face. "I'm probably staying in Queens today."

"I was going to suggest I take us out to lunch, and Orla could come along too."

"Sorry, Killian. That's really sweet, but..." She glances back at the crowd.

My hand flexes around the car keys. "No worries. Got your phone on you?"

"Yup, and I have a football team watching out for me." She grins. "I'll be fine."

That's what I'm worried about.

I grunt in agreement, but I really want to sweep her up, put her over my shoulder, and take her back to my Ferrari. "Call me if you need anything. Do you have the credit card with you?"

She rolls her eyes, just like my teenage daughter. "Yes, *Daddy*."

Now I'm well and truly fucked.

I drive back to Manhattan with Teagan, wondering why I feel so unsettled.

EIGHTEEN

Clodagh

We inspect our outfits in the mirror.

We are out the other side of the what-the-fuck-do-I-wear panic. These days it's more like a case of how-the hell-am-I-gonna-choose rather than shit-everything-I-own-is-falling-apart, thanks to Big Daddy's credit card.

We are having pre-drinks in my studio before we hit a new club in the Meatpacking district.

Orla is wearing tight blue jeans and a lace top. I've opted for a tight green leather dress paired with Doc Martens to give it a more edgy look.

I look great, but I can't breathe.

"I'm going to have a panic attack," I tell Orla, trying but failing to take a deep breath. All my organs are squashed by the tummy control shapewear that comes to just below my chest.

I tug the tight leather dress up past my hips, feeling claustrophobic. "No! Get them off. Get them off!"

"Calm down." She chuckles and snaps the elastic

of the torturous underwear as she tries to roll them down me.

I'm overcome with a ridiculous bout of giggles.

"Quit squirming. You're working against me here. You're in such a bubbly mood today."

I grin through my giggles even though the underwear is still suffocating me. "It's been a good day."

"Uh-huh." She smirks at me. "Obviously, nothing to do with your hot, moody boss joining us for yoga this morning."

"Did you see the yoga group chat? They're going nuts about him."

"Yeah, I had to turn off notifications on my phone. Also, your granny Deirdre keeps sending me articles about murders in Manhattan. It's kind of a buzzkill."

I sigh and adjust my fishtail braid. "I know, sorry. She's adding them to the Kelly family group chat. I think she has an alert on her phone for murders in New York. She'll have a heart attack if you join the police force."

It takes two of us to push the oppressive shapewear down to my knees. I step out of it, sighing in relief as I feel the fresh, cool rush of air between my legs. "I'll wear a thong. My fat needs somewhere to go, and it might as well be evenly spread all over."

"Alright." I chug my last glass of vino. "Let's go. I need to get my phone from upstairs. Behave yourself in front of Killian and Teagan," I warn her.

"I don't know what you take me for," she mutters behind me.

We head upstairs to the lounge area, where Teagan is sprawled out in a onesie on a fluffed beanbag in the middle of the floor, and Killian and another guy—clearly his brother, Connor—are on the couch.

Holy fucking potatoes. God was generous when he handed out genes to the Quinn family.

The younger Quinn is just as showstoppingly handsome as his brother. Surprisingly, it's still the older, grumpier one that does it for me.

My gaze meets Killian's, and he pauses in his conversation with Connor.

God, those icy blue eyes.

My stomach somersaults as his gaze cruises my figure from head to toe, observing me warily. Like I might be contagious. "This is Connor," he says.

No compliments. No pleasantries. Not a hint of a smile, just that severe deadpan.

"Hi, Connor." I flash him a smile in greeting as I collect my phone from the table. "This is my friend, Orla."

"Heyyy," Orla says breathlessly, gawking at the sausage fest on the couch. She's practically salivating. I shoot her a warning with my eyes. No doubt, those two have enough admirers to give them an ego the size of the Empire State Building, without us adding to the pile.

I check my phone quickly. Sixteen new messages from the yoga group. One new message from Granny Deirdre telling me to only buy drinks from a can and use rubbers with gentlemen.

"It's great to finally meet you," Connor says with a grin. "Come and have a drink with us."

"You look hot, Clodagh," Teagan calls, vaguely interested. "Like a mermaid with green scales and a braid."

"Do you always look like a hot mermaid?" Connor jokes. "Or is it a special occasion?"

"This is us all the time," I joke back. "I like to look my best when cleaning. Killian makes a lot of mess in the bathro—"

Oh crap. I was going to make a mermaid joke. My face burns thinking about the mess I saw Killian make in the bathroom.

Killian's jaw grinds, and his nostrils flare so much he might capture wind speed.

"Well, you look lovely," Connor adds.

Still nothing from Killian. I guess mermaids aren't his go-to fantasy. It annoys me that I'm annoyed.

His eyebrows join in a deep frown. What the hell is his issue? This morning at yoga, he was relaxed, and dare I say, *fun*. Now, he's put the stick back in his ass.

"Well done getting my stiff big brother to do yoga in a park." Connor grins, thoroughly enjoying himself as he looks back and forth between Killian and me conspiratorially. "Next, he'll be meditating in Central Park."

"Dad was awful," Teagan pipes up. "He couldn't do half the moves."

"Bottom of the class," I tease as Killian rolls his

eyes. "Not like you, Teagan. You should keep it up."

"Are you sure you can't join us, ladies?" Connor asks. "I need to hear more."

Killian's eyes lock with mine. "We're just about to order pizza and a movie, but obviously, you have other plans," he says flatly.

"Yeah, we're heading to the new club in the Meatpacking District," I tell him, even though he didn't ask. "Vapor. Sorry, Connor. It'll have to wait."

Connor's smile widens as he exchanges a glance with Killian. "Vapor, hey? Great choice. They'll treat you well there. You deserve a good night out after putting up with my brother. So what's it like living with him? He's a pain in the ass, right?" Connor seems to be in no hurry to let us leave.

"The worst." I smile. "If I didn't have Teagan to live with, I'd run away."

Connor chuckles in approval.

Killian doesn't seem to find our banter funny. I'm met with a dark gaze. "Security will escort you." He reaches for his phone.

"It's okay," I try to say, but he cuts me off.

"It's not open for debate."

Jeez. Nothing ever is with Killian Quinn.

***

I've been told there's an art to getting into a New York club. Be chill, be cool, but be in their face.

"IDs," the doorman the size of a truck growls at me. Is it a rule for bouncers to never smile? We get it

—you're in charge, and you're scary.

I hand over my ID warily. I've never been in such an attractive queue before. He might decide we aren't good-looking enough to get in. And since it's an Irish passport, some insist on seeing an American ID.

The doorman reads it, nods to a woman with a clipboard over his shoulder, and passes her my ID.

What the hell?

Are they *confiscating* it?

"Hey!" I protest.

The girl scans my ID, then clicks her fingers. "VIPs go this way."

"Excuse me?" I ask. She must have made a mistake.

She looks at me with deadpan eyes.

"You heard her," Orla hisses in my ear, shoving me softly. "We're very important people. Will you shut the fuck up already? Do not look a gift horse in the mouth, you fool."

We're escorted through the dark hallway by a hostess with such impossibly beautiful dimensions that she looks like a human avatar.

"I don't understand," I mutter to Orla.

At the door cloaked in velvet, a second hostess stands waiting to hand us a glass of champagne.

I blink at her, baffled. Is this an Irish thing or something?

She ushers us into a bar where all the beautiful New Yorkers hang out. I've never experienced a place like this before. The hostess guides us to a table.

"Clodagh, is that…?" Orla squeaks.

"The Hemsworth brothers?" I finish for her. "I believe so."

I might faint. The sight of them is more than my clit can handle.

A siren wails from the bar, and suddenly, four waitresses in cocktail dresses march forth with a tray between them, carrying a bottle of champagne with sparklers. I remember seeing something similar on a night out in Ibiza once when an obnoxious dude bought the most expensive bottle on the menu.

The women turn and start walking toward us.

When I turn my head, no one else is behind us. Where is the obnoxious dude?

"Hi, Clodagh," one of the waitresses purrs. "Tonight, you're our honored guests."

I gawk at her.

Killian. This has to be Killian's doing.

The whole bar watches as a bottle of champagne, with sparks shooting out of it, is placed on the table in front of us.

"Isn't that the crazy comedian who takes cats on stage?" someone near me whispers, staring my way.

I shoot them a hostile glare in response.

Orla looks at me with a dangerous glint in her eyes. "Tonight, we parrrr-teeee."

***

I couldn't keep this wild lifestyle up every night. I've concluded that you have to mix high-end clubs with low-key Irish bars to appreciate both.

We chugged the champagne in a record-breaking thirty minutes. Once I had confirmed that we would *not* be paying for it, it was game over. The second bottle of champagne was a mistake. In hindsight, we should have summoned some more decorum from somewhere inside us, if such a place exists.

Now I'm on the dance floor talking to a gorgeous guy, but I need to break wind. The champagne bubbles have caused severe gastric distress.

I look over at Orla. She appears to be having her face licked by my guy's friend.

They both work at hedge funds on Wall Street. Honestly, I don't know what a hedge fund is. I think of a room filled with people waving tickets and screaming "buy" or "sell," though I'm sure it doesn't work like that nowadays.

My guy doesn't seem bothered by my lack of hedge fund knowledge. He wants a shag, and I'm considering giving it to him.

He's better than the last guy I talked to, who thought I'd split my sides laughing at him doing a fake Irish accent, shouting "to be sure, to be sure!"

Yup, like I haven't heard that one before.

American Andy presses his lips against mine, going for the kill. He's minty enough for me to invite him into my mouth. With his tongue in my mouth, I rub my stomach without him noticing.

He breaks the kiss. His eyes look a bit chaotic. "Wanna fuck?"

I rear back, shocked. Dirty bastard. Chivalry *is* dead.

"Getting straight to the point there," I reply dryly. He's about to lean in for another kiss when abruptly, he detaches himself from me.

"What the hell?" American Andy sneers. "Get lost."

I blink for a second, thinking he's talking to me. Did I relax my stomach too much, and one slipped out?

Then I realize that two doormen surround us. One of them has their hand on American Andy's chest.

"Get your hands off me," American Andy says, his agitation rising. I think he might be on something. His pupils are pretty wild.

"It's time to leave, Clodagh." It's the doorman from outside. Does he have a photographic memory that he remembers everyone's names from their IDs? "Time to go. Your lift is waiting."

I look back and forth between Andy and the doormen, perplexed. "Am I getting kicked out for kissing?"

"No." Doorman number two steps in. "You're getting escorted home."

I feel surrounded. "*Why?*"

"Because my employer says so," doorman one says in a strained voice that says *hurry the fuck up, lady.*

My eyes narrow. "Your employer?"

"Mr. Quinn."

"He's the owner of the club?"

"Yes."

Of course, he never thought of mentioning it to me.

Fuck this shit. It's not even midnight. I'm not Cinde-fucking-rella.

"He's my employer too, but I don't understand. Why do I need to leave?"

He sighs heavily and gives me a sour look. "Look, I dunno, lady. Can we do this the easy way? I don't have all night."

Doorman number two has wedged an arm through mine, and doorman number one is encroaching on Orla's bubble.

"I'm not working now," I snap. "I'm on my own time."

"You'll have to take that up with Mr. Quinn. Good luck," he deadpans as he leads me through the dance floor.

"This is against my constitutional rights!" I think. Killian Quinn can go to hell. Who does he think he is? His arrogance is *off the charts*. He doesn't own me. He doesn't dictate what I do with my free time.

Something stronger pushes through the trapped wind burning me up.

Rage.

Killian Quinn is going to fucking have it.

***

I don't give myself time to change my mind.

I push open his bedroom door and storm toward his bed without turning on the light, until I'm standing with my hands on my hips, glaring at him.

He's awake.

The light from his bedside table casts shadows on his face, simultaneously making him look even more devastatingly attractive and deadly.

The blankets are pushed down to the V of his lower stomach. I'm momentarily distracted by the dark pubic hair. He's naked under those covers.

His eyes flash with anger as he takes me in.

Shivers go through me, but I spread my legs into a defiant stance and square my shoulders. Chest puffed out. Butt clenched.

I'm the alpha here. You don't scare me, mister.

"How dare you!" I splutter.

"What the fuck are you doing?" His voice comes out in a husky growl as he rises onto his forearms.

It's then I notice the book beside him, momentarily disarming me. Hot guys reading... it doesn't get any sexier than that.

I find myself wavering but forge ahead. He's the asshole here. "You can't just demand I come home on my own time. You don't own me. Orla and I were having a lovely night, then I was manhandled and ordered to go home." I gulp in a deep breath. I'm on a roll here. "You can't ground me like you do Teagan. I'm not your *property.*" Spit sprays from my mouth as I hiss my last words.

Attractive.

He responds with a fixed glare, not giving away

any emotion. "Everything in this house is my property."

"Ugh!" I screech in an angry huff because it's all I'm capable of.

It's the sneer on his lips that sets me off again as his gaze burns into me.

I refuse to wither.

"Do you get off on being a jerk? Do you?" I snap, not expecting an answer. "Controlling people is your version of porn. Yes, *Mister Quinn*," I say in a patronizing sneer verging on a baby voice. "Three bags full, *Mister Quinn*. Just when I was getting to know Hedge Fund Andy, you ruined our chance at something special." Lies.

I see his whole body go rigid, every muscle in his massive chest tightening. His jaw clenches. His nostrils flare. Angry breath leaves his lungs.

I *feel* the air crackle with his wrath.

The sheets rustle.

Fuck. He's on the move.

The sheets are flung off, and his legs are out of the bed. He stands to his full height at the side of the bed, treating me to a full moon.

As he comes at me, not giving two fucks that his massive cock is now on display, I realize I have no follow-up plan.

"That'll be all. Good night!" I bark before turning on my heels and skittering out of his bedroom.

NINETEEN

Clodagh

The sound of heavy footsteps coming toward the studio door has my heart doing the bongo against my ribs.

Living with the most arrogant man in New York and a few too many drinks pushed me to the brink. Now my inner alpha has reduced to a scared little kid who wants nothing more than to crawl under the bed and disappear.

He's going to fire me and throw me out onto the street tonight. Immigration will be here to deport me any second now.

I could have kept my fat trap shut, but instead, I—

The door is thrown open and slams hard against the wall.

Killian stands in the doorway, nostrils flaring, and jaw clenched, face like a bull about to charge.

Oh fuck.

My only saving grace is that he put on boxers.

The muscle in his jaw flexes so tight I think it might break. "No, that won't be all," he says in a low, husky drawl. Something gathers in his eyes—not just anger—something that looks a lot like lust.

He takes a step toward me, closing the gap between us.

I'm vaguely aware of myself backing away until I'm pressed against the wall, and his muscular arms form a barrier on either side of me.

"You think I'll let an employee get away with that? You owe me an apology."

"No, you owe *me* an apology, Killian." I try to keep my voice steady, but it catches in my throat.

He's so close my body is literally shaking with anticipation, like he is electrifying me with his presence even though he's not touching me.

His arms remain braced against the wall on either side of me. His breath is hot on my forehead. His whole body is just inches from mine. He smells like his body lotion, the one I sniff every day when I clean his bathroom. He's not even touching me, but my body hums wildly in response.

My breathing is all over the place, my cheeks are on fire, and my core *throbs* with anticipation and desire.

I feel overwhelmed and out of control.

"Why did you make me come home, Killian?" I rasp. "Why do you care if I stay out all night on my own time?"

He doesn't answer me.

His eyes hold mine, and the burst of sexual energy is so palpable I can barely keep eye contact. The way he looks at me makes goose bumps break out over my arms and chest.

"Were your people spying on me?" I press on, knowing I'm playing with fire, but I can't stop. "Why'd you make me come home?"

"I think you fucking know why." His voice comes so breathy and thick with need, as if in pain.

I arch my hips against his thick erection.

Oh.

He lets out a shuddery groan and grabs them, holding them against him so I can't move.

My palms slide over his warm, solid chest. I feel the flutter of his heart.

I'm so done for.

"*Goddammit,*" he groans against my forehead. "What are you doing to me?"

"I dunno," I whisper, our mouths almost touching. "You'll have to explain."

He groans again. "You're on my mind all the time. I think about you at work. I think about you when I'm running. I think about you when I'm watching TV with my daughter, and I *hate* it."

I'm about to ask him to clarify whether that's a compliment when he says, "I need to know what it feels like to be inside you."

God. His voice is so masculine and sexual, I'm *shaking* with need.

"Then find out," I manage to croak, barely audible.

He pulls back to see if I'm serious, his eyes blazing.

When he sees blatant approval, he pulls my leather dress up so that it's to my waist, pulls aside the thong, then slides two fingers deep inside me.

I'm *soaking.* I'm so wet, it's embarrassing.

The sensation of his hands *down there* has me writhing around like it's the first time I've ever been touched.

I arch my back into his hands and spread my legs wider, thrusting into his touch. Thousands of shivery tingly sensations light up my core as his thumb circles around my most sensitive spot.

"Soaking," he says in a ridiculously husky voice. "You're absolutely fucking drenched."

He bends down to kiss my neck as he controls me with his fingers. "Such a disobedient nanny. You want me to fuck you so badly, don't you? It's all you've wanted since you moved in here."

I whimper in response. *Oh God, that feels good.*

"Say it," he breathes against the dip of my neck. "Beg me. Beg me, and I'll give you what you want."

Arrogant ass.

"Please."

"Louder. I can't hear you."

"Fuck me," I gasp. "Please."

"There's a good girl. That wasn't so hard, was it?"

His fingers leave me, and I moan at the loss. Then I realize it's so that he can slide his boxers down and off him.

Then he turns his attention back to me. With a devious smirk, he slides my thong down my legs. I grip his shoulders for balance and lift each foot to free it, barely able to contain my impatience.

Desperate to feel him bare, I wrap my hand needily around his cock. He's so thick; this is going to hurt.

He groans into my hair in response and lifts me off the floor, his hands tight around my backside. My hold on him slips.

The tip of his cock pushes against my entrance.

"Wait," I breathe.

"Dammit," he hisses, closing his eyes as if trying to calm himself down. "Condom. You got one down here?"

Struggling to form words, I wave vaguely toward my purse on the counter.

He leans over and rummages through it until he produces the condom.

Then his cock is back pressed against my stomach again.

God, I'm so ready.

I watch him as he sheaths himself. I'm useless. Incapacitated. A mass of quivering jelly.

He bends slightly to accommodate my height, and his mouth comes down on mine as the tip of his cock nudges my entrance.

I try to kiss him, but I'm too nervous and aroused. I swallow air, whimpering against his mouth.

He lifts my left leg and wraps it around his waist. I'm still fully dressed, including my Doc Martens.

He slides his hard, thick cock into my wet opening, and I gasp at the sudden sensation. My core flutters with pleasure.

"You okay?"

I nod, unable to form words.

His eyes hold mine as he pushes his cock deeper

inside me. His mouth ajar, he lets out a shuddery breath, closes his eyes, and presses his forehead against mine. "*Damn.* I've wanted to do this since I first set eyes on you."

The sight of him so worked up, the feel of him filling me up, his words... I'm in danger of collapsing on the floor.

"*Fuuuck.*" A growl rumbles from his throat as my muscles clench hard and territorial around him.

"Ahhh," I moan as he thrusts. I can't speak. All I know is that this is my new favorite feeling in the world.

His full lips fall open, and he groans my name. It's the sexiest sound I've ever heard. "You feel so fucking good. Amazing."

My hands roam all over his chest, desperate and amateurish. I don't care.

His voice. His skin. His smell. I need it all.

My shallow moans and mewls are joined by his deep grunts. His eyes hold mine as he drives into me, hitting a spot so deep he can't possibly get any deeper in me.

I grip his neck for support.

Killian Quinn is fucking me. Killian Quinn's dick is inside me. I'm so full of him that I can barely remember my own name.

His mouth slackens, and his face softens as he loses control. Seeing him like this just pushes me over the edge even more.

I'm so close.

So, so close to exploding.

"I can't hold it," he says through a ragged breath. "I'm going to come. *Fuck*."

He groans low and deep. His face strains, his jaw grinds, and a muscle in his forehead jumps as he tries to hold out, waiting for me to orgasm.

But he can't.

His face contorts with a mixture of pleasure and pain, and his mouth hangs open as he releases into me with a final jerk, holding my hips in place so I can't move.

I close my eyes and hold him tightly as his body relaxes against mine.

He drops my leg, but his cock stays inside me, keeping me pushed against the wall.

I let out a heavy breath, pressing my head against his chest.

Then something... changes. The air changes, the mood changes... he changes.

His whole body stiffens under my touch. He breaks the embrace, pulling out of me. Now he can't even look me in the eye.

He clears his throat. "I'm sorry. This was a mistake."

"W-What?" I stammer, trying to keep up with his words. "What do you mean?"

My heart thuds as I wait for him to smile.

"I shouldn't have done that," he says, not meeting my eyes as he discards the condom in the bin and pulls up his boxers. His mouth forms a hard line. "Forget this happened."

Is he for real?

I stare at him for a long moment, trying to figure out what to say, but he ignores me.

I feel sick.

"Are you going to look at me?" I cry.

When his gaze meets mine, regret stares back at me. He almost looks *disgusted.* It's painful and ugly and... heartbreaking.

"I'm sorry, Clodagh," he repeats, his voice thicker this time. "I'm really fucking sorry."

He leaves me propped against the wall with sticky thighs and tears in my eyes, feeling more shit than I ever have in my life.

Luck of the fucking Irish.

TWENTY

Clodagh

"You're an idiot," I whisper to the bathroom mirror.

My bare, pasty face stares back at me with its red-rimmed eyes, blotchy cheeks, and a charming new zit as the cherry on top. Lack of sleep, sleeping with your boss, champagne sweats, and being rejected by your boss equals hormonal meltdown.

Blasting hot water over my skin in the shower for twenty minutes did nothing to cleanse my shame.

Fucking. Idiot.

I can't believe I fucked him. I'm the stupid nanny maid who drops her pants for her boss less than *two weeks* into the job.

I wish I'd never invited him to yoga.

I wish I'd never stormed into his bedroom.

And I really wished I hadn't let him use me for a convenience fuck.

I wish the whole damn day had never happened.

Now he has all the power. He marched into my studio, made me beg for him to fuck me, then discarded me like a moldy, rotten spud. He had barely pulled out of me before the revulsion took over.

Bastard.

I twist my wet hair up in a bun with a towel, then walk out into the bedroom and curl up on the bed with my hands wrapped about my knees.

I stare at nothing, feeling my eyes well up with tears again. All I can see is the disgusted look on his face, his words repeating in a loop in my head.

Besides the advice of using rubbers, Granny Deirdre warned me never to let a man control my emotions. I thought I was smarter than this.

I swore I wouldn't let another man make me feel worthless again. My ex walked away with most of my savings and chipped away the self-esteem that I had built up since leaving school. He threw a huge grenade into my life and left a big, ugly hole.

Now Killian has the power to do the same.

What if he doesn't want to see me again and gets rid of me?

My phone pings. Mam on the family group chat. It's dinnertime back home.

I stare at the picture of Mam, Granny Deirdre, and my brothers eating dinner until my eyes are too wet to see it properly.

It's my youngest brother, Mick's, sixteenth birthday.

For the first time since I landed in New York, I feel homesick.

***

I didn't sleep at all last night. Zero minutes. I spent all night wondering how I was going to face Killian. I bet he's already over it. He's probably forgotten we had sex last night.

Orla bounces toward me, dodging dog walkers and joggers. Everyone in Central Park looks so happy. I hate them for it.

I already messaged her this morning to inform her of my major blunder.

"So?" she asks excitedly, handing me a water bottle with electrolytes. "Spill. Have you seen him this morning?"

I swallow a big mouthful of the drink as we stroll by the bronze *Alice in Wonderland* sculpture. "Thanks. You're a lifesaver. No, I snuck out of the house. I'm too haggard after the champagne and lack of sleep to face him today. I still need to work out my communication strategy for dealing with him."

She smirks, shaking her head in disbelief. "Can't believe you slept with him."

"Ugh." I groan in exasperation. "I can't believe it either. This is the worst Catholic guilt I've ever felt."

The guilt has nothing to do with being religious. I only go to Mass when Gran nags me at Christmas. But every Irish Catholic is born with the guilt gene, and it only gets worse if you go to a Catholic school. I get it bad when I slack off on a sick day when I'm not really ill. Or if I don't do yoga three times a week. Or if I have dirty thoughts in inappropriate places like the hospital, as I found out when Gran slipped and fell.

Or a new one—sleeping with my cold-hearted, billionaire boss.

We're silent for a moment as we sidestep a group of roller skaters.

"We all make drunken mistakes," Orla says eventually. "You're not the first person to have accidentally shagged their boss, and you won't be the last."

"This is my second drunken mistake in New York, and both times, I dropped my pants. I need to get my shit together." I chug down the bottle of water. "I can't even blame the alcohol. On a drunk scale, I was buzzed but not wasted."

"Come on, you're being too hard on yourself. From how Killian looked at you at yoga, there's something there. He's not a complete robot."

"No, seriously, Orla, if you'd seen his face after... one minute, he's banging me like we were the last hope for mankind's survival, and the next minute, he's gone, and I'm standing in the middle of the room, bawling like a child." I turn to her. "How am I going to even look him in the face again?"

"It'll be fine." She squeezes my arm gently. "You'll be grand."

Grand. Bah. Like hell, I will.

"The worst part is he sent flowers to another woman only this week." God, I feel sick just saying it out loud. In my lust haze, I'd forgotten that he might have a girlfriend. How will I feel when he brings

Maria back on Tuesdays, as the manual says?

"I don't even know how serious they are. Sam said they've been out a few times. Maybe they're exclusive." I sigh for the millionth time today and bring up the source of my torture on my phone. "This woman."

Orla stops in her tracks to examine the photo on my phone. She physically blanches, and not because Maria is painful to look at.

No, Maria is an absolute stunner. I'm ashamed to admit that I spent an excessive amount of time researching her this morning.

"I guess it's not a surprise." Seeing my expression, she bites her lip. "But, Clodagh, you're stunning too."

She's trying to make me feel better, but it makes me feel worse. "Listen, be careful. I don't want to see you get hurt again. We were all worried about you when you split up with asshole Niall. You lost so much weight and were quiet all the time."

"Yeah, you'd think I'd learn to stay away from men who can hurt my heart. Anyway, it's fine." I shrug, picking up the pace again. "I'll only be working for him for another few months. The cowboy agency thinks they have another au pair position for me in Brooklyn."

Best I move off the topic of Killian. "What about the guy from..." I rack my brain, trying to recall our conversation from last night. Which state was it? The middle states are a bit of a blur to me.

Now it's Orla's turn to look tortured. "Kansas."

Last night, three of us left with security. Me, Orla,

and her hedge fund guy.

"I took him home with me. I have a bad dose of the Catholic guilt too. Last night, I brought home a solid ten, but this morning, I woke up with a four. I didn't fancy him at all. I'm shallow, aren't I?" She whimpers, looking at me to make her guilt disappear.

"You're not," I say soothingly, trying to hide my smirk. "You seemed quite taken with him last night."

"Ugh, don't remind me. I'm so relieved Uncle Sean isn't home right now. I'm twenty-five, but I still want him to think I'm a virgin. It wasn't even worth it. I got really freaked out during the sex because I started thinking that Auntie Kathy's ghost might be watching. She died in that room, you know?"

I groan. "I'm glad I didn't know that when I lived there."

"Let's forget last night ever happened for both of us."

I snort. "If only. I still have to live under the same roof as my mistake."

We walk on in silence for a bit, reflecting on our mistakes.

"Was yours good, at least?" Orla asks with a sly grin.

"Yeah," I say with as much flippancy as I can muster, thinking about Killian's eyes blazing into mine.

My stomach churns as the unease I've felt since last night returns. I'm too soft to handle this.

It wasn't just good. It was the best sex of my life.

And that realization is terrifying.

***

I spend the rest of Sunday hiding in my studio. Killian doesn't trouble himself to seek me out.

My only reprieve of the day is when my first shipment of wood and tools arrives.

As soon as my beautiful selection of hardwoods was deemed "non-explosive" (I wasn't kidding when I said Killian had more security protocols than JFK airport), the security team handed them over.

Sam personally delivered them to me. He wanted to hang out, but I fobbed him off by saying I was feeling under the weather. My mood isn't conducive to talking.

Having no workshop here limits what I can do, but I have saws, clamps, and wood glue to make a decent birthday gift for Teagan. It's a nice distraction after dicking around all day, mourning something that doesn't exist and feeling sorry for myself.

It's time to snap out of it.

I'm just making her a box but sprucing it up with a window for pictures and some custom Celtic designs. God knows what Killian is buying her. Teagan has more electronics and accessories at thirteen than I do at twenty-four.

It's small, so it won't take up much space if she doesn't like it. My mom used to tell me that the beauty of a box is that it can be whatever you want it to be.

Back when I was living in Ireland, I made them out of farmers' disused pallets and sold them as vintage items. Although I wasn't exactly rolling in money, there was a sense of gratification in what I'd created.

My ex filled my head full of shit that I could make a business out of it.

The following two hours are spent constructing my design, taking measurements, and carving and sanding the wood. I use grit sandpaper rather than tools to sand the wood since it's a lightweight, delicate wood that easily marks.

This is as much for my benefit as it is for Teagan's. Sanding helps me release some of my pent-up tension.

Carving Teagan's name and the Celtic Knot takes about an hour.

After finishing the job, I send a picture to the Kelly family group chat and smile for the first time today.

Mam messages back. **How wonderful! Your American family must love you! X**

That's all it takes for my smile to die.

***

I'm late. Shit. I run through the hallway into the kitchen to see Killian is already back from his run. It's six o'clock.

I brace myself as he turns, scowling. He's not

happy.

"Morning. I'm so sorry. I slept in."

I avert my eyes from the distracting sweat glistening on his thick bare biceps. Now I know they feel as good as they look. Lucky for me, he's wearing a T-shirt. His stubble is thicker than it usually is as if he hasn't shaved in a few days. It suits him.

His eyes move over me, reminding me he knows what I look like naked. "Week three, and you're taking liberties already?" He raises an annoyed brow.

My face reddens. "Sorry. I didn't sleep well last night." *Because I was running through every possible outcome of this morning in my head.*

"Don't think I'll let you take advantage because of what happened between us."

I gape at him. I can't believe I thought I was falling for this guy. Am I a glutton for punishment? "It's got nothing to do with what happened. Like I said, I overslept. It won't happen again," I say with more steel in my voice. Can't he drop it now?

He sighs, and his expression softens somewhat. He looks like he didn't sleep well, either.

"Teagan and I are heading out tonight for dinner, so you don't have to worry about making something. That'll give you time to catch up on sleep."

"Sure," I say, forcing a smile. Is he trying to get away from me? "Do you want your breakfast now?"

"Since you slept in, I don't have time."

His tone, his stance, his eyes. All cold as ice.

Freezing.

I get a flashback of the heat in his eyes when we were fucking. Of how his large hands roamed my body like he worshiped it.

"Sorry." I cringe. How many apologies can one make in a single morning?

"Should we talk about what happened on Saturday night?" I immediately regret asking the damn question the moment I see his jaw tighten.

"Let's put Saturday behind us and move forward, okay?" He says it in the same tone he uses to ask Teagan to remove her eyeliner. "Can you do that?"

I feel fucking patronized.

Of course he doesn't want to talk about Saturday night; it meant nothing to him.

I attempt to mask my hurt. I know he can see it. I don't know why I feel so burned. I had a few one-night stands before but always managed to walk away just fine. Maybe this situation is different because he's my boss, and I can't simply walk away.

I hate that I wear my feelings on my face.

I hate that Saturday night meant more to me than him.

I hate that I'm the naïve, small-town girl who imagined this whole scene would end with Killian apologizing to me.

"It's fine," I joke weakly. "Sex with the nanny isn't in the manual."

He manages a slight smile. "No, it most certainly is not."

I busy myself with loading the dishwasher as he

drinks down a glass of water behind me. At least this way, he can't read my face.

The tension in the air is unbearable. I need him to leave.

"From now on, I promise to keep my hands to myself," he says softly behind me.

My heart flutters.

"It's all good, Killian. Let's go back to how things were before." I plaster a false smile on my face. I have to protect my heart. We are two puzzle pieces that don't fit together. "Pretend it never happened. I'll only be working for you for another two months."

I especially hate that he looks so relieved.

TWENTY-ONE

Killian

Connor swings the door to my office open, grinning wide. "Miss me?"

He looks far too fresh to have spent three days in Vegas. Then again, at thirty-two, he's got an advantage on me.

"I'm surprised the place didn't go up in flames while you were away," I say sarcastically, looking up from my screen. "Successful trip?"

He strolls in and rests a shoulder against the wall. "Expansion of The Regency Casino finally agreed. I thought we were going to have another situation with the building contractors. But way more importantly, I got to squeeze in watching the fight at the MGM. Best heavyweight title fight I've seen in decades."

I nod in agreement. "I caught the last half streaming. Tyson's a legend."

"Big brother needs to get out more. All this streaming is turning you into a boring old man."

"You may be on to something." I stare at him deadpan. "I slept with my nanny. I slept with

Clodagh."

His eyes widen, and he breaks into annoying howls of laughter.

Frustrated, I slam my laptop shut. "Yes, yes, when you're ready," I snap. There's no way I'll accomplish anything now.

His laughter dies down to a chuckle. "She's not *your* nanny. I have a disturbing image now."

I heave a sigh. "You know what I mean. I fucked my employee. Clodagh. I'm that guy." Is this what a midlife crisis looks like?

"Saturday night?"

I nod.

"I'm not surprised by the way you were so fired up. Don't think Teagan didn't notice either. She's twelve, not stupid."

Shit.

He tilts his head in an amused smirk. "Why?"

"Why what?"

"Why'd you fuck her?"

Connor asks some stupid questions for someone with a high IQ.

Because all I want to do is fuck her deep and hard every single day of my life, then cuddle her afterward, and it still won't be enough.

"Why does any man fuck a woman?" I snap.

"Fair enough." He shrugs. "Where?"

"In the house." I'm a moron.

His brows lift.

"I know, I know," I cut in before he can speak. "I don't do it in the house when Teagan's there. I broke my own rule. I followed Clodagh down to her studio and…" I slump in my leather wingback chair. "I got carried away. Now she's barely making eye contact with me and tiptoeing around ever since."

Guilt washes over me.

It's been three days since Clodagh and I had sex, and the tension between us is so palpable you could slice it with a blade. She only speaks to me about chores in polite but terse tones.

I feel like shit. I went too far, all to satisfy my own selfish needs. I shouldn't have followed her to her studio. I want her to feel safe and at ease in my home, and for the past few nights, she's looked almost tormented.

This evening after work, I'm going to meet with Teagan's ballet teacher to see if Clodagh's instincts are correct. Maybe it's for the best to create space between me and Clodagh.

His mouth twitches into a smirk. "So what happens now? Are you two in a 'nanny with benefits' relationship? She seems like a nice girl; you shouldn't treat her badly."

"I'm not trying to treat her badly. I'm trying to be professional," I say, my chest growing tighter with each word. "She and Teagan are getting along better than the other nannies, so ideally, I don't rock the status quo."

"I think it's safe to say the status quo has been rocked, Killian."

"We're both back to being professional. It was a mistake."

"If you say so," he says, still smirking.

I narrow my eyes on him, contemplating strangulation. "What the hell is that supposed to mean?"

He folds his arms across his chest lazily. "If you run your hands through your hair any more, you'll trigger premature balding."

"I regret telling you now. Look, in eight weeks, Clodagh will be gone." My jaw clenches at the realization. I imagine the house without her dulcet tones, her laughter, her scowls. Nothing left of her.

I shake my head, willing myself to get a grip. "Mrs. Dalton will be back, and that's better for Teagan."

He makes a humming sound but drops it.

"Don't forget Teagan's birthday dinner on Friday night. Then I have a teenybopper concert to attend. So don't tell me I'm boring, buddy. We're going to see..." I think for a moment. "Hayden Agu... fucking something or other."

"*Cayden.* Even I know his name. I told you; you need to work harder at being a cool dad."

I roll my eyes. "Yeah, well, next week it will be some other pop star dickhead."

He smiles. "She's growing up so quickly. It feels like just yesterday she was swooning over the ponies at the city farm. Now she's swooning over a guy with a ponytail."

"Don't start," I groan. "She'll always be my little girl. And any swooning will be done under my watch."

I sometimes stare at Teagan, and it feels surreal

because I can't believe she's nearly thirteen. It seems like yesterday that she was four years old.

He pushes off the wall and readies himself to go. "It's in my calendar. Dinner, I mean. If you think I'm joining you to see Cayden Aguilar, you've got another thing coming."

"Yeah, yeah." I wave him off.

My phone beeps. I frown, seeing the sender. "Maria." It's another lovey-dovey message. "She's got the wrong impression of me. I sent her flowers, and she's acting like I proposed. I don't know where this has come from."

"A million guys would kill to be in your shoes." He shakes his head and opens the door wider. "Is she still coming to dinner with the mayor to grease the slimeball up?"

"Yeah, she's friends with his wife. Should be a good dynamic between them."

I stare at the message.

It's just a pity my ugly dead heart doesn't feel a smidge of excitement about that.

**

I rap my knuckles on Teagan's door and push it open, not expecting her to be awake at seven o'clock. I take a seat on the edge of the bed, and the lump beneath the covers stirs.

"Good morning, princess." I lift the covers from her face.

"*Uh.*" Eyes closed, she screws up her face as if in

pain.

"Time to get up, birthday girl."

She finally opens her eyes, smiling sleepily. "Morning, Dad."

"Happy birthday. A big thirteen today." God, I almost sound choked up. I pull her into a hug. "You're growing up so fast. But you're still my little girl," I say into her hair, then lean back to kiss her forehead. "Even when you're fifty and looking after me."

"Ew. I can't wait, Dad."

Stretching out, she sits up in bed. Her face and features are becoming more and more like a young woman's, and it almost scares me. She's the same height as Clodagh. "I wish your mother could see you," I say with a sad smile. "She's still with us every day, you know. She's watching over you."

"I know."

"You know I love you more than anything in the world, right? It doesn't matter how old you are."

"*Dad.*" She groans. "I can't handle you like this."

"I'll have you know I'm a very cool dad."

I receive my first eye roll of the day. "Sometimes. You're not as bad as Becky's dad. He does awful silent farts and thinks no one notices."

"Glad to hear the bar's so low." I chuckle. "Your roller skates and photo printer are downstairs." At thirteen, I have to ask her what she wants because there's not a hope in hell I'll get it right. "But this is something extra I wanted to get you. It matches your beautiful eyes."

She takes the necklace with her name engraved in blue stones. "It's beautiful, Dad. Thank you."

As she wraps her arms around me, I scoop her up for a bear hug. There's no better feeling in the world.

"Are you excited about meeting the floppy-haired pop star kiddo tonight?"

"Stop calling him that." She huffs. "He's like *the* best singer *ever*." Her eyes glaze dreamily. "This is going to be the best night of my life."

Christ. No pressure. The floppy-haired popstar better be nice to my daughter. He's getting enough money from me.

"We have dinner with Gran and Connor first. Make sure your friend Becky is ready by six o'clock."

She nods. "Should I invite Clodagh?"

I frown. "It's a family dinner. Your grandma will be there." I pause for a moment, swallowing hard. "Do you want to invite Clodagh?"

She shrugs. "She said the restaurant was on her bucket list. She seemed really jealous when I told her I was going for my birthday. She's kinda okay." Coming from my daughter, that's a massive compliment.

I should be thankful Clodagh and Teagan get along. "Invite her if that's what you want. I want you to be happy." I pause. "There's something else I want to talk to you about."

Her eyes widen, and I can see the wheels turning in her head, wondering if she did something wrong. "What is it? Am I in trouble?"

"No, I am," I say. "I'm sorry for not listening to

you. I met with your ballet teacher last night. It turns out, she knows me and has an issue with me."

Her teacher's husband once worked for me and got fired. Had I known that, I wouldn't have sent her there. Since she still uses her maiden name professionally, I didn't make the connection.

"Does she have something against me?" Her big, worried eyes break my heart. I'm a terrible father; everything I do impacts my baby girl.

"Princess, it's me. It's all me, not you at all. We'll get you into a different class."

And I have Clodagh to thank for bringing my mistake to my attention.

I kiss my daughter's head and stand from the bed. "I'll meet you for breakfast in twenty, okay?"

***

I walk into the kitchen to find Teagan and Clodagh talking loudly.

"You two seem happy," I interrupt, eyeing the pancake stack with cream and fruit, topped with a lopsided candle. "What's this?"

"Clodagh made a birthday breakfast," Teagan chips in cheerily before Clodagh can answer.

I lock eyes with her as I take a seat at the kitchen island beside Teagan.

"She doesn't have to eat it all," she says quietly. "I know it's a bit naughty for breakfast."

"That's very thoughtful of you."

"Check this out, Dad. Clodagh made it for me."

Teagan pushes a wooden box in my direction. Inside it are tubes and bottles of hair products.

I turn it around, trailing my fingers over the Celtic design. "You made this?" I ask slowly, pausing to look at Clodagh. She even engraved Teagan's name on it. Did she do this in her studio?

She nods shyly. "It's just a little token. Nothing fancy. It's made with a kind of wood we call 'Irish mahogany' coz it's used in a lot of furniture at home."

"It's beautiful," I say quietly, my voice thick with emotion.

Something twists in my stomach as I slowly turn the beautifully crafted gift over in my hands. I'm a horrible fucking man.

"Be careful, Dad. Those are the products Clodagh uses in her hair," Teagan announces proudly, looking shyly at Clodagh. "So I'll be able to do my hair like hers."

"That's great," I say, trying to keep the emotion out of my voice. I set the box down and reach for a pancake, my heart swelling with joy from seeing Teagan so happy. "Just use a tiny amount first to make sure that you don't have an allergic reaction. You don't need to use stuff like this at your age."

"You have no clue about hair, Dad!" she tells me, outraged, and then turns toward Clodagh. "Dad said you can come with us to dinner tonight if you want. Are you coming?"

"Uh." Clodagh's eyes turn into saucers. "I don't want to impose on you guys."

"I insist," I say after clearing my throat awkwardly.

She stares at me for a while, trying to decide whether I'm sincere. Eventually, she nods and murmurs, "Okay."

"Awesome!" Teagan squeals excitedly.

"Can I get a minute with you?" I ask Clodagh, inclining my head toward the patio.

Despite her apprehension, she follows me outside.

"It's fine, Killian," she starts before I have a chance to speak. "If you don't want me at dinner, I won't come. I can tell Teagan I'm not feeling well, so she won't be upset."

"No, that's not it. I want you to come. Look, I went to see Teagan's ballet teacher, and I need to apologize to you." I smile wryly. "It turns out I fired her husband. Things got nasty. She clearly has a chip on her shoulder and is taking it out on Teagan. I've moved Teagan to another class and filed a complaint against her teacher."

"Oh." She seems taken aback. "Cool. Glad I could help." She pauses, chewing on one side of her lip. "Anyway, if you don't mind..." She looks at me with caution. "So, uh... if it's okay with you, can I give you some more advice?"

My brows lift. "Go ahead."

"I get I'm no Nanny McPhee, but just hear me out, okay?"

My lips twitch.

"Maybe you should ditch the whole 'princess'

thing if she doesn't like it." She looks up at me. "It's like you're dismissing her as her own person if you ignore what she wants. You want her to listen to you…" She gives a little shrug. "But it works both ways."

"Come on," I scoff. "I…" I rub the back of my neck, agitated. I what? I want to call her princess because *I* like it? Because I don't want her to grow up and leave me?

I inhale, releasing the breath slowly. "You make a valid point."

She barely disguises her surprise behind a guarded smile. "Is there anything else, Killian?"

Yes. I want to take you in my arms and never let you go. "No. You know, you don't give yourself enough credit."

"You don't give me enough credit either."

Her face tightens, and the guilt strangles me. I want to say so much, but nothing comes out.

"I'm sorry," I say in a low tone, hoping to show how serious I am. "I'll do better."

She nods, and I watch her walk toward the patio door. "And I do want you to come to dinner," I say to her back.

She turns, and I see a genuine smile, one I haven't seen in days. Suddenly, I feel breathless, as if I've just been punched in the chest.

***

Three Hours Later.

"I thought you'd want to see this." I stare at the smiling photo of Harlow on the tombstone. "It's got Teagan's name in Irish on it. You would get her something like this. You always bought more thoughtful presents than me." I chuckle. "I just throw money at a problem."

"*It's beautiful,*" she answers me. "*I love it.*"

"Clodagh made it. She's got talent. She could make a go of it if she had some business mentorship. I've been thinking about offering her help."

Harlow remains silent.

I guess I shouldn't tell her about someone I was intimate with.

I put Clodagh's present under my coat as spits of rain come down.

"She's thirteen, Harlow," I whisper. "She's growing up too quickly. Soon, she'll want to leave me too."

"*You can't keep babying her, Killian,*" she scolds me. "*You have to let her make her own mistakes. She needs more freedom now.*"

Inhaling deeply, I close my eyes. Even the pretend voice of Harlow makes me feel guilty.

The fucking guilt never goes away.

The guilt of failing to protect Harlow.

The guilt of being a shit father.

Now I have the guilt of crossing the line with Clodagh.

The guilt of feeling something I shouldn't.

I don't believe in ghosts. The souls of the dead do not rise from the grave to take care of their loved ones.

Harlow lives only in Teagan's and my imaginations. Harlow is now nothing more than my eternal guilt.

The humming of the lawnmower is the only thing that breaks the silence as I walk away.

TWENTY-TWO

Clodagh

Orla: What did you get?

I smile to myself as I meander through Central Park, typing a response to her.

Me: Everything. Underwear. Shoes. Black sexy dress.

I send her a picture of me in my fuck-you-Killian-Quinn outfit.

Fuck you, Killian Quinn.

Fuck you and your ridiculously blue eyes, stupid, handsome face, and big dick.

And fuck me.

Fuck me for obsessing over you and your ridiculously blue eyes and your stupid, handsome face and your big dick.

And for letting myself become a miserable emotional wreck because of a guy. *Again.*

This outfit reflects those thoughts perfectly.

It's a slim black bodycon dress with a lace finish. I picture the woman he was with in the hotel wearing the same dress, the woman who strode out of the hotel with him like she owned it.

I'll need to don my body-control underwear to keep all my bumps in the right place.

Orla: Nice. Is it a bit sexy to be meeting his mam in?

Maybe. But what does it matter? I'm not meeting his mum as a girlfriend. I'm being offered a seat because Teagan wants me there.

Killian's expression this morning made that clear. He had a face like a constipated grump. Seriously, what was up with him? He was even weirder than he had been these past few days.

Me: I'll wear a cardigan—

Ahhhh!

I collide full force into a solid body, eliciting a grunt from the person I've walked into. I look up in horror to see I've walked into a guy holding a fast-food drink. He's tall and broad-shouldered, wearing a white T-shirt that molds nicely over muscle, now soaked in fizzy liquid.

My hands fly to my mouth. "Oh my God, I'm so sorry."

"Forget it." He sounds way more forgiving than I deserve.

His grin catches me off-guard more than the fact that I've doused him in his own drink.

Flustered, I fumble in my bag for a napkin. "I didn't look where I was going." I groan, feeling my cheeks heat. "Can I pay for your dry cleaning or something?"

"Relax," he drawls, his hand coming up to stop me. "Seriously, it's fine."

I sigh harshly. I'm sure karma will bite me later for this.

"What's your name?"

"Clodagh."

"Lovely name. I've never heard of it." His eyes gaze leisurely over me. "It suits you."

I smile at the hot stranger, feeling a bit off-kilter. *Is he flirting with me?* "It's Irish. And yours is?"

"Alfred." He holds out his hand to me. "Tell you what, Clodagh, I'll forgive you if you give me your number and let me take you out for a drink."

Oh.

An unattractive snort escapes me as I take his hand. I'm about to respectfully reject him when I stop and think.

Why wouldn't I accept?

"Sure, Alfred. I'd love to."

***

Bucket list number four: the exquisite *L'Oignon du Monde* restaurant. Translation: The world's onion. Everything sounds more glamorous in French.

It's like I've stepped inside a French palace.

Reservations here are like gold dust. There's a one-year waiting list, so I don't know how they slipped me in for Teagan's birthday. Maybe Killian has his own list. The billionaires' waiting list involves no waiting, while the ordinary people's waiting list involves a year of waiting.

Killian motions for me to sit between him and

Connor. That's great; I'm in the middle of a Quinn sausage sandwich.

Teagan sits opposite me, flanked by her grandma and her friend Becky, who she talks about constantly. I can't believe I fucked her dad. I'm a trollop nanny. I can't look her in the eye without feeling severe Catholic guilt.

Killian's mum is a timeless beauty. Since we entered the restaurant, I haven't had a chance to speak with her properly, but my gut tells me I like her. Maybe it's because she was polite to the hostess as she took her coat off, while the snobby woman in front of us practically hung hers on the hostess's head.

Just as I'm about to take my seat, a server appears behind me, and then there are six servers at the table, one behind each chair.

What the fuck is going on?

This is over the top. I restrain myself from laughing as they help us all into our chairs. No one else seems to find it funny.

"You're welcome," I say with a wide smile to the server who assisted me in my chair and set a white napkin onto my lap.

Wait, what?

That didn't make any sense. I meant to say *thank you*. My words are all jumbled up because I'm nervous.

But before I can apologize for my verbal faux pas, he's gone. Talk about embarrassing.

A flurry of activity ensues as the servers scurry

around us, offering us water, breadsticks, olives, and little amuse-bouches.

People at the next table nudge each other. "The Quinn brothers," a guy says loudly.

I glance around at the other tables, and all eyes are on us. Women are staring at us. *Correction*, ogling Killian and Connor.

I've seen more subtlety at strip clubs.

Teagan barely bats an eyelid. At thirteen, she's used to this?

"You okay?" Killian asks in a lowered voice as Teagan and Becky chatter excitedly about meeting the pop star. They're obsessed. If I never hear about bloody Cayden again, it'll be too soon.

I side-eye Killian. "Yeah, I'm great."

His arm comes up to rest on the back of my chair. It settles there. I don't know if he means to be so close, but it's giving me goose bumps. He's so big that his thigh brushes against my bare skin every time he shifts.

I could tell him politely to stop manspreading, but I'm a glutton for punishment.

The servers appear again to take our orders. They never really leave; they seem to be waiting behind the curtains, ready to jump whenever we need them.

While everyone else mulls over the menu, I don't have to bother. Fancy restaurants and their pretty fonts make it impossible to read the menu. It's like they don't *want* you to know what's on offer.

"I'll have the half-young cockerel for starter and the steak tartare for main," I tell the server. "Oh, and a side of purée d'échalote caramélisée, please." I'm 99 percent certain I've pronounced it correctly because Siri and I practiced it a billion times.

Killian raises an eyebrow as if mildly impressed.

My lips purse. The arrogance of him to assume that I can't pronounce things correctly in French. Disclosure: I practiced this afternoon.

I'll never relax with him being in such proximity. Nervously, I pop a soft cheese ball in my mouth. Delicious.

Connor chuckles as the servers retreat. "A woman who knows what she wants." His eyes twinkle with amusement.

"I checked out the menu this afternoon," I tell him.

"I couldn't do that. It would make me hungry and impatient. And I'm fickle. I'll change my mind two hours later."

"It's because I have dyslexia," I explain. Until a few years ago, I wouldn't have revealed this, but now I feel comfortable discussing it. "The fonts can be tough to read, so if I know I'm going out to eat at a restaurant, I'll look at the menu online before I go."

The whole table is listening now. I blush as I become the center of attention.

Killian's mum looks genuinely curious. "It must be tough, darling."

"You never told me," Killian murmurs beside me. I tilt my head to see a deep frown on his face.

"What's it like?" Teagan asks. "Being dyslexic, I mean."

"It's hard to describe. It's like your brain plays tricks on you, and the letters all get mixed up and jump around." I take out my phone and scroll to the article I use to explain to people. It's much easier if they can see for themselves. "Here, have a look." I pass over my phone to Teagan.

Her eyes widen as she stares at it. Becky gazes at it over her shoulder. "This is insane. Things are moving. Dad, look at this!"

Killian's arm tenses against mine. He takes the phone from Teagan and studies it, his frown deepening. "Do you have everything you need to be comfortable at home? You should have told me about this."

"It's fine." I wave a hand in dismissal, my heart stupidly fluttering at Killian saying *home.*

And it really is fine. I know how to cope with it by myself. Otherwise, I'd be screwed.

"Sorry," I say, looking around them. "You guys didn't come out for dinner to talk about my issues."

"Nonsense." Killian's mum waves a hand. "It's so nice to meet you, Clodagh. I think it's wonderful for Teagan to have some young female company in the house."

Killian's mum pronounced my name right the first time because she's Irish. You could easily mistake her for an American until a few words slip through with her Irish accent.

"You're not imposing," Killian says gruffly beside me. "Teagan really wants you here."

But do you?

"Yes, we're delighted to have you here." Killian's mum tents her arms on the table and smiles warmly at me. "Tell me all about yourself, Clodagh. Killian tells me you're a trained carpenter."

He did?

All the blue-eyed family are watching me now.

"Hmm, yeah, a carpenter by trade," I say, fiddling with my fork. "I'm taking a career break while I settle into New York. Trying something new." I can't say that the only reason I took the job was to get a visa.

I bite into another soft cheese ball and get a funny look from Killian.

"Is there a reason you're eating balls of butter?"

"What?" I gasp, gawking at the ball. "I thought it was some sort of gourmet cheese!"

"No, it's butter."

Killian's mum winces. "Jesus, dear." She reaches for my hand. "If you keep eating like that, you'll never keep your figure."

Mortified, I return the butter ball to my plate, my face burning hot with embarrassment. I'm an idiot. They're going to think we don't have any fancy restaurants in Donegal. I'll never get through three courses with the Quinn family.

Next to me, Killian lets out a low chuckle.

"I remember my first day in New York," Killian's mum starts, thankfully moving on from my embarrassing butter faux pas. "I was willing to do anything for work when I came over. *Anything.*" Guess she has me all figured out. "I was eighteen.

Fresh faced off the plane from Dublin. So young." She sighs wistfully. "The seventies were wild in New York. It was a really special time."

"Everyone was doing drugs, and smoking was good for you," she adds mournfully.

Killian erupts into a cough beside me. "Mom, for fu—flip's sake."

I hide a smirk. I don't know why I hid my tattoos under a lace cardigan over my dress now. I even took out my nose ring, thinking his mum would be posh as hell.

"Oh stop, Killian." She waves her hand dismissively and gives Teagan's shoulders a squeeze. "Teagan knows better than to take drugs."

Teagan smiles innocently at her gran.

Killian's mum turns back to me. "Tell me, dear, where are you from originally? I can tell you're a northerner."

I smile. "Donegal."

She looks delighted. "Do you know any O'Sullivans from Donegal town? They used to..."

Here we go. The 'do you know this family' game.

I smile at her.

My eyes stray to Killian, and as if he can sense it, he moves his attention from his mum to me and raises his eyebrows in question.

My cheeks heat, and I quickly look away.

Five minutes later.
"Do you know any Maloneys?"
"Yup, I think I know that family."

"Lovely," she squeals. "Do they still own the bakery in Donegal town?"

"I think so," I fib as the army of waitstaff arrives with our starters.

My stomach growls in response; I had skipped lunch in anticipation of this moment. I quickly take a photo with my phone to send to Orla.

Half an hour passes, and I'm feeling relaxed. Different conversations at the table sometimes cross over each other. Killian's mum is fun, and Connor uses every opportunity to wind Killian up.

Even Killian is relaxed and laughing. He may not smile often, but it's worth the wait when he does.

I'm starving by the time the mains arrive because the starters were the size of a pea.

"Your tartare, ma'am," the server declares, placing my dinner before me.

I squint in confusion, unsure of what I'm looking at. It looks like the mincemeat my mum buys at the butcher's.

I take a bite and cough.

It's slimy. And cold. Why is it cold?

My fork trails through the weird meat. This is fucked up.

"Everything okay?" Killian murmurs, watching me.

"Yeah." I squirm in my seat because the tummy control pants are chafing. "It's just not what I was expecting."

"You know tartare is raw, right?"

"Like rare?"

"No. Raw. Uncooked."

I stare, transfixed at my plate in horror. I blew my chance at the World's Onion for this? "I thought it was like a bourguignon," I mutter, taking a swig of water to get rid of the taste of the raw meat in my mouth. They should fucking highlight that fact on the menu. "Why would I want to eat raw meat? I'm not a dog. Is it even safe?"

"They blend raw egg and raw beef with seasonings. It's an acquired taste." The corners of his mouth quirk into a light smile. "In a restaurant like this, it's safe."

Raw egg and meat blended together? Sickos.

I tentatively gather a small sample of meat onto my fork and take a bite. This is a disaster. If I don't think too much about what it is, I might not projectile vomit. "Sounds yummy."

I eye Killian's succulent steak with triple-cooked fries and peppercorn sauce.

I might cry.

How am I supposed to enjoy my potatoes with this vomit-inducing muck on the plate?

I take a big swig of wine and wonder if I could get away with requesting a neat whiskey and pouring it over the abomination on my plate to disguise the taste.

"You don't have to eat it if you don't like it." Killian nudges me. I wish he wouldn't watch me. This is traumatizing enough as it is without spectators. "Do you want to order something else?"

"I can't," I groan in despair. "I have to finish everything on my plate because I'm doing it for all the starving children in the world who can't." Damn Catholic guilt.

He nudges my hands away from my plate as the others are caught up in Teagan's and Becky's gushing about the pop star dude.

"What are you doing?" I ask, confused, as he swaps my plate for his. "No! I can't let you do that."

I'm tortured between taking a bite of the steak and doing the right thing and swapping the plates back. "Do you even *like* steak tartare?"

He takes a bite, the picture of ease. "Love it," he says with a wink.

"Liar."

"What are you two doing?" Connor interjects, watching us.

"I've changed my mind." Killian shrugs, a smile playing on his lips. "I fancy the tartare."

My cheeks flush as I look at Connor, and give a dismissive shrug. I bite into Killian's steak. Fuck that, there's no way I'm giving this back.

As he loads the next forkful of raw food, his arm brushes against mine. Wow, that was sweet. The guy is eating raw meat for me. It must be the dad side of him.

I don't know if it's my pride, ego, or something else, but I wish he would see me differently.

I'm just a quick one-night fling. *Correction.* A fifteen-minute fling, a mistake, not a serious proposal.

My core heats as I imagine him forcing me up against the wall of my studio and fucking me.

Now I feel as raw as the damn meat.

Feeling someone's eyes on me, I shift my gaze to the next table. They're talking about Killian.

One woman stares at me as if she wants my organs. I narrow my eyes at her. *Back off, lady. I'm his nanny maid. I don't need negative vibes in this fancy restaurant.*

"People are talking about you," I say in a hushed voice.

His eyes crinkle. "Are they? Hadn't noticed."

His face is warmer this evening. He's in a good mood. Being out with the Quinns is less weird than I expected. Killian's mother is down to earth, despite having birthed two billionaires. Connor's a lot of fun, too.

"So, Clodagh," Killian's mum begins, her eyes full of mischief. "Have you met any nice men in New York?"

Killian's not interested in me. I might as well show him the feeling's mutual. I swallow my bite of steak and say, "Actually, I met someone recently."

Killian's thigh presses hard against mine under the table as if in warning.

Oh my God, he thinks I'm talking about him.

I almost want to laugh. Does he think I'm going to blurt out about our one-night stand to his family?

Feeling his intense stare on my cheek, I carry on. "Just today, I met a nice guy in the park who wants to go out. We exchanged numbers."

Killian's leg pulls away from me. The drink hovers over his lips for a moment before he takes a sip.

I dare not look directly at him.

"I'm not surprised," his mum drawls. "You must have guys queuing up in Central Park. You won't stay single for long."

"He'll need to be vetted," a low voice rumbles next to me.

I tilt my head to Killian.

With his cold eyes locked on mine, he takes an aggressive swig of his beer.

"We're just going for coffee," I say, wondering why my heart is racing. "I'll tell you if it becomes serious. I won't let him near the house without your approval."

For the first time this evening, Killian's expression contorts into the familiar scowl of irritation I know all too well.

***

"Ouch." My shin slams against the toilet bowl as I attempt to squeeze the shapewear panties up over my thighs. Did the steak add fat to my ass already? "Fuck's sake."

I've been in here so long the Quinns will think I'm doing a number two. I don't want Killian to know I poo.

The main bathroom door opens, and heavy footsteps approach the cubicles.

"Clodagh."

My stomach dips. "Killian?" I squeak.

"I'd like to talk to you."

"Er." I look down at my shapewear stuck around my knees. "Just a minute," I say in my best singsong voice.

My thighs shudder a bit as I pull on the underwear. The grunts will definitely give him the impression that I'm doing my business.

It's pointless. Mission aborted.

I roll them down my legs and step out of them, shoving them into my bag.

"Hey," I say breathlessly as I open the cubicle door and step out. "I was just…"

Just what?

Now I've made it even worse.

"What are you playing at?" he says with an angry scowl.

"There was a queue for the ladies," I lie, mortified. "That's why I've been in here so long."

"That's not what I'm asking about," he growls. "I'm talking about you giving out your number to random guys in the park. Is this to make me jealous?"

"What?" I hiss, gawking at him in disbelief with bug eyes. "No. It's to make me happy!"

He moves closer until he has me pinned against the bathroom door with his arms on either side of me.

My heartbeat goes fucking wild. The tightness in my chest cannot be ignored.

I need a doctor.

"It's not all about you," I say breathlessly,

dropping my bag to the floor. "Arrogant ass boss. Boss ass." Ugh. "You've made it clear you're not interested in a rematch." I keep talking. "Why wouldn't I date? I'm not breaking your rules."

He dips his head so that his icy blue eyes are only inches from mine.

I feel a rush of heat between my legs, which is an issue because I've got no panties to cream.

"You're not dating." He moves his face even closer to mine so that his minty breath is hot on my face. "No Sam, no Liam, no other fucking young idiot. While you are living under my roof, you don't date."

"But you said I was just a mistake. Why shouldn't I date?"

His face darkens even more. "Fuck," he hisses.

I've no idea what is going on, in this bathroom or his head.

"Because it's in the manual? Is that why I can't date?" I say, my voice hoarse.

We're touching now. His thighs rub against mine. My chest brushes against his.

I squirm against him, trying to catch my breath.

"It has nothing to do with the fucking manual." As if he feels the need to cage me further, he widens his stance to trap my legs between his. "You were mine the moment I came inside you. As long as you live beneath my roof, no one else can have you, understand?"

On impulse, I thrust my hips against him.

Holy shit, he's hard.

"Understand?" he repeats more forcefully.

"Yes," I squeak out.

"Good girl," he growls against my lips, pressing his erection against me.

Gah. He's killing me. I *am* a good girl. My legs are already opening for him.

His lips press firmly against mine with an intensity that feels like a declaration of ownership rather than a kiss.

Stop this. Push him away.

I'm in the bathroom of a fancy restaurant.

Before I can stop myself, I widen my legs and push my hips into his so his hard dick is between my legs.

His hands roam, trying to feel my ass through the dress.

He groans into my mouth. "You're not wearing any underwear."

"Not anymore, no," I rasp.

He pulls back abruptly with a sharp exhale of breath. For a long moment, he stares at me, breathing heavily.

Then he runs a hand through his hair, gives me one last hard look, and storms off, leaving me stunned and pantiless in the bathroom.

TWENTY-THREE

Clodagh

"I'll need you around this evening," Killian informs me as he saunters into the kitchen shirtless. "I hope you haven't forgotten."

"Nope. I haven't."

Have you forgotten how you kissed me last night? my eyes scream at him. *Can you tell me what's happening between us?*

My body still throbs with the memory of his kiss last night. After we left the restaurant, he went to the concert, so I haven't seen him since. Now he's standing in the kitchen displaying his broad shoulders and bare chest and those abs that make my vagina flutter.

My gaze follows the treasure trail of dark hair disappearing into his running shorts. Treasure I'm unlikely to see again.

This isn't playing fair at all.

I hand him his smoothie. "Did you have fun at the concert?"

He scowls at me. There's a pattern here. After

every scorching-hot spell with Killian, temperatures plunge to sub-zero and arctic conditions.

"Sixty thousand screaming teenage girls and their horny moms aren't my thing, so no."

I smile for both of us. "Did Teagan have a good time? What did she think of Cayden?"

He sighs, scrubbing a hand through his hair. "Teagan was the worst of the screaming teenagers. My ears are still ringing." He takes a large gulp of the smoothie as if he's dehydrated. "Apparently, meeting the little pop star runt was the highlight of her life. I'm sure she'll tell you about it, so I won't spoil the surprise."

"I can't wait." I groan. "Your mum is fun. She's down to earth for having birthed billionaires."

"She liked you a lot, too."

Oh. This makes me feel all warm and fuzzy inside.

I clock the dark circles under his eyes. "You look exhausted. Just one day, I expect you to sleep in. I'll get the coffee ready."

He slides onto a barstool. "My body won't let me. I'm programmed to wake up at five."

"And the manual can't be overridden."

Silence.

My little joke bombs.

He ignores me. "After breakfast, take the day off. Don't worry about any tasks since you're working tonight."

"Thanks." I beam. "Awesome."

"Why are you so cheery?" he asks gruffly, as if it's a crime.

Our gazes connect, and his eyebrows furrow as he realizes the truth as to why I'm so chirpy this morning.

"No reason," I say as I flick the switch to start the coffee machine.

"Catering will arrive at seven with the food. I need you to be around to let them in. They've been here before, so they know their way around the kitchen. Be around the kitchen if they need anything. At dinner, I need you to keep people's drinks topped off. Oh, and Teagan's staying with Mom."

"Sure," I say as I set his coffee in front of him.

I get a once-over from him before he opens up his laptop. "The mayor will be here, along with a few important council members and my business partners. The mayor's an old-fashioned kind of guy. Can you dress accordingly, please?"

My jaw drops open at the arrogance of it. "Do I not usually dress *accordingly*?"

"Not in that T-shirt, no."

"I do have *some* knowledge of social etiquette, you know," I huff, folding my arms across the bunny. "I didn't wear my bunny T-shirt to dinner last night, did I?"

"You didn't wear any underwear either."

"I had it on," I grumble. "I just took it off because... never mind, alright. I'll wear something appropriate for the mayor. So what's dinner for? Why isn't it taking place in one of your hotels?"

"I didn't realize I needed permission to have dinner in my own house," he mutters, eyes glued to the laptop. "It's business. We're having some technical issues with the new casino build in Brooklyn. It's best that we discuss them in private." He glances up. "Remember your NDA. Anything you overhear tonight is confidential."

"Don't you trust me yet, Killian? Killy?" I add playfully, because this morning, I can't help myself.

The expression on his face is almost one of disappointment. "We've known each other for a few weeks, Clodagh. You shouldn't trust someone in that space of time. And I told you if I heard that ridiculous nickname again, you'd be out of a job."

"Fine." My eyes narrow. *But you know me well enough to stick your cock in me.* "I remember my NDA, sir."

He drains his cup of coffee and slams his laptop shut with a frustrated sigh. "And stop running at the automatic doors to test them."

Shit. I cringe. Okay, so maybe I've done that once or twice.

"I've no idea what you're talking about." I bristle. "Are you spying on me?"

"No," he says as he stands up. "The security system detected unusual activity in the lounge area."

"Did they detect any other unusual activity over the past few weeks?" I ask with a hint of sarcasm.

His eyes meet mine in a warning. So it's okay for him to talk about what happened between us, but not me.

Without another word, he strides out.

***

"Want to grab a coffee?" Sam asks as we stroll lazily through Central Park. After a sun-soaked yoga session, I'm in a very chilled-out mood. Maybe it's because Sam is the opposite of Killian; he's friendly, charming, and allows my pulse to remain at a healthy rate.

"I can't," I moan. "I have to go shopping. Killian wants me to look presentable tonight to serve drinks at his fancy dinner." I roll my eyes in disgust. "The way he looked at me this morning, you'd think I walked around with butt cleavage or something."

"Butt what?"

"Butt cleavage," I explain. "It's where you show some of your ass like you would breasts. Like a half moon."

"Right," Sam splutters. "Yeah, the mayor might have a heart attack."

"As if anyone's going to be looking at me, anyway. But if that's his wish, then it's only right I hit the designer shops."

"Do you want some company?"

I eye him skeptically. "Are you serious? You want to come shopping?"

"I like spending time with you, but..." He smirks. "An afternoon in Bloomingdale's isn't my idea of a good time."

"Tell me about it. I like the idea of shopping. Then, after ten minutes, I want to get the hell out. I'll just flash Killian's credit card and ask someone to pick something that suits me. I want to spend the rest of the afternoon working on some new furniture designs." I sigh guiltily.

It's time to get my life plan in order.

This life is temporary.

My chest tightens. Two months from now, I'll no longer work for Killian. The au pair agency is searching for another family, but they could be based anywhere in the state.

I need to work out how to stay in New York and do what I love.

"What should I wear to make an impression in front of a mayor? I'm aiming for a First Lady-style look." Like the woman from the hotel. Has he seen her since? He hasn't had any Tuesday sex transactions since I moved in.

God, if he did, I don't know if I could handle it. What if he has sex a few floors above me?

Could he be so cruel?

The pangs of jealousy are back.

Sam looks me up and down and winks. "Doesn't matter what you wear, you'll look gorgeous."

"Yeah, right," I scoff. "But thanks for the ego boost. So give me the lowdown. Who'll be at this?"

"Tonight? Connor and his date. His other business partner, JP, short for John Paul. You probably haven't met him yet; he lives in Vegas and runs the office there. If you think Killian is ruthless, JP is on an entirely different level. Try to steer clear of him. He's the wolf in Quinn & Wolfe." He thinks for a moment. "Mayor Williams and his wife. Counselor Menendez and his wife."

I shrug; these names mean nothing to me. I've no idea about state politics.

We veer around the pond toward the park entrance.

"Oh, and Killian, of course, and Maria."

I stop dead on the pavement. "Maria?"

"Everything okay?"

"Yeah." I want to vomit. "Just a stone in my shoe." I pretend to fix it, then carry on walking.

"Maria Taylor, his date," Sam continues casually, oblivious to how he is twisting a knife into my heart. "She's friends with the mayor's wife."

"Right," I say slowly. "So things are heating up between them? Is she his girlfriend?"

He shrugs. "Maybe. Who knows with Killian?"

"Did he vet her?" That seems to be his go-to operation for bringing people into his inner circle.

Sam chuckles. "Nah, he doesn't vet his own girlfriends."

Double standards.

Sam grins at me, not knowing how much he has kicked me in the guts.

I force a smile back because why wouldn't I? It would be weird to be upset about my boss' maybe-girlfriend.

Killian Quinn is a jerk. Days after sleeping with me, he's going to parade another woman in front of me. In the *house*.

"Has he slept with her?" I blurt out.

"I don't know." He frowns. "That's not info the security team is privy to."

"There are cameras in his bedroom. He spied on me one day."

"He turns them off before bedtime." He gives me an odd look, the corner of his mouth twitching. "He wouldn't let us watch him get intimate with someone."

"Sam, I have to go," I say with a fake smile. "I'll see you later."

He looks confused. "Let me walk you—"

"It's fine." I wave him off and sprint away, leaving a perplexed Sam in my wake.

My phone vibrates as I make it out of the park.

What the hell does he want now? I'm not supposed to be working this afternoon. I pull it out of my bag.

Central Park Alfred: Let me show you the sights of Brooklyn. Next week? Name a date.

Yes, Alfred, that definitely fucking works for me.

My anger bubbles in the pit of my stomach. Killian can go to hell.

You were mine as soon as I came inside you. As long as you live beneath my roof, no one else can have you.

Killian Quinn will learn I'm not his possession.

Starting with tonight.

***

As I clack my way up the stairs from my studio in my high heels, I hear voices, and the dread bubbling in my stomach since I left Sam rises to the surface. Fifteen minutes was all I had to get ready for dinner since I'd let the caterers in.

Taking a deep breath, I walk into the lounge.

Killian leans against the fireplace in a dark-blue suit with one hand tucked into his trousers and the other against the fireplace. Underneath, he's wearing a vest.

His presence puts my already tense nerves on edge further.

In an instant, I forget all of my social skills and just gape at him. Killian Quinn in running gear is sexy as fuck. Killian Quinn in a three-piece suit is downright showstopping.

I'm equally depressed and flustered.

I don't miss the double take he gives me. Bingo. Except I can't figure out whether he's angry or horny. Maybe the two are interchangeable.

I snap out of my lust daze and regard him coolly.

Connor sits in the armchair with a glam six-foot Amazonian model casually perched on his armrest.

Maria isn't here.

Maybe she's not coming.

"Clodagh." Connor stands up to greet me, giving me an appreciative once-over. "You look stunning. Are you joining us for dinner?"

My cheeks burn. I've overdone it. "No, I'm serving the drinks."

Connor winks. "Looks like everyone will be getting frequent top-ups then."

A nervous giggle escapes me, sounding unusually

high-pitched due to the bodycon underwear crushing my organs. I should have learned my lesson at the restaurant, but beauty is pain.

"There was no need for you to dress up."

I turn in the direction of the low husky drawl that induces the pesky flutters and glare at him. "You told me to look presentable. Do I not look presentable enough for you?"

His blue eyes blaze with heat. "I told you to dress accordingly."

I consider whether to kick him in the nuts or run down the stairs crying.

Connor looks at Killian with a frown.

Killian's eyes slowly travel up my body, starting from my toes and finishing at my head. "Yes, Clodagh," he says slowly. "You look presentable. You look... very nice."

I'm flattered. "Charmer of the century," I mutter under my breath.

I saunter past him in my green Chanel dress. Okay, I may have gone overboard. In fact, the effort I put in just to serve drinks is downright outrageous. I look like I'm auditioning for a starlight role in a Hollywood blockbuster, if I say so myself. I even removed my nose ring to look *ladylike* for the old mayor frump.

"I'll be in the kitchen with the caterers," I say haughtily, not bothering to glance back at him.

I don't need to, to know his eyes are burning into the back of me. I can *feel* it.

One point for me, zero points for Killian.

***

The doorbell rings. That's my cue. I make my way to the entrance hall.

The hallway fills with perfume and cologne as they stream in together. Killian is at the door greeting them.

Counselor Menendez and his wife. JP Wolfe, the Quinns' third business partner, arrives alone. He looks Spanish or maybe Italian and has the lowest drawl I've ever heard.

"Clodagh," Killian murmurs as I come up behind him. He puts his hand on my lower back. "Would you mind taking their coats, please?"

Killian helps Mrs. Menendez remove her coat, engaging in small talk with the couple.

Huh. So he can be charming. Just not to me.

I take the ridiculous fur coat from Killian just as the bell goes again.

Folding the coat over my forearm, I open the door.

My heart plummets.

Maria.

TWENTY-FOUR

Clodagh

Maria.

The beautiful brunette from the hotel. Her dress goes past her knees, but the slit leaves nothing to the imagination.

Everything is perfect. Her brown hair is styled in curls that float around her face and shoulders. Her beautiful features are done up in natural makeup, while her tailored, royal-blue dress hugs her body. Is she trying to match her outfit with Killian's eye color?

There's no way a guy wouldn't find her attractive.

Her eyes scan me, assessing me.

"Hello. And you are..." she asks in a clipped tone.

"Clodagh's my staff," Killian casually announces behind me. "She's serving drinks tonight."

"Hello," I say just as stiffly back.

Upon learning I'm *just staff*, Maria's annoyance immediately dissipates.

She walks past me into the hallway and pulls Killian in for a hug, kissing him on the cheek.

Laughing, she murmurs something to him so I can't hear it. He chuckles back.

"Let me take your coat," he says, helping her lower it.

My heart burns with pain as I watch their exchange. Killian puts his hand on her lower back, just as he did with me. There's an intimacy shared between them as if they've slept together.

He leads her into the lounge, but not before handing her coat to me, mouthing a "thank you."

Turning away, I put the coat in the closet.

How could he do this to me?

How could he make me watch him with another woman?

Because my feelings don't count.

As long as I live in his house, I can't date anyone because I'm his convenient fuck. But not if there's a better alternative. Everything is starting to make sense.

Teagan isn't here. Oh God, he's going to have sex with Maria. She'll stay over.

I feel sick. This is why I need to go out with Alfred, the cute guy I met in the park. That's what I need. A guy who is straight up and doesn't blow hot and cold. And Killian can't stop me. I have a constitutional right to pursue dick.

I slam the coat hard onto the hook.

I hope it rips.

Again, the bell rings, and I resist the urge to groan loudly.

I open the door to a tall skinny man with a thick

mustache. "Good evening, sir. You must be Mayor Williams."

He flashes me a lecherous smirk. "And who are you, lovely young lady?" he asks, taking my hand and pressing his lips to it.

"Clodagh." I pull my hand away as soon as I can, my skin crawling.

Ew, as Teagan would say.

"Mayor Williams." Killian walks up behind me, and the mayor steps into the hall. "Where's your beautiful wife?"

"She's feeling poorly, I'm afraid," he booms. "Her varicose veins are acting up." When he explains this, the mayor eyes me for some reason, so I make a sympathetic "oh" sound.

"This one's too young to worry about that." He takes a moment to admire my legs, free of varicose veins, and licks his lips.

Ew, again.

"And how do you know this lovely one, Killian? I do hope she'll be dining beside me tonight."

Killian places a hand on my back again, and I tense up.

I can't bear the thought of him touching me, knowing he's going to have sex with another woman when dinner is over.

"Clodagh's my live-in assistant."

"Nice to meet you," I say politely. Please fuck off into the lounge. You've already kissed my hand.

The mayor's face lights up. "Ah, you're Irish! I can hear it now. Of course, you are, with beautiful red hair like that. I'm Irish too. My great-great-great-grandfather came from Dublin." For fuck's sake. One of those dudes who wants to explain his Irish ancestry to me. "Where are you from? Dublin?"

I bristle.

Assuming every Irish person is from Dublin is as insulting as assuming a Canadian person is from the States. "No, up north. Donegal."

He lets out a bellowing laugh even though I'm not trying to be funny, then turns to Killian. "I did a tour there once. Beautiful scenery but the transport and amenities are terrible. No trains, just old cars for rental, and the roads need some real repair. It's such a slow way of life," he drawls, patting Killian on the arm.

I snatch his coat, glaring at him. He's making us out to be like country bumpkins with no teeth.

"You're better off staying down the south coast," he adds helpfully.

"I'm sure Clodagh's homeland is well worth visiting." Killian runs a hand over his strong jawline and actually looks pissed.

I trail them toward the lounge area, steam rising from my head.

Insulting someone to their face is bad but not as bad as insulting someone in front of their face TO SOMEONE ELSE'S FACE. That takes it to a whole other level of assholery.

Except Mayor Moron isn't finished. He turns to me, licking his lips again, and says something gibberish in appalling Irish. "Did you understand that?"

"No," I grit out. "I have no idea what that was." See, *this* is the type of guy I imagined when Marcus first told me about the job. I have a horrible vision of the mayor wearing a diaper, asking me to sing to him.

Killian's scowl deepens. "Let's let Clodagh get back to work."

Can't I just hide under all the obnoxious coats?

This is going to be a long fucking night.

***

With every minute that goes by, I get angrier, and they get drunker.

Every laugh, every stolen glance, and flirty smile makes me want to pour the wine over their heads.

With the caterers gone and dinner done, I'm alone in the kitchen, watching the party through the double doors.

Fuck. Maria is waving me over again.

Why doesn't she allow me to pour her a large glass of wine like a normal person rather than top her up with a trickle every five minutes? Because she wants to look like a dainty wee bird in front of Killian, that's why.

I march back to the dining area with two bottles of wine and make my way to Maria as two conversations compete loudly across the table.

NDA? I wouldn't fucking wish these conversations on anyone; they're so dull.

Every time I come over to fill Maria's glass, she's sitting closer to Killian. Soon enough, she'll be on his lap.

She's an advanced flirt, never missing an opportunity to 'accidentally' brush up against his arm. She knows she's high value and is going for the money shot.

And Killian lets her. He's barely looked at me except to give orders for drinks.

Tears prick my eyes, but I keep them in check.

Maria leans over to Killian, saying something to make him smile.

I stiffly lean over to pour more wine into Maria's glass as she touches Killian's hand.

She smiles at me gracefully, probably for Killian's benefit. She crosses and uncrosses her legs under the table, and I know her leg has touched his.

I want to scream.

I want to vanish from the scene.

I hate him.

I absolutely hate him.

My hair grazes Killian's shoulders as I lean over to top up his glass.

He tilts his head in my direction, almost touching his lips to my jaw.

"Thanks, Clodagh," he says, locking eyes with me. "You're doing a great job. I don't know what I'd do without you. Clock off in thirty, okay?" He pauses. "I won't need you anymore."

I stare back at him silently. *No, you won't. You've made that loud and clear.*

I knew he was cold-hearted and ruthless, but I didn't think he would go to this level.

He said we were a mistake, yet I'm not allowed to date anyone else under his roof while he can parade someone in front of my nose.

The whiplash is brutal.

"I think some of the staff have a little crush, Killian," Maria says in a voice that carries. "You should be careful. Of course, it's completely understandable."

Killian's brows form a deep frown as he takes her in. He doesn't like this comment one bit.

I don't see how he responds, because Mayor Moron calls me over. *Summons me with his fingers.*

"Be a doll and bring me another scotch." He squeezes my hand creepily with his sweaty one.

Gross. He's drunk now; I can see it in his glazed eyes. He's managed to get crumbs all over the floor.

"Any chance of a pint of the black stuff?" he slurs, thinking he's funny.

"We don't have Guinness," I snap. *But I'll give you a black eye if you want instead.*

I drop to my knees to clean the crumbs off the floor and lock eyes with Killian.

The only way I'll get through this evening is if I turn into a husk of a human, void of the ability to feel.

I leave the dining area and head to the main bathroom on the ground floor, trying to pull myself together.

Maybe I'll take a bottle of wine down to my studio.

That way, I'll forget about Killian and Maria having sex a few floors above me.

Minutes later, I walk out of the bathroom and collide with a chest.

"Hello, angel," the mayor says in a voice that makes my neck hairs stand on edge.

He takes a step closer, his eyes sweeping up my body.

I bluntly move away from him, but he puts his arm up across my stomach to stop me.

What the fuck is happening?

"Excuse me." I forcefully try to pull his arm away.

"Killian said he has an Irish present for me." He smirks, pressing his hand to my hip. "I didn't expect it to be so lovely."

I freeze, feeling bile rise in my throat.

"Get off me, you sleazy old bastard," I screech, pushing his hand away. My legs are shaking, my arms are trembling, and my pulse is pounding.

He *chuckles.* He has the audacity to chuckle as if this isn't the first time he's been called that.

"I like the fighting Irish spirit," he drawls behind me as he walks into the bathroom. "This isn't over, doll."

With shaky legs, I sprint down the stairs to the lounge.

"Clodagh," Killian calls after me as I'm about to escape into the kitchen. "Can you open another bottle of red, please? Then call it a night."

"Yes, sir," I say in a very loud, strange-sounding voice, causing a few of them to give me a second glance. The room is a blur; I can barely see people. "It would be my pleasure." My voice betrays me at the end and comes out wobbly.

I hiss another "*sir*" at Killian.

His eyes widen, and his glare changes to something perplexed.

I storm into the kitchen and pull the cork out of a bottle of red with such force the wine nearly sprays everywhere.

An Irish present?

How dare he.

How dare he think he can *pass me around to his colleagues?*

He can go to hell.

I march into the dining area and head straight to Killian.

I'm beyond caring about my visa.

"This is the last time I'll serve you and your fucking sleazy buddies," I say with such saccharine sweetness that Killian looks confused.

The entire room goes dead. The only sound is the ticking of the large clock on the wall.

He's about to talk when I see fucking red.

In one smooth motion, I tip the bottle of wine all over his lap.

It's like I've detonated a bomb in the room.

Sharp gasps.

Silence.

The wrath of Killian Quinn cutting through me.

I set the bottle down on the table with a thud, turn on my heel, and stride out of the room.

TWENTY-FIVE

Clodagh

I have no idea what my plan is. Just get out of here and process it later.

I need to get away from Killian with his cold dead heart, Maria with her long pins, and Mayor Perv, who probably has the power to have me deported.

A sob emanates from my throat.

I'm never opening my legs for a man again.

I hear commotion upstairs, and my stomach lurches. *Just get out of the house.*

I scoop up my phone and my bag. I can barely see through the fat, angry tears streaming down my face. There's no time to change out of this dress.

Underwear. Toothbrush. Reading pen. I can't think straight.

I'll get Sam to pack up the rest of my things.

I'm headed for Queens.

I'm not fast enough. Even his footsteps sound angry.

I brace myself as the studio door crashes open.

"What the hell was that, Clodagh?" He stands in the doorway staring at me, looking as bewildered as he is infuriated. It looks like he pissed red wine all over his trousers.

My stomach twists further, and I forget I was justifiably standing up for myself because his wrath is downright petrifying.

Tears blur my vision as I choke back a sob. "You—" I try to get out.

He moves closer to me and tips my chin up. "Clodagh?" he asks more calmly.

I jerk my head away from his touch. "You don't own me!" I spit out. "You're not better than me."

He rakes a hand through his hair, bewildered. "I know you're a much better person than I am. But that still doesn't explain why you decided to dump a bottle of wine on me in the middle of dinner. Or why you're so upset."

"I'm not your property to pass around, Killian!"

"*What?*"

"Your sleazy buddy, the mayor?" I push away from him, letting out an unattractive snort. "You told him I was his Irish present."

"His Irish present..." he murmurs, frowning as if not understanding.

Something changes in the air as recognition flashes across his face.

"His Irish present is a bottle of Irish whiskey," he says in a rough voice, rearing back to stare at me. "*Christ*, Clodagh. What kind of man do you think I am?"

"Yeah?" I shove my toiletries into my bag with force. "Well, that's not what Mayor Perv said."

He stiffens, every muscle going rigid. He doesn't speak. His jaw slams shut and hardens.

"Did he touch you?" he asks in an almost too calm voice.

I jerk my head in a no. "I didn't let him. I ran off."

He nods. "Stay here," he says in a low voice, his eyes locking with mine. "Don't leave your studio until I come back."

"I'm going to Queens."

"Please, Clodagh. Please."

He says it with the same air of authority I'm used to hearing in his voice. But his eyes are different this time. I see something I haven't seen before.

Maybe fear?

Anxiety?

Pain?

"Fine," I say quietly with a sigh.

I watch as he turns his back on me and strides out of the studio, slamming the door.

I exhale heavily and collapse onto the sofa.

What the hell is going to happen?

I can't keep the door closed. I have to know what's going on.

With shaky legs, I walk through the studio door and up the stairs, hovering out of sight on the top stair.

They're still in the lounge. Their voices are hard to distinguish in the burst of noise. A male tells someone to calm down.

"Get the fuck out of my house." It's Killian. His voice isn't raised; it's cold as ice. "If you ever so much as lay eyes on any of my female staff again, I'll kill you."

"This is absurd. Your deal is dead in the water, Quinn. You'll regret this!" The mayor storms out of the lounge area into the hallway, face twisted in rage and breathing hard.

I almost have to laugh as he rummages through all the coats, searching for his own, muttering relentlessly. "You forget who I am, you arrogant fuck."

I crouch down on the stairs so I don't have to see the cretin.

The hallway is a flurry of activity as people hurriedly put on their jackets, almost tripping over each other to make their way out.

Why is everyone leaving?

Everyone, of course, except for Maria, who stands with Killian in the hallway.

For a moment, neither of them speaks, unaware of me hiding on the stairs. Killian stands with his hands on his hips, facing away from me and staring at the ground.

Maria places a hand on his forearm. "Are you sure this maid is telling the truth, Killian?"

My gut clenches. I can't bear to listen to them talk about me, so I inch back down the stairs and melt into the shadows, my mind racing. She doesn't look like she's going anywhere anytime soon.

I can't stay. I'm not staying here while Killian sleeps with her. He might not have offered me on a platter to the mayor, but if he sleeps with another woman when I'm in the house, it'll destroy me. I'd prefer to spend the night on a Central Park bench.

I want him. That's the shitty thing. How can one person feel something so one-sided?

I let myself become too attached, and now I'm vulnerable. The ache in my heart spills out through tears as I race into my studio and collapse onto the couch. I would rather feel nothing than be riddled with this pain.

The knock on the door makes me flinch.

"I'm fine," I shout, trying to sound as upbeat as possible. "Let's talk tomorrow."

Right now, I don't care if he fires me.

Silence.

Just when I think he's left, his deep, husky voice drifts through the door. *"Please."*

"Go away."

"I'll wait out here all night if I have to."

I wait for what feels like an eternity to figure out it's an idle threat.

When I hear him still leaning against the door, I wipe my tears with my hand and move toward the door to open it.

Killian stands rigid in the doorway, his blue eyes blazing into mine. The lighting throws shades on his jawline, making him look equally beautiful and predatory.

His expression twists into concern as he takes in my blotchy face.

Please go away.

"I'm sorry," I force out, maintaining a steady tone

as I stand awkwardly by the table. "I didn't mean to make you lose your deal."

His frown deepens, as if my words have wounded him. He takes a purposeful step closer. "I don't care about the damn casino, Clodagh."

"You're not the one that should be sorry," he continues quietly. "I should never have put you in that situation. I swear, Clodagh, if I thought that would happen, I would never have invited the fucker into my home."

I try to swallow the massive lump in my throat. "It's fine."

"It's not fucking fine. I promised to keep you safe, and I didn't. I'm so damn sorry, Clodagh."

"Look, I just want to go to Queens, alright?"

He watches me for a long moment in silence.

Then his face darkens, and he nods, almost dejectedly. "You don't feel safe here. I should have protected you. I failed you."

He looks so devastated that I almost feel sorry for him. Almost.

I grab my backpack and give him a faint smile. "It's not the mayor. I've had my share of sleazy guys before. I just need some time out, okay?"

"It's me. You want to get away from me."

I sling my backpack over my shoulder and grip it tight for support.

Can't he leave it?

"I can't stay here while you sleep with Maria." My voice breaks on her name. I study my feet because I can't bear to look at Killian. "I know there's nothing between us, but I can't shut off my emotions like you can. I figured that out tonight."

He makes an ugly sound that sounds like a laugh.

The callous bastard actually fucking *laughs* at me.

"Can you just fuck off, Killian?" I say in a sob, glowering at him through my tear-filled eyes.

"Wait." His arm shoots up, and I am jarred back against his warm body. He stares into my eyes and slowly slides my backpack off my shoulder. His arm tightens around my waist, making it impossible for me to escape. My head barely reaches his chin.

I go rigid as the warmth of his body and the smell of him surround me.

My heart starts pounding in my chest. My face flushes hot, and I hate his effect on me.

He's not playing fair.

"Maria's not here," he says gruffly. "She's gone. She was never going to stay. I took her out for lunch yesterday and told her things would only remain friendly between us." His warm breath blows against my forehead as he heaves a sigh. "Even I'm not that big of a bastard, despite what you think of me."

"Yeah? She didn't look like she got the memo," I snap.

"I'm sorry." His strong hands grip my lower back, holding me flush against him. "I'm sorry you thought there was something between Maria and me. I've taken her to lunch a few times, but that's it. There's no connection. You are the only person I saw in the room tonight." He almost seems frustrated with himself for his feelings toward me. "You're the only person I notice in any room these days. You consume my thoughts more than I care to admit."

"Why is that such a bad thing?"

"I can't give you what you need." He caresses my cheek with a sadness in his eyes that makes me want to scream *why? Why not?* "You deserve more."

Instead, I muster a weak smile like it's no big deal. "I know, Killian. You've been upfront about that. You don't want anything serious with me."

His expression turns grim. "It's not that cut-and-dry. I'm not a good guy for you."

"You don't commit."

"I can't commit. There's a difference," he counters, as if it justifies everything.

His face clouds over. I want to ask him what he means, but I'm afraid he'll close down.

And right now, he wants me. He hardens against me as I run my hands down his chest. His breathing is ragged, and his nipples harden as my fingers trace over them.

I get on my tiptoes, so his hardening cock is closer to my core, and I can run my hands through his hair.

I want him to fuck away my pain. I want him to fuck away my tears.

Even if only for tonight.

"I didn't come here to fuck you." He groans against my forehead, his expression clouding with what I think is regret. "I came here to make sure you're okay."

"Then make me feel good," I murmur, angling his

head down so our lips almost touch.

He groans again, then grips the back of my hair and drags my mouth to his. I open wide, my tongue pushing hungrily against his.

His stomach muscles jerk as I push my hand down his abs and into his underwear. I need to feel all of him. *Now.*

Holy shit, he's fully erect. His thick, heavy cock strains in his trousers, jerking against my touch, and I love how affected he is by me.

I curl my hand around him possessively; the sensation sending shivers through my body. I'm aching for him to destroy me, to rip me to pieces.

"Wait, Clodagh," he says as I fumble with the buttons of his trousers. His voice is coarse, thick with need. "*Fuck.* This is all about you, not me."

He slowly unbuttons his shirt while I stand there, panting and desperate, with my hands gliding across his skin. The shirt joins the rest of the clothes on the nearby table as he grabs me with one arm and carries me into the bedroom.

"Let me show you how sorry I am about tonight, beautiful."

Every atom of my body shivers in anticipation as he gently lays me down on the bed. My arousal is so strong I'm almost embarrassed.

I try to sit up, clumsily reaching for the top of his trousers. I need him naked.

"Not so fast," he growls as he climbs onto the bed and grabs my wrists, trapping me in his embrace.

My hands slide over his toned chest as I

impatiently squirm beneath him.

He gently inches my dress up above my waist and over my head, murmuring, "Sorry, baby," when my hair gets caught in the fabric.

I suck in a deep breath. I can't wait any longer. I've needed this since the night he left me standing with my dress bunched up around my waist.

"What the hell are these?"

I freeze at his surprised tone and follow his line of sight down to where the tummy control shapewear clings to me like a second skin.

Uh-oh.

"Don't worry about those; they just help flatten everything out. Take 'em off."

He slides them down my stomach, and his eyes widen when he sees how tight they are. "Clodagh, these aren't good for you. You have red marks on your stomach." He bends down to kiss my stomach softly. "I don't know what you mean by 'flattening out', but I do know you don't need it."

I don't know whether to swoon or die of mortification.

"Yeah, yeah," I say awkwardly. "Can we get back to what we were doing?"

He chuckles quietly and unhooks my bra.

Now I'm completely exposed and his for the taking.

What are you waiting for?

I spread my legs, willing him to climb on top of me.

TAKE ME.

Killian has other ideas.

"This time will be slower," he murmurs, talking to himself as much as me.

He gently spreads my legs, and his eyes roam over me from above with a look so predatory, tiny shivers erupt over my body.

He starts at my mouth, kissing me slow and deep, then travels down at a torturous pace. Down my neck and across my collarbone to my breasts. My nipples are so hard it hurts.

I moan out in pleasure and instinctively arch my back as he takes my nipple in his mouth. I grip the back of his neck, my fingers entwined in his thick locks of hair as he teases one breast and then the other with his tongue.

Then he's on the move again, his beautiful mouth trailing kisses down my stomach, delivering chills across my skin until his stubble tickles above my clit.

"Wait, Killian." I put my hand on his face before he can travel farther and clamp my legs against his shoulders. "There's no point in doing that."

This makes him freeze. He blinks up at me, bewildered. "No point?"

"I, uh, don't find it easy to come that way," I say in a small voice. "It never worked with my ex."

"Never?" He searches my face, and a wave of regret washes over me as I realize I said too much.

I shake my head slowly, my cheeks burning.

Immediately, his expression softens. He kisses my stomach as he looks up at me. "There's no pressure for you to come."

"I won't." I can't believe I'm admitting this. "I've never gotten there with a guy going down on me. I don't know if it's me or them... I get too locked in my own head."

He smiles and comes up to plant a kiss on my lips. "That's okay. But will you let me try because I want to?" His gaze darkens with lust. "I can't stop thinking about what you taste like. But I won't do it if it makes you uncomfortable."

I give him a shy nod in response. What if he doesn't enjoy my taste?

He must sense my unease. "Hey," he murmurs below me, his brows pulling together in a frown. "There's nothing you can do to make me want this less. All you need to do is close your eyes and relax, okay?"

I bite my lip as he stares up at me intently. Doing as I'm told, I take a deep breath and squeeze my eyes shut.

He travels down again and places one hand on each of my thighs to keep them apart.

His tongue and lips brush over my clit, and I nearly jump out of my skin at the sensation. Immediately, a deep, primal growl comes out of him, making me want to giggle, but I hold it back. He has no qualms about showing me how much he's enjoying himself.

He starts off slow as if he's testing the waters to make sure it feels good for me.

My pulse quickens, and I will myself to relax. I resist the urge to close my legs as he eats me.

Fuck... that's nice.

Killian knows exactly what he's doing: the perfect amount of pressure to use, the alternating rhythm of slow and fast, how to use his fingers to massage my slit while pleasuring me with his tongue.

A delicious heat builds between my legs, but I know I won't reach orgasm. I'm close, but I'll not get there. I never do.

I try to push away the negative thoughts infiltrating my mind. What if I don't taste good? What if he hates it? Does he think something is wrong with me? *Is* there something wrong with me? Why can't I come with guttural moans like they do in the movies?

His groan vibrates against my skin, and when I look down, his mouth closes over me, and the look on his face is so full of lust and pleasure that the heat in my core intensifies.

"Clodagh," he murmurs in a low baritone. "You taste incredible. I love this."

Our eyes meet, and the connection sends more delicious thrills through me. I didn't want our stare to end, but the moment's intensity is almost too much.

Holy hell.

Every sensation is heightened.

My skin tingles everywhere his tongue caresses me.

His scent lingers all over me.

My legs involuntarily jolt whenever he utters my name in that deep husky growl and tells me I'm the sweetest damn thing he's ever tasted.

Fuck.

Fuck.

"Oh, fuuuuuuuck," I moan in pleasure.

Shallow breathing. Remember how to breathe.

I buck as he does something with his tongue I can't even describe.

"Too much," I pant out, unsure if I want him to stop or keep going.

"Really?" he breathes beneath me.

"No. Yes. I don't know! No."

God... it feels amazing.

Maybe... just maybe...

"Let go, beautiful," he says softly below me. "I can feel that you want to."

My body quivers. Killian is relentless. He's not stopping until I come. It feels like this could go on forever.

I don't know if it's the pressure building in my core or the look of pure pleasure on his face that tips me over the edge, but... wow, this is actually happening.

I'm there.

"Yes, beautiful, let it happen. You deserve to feel so good."

I'm coming... I'm coming on his tongue.

My legs spasm as I let out breathy, jerky moans, gripping his hair tightly as the flutters in my core become intense waves of pleasure throughout my body.

I collapse onto the bed, my arms and legs like jelly.

"You did it," I gasp, staring at the ceiling. "Thank you."

He chuckles low and husky as he brings himself level with me. "No need to thank me. The pleasure was all mine."

I give him a silly grin. "You must have a really strong jaw."

"Nah." His blue eyes shine at mine. "Just a really big appetite."

I don't remember falling asleep. But when I wake up in the morning, I'm under the covers, and Killian is gone.

TWENTY-SIX

Killian

Two Weeks Later

"Eyes locked on me," I command.

She obediently lifts her chin and locks her gaze onto mine as she takes my hard shaft down her throat.

"Yes, that's it. Show me how much you want it. Take me like a good girl."

My mind savors the sight of her; her vibrant emerald eyes alive with emotion, her freckled nose and voluptuous lips enveloping my cock in her mouth. This vision has been playing in my head nonstop, stealing me away from work.

How could I not after the filthy few weeks we've had? My cock has had so much stimulation that I'm amazed it's still intact.

"Yes, beautiful," I groan as I hit the back of her throat and shudder. I clench her locks in my fingers, resisting the temptation to thrust even harder. "That's it. Keep doing that. Good girl."

Damn.

Sensory fucking overload. Every suck feels incredible, sending tingling vibrations straight down my spine. The warmth of her pretty mouth, the little whimpers she makes, the look in her eyes that shows how much she wants to please me as the water drips off her face and chest from the shower.

Am I wrong to find her gagging so arousing?

Her pace quickens as she slides my throbbing cock in and out of her mouth, devouring me from base to tip.

"So. Damn. Good," I pant through gritted teeth, pressing one hand against the shower wall.

Now I've taken control. I'm fucking her mouth. I let out a hard, heavy groan and fist her hair tighter as I thrust into her mouth.

She makes a soft mewling sound. I have to force myself to check that she's not in pain, but when she looks up at me with those big green eyes, all I see is that she wants to please me.

"I'm close," I growl through grated breaths, my gaze fixated on hers. I should warn her that if she keeps this up, she'll be choking on my cum.

The intensity builds within me until I can no longer control it. Every muscle coils tightly, and my body shudders with pleasure as I emit a guttural groan. My balls feel like they're going to explode.

"*Fuck.*" My cum pulses out, filling her throat, and I grasp her head so she takes it all.

"Damn, Clodagh." I let out a husky laugh as my breathing returns to normal. "I'd die a happy fucking man tonight, sweetheart."

I raise her gently off the shower floor and into my arms. Her cheeks are flushed, and her hair clings to her forehead. "Breathe, sweetheart. Relax."

"I think I'm going to have to practice by holding my breath in the bath. You're a big guy."

My low laughter rumbles through the shower stall as I lace our fingers together and step out. Neither of us says a word as I wrap her in a fluffy towel, drying her body with gentle touches. Fucking hell, feeling her curves is making me hard again already.

She stares at me as I carry her to her bedroom, her lip twitching as if she wants to say something but is lacking the words.

"Everything okay?" I ask.

She smiles and nods.

I lay her out on the bed, naked and ready for me, and climb on top of her. Softly, I kiss her neck, the curves of her collarbone, the swell of her breasts until I feel her nipples harden and her back arch in response.

"Too soon?" I ask, searching her face.

"No," she breathes. "I want you inside me."

I thrust my cock into her, relishing the sensation.

She winces, her hands pressing against my back in resistance.

I groan as her muscles clench around me, squeezing my cock. It feels so good; I could just stay inside her and never come out. The more she tightens around me, the quicker I'm going to come.

I wait until the tightness in her relaxes a bit, fighting hard not to thrust into her wet warmth.

"Easy," she moans a bit as she adjusts her hips to take me all in.

"Breathe, Clodagh." I smile down at her, running a finger over her bottom lip. "Relax."

Her pussy clenches around me, and it feels fucking amazing. It always feels amazing. It drives me wild knowing I'm the only man who has made her orgasm.

She makes me feel like I'm in a warm, delicious bath, spending Christmas in St. Barts, running the New York marathon, opening my first hotel. The best fucking feelings in the world all rolled into one.

I slide deeper into her sweet little pussy, staring into her eyes.

My hands tighten around her hips, and I can tell by her face that I'm grinding against her clit with each thrust.

"Ahhh, you're so deep," she moans, her fingers digging into my back. "You feel so good inside me."

A deep, throaty groan escapes me. Her whimpers are enough to send me over the edge.

She knows exactly what she's doing and exactly how to push my buttons.

I come hard in her tight little pussy, my hips shuddering and shaking with the force of my release. Coming like I won't stop. Because the Neanderthal in me wants to own her. Wants to make sure she's full of my cum.

Finally, I let out a deep breath and collapse on top

of her, our bodies still intertwined. I press my face tightly against her neck, devouring the scent of her skin.

She purrs in contentment against my forehead. Her legs wrap around my waist like she has no intention of letting go.

I pull away a bit to look into her eyes. "You didn't come. But we'll get there. Soon, you'll come all over my cock."

She takes her lip between her teeth and drops her gaze to my chest. "Sorry."

"Don't apologize." I place my finger under her chin and make her look at me. "You don't have to be sorry for anything. Alright?"

She nods shyly with a small smile.

"Good girl." I press a kiss to her nose. I never want her to feel like there is a problem because she doesn't climax during sex. But I'll be damned if I don't die trying. Because I'm the one who's going to get her there.

And the only guy who'll have the privilege of making her come. The thought enters my head abruptly.

I take my time with my mouth exploring her jawline, breasts, her soft stomach, and the skin just above her swollen, beautiful pussy until I can feel her breathing change and her lower stomach quiver from desire.

I gently push apart her thighs again. Her legs tense a little as if she wants to push me away, so I have to go slow. Be patient. All good things come to those who work for them.

I glance up to see her eyes closed and her arms splayed on the pillow. Slowly, I make my way to the sweet spot between her legs. I move back and forth with my mouth, my tongue flicking against her clit each time.

I don't stop until I hear those beautiful whimpers of pleasure and feel that sweet pussy let go for me.

Only me.

I watch her face contort and her breathing become jagged as she arches her back and really rides my face. She squirms and writhes above me, letting out little grunts and moans that send me wild.

"Killian," she cries out. "Oh God."

I'm certain nothing is better than this little green-eyed vixen's legs spread open for me.

She has the most beautiful pussy. Her scent, her taste, her feel... I'm fully erect again.

She shudders as she lets go of control, and I fucking own her climax. Every whimper, every breath, every shudder is mine; I own them all.

Mine.

***

Fifteen minutes later, I rouse my head from the pillow. "I should go."

"You could stay," she replies, feigning nonchalance. "It'll save you the trip home," she adds jokingly, although there's an unspoken question in there as well. "And I'll even make you coffee and breakfast in the morning."

Every night, I come to Clodagh's studio to have sex with her, but I never stay. It's a boundary I haven't crossed.

"No, I better not." I kiss the top of her forehead to soften the rejection. "But yes, you will make me coffee in the morning or else you'll be punished." I'm trying to lighten the tension of the elephant in the room.

She gives me a strained grin. "Tell me about it. My boss is a nightmare."

I haven't told her my plans to help her secure a green card, allowing her to stay in the US without issue. In a few months, when Mrs. Dalton is back and I'm no longer part of her life, she can pursue her carpentry wherever she wants.

I'll move on from this fling and be free from ridiculous daydreams about my red-haired, inked carpenter.

I think about her at work. I think about her on my run. I can't take a shower without jerking off.

My mind shifts back and forth between guilt over fucking a member of my staff—my live-in staff—and fantasizing about when I'll do it again.

It's the most obsessed I've been over a casual fling.

Which is why it needs to end.

***

It must be a midlife crisis.

That's why I'm sitting in the boardroom

321

surrounded by my business partners discussing the stalled Brooklyn casino disaster when I can only think about Clodagh.

Images run through my head. The most random, unhelpful shit.

Clodagh in her black dress at Teagan's birthday. Clodagh in her yoga pants. Clodagh scolding me for being grouchy. Clodagh's studio covered in wood. Clodagh realizing she's eating balls of butter. I smile.

"Killian?" JP's voice booms from the other end of the table, snapping me back to reality. "You know what needs to be done to get this moving. There needs to be some serious groveling on your part."

Fuck's sake. He's right. There's only one way to fix it. The mayor metaphorically has me by the balls and is squeezing tight.

"Like hell I do," I sneer. I'll be damned if I'm going to grovel to that smarmy jackass.

JP's dark eyes blaze with anger as he exhales. "You're allowing emotions to interfere with your business decisions. It needs to be fixed."

Anger flares in my chest, aimed at JP, the mayor, myself. I can't decide who I'm madder at.

"This has nothing to do with emotions," I snap. "This is about that idiot disrespecting my staff. In my own house, I might add."

"Look, just because you're losing your mind over your nanny in some ridiculous midlife crisis doesn't mean you can drag the business down with you."

Well, that confirms it, then. I must be as obvious as those old men who come into my hotel bar with much younger women draped over them.

"This isn't just about you, Killian," he continues, sounding tired. "We all have a vested interest in this casino." He turns to Connor. "Help your brother see reason, will you?"

Our standoff is interrupted by a heavy knock on the door.

Marcus appears at the doorway. "Killian, I need to talk to you. I've been trying to get ahold of you all day."

Now this is a guy who has been through multiple midlife crises.

I beckon him inside, glad for the distraction from the conversation about failed casinos. "Go ahead. What is it?"

He looks from me to Connor and JP, debating whether to speak in front of them.

"Out with it," I say impatiently.

"We did a police check on Clodagh. There are two different police forces in Ireland, the Northern Irish police and the Republic of Ireland police."

"I'm aware of that, Marcus." I sigh. Where is this going? Is everyone determined to piss me off today in this office? "I don't need a geography lesson. Get to the point."

"I screwed up. We marked the vetting process as done once the Irish Republic police force returned their response. The Northern Irish police sent theirs in afterward." He hands me his laptop, looking like he's about to wet himself with fear.

"You need to see this."

For a moment, I fail to understand what he's talking about until it hits me like a ton of bricks.

"We'll revoke her visa immediately," Marcus says quickly. "She never disclosed it at the time. I'm sorry, Killian. I'll have a replacement ASAP."

Connor and JP stare at me with wide eyes.

My nostrils flare as I read through the report. "No. I'll deal with it."

***

"Clodagh?" I shout, striding through the house. My gaze stops at the doorway of Teagan's room, where Clodagh is tidying up and bobbing her head in time with her headphones.

I tap her on the back, and she screams and jumps. "You startled me. What are you doing home so early?"

My angry expression wipes the smile off her face.

"Is there anything you want to tell me?" I ask her, barely managing to keep my voice even.

She grimaces. "Is this about your underwear? Do they feel tighter now?"

"No, not my damn underwear. Though, yes, you have managed to shrink them. *You stole a fucking car?*"

Any remaining color drains from her face as she sets down Teagan's pillow on the bed. "It's not as bad as it sounds."

"I'll be the judge of that." JP is right. My emotions are clouding my business judgment.

She cast us all under her spell. Teagan seems to idolize her now, and if she catches wind of this, it sets a terrible example.

And me?

I'm a fool. I was sucked in by her pretty face and infectious laughter, and I don't even know the person sharing our house with my daughter.

"Explain," I demand.

"Okay, okay," she whimpers, flapping her hands in the air. "Just give me a chance."

"I'm waiting," I say through clenched teeth, trying to remain calm.

She swallows hard and nods. "I was living in Belfast at the time. I told you my ex screwed me over. I was so pissed off when I left his place that I saw he'd left his keys in his shiny new car, and, well, I figured I'd take it." She lets out a little bitter laugh. "Only it wasn't his car; it was his neighbor's."

This is the most ridiculous story I've ever heard. "For fuck's sake."

I watch as her face crumples and the first of a fat tear rolls down her cheek. "It was supposed to be leverage to get some of my money back. That asshole had all my savings, and I was broke as shit. Unfortunately, the police won't accept one crime for another."

I glower at her. "How did you get past immigration? Did you lie on the form?"

She chokes back her tears. "You don't need to declare smaller offenses."

"You might be able to get away with that on a

vacation visa, but if you have anything criminal on your record, your work visa is as good as gone. We can't sponsor you anymore."

The full weight of my words hits her, and the tears flood down her face uncontrollably.

I stand rigidly; torn between wanting to comfort her and the knowledge that she lied to my company and me, and she shouldn't be in my house.

"I'm really sorry, Killian. I made a mistake," she sobs, her voice muffled as she wipes her nose on her sleeve. "I didn't know how else to get my money back."

I stare at her intently, knowing this is my perfect opportunity to end this fling between us so no one gets their heart broken.

But then those deep green eyes of hers lock on mine, and I hear myself say, "I'll fix it." Even though I know fixing this will take a miracle.

This isn't a guy I can bribe; this is immigration.

And that's when I realize that I'm much deeper into this than I thought, because the look of relief on her face melts my heart into goo.

Clodagh

I'm falling.

And not because the man has agreed to do something dodgy with my criminal record for me, but because every day I peel back another layer of Killian Quinn, and underneath the grump is actually a protective sweet guy.

TWENTY-SEVEN

Killian

A Few Days Later

"Clodagh?" I shout as I enter the kitchen. I hear noise coming from upstairs.

Coming back from work unexpectedly is becoming a habit. I tell myself today's trip is because I forgot my phone.

On the island counter are two bouquets, which weren't here when I left for work this morning, and the cards are open.

Mildly curious, I grab one and read it.

Happy birthday, Clodagh, from Sam and the security team.

Hold up, it's her birthday today? My jaw clenches. Why on earth didn't she tell me?

I pick up the second card. When I see it's from the Irish idiot who tried to kidnap her, my temperature rises further.

Why are all these men sending her flowers?

Why the hell did she tell everyone but me it was her birthday?

"Hi, Killian," comes a soft Irish voice behind me.

I turn almost defensively. "Clodagh," I say, gruffer than I meant to. "It's your birthday today?"

"Yeah," she mumbles, quickly pulling her hair up into a bun as she passes me to get to the sink.

I stand there stiffly, watching her load the dishwasher. "Why didn't you tell me?" I ask, heat creeping into my voice.

She pulls a weird face and shrugs. "I didn't want to make it a big deal."

My gaze moves toward the flowers on the counter. "But everyone else seems to know about it."

She shrugs again, like she has no explanation for that.

"I don't want you working today."

She stops loading dishes for a moment and searches my face. "Killian, you're supposed to say happy birthday. You sound kinda mad."

"I'm..." I *am* mad.

I don't say that.

She turns back to the dishes, and I stand there, wondering what the hell is wrong with me. I want to take her in my arms and tell her I'll give her the world today.

"Happy birthday," I eventually say, though my voice sounds strange. "What are you doing to celebrate?"

"Nothing glam," she answers easily. "I'm going out for dinner at a cool place in Brooklyn that has rave reviews, then we're heading over to the pub I used to work at in Queens. Funny how I've been missing it lately."

"Go ahead and use the credit card for whatever you want. You deserve it."

Her gaze meets mine for the first time since I questioned her about her birthday. "Sure. That's very kind of you, Killian."

Is it my imagination, or does she look hurt?

"Have a good time," I say in a neutral tone, then I slip away upstairs to get my phone so I don't have to witness the disappointment on her face anymore.

And maybe so she can't see mine.

***

"Put the damn phone away, Teagan," I grumble, pouring too much salt on my steak. I've trained myself not to say princess, although it's slipped out a few times. "You know it's not allowed at the dinner table."

Teagan stares at me like I asked her to put needles in her eyes.

"Becky's messaging me," she wails. "I *have* to reply."

I set the saltshaker aside and lean forward to take the phone away from her. "You see Becky every day. Seven hours a day. How can two thirteen-year-olds have so much to say to each other?"

She narrows her eyes at the audacity of the question.

I look to Connor for support, but he's busy scrolling through his damn phone. He doesn't care; he gets to be the cool uncle.

"When I was your age—"

"I didn't even have a phone," Teagan interjects, rolling her eyes as she mimics me in a gruff voice. "I know, Dad. You got a lump of coal for Christmas. Your emojis are so lame that you shouldn't even be allowed to have one anyway."

"You're the only one privy to my emojis." I shake my head and look at Connor. "Did we give Mom this much attitude when we were Teagan's age?"

Connor chuckles as he piles more fries on his plate. "I did. I was the cheeky one."

I turn back to Teagan. "I spoil you. You can have your phone back after dinner."

"Ugh." She stabs her steak with her fork. "Why are you so grumpy tonight?"

"I'm not grumpy."

But maybe I am, a little bit.

I get a vision of Clodagh in her blue jeans and lace white top, leaving the house to go to dinner. It's nine o'clock already; she'll probably be done by now, on her way to the pub where she used to work—surrounded by horny young Irish football players.

Without thinking, I fire off a text: **Do you need a ride home?**

"That's not fair!" Teagan screeches. "Uncle Connor, do you freaking see this? Dad's using his phone!"

"Work stuff," I mutter, eyes still on my phone

screen. "I'm checking in with Clodagh."

The tiny dots on the screen indicate that Clodagh is typing, then they disappear without a reply. My hackles rise.

"Where is Clodagh?" Connor asks. He knows we've been... we've been what? Fucking?

"It's her birthday." I reach to open a new beer, annoyed that Clodagh is ignoring me. Then I remind myself that she isn't working today. She isn't on the clock and isn't obligated to answer me.

Still, manners are for fucking free.

"She's in Queens."

"Uh-huh." Connor stares at me with that knowing smirk of his.

"What?" I snap.

His brow arches. "Maybe you should check in on her, make sure she's okay?"

Connor's right: I should go check on her. "The Irish idiot that ambushed her at the house might be there."

He'll try to hit on her for sure.

I should go.

Except... this is a ridiculous idea. Clodagh's a grown woman. What am I going to do, pop in unannounced at her birthday party to make sure she's okay?

"Send one of your security team if you're really that worried," Connor says casually with a hint of amusement. "She and Sam seem to be close."

My entire body goes tense.

He grins helpfully, and I feel a sudden urge to

wipe it off his face.

Fuck that. I can't sit here all night on edge.

Finishing the beer in one gulp, I stand. "Teagan, do you mind looking after your uncle Connor while I pop out?"

"She's way too cool for you, Dad," she drawls. "She's not interested."

Alarmed, I look at Connor. Teagan knows something's going on between Clodagh and me? Could my daughter be perceptive enough to tell?

He raises a brow at me in silence.

I swallow hard, my heart thumping in my chest as I look at my daughter. This is exactly the disaster I didn't want to arise.

"Clodagh and I are just... buddies," I tell her cautiously, feeling shit for lying to my own child. "I want to make sure she has a nice birthday."

My little girl lets out an eye-rolling smirk. "Yeah, yeah, whatever. She's still too cool for you."

My chest tightens as I stand there, gripping the back of the chair tightly. I shoot Connor a fleeting look of panic.

The last thing I want is for Teagan to know something's going on between Clodagh and me, the young woman who lives in our home and is supposed to be caring for my daughter. It feels like an act of betrayal to her. Maybe I want her to think of me as a dad only, not as a man or a letdown.

I study her face, feeling more flustered than I have in a long time. Should I deny it?

"You need to get her something," Teagan says.

"What?"

"Jeez, Dad, you're clueless." She rolls her eyes again with exaggerated exasperation. "It's her birthday."

Christ. She doesn't seem particularly bothered by it at all.

Connor smirks at me. "Tiffany's is open late tonight."

My face contorts into an awkward smile as I meet his eyes. He gives me an encouraging look in return.

"Okay." I give a curt nod, focusing on Teagan. "I'll see you later."

"Good luck!" she calls after me as I leave. "You'll need it."

***

Ninety minutes later, I'm walking into an Irish pub in Queens for the first time in years and am instantly deafened.

The Auld Dog – it brings back unsettling memories of O'Shea's, the pub where I had a fight before Harlow died. The first pub I ever owned. The pub that started my business. It's like opening a time capsule—all the sights, smells, and sounds bring me back to that horrible night.

The smell of stale beer hangs thick in the air. Drunken laughter drowns out the Irish band in the corner. An old man stumbles forward, trying to clumsily imitate a jig while his pals cheer him on. He teeters and then tumbles into a nearby table, knocking over a tray of beers that shatters on impact. No one seems to care.

"Fuck ye..." another old guy shouts beside me. "Are you young Joe Byrne?" Christ. Literally Christ. He's wearing a priest's collar.

"No, Father," I reply curtly.

I shake my head in disbelief. It's been a while since I've been in a pub like this.

"It's Clodagh's boss from Manhattan."

I glance behind me to see one of the ladies from yoga brassily touching my back. I give her a reserved smile before scanning the room.

"Are you coming back to yoga, honey?"

"Maybe," I murmur distractedly. I don't have time for this. I'm here for one reason only.

And there she is.

My stomach churns with the force of seeing her. My heart races, and my palms feel clammy. It's terrifying.

I watch her grab the arm of a guy who looks vaguely familiar; one of the football players. Jealousy surges through me as he touches her lower back. He says something to her that must be hilarious because she tosses her head back and flashes him her wide smile that should only be directed at me.

She's glowing.

She's happy.

I want to pull her away from the guy and everybody else and keep her all to myself.

As if sensing my heavy gaze, she turns.

And her jaw hits the floor.

TWENTY-EIGHT

Clodagh

Glacial-blue eyes burn into mine with unapologetic intensity.

Everything and everyone around me fades away. The noise in the pub recedes into nothing. Time stands still. Aidan is talking to me, but I'm not listening.

I stare at Killian across the pub, my heart in my throat. He's wearing a baseball hat and a low-key blue T-shirt, but nothing can hide how devastatingly handsome he is.

He nods in acknowledgment.

With a hitched breath, I watch as he navigates through the crowd of drinkers toward me. With every step he takes, our gazes remain connected as if tethered.

What the hell is he doing here? I knew something was off this morning. His annoyance was barely concealed under his cool, detached exterior. I didn't understand why.

It's then, as he walks toward me, that I realize I'll never get over this man. Never get over how handsome he is or how he makes me feel. On my twenty-fifth birthday, I'm living legally in New York. I've had an amazing meal and am surrounded by my best friend and people who care about me. I've never laughed so hard in my life.

But *nothing* comes close to how I feel right now as Killian Quinn approaches me.

I'm doomed.

And then he's right in front of me, within touching distance. So close I can smell his cologne, and I swear I can feel the heat emanating off his body.

"K-Killian?" I stutter as if he might be a figment of my imagination from drinking The Auld Dog's bad wine.

"Clodagh."

Is he here for happy hour?

"Your bloody boss is here?" Aidan grumbles beside me.

"Sorry, Aidan." *Please fuck off.*

I step away from Aidan toward Killian.

"What are you doing here?" I sound breathless, like I've inhaled a cigar deep into my lungs. Nervously, I tuck a strand of hair behind my ear. I need to get a grip, but Killian standing in front of me in Queens is making me go to fucking pieces. "Did I forget to do something at the house?"

"No." He looks so uncomfortable that I worry he's here to deliver bad news from Ireland like Granny Deirdre has passed away. "I'm sorry I never said happy birthday properly before."

"Oh, right." My pulse races, and I laugh nervously again because it's all I'm capable of. "Don't worry about it."

Someone shoves me from behind, and Killian grabs my arm to steady me. He pulls me closer, his glare directed over my shoulder.

Now his mouth is nearly touching my forehead.

I blink up at him, defunct of all social skills.

He tilts his head so our eyes meet, then says into my ear, "I have a present for you."

"For me?" I squeak. "You didn't have to."

"I'll give it to you and be out of your way." He looks around the noisy pub before meeting my eyes again. "You seem to be having a great time."

He rummages through his pocket with a strange look on his face.

Am I imagining it, or is he nervous?

I watch as he takes out a small box wrapped in Tiffany-blue paper.

"Here." He hands it to me. "Don't get too excited. It's nothing much."

I tear off the wrapping with fat fingers, embarrassed at my trembling hands. It must be a side effect of the wine.

"Killian," I gasp, staring down at the silver chain with a green heart. Blood floods my cheeks. "It's... beautiful."

He shrugs dismissively, but the corners of his mouth turn up in a smile.

"It matches your eyes!" someone shouts behind me.

I turn around to see the women from yoga and Orla hovering, watching us.

My brow arches as I give Orla a harsh glare. "Are you guys listening in on our conversation?"

She smacks her lips together to tell me I'm a moron. "Of course we're bloody listening."

I let out an exasperated sigh. "Go away," I hiss, shooing them away before turning back to Killian.

He smiles as he takes the necklace out of my hand. "They're right. It does match your eyes. Now turn around so I can put it on you."

I rotate, making eye contact with Orla and the women, still watching me and winking. His hands are on my neck, fastening the chain. I touch the heart and nearly jump out of my skin when I feel his lips brush my neck. A delicious shiver of pleasure runs through me.

He turns me back around to face him.

"Thank you," I choke out.

The band launches into a bad rendition of a Dropkick Murphys' song, and the pub goes wild with whooping and cheering.

I let out a girly laugh and stare at Killian. It's safe to say he's the only billionaire the pub has ever seen. It's a far cry from his fancy hotel bars.

I might be a little hysterical.

He runs a thumb possessively over my bottom lip, looking lost in thought. For a moment, I think he's going to bite it. My lips part involuntarily, and I exhale an uneven breath, my heart pounding away.

I've been sleeping with Killian for weeks.

During the day, he's still my grumpy boss, barking one-word demands and sending cryptic text messages.

Every night, he comes to my studio, and we have the most out-of-this-world sex. Going at it like horny primates. I feel all shagged out.

Every night, he leaves to sleep in his own bed. He's never promised me more than a fling.

But here, under the lights of the pub with everyone I know in Queens looking on, this moment feels like something more.

There are a million questions I want to ask. A million answers I need.

Instead, I ask, "Do you want a pint, Killian?"

He opens his mouth, but before he can respond, Liam is in our faces. "I've done some digging on you, Quinn."

"Back off, Liam." I hiss, glaring at him. Bloody Liam cockblocking me. Seriously? Why is everyone in this bar so nosy?

Liam addresses me and ignores Killian. "Don't do anything you'll regret, Clodagh."

I never lift my glare from Liam. "Do you want flowers stuffed in your mouth again?"

"You heard the lady," Killian growls in a severe tone, flashing angry eyes at Liam. "Get lost."

Liam's undeterred. "You're dangerous. I fucking know all about you."

I stare at him, clueless as to what he's blathering about.

"And now you're after our Clodagh."

"*Our* Clodagh?" I hiss at Liam. The cheek. "Who exactly are you talking on behalf of?"

Killian's arm tightens around me. "She's not your anything," he snarls, his voice dropping to a low growl. Conversations around us cease as eyes turn to us. "She's mine. Now get out of my face before I do something we'll both regret."

But Liam isn't done yet. My heart skitters as he edges closer.

I tug on Killian's shirt to get his attention before things escalate out of control. His muscles tense, and his chest rises and falls as his anger threatens to boil over.

"Let it go, please," I plead, trying to defuse the tension.

To my relief, Liam decides I'm not worth fighting for after all. He puffs out his chest but steps back, not looking so sure of himself. Perhaps because Killian is easily a head taller than him.

"Let me know when you come to your senses," he hurls at me before marching away.

I huff indignantly in response.

"I'm serious, Clodagh," Killian says in a low voice, his gaze fixed on me. I feel it right between my legs. "You belong to me." The intensity of his words hangs in the air, overshadowing any trace of Liam's outburst.

I bite back a goofy smile.

Before I can reply, his lips crash down on mine with a ferocity that takes my breath away. Every nerve in my body comes alive as I'm suddenly entangled in the most intense kiss of my twenty-five years on earth, right in the middle of The Auld Dog.

*****

I wake up in a cage.

A sexy man-cage with a muscular thigh wrapped around my hip and a heavy arm draped over my stomach. Stubble tickles my shoulder blade, and a warm chest rises up and down against me. Warm breath caresses my neck, making my nipples pebble.

God, he smells good.

He's fallen asleep in my bed. The last thing I remember was melting into his hot body and falling asleep naked in his arms.

He mumbles something near my neck.

"What?" I ask softly, confused.

"Teagan's tutu," he breathes. "Pink tutu."

"Uh, sorry?"

"It's at the buffet."

I stare up at the ceiling, trying to stifle a giggle. I remember him speaking gibberish last night; Killian is a sleep-talker, it seems. He only had a few beers last night, but he must have conked out cold. He never stays the night with me. Each time he shuts my studio door behind him, I'm reminded of the uncertain nature of our relationship; it almost makes me feel like a prostitute, considering he supplies me with a credit card.

I tilt my head, trying not to make any movement, but it's hard when his face is buried in the crook of my neck.

The clock reads six o'clock, making me an hour late for work. He's late too. He said he can't sleep past five, yet here he is, snoring and talking shit in his sleep.

So he is human.

Is it okay to tell your boss you're late for work because he's on top of you?

As if sensing my thoughts, his thigh tightens around me, and the cage gets smaller. He stirs, and I can feel something hard against my leg. Is that...?

Yes, my boss's hard dick is against my leg.

Heat floods my body, a weird combo of arousal, warmth radiating from Killian wrapped around me, and nerves at what he's going to say when he wakes up to find he's slept over.

I angle my head to get a better view of his handsome face. He has such a masculine profile. The sexy scar running through his thick brow, the strong nose, his powerful jaw, his luscious mouth —which is just as appealing whether he scowls or smiles. The formula makes for a beautiful man.

His blue eyes are hidden beneath thick lashes, and his mouth hangs open slightly. He looks more vulnerable when sleeping, like his tough exterior has dissipated.

I can study him now without hiding my feelings on my face.

Sadness washes over me. I know what we're doing won't last; it's a fling, and it'll be over when I leave this townhouse. I'm not naive. I thought I'd accepted that. I thought I could live in the moment. It's what I tell myself every day.

Yet I can't help the pang in my chest when I think of our expiry date.

I don't want to let you go.

At least when Killian and I part ways, I'll be left with one positive—I know I *can* orgasm with a guy. At least when he uses a skilled tongue.

"Are you watching me sleep?"

I stiffen beneath him. "No. How would you even know that? Your eyes are closed."

His lips curl into a smile as he slowly opens his eyes. As he stirs, his hard cock presses more firmly against my thigh, rousing him fully from sleep. "I can feel you watching me."

"Not in a stalker way," I huff, wriggling beneath him. "You know you talk in your sleep, right?"

I study him, waiting for a reaction. Relief floods me when he doesn't freak out about the fact we spent all night together.

"Did I say anything interesting?" he asks, his voice drugged with sleep.

"Something about Teagan's pink tutu."

"Ah, sounds like I was stuck in the last decade. Teagan hasn't worn a pink tutu since she was four." His mouth brushes softly against my neck.

Does he not care that he spent the night in my bed while Teagan is upstairs? I thought he hated the idea. I expected him to leap out of bed like he was in the military. Instead, he slowly lifts himself onto his forearms with a grunt.

"It's already six o'clock," I croak, waiting for him to freak out. "You overslept. And I'm late for work."

"Uh-huh," he murmurs in my ear, his face close to mine. "What excuse are you going to tell your boss?"

Have little green leprechauns taken over Killian?

"I have no idea," I whisper. "He's a real bastard."

He lets out a low chuckle.

"Seriously, are you not concerned about Teagan finding out?"

He sighs and drags a hand through his bed hair. "She knows something is going on between us. She didn't seem too upset. Maybe I'm overthinking the whole thing."

What?

Am *I* dreaming and talking in my sleep? I drop it even though *I'm* freaked at the thought of Teagan finding out.

Killian lets out a contented yawn and props both hands behind his head. He looks like he's in no rush to leave. He smiles at me. "Wow."

"Wow, what?" I wipe my mouth in case he's talking about drool on my chin.

"Your eyes. They never cease to take my breath away. I can't get over the color of them."

Oh my God, swoon alert. Be still, my poor heart. I fight a giggle. "It's because I'm a mutant. I don't know the science, but green eyes are a mutation, apparently. Did you know only two percent of the world has green eyes? I'm unique."

"That you are. Sexiest mutant I've ever seen."

Since the leprechauns are in control, I may as

well extract what I can from him. "Hey, I have a question."

"Mm-hmm," he murmurs lazily.

"What was your first impression of me when we met in the hotel? I've always wondered."

I brace myself.

"I was surprised that a beautiful young woman asked for my advice on underwear." He smirks as if remembering. "Then you started breaking shit in my hotel and dropped to your knees."

"You were very grumpy," I say with a small pout.

His brows rise. "Like I said, you were breaking shit. And you're a little thief. What else have you stolen besides soap and cars?"

"Nothing! Anyway, stuff in hotels is fair game."

"Not unless you're a resident. Which you were not." He chuckles. "But I'll admit that I have thought about you wearing that lingerie and choker quite a few times since then."

Oh. My insides are turning to goo. "Good thing I bought it then."

He seems to like this idea as his eyes blaze with heat. He rises onto his forearms, holding his weight up, and impatiently pushes my legs apart with his thigh. "Fuck my early morning meeting. Fuck them all; they can wait. This can't."

I feel a tiny shiver of nervous excitement. He's all man. He would crush me if he let himself drop.

"Next time, wear the choker," he growls as his hand travels down my stomach until he finds the sensitive spot between my legs.

My toes curl as his fingers tease my clit, pleasure rippling out in little waves through my body. "Yes, sir," I breathe, looking right into his eyes. "Whatever you want."

This seems to tip him over the edge. His hand closes over my jaw as he pushes himself into me.

I tense up a bit before my body relaxes into the rhythm of his thrusts.

God. *This man feels so good inside me.* My legs wrap around his waist, my feet digging into his butt.

"Clodagh," he groans, and I swear there is a hint of love in his voice and the way he looks at me.

In this moment, we have an invisible bond that only we can feel. I feel warm and happy and content. If I were a poet, I'd say our souls were speaking.

The muscle in his jaw jumps as his gaze drops to my breasts, bouncing with each thrust; I can tell he's close now. He breathes heavier, his focus slipping. His face contorts, beautiful jaw slacking, eyes drowning in lack of control.

With a heated growl into my neck, he explodes inside me.

No, Killian Quinn. I'm not giving you up.

***

"What are your plans for when Mrs. Dalton returns, and I no longer need you?"

My smile drops. Now he's half dressed and back in business mode. An unpleasant feeling rises in my stomach. I know he's talking about the job, but his words feel personal. They cut.

I slowly climb off the bed and reach for my leggings. "The agency might have found me a couple who need an au pair," I say, hoping he can't hear the edge to my tone. "It's only three days a week, so the other two days I'm going to focus on building up some inventory to sell. Orla and I are going to try to find somewhere affordable in Brooklyn. Not the fancy part, obviously. We're checking out the cute district with the large Polish and Hungarian community." I'm rambling. "Do you know it?"

For some reason, this irritates him. "I know it." He pulls his T-shirt over his head and looks at me. "Do you even want to be an au pair?"

"Not really. But not everyone loves their job, right? I want to stay in New York, so this is a compromise."

"I'm working on a permanent solution for you."

My hand freezes as I reach for my vest top. "What?"

"A green card," he says as if he were talking about getting me a hot dog from a street stand. "Not tied to the hotel. A green card that means you can work anywhere you want and stay for as long as you want." His brow furrows like he's scolding a child. "And you should start charging for those yoga classes on Saturday, by the way."

He says it so casually.

Green card. Like it's a bus pass or something instead of a permanent pass to the States.

My pulse skyrockets.

Don't get excited.

"Really?"

He nods. "Really. I'll help you put together a business plan."

"Business plan?" I squawk because, apparently, I'm a useless parrot now.

He slips his foot into a shoe. "For how you'll make carpentry work for you in New York. Quinn & Wolfe has a team that helps small businesses get on their feet; we'll get you in to pitch. I can be there if you need me to."

I might actually wet myself if he keeps talking. Or cry. Or pass out.

All these magical words coming out of his mouth. He can't just bounce around suggestions like these and not expect me to have a meltdown.

"I..." I struggle around the lump in my throat, too overwhelmed to process anything. "I don't know what to say. Thank you."

"It's fine," he says grumpily, now fully dressed. He smooths down his T-shirt. "Right, I'd better get—"

"Why, Killian?" I ask loudly. I never interrupt him.

"Why what?"

"Why would you do this for me?"

"Because I can."

"Not because you care about me." My voice is barely audible, but I have to press. He has to give me something.

His brow furrows. The muscles of his face tense visibly. "Of course I care about you."

"I don't understand where I stand with you," I say,

embarrassed to feel hot tears in my eyes. "I've turned twenty-five; I'm supposed to be sowing wild oats. I know this is just a fling. But…"

But what?

He edges closer and speaks, his voice almost a growl. "You don't believe your Irish idiot? That I'm dangerous?"

My eyes widen. "No! Of course not. And he's not *my* idiot."

He takes a long look at me, scrutinizing my face. "Do you know what he meant?"

"I think he was talking shit."

"He wasn't." His jaw hardens as he crosses his arms and towers above me. "You should take him seriously."

"What do you mean?" I ask in a small voice, a trickle of fear running through me. Is Killian about to tell me Mrs. Dalton is locked away in the attic or something morbid?

He gazes at me for another long beat, debating whether to tell me something.

I watch his Adam's apple bob thickly in his throat and stay silent.

"It's my fault Harlow died," he finally says in a husky voice. "She was shot in a botched robbery because I gave her an engagement ring worth a quarter of a million dollars. Something she didn't even want." His lips twist into an angry grimace. "She was killed because she had diamonds and no security. Both my fault. Both led to her death."

"Oh, I didn't… I didn't know that." Shit. That's

horrific. What the hell do I say? My mind goes blank as I try to come up with something comforting. Unease creeps up my scalp as I scramble for the right words, wishing I knew how to make him feel better.

I reach up to run my fingers through his hair, but he tenses up. "It's not your fault, Killian. You can't blame yourself," I say, trying to reassure him, but it doesn't do any good. He's stuck in his own self-blame spiral.

He grunts in response like he's had the conversation before.

I'm lost for words. After a long pause, I ask quietly, "Is that why you have so much security?"

It makes sense now.

"I had security back then, not a ton, but it would have been enough." His throat bobs. "Harlow and I split up. She moved out, and her new place didn't have security. I didn't think she needed it."

He takes a deep breath and shakes his head, a dark laugh slipping out. "I was wrong," he says flatly. "Very fucking wrong. The only saving grace is that Teagan was at Mom's."

My heart breaks for him. I can't imagine what it feels like, but if the haunted look in his eyes is any indication, I never want to experience it.

"But that doesn't make you dangerous. It wasn't your fault." I shake my head in disgust. "I'm going to wring Liam's neck for saying that to you."

He gives a slight shrug. "A stupid rumor went around Queens. I went to her apartment that night and had a massive argument with a guy she was with. People saw us fighting and thought I had something to do with what happened next. It pops up every now and then, usually when someone's trying to stir up trouble."

I exhale heavily as the gravity of his situation sinks in.

"So now you know." His lips tug into a weak smile, though it doesn't quite hide the sadness in his eyes.

"I'm sorry, Killian," I say, burying my face into his neck. I wrap my arms around him, knowing it will take much more than a hug to get rid of his demons.

"You make me feel safer than anyone else in the world," I whisper.

TWENTY-NINE

Clodagh

One Week Later

For the first time since I've moved into the townhouse, Killian is working from home. He *never* works from home.

I'm suspicious. Is he keeping tabs on me? But he's got cameras for that. He promises he doesn't, but I don't know...

Occasionally, he surprises me over the speaker. Sometimes hearing his low, husky American drawl pumping through the speakers is pretty sexy. A nice distraction from bed making.

Sometimes it's not.

Last week, I farted loudly, and two minutes later, Killian spoke to me over the loudspeaker. I've been agonizing over whether he heard me or not since then. I'm pretty confident Americans don't fart as much as the Irish. My ex thought letting one rip in front of me was a rite of passage.

353

But since I moved in with Killian, I haven't heard him release any.

My phone buzzes for the millionth time today.

Killian: Water refill.

Demanding git. I've been running around all day for him, bringing up cups of coffee and tea and lunch and smoothies. If he were a boyfriend, I'd tell him to refill his own fucking water. But he's not. He's my arrogant live-in boss who I'm having a casual fling with.

And I'm a weak woman because it's turning me on.

He looks so grumpy every time I visit his office to fulfill his latest demand that he might as well have "do not disturb" tattooed across his forehead. He's always on the phone yelling at some poor schmuck. I love my new American vocabulary.

I smirk to myself. Perhaps I need to liven his workday up a little.

Yes, sir, I text back.

I hurry down to my studio and slip into the lingerie and choker ensemble Killian had caught me fawning over in the hotel that first day we met. I douse myself in perfume, brush my teeth, and touch up my makeup.

A quick mirror check says I look good. No stray hairs. No belly bloat.

Efficiency is key. I only have twenty minutes before I need to be out the door. He's given me the most mundane task ever. I have to wait at City Hall to get some paperwork done, so I can't even have lunch. What a tyrant.

I head back upstairs, my heels clicking on the marble floor. I *really* hope the security guys aren't watching through the camera.

I pause outside his door, adjusting my bra, and then knock. It's hard to predict how this'll go. He could go nuclear on me and throw me out for interrupting his work.

"Come in," he calls.

I step inside with the jug of water.

He's behind his huge desk, a frown etched over his face as he glares at the monitor. Fortunately for me, I'm out of sight, so if he's on a video call, no one can see the lingerie-clad nanny maid who has entered the room.

For a moment, he doesn't even glance up. "JP, stop going around in circles." His lips press together tightly. His gorgeous, thick dark locks flop over his forehead, and I resist the urge to swoon.

I'm a powerful temptress.

"I've found a way around the mayor's—fuck."

Fuck is right.

I have his full attention now.

Jaw hits floor. Smack. Fucking. Bang.

His mouth hangs open as he takes me in with his eyes, from head to toe.

It's possible I didn't think this through. There has always been something intimidating about him, but now he looks downright dangerous.

I strut forward with slight apprehension as I try to figure out whether he's angry, aroused, or a bit of both.

"Killian?" a male voice, possibly JP's, says from the speaker system. "Is someone there, or am I boring you?"

"Yes," Killian says in a low voice, eyes on me. His hands tighten around the edge of the desk.

"Yes, I'm boring you?" JP sounds really pissed now. "What the fuck are you looking at? We have twenty-four hours to sort this out, or the casino is dead in the water."

Fighting a giggle, I innocently set the water jug down on his desk and resist the urge to lean over and wave at JP. It would make for an interesting story.

Killian glares at me so ferociously I'm surprised I haven't been stripped of my underwear.

"Alfred Marek sent us a letter backed by the fucking mayor himself," JP rants, oblivious to my presence. "Going by the expression on his face when he stormed out of your house, I don't think it's an idle threat. This isn't just a silly little local protest now."

Huh. Seems Alfred is a more common name than I thought. Like the guy I had to ghost from Central Park.

Killian mumbles something about casino builds. I don't know what; I'm too focused on clenching my ass cheeks together and looking seductive.

"That made no sense," JP barks. "Are you even listening?"

"No," Killian says, still staring at me instead of the screen. Boobs. That's what he's thinking.

He taps something on the keyboard. "I'll call you later."

Since I've fulfilled my duty of delivering him his citrus-infused water, I turn to leave.

"Wait," he growls, beckoning me like a king with his servant. "Come here."

I turn to face him.

"Sorry I interrupted your call," I say, smiling innocently at him. Lies.

"It can wait." He grabs my hand and pulls me until I'm straddling his lap. His fingertips skim along the edge of my lingerie, sending a jolt of pleasure through me. "This is a nice surprise, my little car thief."

His dick thinks so too. It pushes against my crotch like a hard, immovable rock.

I sling my arms around his neck and press my hips up against his. My plan is to cocktease him for a few minutes, then leave. Payback for making me wait ninety minutes outside city hall.

"Is the mayor giving you shit because of what happened at the dinner party?" I don't like that thought. How did I end up triggering a feud over a casino?

His grip on my lower back tightens. "Just some hiccups with the build. Nothing to stress about. One of the local businesses is protesting the construction."

"Why?"

He shrugs. "They don't want us to build there."

I think of the times that Orla and I have

visited Brooklyn for dinner or walked alongside the Brooklyn Bridge Park and stared at the tall financial towers in the city. "I get it."

"What do you mean, you get it?"

"Imagine if some big shot wanted to bulldoze The Auld Dog and Tony's bagel store. The whole area would go nuts."

"That pub looks like it should have been demolished years ago. The restroom was a biohazard."

I roll my eyes. "Tell me about it; I used to clean those toilets. I saw the worst side of humanity. Anyway." I jab him in the chest with my finger. "That's not the point at all."

He quirks his brow. "What is the point?"

"You know some of the older men there have nowhere else to go? It's the only place they get to talk to people. Like Mr. McNearney—he's seventy-five, his wife passed away years ago, and he has no family left. He goes there every single day, even on Christmas Day. The pub stays open just for him and a few others, and they do a wee roast for them. Community is so important, you know?"

Killian stares at me intently for a long time, and I wonder if I've smeared lipstick on my cheek or something embarrassing like that.

"Would *you* want to live beside a casino?" I ask him.

He doesn't answer me.

My fingers close firmly around his strong jawline. "Are you alright?"

His response is a slow nod.

His eyes drop downward, and a tortured groan erupts from his throat. "We don't have time for this."

"I know," I huff. "I'm going to City Hall now."

"You're not. You're going on a helicopter ride over Manhattan."

"Say what?"

"I found your bucket list."

"Oh my God! How?"

"It was quite easy, considering you left a piece of paper with a huge title called 'Clodagh's New York bucket list' on the table in the kitchen."

"So I don't need to wait in line?"

He chuckles. "Nope. That was a ruse."

I let out a loud screech and jiggle my legs. "You know that this could be considered pretty romantic, right?"

"Calm down," he grumbles. "It's just another commute for me."

Whatever. I'm flying over the Empire State Building.

As I smile in glee about my helicopter ride (Granny Deirdre is going to lose her shit), Killian unclasps my bra and latches onto my nipple.

Boobs.

What is it with guys and boobs?

I think they want what they don't have.

I think back to my first conversation with Marcus, where I was worried about having to let some rich old billionaire suckle on my breasts.

Ha. It's funny how things turn out.

***

"No shit, Orla, we were so close to the Empire State spike I thought it was gonna skewer us!"

Bouncing. It's the only way I can describe how I'm traveling down Fifth Avenue to the townhouse. I'm buzzing after my bird's-eye experience of New York.

Now I'm by myself, talking to Orla. Killian had to go back to the office.

"I'm so jealous," she moans down the line.

"And we passed that huge apartment complex. We always wanted to know what the inside was like. Well, now I know! I took some pics for you. I'll send them over. Killian said he owns some apartments there."

"Next time, take me with you, for fuck's sake."

"I will. I didn't even know we were doing it today." Now I know why he was working from home—to surprise me.

"Did he say anything more about the green card?"

"No. I don't want to press him. He said it so casually, like it was no big deal." I blow out a breath as I reach Killian's house. "I just don't know. It means he has all the power. What's worse? Killian deciding my fate or a random au pair agency? It feels weird now that I'm sleeping with him." I pause for a moment. "Maybe I should take the nanny job."

"Bollocks. That's your Catholic guilt talking. When a billionaire guy wants to give you a green card, you take the green card."

Someone clears their throat behind me.

Still holding the phone, I turn to see familiar light-blue eyes. It takes me a moment to register... The last time I saw him was that day in Central Park.

The guy I was supposed to go on a date with. Alfred.

He stands watching me with a smirk, his hands in his pockets. My female spidey-senses activate.

What are the chances of him walking past here?

"Orla, I gotta go. Someone I know is here."

My pulse quickens as he smiles at me, waiting for me to get off the phone. In hindsight, I should have kept Orla on the phone.

Relax, Clodagh, you're being ridiculous. This is *Fifth Avenue.*

He smiles. "Fancy seeing you here."

I swallow and give a tight smile in response. "Hi. How are you?"

"Great."

An uncomfortable silence hangs between us.

"Er, what are you doing in the area?" I finally ask.

He gestures up the steps. "This is where you live, right? I figured I'd come and see how you were doing."

What the fuck? Who does that?

My spidey-sense radar goes off the charts. I climb another step of the townhouse, my heart pounding. "That's not cool. How did you find out where I live?"

I think over our text conversations. I told him I worked for Killian.

"What's the matter?" he says with an irritated

edge to his tone. "You seemed interested. Why the change of heart?" He takes a step up the steps to the townhouse. Too close, jackass. "Aren't you going to let me in?"

"No." Fear creeps up my spine. This guy is nuts. It's time to end this conversation. "I'm not interested. I'm seeing someone. And it's downright creepy to come to my address."

Do I go in the house or make a mad dash down the street?

He knows I live here, and I'm not sure I could outrun him.

Plus, I can always press the panic button if I'm in the house.

My heart pounds as I quickly move toward the retina scanner at the door.

In the reflection, I make out his face directly behind me.

Jesus Christ, this is actually happening. I'm going to end up in someone's attic.

The door buzzes open, and I lunge at it.

THIRTY

Killian

Now I understand what "rose-tinted glasses" are. I've seen New York a hundred times from a helicopter, but not through Clodagh's eyes. Her squeals of delight were so distracting I worried we were going to career into one of the skyscrapers.

It was the most excited I've seen anyone since Teagan met the pop star runt.

I look forward to making more items on her bucket list happen. I want her to have all the experiences she's dreamed of. And I'd like to be there to see at least some of them. Except for the *Sex and the City* tour.

"What are you smiling about?" Connor interrupts my thoughts.

I snap my eyes from the skyscrapers outside the boardroom window to Connor and raise a brow. I'm now back in the office for a late afternoon meeting. "Am I not allowed to smile?"

"It's a little weird when we're discussing the mayor filing a lawsuit against you for an alleged physical altercation. Especially when you're doing the smiling, Killian."

I roll my eyes in disgust. "It was a gentle scuffle. I've seen worse at a Red Sox game."

"Yeah, well, he's pissed, and he wants to have something over you," JP grates over the video link. "And our application fee to the state is in danger of going from one mil to two because of this."

"He can go to h—" The shrill tone of my phone cuts through my chest like a knife. Jesus Christ.

Code red. It's the sound I only expect to hear during a drill test.

I snatch my phone up from the table as Connor looks at me, alarmed. "Yes?" I ask sharply.

"Sir," Angus, one of the security team, says on the other side of the line. "An intruder attempted to break into the property. The police have been informed. He tried to tailgate behind Clodagh."

I instantly freeze. "Is she okay?"

"Yes, sir. She took a tumble down the steps, but she's fine. Her wrist is swollen, so we're on our way to the hospital to check if it's broken or sprained. The property has been checked and remains secure. It's fine."

"It's not fucking fine!" I roar. This can't be fucking happening again. "Where is she?"

"Mount Sinai hospital on 5th, sir. She didn't want to go, but we insisted. She kept talking about a magic, hmm, some magic show she wants to go to this evening."

"Magic Mike." I heave a sigh of relief. If she's

arguing with the security team about what's next on her bucket list, she can't be severely hurt.

"Who's the guy?" I ask in a lower, calmer tone. "What was he after?"

I've had a few nutcases attempt to break into my townhouse over the years.

"The guy's name is Alfred Marek. Sam said he was linked to the family causing trouble with your casino in Brooklyn."

Every hair on my body stands on end, and I'm on my feet in an instant.

"Killian?" Connor asks, worry lines creasing his brow.

"A guy in his twenties?" I bark into the phone.

"That's correct, sir."

My jaw clenches in anger. "Where is Marek now?"

"He's with the police being questioned. It's doubtful we'll get anything to stick. We got there before anything could escalate."

"See you at the hospital. Make sure Clodagh has people with her until I'm there."

I buzz Mandy on the intercom, my heart pounding in my chest. "Mandy, have a car waiting downstairs. I'm going to the hospital."

I don't even stop to acknowledge Connor and JP. Standing up, I stride out the door, the smile well and truly wiped from my face.

***

I hear her before I see her. My stride quickens. She's

laughing. Her distinct Irish lilt provides a welcome respite from the suffocating dread that had built up within me on the way to the hospital. It echoes down the hospital hallway, leading me to the room where Clodagh is.

Clodagh is perched on top of the bed when I walk into the room, legs swaying back and forth over the side. Sam and Angus lean against the wall, chatting with her.

They immediately stiffen when they see me. I give the guys a nod of acknowledgment and turn to Clodagh.

"Are you okay?" My voice comes out hoarse.

"Yeah," she says breezily. "Private healthcare is sick, as Teagan would say. That means good. I feel like I'm in a spa here. You know, even the colonics on those posters out there look appealing. I might add one to my bucket list." She leans back in the bed. "Oh, by the way, did you know we're in the plastic surgery ward? That's why all the patients are so good-looking."

"Really?" I mumble with a small smile, standing awkwardly in the hallway.

A lump lodges in my throat as I struggle to keep a tight rein on my emotions. I'm afraid if I step any closer, I won't keep them in check. She has no idea what's going on in my head. "I let you down again. I failed to keep you safe."

"What? No! This one's on me." She stops swinging her legs and looks at me a bit sheepishly. "Sorry, Killian."

I frown, taken aback. "What the hell are you apologizing for?"

"I lied when I said no more guys were going to kidnap me." She winces. "I attract *cray-cray*," she says in a weird high-pitched voice.

I have no idea what that means. "What?"

"*Crazy.*" She rolls her eyes, smirking at me. "I forget you're an old guy sometimes. Teagan taught me it."

I give her a small smile in return.

Her brows scrunch together in confusion as she studies me. "What's wrong? Are you mad? Did I breach some security rules or something?"

I pinch the bridge of my nose and almost laugh bitterly at her question. She's asking if *I'm* mad at *her*? Her wrist is bruised and swollen, and it's my fault; she was lucky nothing worse happened to her. I'm the worst thing that could have happened to her.

"No, Clodagh. Of course, I'm not mad." I take a step closer to her. I want to take her in my arms and kiss her. "This is a direct result of living with me. This is all my fault for putting you in this situation."

"Nah." She shakes her head. "You didn't. He asked me out a few weeks ago, and when I stopped talking to him, he didn't take it well."

"Wait, what?" My eyes widen. Son of a bitch. "He was the guy messaging you? The one you mentioned at Teagan's birthday?"

"Yeah. I was gonna meet him until..." Her cheeks flush as her gaze travels over to the security guys trying to pretend they aren't eavesdropping. Except for Connor, no one knows about us, and Teagan only has a vague idea.

She turns back to me, looking pensive. "He was on the street when I came back this afternoon. Just waiting around. You should have seen his face when the security squad came out of nowhere. It was like a Bond movie."

I take a deep breath, my mind racing with questions. What was the fucker planning? "The guys said you tumbled down the steps."

"I'm not sure who to blame for that. I might have fallen backward myself."

I'm silent for a minute, studying her.

"It seems he was tailing you. The team explained to me on the way here. He knew you worked for me and lived here." I feel sick saying it out loud. "He was using you to gain access to the property."

Her mouth forms a little O, and the light in her eyes fades slightly.

Her phone beeps beside her on the bed. "Ugh," she mutters, reading the text message. "I told Orla, and Orla, the snitch, told my mum. Now Granny Deirdre is blowing up the family group chat."

She holds up her phone so I can see it.

"Read it out to me," I say quietly, too uneasy to focus on the screen.

"She says New York is full of hoodlums, and my life is in danger. She wants me to take the first plane back home," she recites while rolling her eyes. "This is all Orla's fault."

I stare at her. "Right."

"Jeez, you're grumpy," she mumbles under her breath. "You were fun on the helicopter."

A doctor appears in the doorway. As soon as he sees me, he does a double take. "Mr. Quinn." He glances back and forth between Clodagh and me. "I'm here to talk to Clodagh."

I nod and gesture for him to come in.

He moves forward, smiling. "X-ray looks good. You have some deep bruising but no sprain. Take it easy on your wrist for the next week or so."

Grinning, Clodagh pumps the air with her uninjured hand. "Does that mean I get to go?"

"You can indeed."

"Awesome." She hops off the bed. "Teagan will be home from school soon. I need to make dinner. I hope you're not expecting a gourmet feast from a one-handed chef."

My stomach clenches as I watch her. "You're not cooking. I'll cook."

"Shut up." She laughs. "That I have to see."

My jaw locks tight. She's so carefree, so oblivious to how differently this could have gone. The naivety of someone who has never experienced deep tragedy. A crushing guilt descends upon me like a physical presence in the room.

"Boss," Sam says from behind me. "Sorry, we shouldn't have called a code red. It wasn't this time."

This time.

I failed her again.

This ends now. I know what I have to do, even if it means shattering my heart in the process.

THIRTY-ONE

Clodagh

I follow the sea of suits through the revolving doors into the elegant lobby of Killian's glittering skyscraper. It's funny how I can forget that Killian owns a chain of hotels and casinos and isn't just a snarky, hot, grump with an OnlyFans subscription he likes to use in the shower.

Click, click, click. Tap, tap, tap. There is no way I could listen to that sound all day long. There's nothing worse than the incessant clicking of a stiletto heel on a hard surface.

If I had to work in an office, I'd want to work in a cool, dog-friendly, hipster office in a converted warehouse where you can wear jeans.

Everything here is evil high-gloss gleaming with the malicious shine of a corporate establishment. The water feature in the center of the reception area does nothing to create the calming and tranquil feel it's designed for.

I scuttle along in my squeaky sneakers toward the sexy reception desk dodging busy businessmen and women coming from all angles.

Huh. Sneakers. I didn't think "trainers" first in my head. I'm so American now.

"Hey." A guy suddenly cut across my path, making me stop. "Do you have any of those small sausages with leek filling?"

"Erm, excuse me?"

"Sausages," he repeats himself louder. Alright, so I heard him correctly the first time. "With the leek stuffing."

I rack my brain for a task I've missed. Is this what I'm here for today? Killian wants sausages filled with leeks? It's a bit random, but he's been acting strange the past few days, so anything is possible.

"No, sorry. I don't have any on me."

"Okay, when will you?" he snaps.

"Hmm, is this for Killian?"

He looks at me like I've sprouted an extra head, and then a light bulb seems to go on in his brain.

"Oh. You're not the trolley girl."

"Nope. Not her." I glare at him. "But if I see a girl with sausages I'll be sure to send her your way."

He grunts and walks on, no further use for me.

What a charmer.

I reach the sleek reception desk with a man and a woman behind it. It's so large they must have to use microphones to talk to each other.

"Hi," I say to the receptionist lady, in the same voice I use with Siri. "I'm here to see Killian."

She gives me an amused once-over. The humans here are all so intimidating. I feel a tad self-conscious. In my defense, the holes in my blue jeans are by design. I'm wearing the bunny T-shirt because I know it drives him crazy. In a good way, I think.

She laughs in my face. "*Killian*? Killian who?"

A video of Killian and Connor being interviewed plays on the large LCD screen behind her. It's distracting.

In return, I smile sweetly. "Killian, whose name is on the big sign outside the building? The guy on the widescreen behind you."

She sees my sweet smile and raises it with her own saccharine passive-aggressive smile. "I don't think so, honey. Please leave."

"No, wait," I start before she can alert security. "He asked me to come. I can call him if you don't believe me."

Her brow arches into a severe line with as much belief as if I told her a group of little fairies was outside. "And you are?"

"His beck-and-call girl," I say sarcastically. "Clodagh Kelly."

Her eyes narrow. "I'll call his receptionist and find out, beck-and-call girl."

She picks up the phone and talks to someone. "A Clodagh Kelly is here to see Mr. Quinn."

"Uh-huh." She talks on the phone, narrowing her eyes so much that I am surprised she can see. "Uh-huh." There's a pause as she stares at me. "Uh-huh." Her face screws up with an array of emotions ranging from confusion... irritation... curiosity, and finally... is that *jealousy*?

The phone is slammed down.

"Here's your visitor's pass." She hands me the pass over the desk, devastated that I'm allowed up. "Take the elevator to the seventh floor. Someone will meet you there."

No retina scan. I'm surprised.

"Thank you." I smirk at her, resisting the urge to blurt out that I'm boning the boss.

Taking the pass, I make my way to the lift.

My ears pop as I ascend. The elevators have nice music and show surround video of New York as I travel, like the Empire State Building does.

The elevator dings as the doors slide open. Thankfully, someone with a friendlier face is waiting for me.

"Hi, Clodagh," the lady says to me. "I'm Mandy."

"Hi. We've talked on the phone a few times."

"I know. I couldn't forget your accent. Come on, I'll take you to his office."

I hope that's a compliment.

She smiles and motions for me to follow her. Nerves take over as I walk through the bustling open-plan office. A million conversations are going on.

I feel so out of place. Why couldn't Killian call me instead? This is weird.

I see a face I know. "Hi, stranger," I call out to Marcus.

He twitches slightly, then tries to cover it with a smile. "Clodagh," he says, stopping in front of me. "Lovely to see you again."

"You too," I say cheerily. "I never got to thank you properly for giving me a chance."

He looks at me wearily. Has Killian told him about us? "I hope you've enjoyed your time in New York so far?"

"Yeah." I start to tell him about the things I've done on my bucket list, but I cut it short when I sense he wants to run away from me. He's practically edging away while we talk.

"That's... nice," he says with a nod. "Just make sure you make the most of it."

He sets off in a trot down the hall. He was way more composed the last time I met him. The man can't get away from me quick enough.

Very weird, indeed.

I follow Mandy to the offices around the corner from the open-plan area. I've never been in Killian's office before.

I smooth out my T-shirt and fix my hair as Mandy knocks on his office door.

"Come in," a deep, husky voice calls out after a minute.

Killian stands staring out the window when I enter, his feet spread apart and a palm pressed against the glass. An ass begging to be squeezed by me.

My knees buckle inward ever so slightly, and my spine shivers. So this is what a physical swoon is.

Pull yourself together, woman.

"Hi, Killian," I say brightly.

He doesn't turn his head to look at me. Maybe it's a

requirement of the job to be aloof and distant in the office. It would fit with all the movies I've seen.

I didn't even think "*film*." I'm so American.

Without glancing in my direction, he orders me to take a seat.

Since he's not even looking at me, I assume it's the seat on the other side of his desk.

I take a seat, crossing my legs, and Killian finally turns to meet my gaze. His expression is entirely blank.

I shift in my seat, feeling a tad uneasy. What's wrong with him? I thought he was quiet this morning, and last night, he told me he wanted me to get a good night's sleep, so he didn't come to my studio.

I know this is his office, but no one is here, and he is the boss, after all, so I'm surprised I didn't get a kiss. Or ideally more, because he looks so handsome in the dark-blue suit.

He takes a seat behind his large desk. Maybe he's really strict on upholding his own company policy? His eyes wander to the bunny on my T-shirt, then return to meet mine.

"What's up?" I ask, a bit of fear creeping into my voice as my female intuition sounds off.

"How's your wrist?"

"It's fine," I reply, not for the first time. I suppress the impulse to roll my eyes because he's being sweet. He asked me if I wanted to go to *therapy* yesterday to get over what happened with Alfred. He's being a tad dramatic.

"Look." He tents his hands together on the table. "This may seem callous to do here, and for that, I apologize. I'm not trying to hurt you. I thought it better to do this away from the house."

"Do what?" I ask in a strangled voice.

He pauses. "Clodagh, you knew this wasn't going to be a long-term arrangement. You understand that, don't you?"

I blink at him, confused. "Are we talking about us... or my job?"

He doesn't answer. A brief flicker of emotion passes across his face before settling into a stern mask.

I feel a pit form in my stomach. I don't speak. I wait for the bombshell to drop: job or us?

"With everything that's happened, it would be best if your time with Teagan and I ends ahead of schedule."

I may as well have inhaled knives; his words are so painful. I stare at him, aghast. "Y-You mean you're firing me?" I stammer out.

He frowns. "I don't want you to see it like that. You'll still be paid up to the last day of your contract. The circumstances have changed, and it's not a good fit anymore."

"Not a good fit..." I repeat, my head spinning.

I don't understand. He wants to get rid of me?

Why is he talking like this? Why is he being so cryptic?

I sit very still and try not to cry. Because what did I expect? This was inevitable. This is stupid, why am

I reacting like this? I'm not on my period. It's just a job. It was going to come to an end in a few weeks.

"Clodagh, I care about you. I want to make sure everything is smooth for you. I have some apartments in Manhattan and Brooklyn ready for you and Orla to pick from today. Rent will be covered, of course, and you'll have a green card guaranteed."

I tuck my foot underneath me and grip my knee as I try to read his expression. He's distant and closed off.

So he wants me to live in an apartment, paid for by him, but not work for him? I feel like a hooker.

Is this because he wants us to make a proper go of our relationship, and he doesn't think it will work if I'm working for him?

"I thought we were doing okay living together and seeing each other," I murmur, attempting a smile. "I didn't think it caused problems."

"It does for me." His eyes hold mine. "We made a mistake. *I* made a mistake. This is all on me. I should never have put you in a compromising position."

"I'm not in a compromising position," I argue back. Why is he saying all this stuff? "It's fine."

He looks away from me and down at his hands. "You won't need to worry. You'll have an apartment, visa, eventually a green card, and the same allowance as you have here for as long as you need." He smiles sadly. "You'll have time to pursue your carpentry career again."

My eyes widen. I want to get up and shake him by

the shoulders. "I'm not after a sugar daddy, Killian. Do you not get how this sounds? Bloody icky."

He stares at me with the same coldness he had when we first met. "It won't be like that. You and I won't see each other anymore."

My breath stalls in my lungs as the reality of his words hits me. "Are you breaking up with me or firing me?"

He shifts uneasily in his seat, and I have my answer.

Stinging tears prick my eyes. "Oh my God. Both."

I'm such a fool. He doesn't know the stupid fantasies going on in my head. How foolish of me to think that we had some kind of future together, that he was mine, that we could be something more.

For weeks, I've been living in this stupid rosy bubble as I bounce around New York, fulfilling my bucket list and spinning dreams of a future shared with Killian.

"Is this about Alfred?" I ask, my voice barely staying level. "I stopped messaging him as soon as we became exclusive. I—"

"No," he cuts in sharply.

I search his eyes, looking for the truth. None of this makes sense. This past week, he was opening up to me. I *know* I saw emotion in his eyes.

"It's about him confronting me, right? You're spooked because you think you put me in danger. I don't care, Killian. I'm fine. I—"

"It's not that, Clodagh."

His gaze is so icy that I believe him. I saw what

my heart wanted to see because I was falling in love with him. It wouldn't be the first time.

"So it really was temporary." I laugh bitterly. "The sex was just a side perk of the job."

"I never promised you a future."

I stare at him, waiting for some type, any type, of emotion. Begging for a sign to show he's affected by what he's doing. How can he sit here watching me, so stoic and detached, as my heart shatters?

His jaw tightens; it's the only sign of emotion visible on his cold face. "A replacement starts in three days."

I grip the edge of my seat for support. It would have been less painful if he had slapped me across the face. A horrible vision comes to mind of another girl in her twenties moving in, rubbing arms with Killian in the morning, sharing dinner, sharing a bed.

"Why are you really ending this, Killian?"

"It's not good for either of us. I can't give you what you need. What you deserve. You'll thank me in time."

"Sounds like a line," I sneer. How many times has he said this before? I jump up from the seat. I can't bear another minute of this agony. "Fine. I'll go home and pack my things and be out of your way. You can stuff your visa, your apartment, your allowance, and your bloody blue eyes, and your..." I draw in a sharp breath. "Your fancy tartare restaurants up your arsehole!" I shriek. I don't want the American Dream that way.

His eyes glint as he stands abruptly. "Clodagh—"

"Don't get up." This time, it's my turn to cut him off. I give him a look that I hope is as cold as his. "I'll show myself out."

Feeling faint, I march toward the door and flip him the bird before slamming the door behind me.

My exit is met with a loud crash from the other side of the room, like a fist hitting a desk.

***

Due to my zombie-like state, it takes me an extra hour or so to get home.

Home.

What the hell am I talking about? Killian's Fifth Avenue townhouse isn't *my* home.

Where the fuck did it all go wrong? When did I let my feelings get involved? I ignored the expiration date I knew we had and blew this fling up to be something more in my head.

Killian never truly cared about me.

Sure, he wanted me to feel protected. He wanted to show me New York. He wanted my company and body, but he didn't want to be with *me*.

That's where I went wrong.

I stand in front of the retina scanner at the door of the townhouse, wondering if it can detect my identity past the mess of red eyes.

Sam is picking me up in an hour to take me—air quotes—"anywhere I want to go." Anywhere so long as I'm gone by the time Killian is back from work.

I have some decisions to make now. Last minute, the only option that the dodgy au pair crew has is nannying for a family with triplets, a teen just out of the correction center, and two Rottweilers. I would have doggy daycare duties as well as nannying.

It sounds bloody awful.

Just as I'm about to call Orla again, a number flashes on my phone.

Shit. Teagan.

Do I answer it? I'll be gone by the time she's back.

"Hi, Teagan," I answer with false cheeriness.

"It's Dad's fault, right?" she cries.

I pause. The less I say now, the better. "He decided it wasn't for the best."

"What? Did something happen between you two? No cap! You hear?"

I smile for the first time since I entered Killian's office. Teagan makes me laugh. No cap means *tell me the truth*, apparently. How the hell does Siri understand teenagers?

I can't tell her the truth because I don't know it myself. Killian was distant and ambiguous, so I don't truly understand why he fired me.

I'm looking for a grand explanation that will make me feel better. Maybe he was worried about Teagan. Perhaps he felt responsible for Alfred's behavior or was uncomfortable with our age gap. Anything to make me feel better. But the reality is, he probably just got bored with me or had always planned for this to be a short-term thing.

"I've no idea. He said..." What bullshit did he use?

"We didn't fit. It's probably best if you talk to your dad."

"That is so stupid," she wails, and my heart breaks a little more at the fact that Teagan cares.

"How did you know so quickly?" I ask tentatively. "Did your dad tell you?"

"Yeah." I hear her sigh down the phone. "He called me. He wanted to make sure that he was the first to tell me. I think he felt bad."

"I'm sorry. We can still stay in contact, though."

She hums unhappily. "What are you going to do now?"

Fuck if I know.

"I'll be grand," I tell her because this is the perfect moment to apply the useless word.

***

One Week Later

"Flight BA4703 to Belfast is now boarding at gate 10," the American flight attendant announces over the intercom. "Please have your boarding pass and passport ready."

The waiting area becomes a flurry of activity as people stand and rush to the gate, juggling duty-free bags and luggage.

In front of me, a line forms. The other passengers look relaxed. Normal. Too content to be leaving. The lucky ones are going on holidays.

They don't look like they're leaving their hearts

behind in New York.

On the outside, I'm sitting, staring at nothing, not eating the egg-and-cheese sandwich I'm holding because I haven't had an appetite in a week. A frozen statue in this sea of hurry.

On the inside, I'm drowning in pain. Consumed with so much of it that I've tricked my body into a daze so I don't break down in public.

I leave behind Orla, the Quinns, and all my hopes for a new life here in New York.

And my heart.

Goodbye, New York.

THIRTY-TWO

Clodagh

One Month Later

"They're giving it to rain tomorrow."

I look up at Tommy as he does the final sanding to the chest of drawers he's working on.

I've been helping out at the furniture store in the village for three weeks now. It feels like three years.

"That's the good weather gone now," he says around the pencil clenched in his teeth as his arms move back and forth in a steady motion, sanding the curves. He always has a pencil in his mouth, like a child with a dummy. "The days will be getting shorter and darker. This is probably the last good day we'll get this year."

Bloody hell. It's the beginning of August. I didn't come here to be even more depressed than I already am.

We Irish love to talk about the weather. We take it very seriously.

"Ack, sure, a wee drop of rain won't do us any harm," he says, not looking up at me.

"Aye," I mumble and continue with the varnishing of the cabinet because what else am I supposed to say?

I look out the window at the grayish sky, where a sliver of sunshine peeks between clouds.

Here, I work hard to distract myself. It's difficult when we only get a few orders a day, but if I manually tire myself out, I might sleep at night. My only purpose each day is to exhaust myself to the point of numbness—no longer thinking, no longer feeling.

No longer realizing that I'm stuck in the same place I was four years ago, living with my mam and gran, doing the same old routine day after day. I've had zero inspiration to create new inventory. Even yoga has become an empty ritual, void of any satisfaction.

My only social life is when Mam drags me along to funerals or one of my brothers asks me to collect them from the pub because they're too drunk to drive.

I'm still part of the Queens yoga group chat. Sometimes when I read the messages for a fleeting second, I forget where I am, and I'm teleported back to New York.

Then I remember and feel a sharp stab of pain before the emptiness sets in.

I have no tears left. He drained them all.

Now I'm hollow.

I get up, go to the furniture store, come back, have dinner with Mam and Granny Deirdre, watch TV, and try not to stalk Killian online.

Sometimes I think I should have accepted his offer. After my feelings for Killian fade away, when he's just an entertaining story, I'll kick myself for not taking the green card.

Orla begged me to stay until she was blue in the face, but the only way I could stay was to accept Killian's charity. Those last few days in New York were a blur. Killian and I went from one hundred to zero in twenty-four hours. An emotional roller coaster—one minute, I'm soaring high above the clouds in a fancy helicopter, and the next, I'm plummeting back to earth at breakneck speed.

I went from seeing him every day to never seeing him.

I didn't even tell him I was leaving New York. What was the point? After the fight in the office, he didn't reach out. He didn't care.

Inhaling the familiar scent of sawdust and wood, I take a deep breath and tell myself to get a grip.

This, too, shall pass.

I mean, we were only together for a few weeks, for Christ's sake, and I'm twenty-five. The world is my oyster. Plenty more fish and all that jazz. When I'm Granny Deirdre's age, I'll remember it as a really sexy time in my life, that's all.

My Fifth Avenue fling with a billionaire, something to laugh about in the pub.

This, too, shall pass. Yet no matter how many

times a day I tell myself that, the dark cloud follows me.

The bell at the front of the shop rings to warn us someone is in the shop. Usually, Mam is out the front —yes, I'm working with my mum again—but she's on her break.

"I'll get it," I say to Tommy and stroll up to the front of the shop.

As I approach the woman waiting at the till, my smile is met with a discontented scowl.

"Hi, how can I help you?" I greet her cheerfully. I fucking hate sales. Almost as much as cleaning.

"I've got a problem with the phonebook table I bought from here," she says curtly. "I'll need to return it."

"Oh. What's the problem?"

"It's too big for my hallway! It won't fit!"

I keep my smile steady. That's hardly our bloody fault.

Why does she even need a phonebook table?

Who needs to use a phone book these days? I didn't realize they still made them.

I sigh heavily. "Bring it in."

"Do you not do pickups?"

"No," I say through gritted teeth. "Not for refunds unless something is wrong with it. Is there anything wrong with it?"

"This is very inconvenient." She ignores my question. Her eyes narrow as she waits, expecting me to say something. "McKinney's furniture store has better service. I'll have to take my business there from now on."

Fuck, I need to get out of here.

"You're welcome," I mutter as she struts out of the shop. Moody old bag.

I glance at my watch. 2:00 p.m. It's morning time in New York. I can't look at the time without converting to New York time and thinking about what everyone is doing there. Teagan. Orla.

Killian.

Orla has her civil service examination in a few hours. The first step of her becoming a New York cop. It'll be really slow going because she'll have to have been in the country for a certain period. I'll never sleep if she ends up patrolling the streets of New York.

I give her a call to say good luck.

She answers right away. "Hi!"

"Hey, I wanted to wish you luck with your exam this morning."

"Ugh." I hear her sigh heavily. "I haven't taken an exam since school. And the first part is math. Like who adds up things manually these days?"

I smile, pushing away my own worries for a moment. "You'll be fine. You've done the practice test."

"How are you feeling today?"

"Great," I lie. "I'm pretty decided on London now." I've been talking to Orla about this for a couple of days and she's become worse than Granny Deirdre, sending me articles about the less-than-ideal aspects of life in London. A rat spotted in a restaurant. People renting out rooms the size of cupboards for exorbitant sums. Not helpful.

Orla hums thoughtfully in response. "I don't want you to give up on New York. It's not the same here without you."

I close my eyes and take a breath before responding. "I miss you, too. I'll start saving and come for a visit in a few months, I promise."

"Christmas in New York?"

I was so looking forward to my first Christmas in New York. Ice-skating at the Rockefeller. Mulled wine in Central Park. "I'll check how much flights are."

"By the way, we had a visitor at The Auld Dog last night."

"Oh yeah?"

She pauses. "I wasn't sure if I should tell you because it seems like you're getting over him."

My heart races. I clutch the phone tighter.

"Connor Quinn."

"Connor, Killian's brother?"

"Yeah."

"What did he want?"

"I'm not sure. He said he was in the area." She pauses. "He was asking about you."

"What exactly did he ask?" I ask, hysteria creeping into my voice.

"It was vague. He recognized me and said hi. He wanted to know where you were living now and how you were doing. I told him you were thinking of moving to London. Honestly, it seemed like small talk. Sorry, Clodagh."

I want to scream down the phone at Orla that she needs to tell me every single minute detail about their exchange. What did he say? What mood was he in? What was his tone like?

Why? Why was he there?

"Careful," I joke instead. "They probably have their ear on bulldozing the pub to put a casino there."

She laughs. "Over Uncle Sean's dead body."

We both fall silent. The thought of Connor being in the pub makes me sad.

"Did he mention Killian?"

"No. He said that Teagan's upset that you're gone, though."

I smile. Teagan and I have been exchanging emails, although I try not to bring Killian up. She sometimes talks about him—like how he doesn't let her do something or how he's in a bad mood. Superficial stuff. I couldn't handle anything deeper.

I'm sure we'll lose contact sooner or later now that nothing holds us together anymore.

"I gotta go, Orla," I say as Mam walks into the shop. "Good luck. You'll do brilliantly."

I hang up the phone.

"We have a funeral to go to," Mam cheerfully informs me as she sets her handbag down on the counter. "Your neighbor's dead. Passed away in his sleep last night. Ninety."

"Oh wonderful," I reply sarcastically. "I can't wait. I don't even know the man well; why do I have to go?"

"He's your neighbor." She scowls at me. "Besides, his nephew will be there. The good-looking one with the limp. He's single, you know."

Oh, for God's sake.

So now my mum is trying to play matchmaker for me at a dead guy's goodbye party.

Her scowl deepens. "Although he won't be interested in you with that ridiculous hoop through your nose."

Fuck my life.

THIRTY-THREE

Killian

Clodagh's right about the subway; sometimes, it is superior to an air-conditioned SUV.

Since we've been at a standstill on the Brooklyn Bridge for twenty minutes, I'm tempted to jump out and walk the rest of the way.

I used to love coming to Brooklyn when I was a kid. Mom would take us to Coney Island Beach, only fifteen miles away from our home in Queens, but that would be our summer vacation. I hadn't been outside the *state* when I was Teagan's age. Teagan has traveled all over the world.

It's always a fear of mine. When you bring your kids into wealth, and I mean *extreme wealth*, are you really giving them a better life? Teagan has never had to hope or wish for anything, even if I impose limits on her pocket money.

But where is her passion and desire to accomplish her ambitions if nothing ever presents an obstacle? Am I raising her to expect everything to come easy?

"Traffic is clearing now, boss," my driver says with

a hint of relief.

I let out a quiet hum in response and lean back in my seat.

Good. I've had too much time to think on this journey.

My gaze dips to the image on my phone. Teagan would be shocked if she knew how much time I spend scrolling on social media; no doubt I'd be accused of double standards.

Except I'm not here for likes, connections, or any other way others get their dopamine hit. All I feel is pain. Every post is a stab in the heart, a reminder of what I've lost.

Because I spend my time staring at pictures of a red-haired Irish vixen with gorgeous green eyes. My fear intensifies with each swipe that the next will show she's moved on, that I'm nothing to her now.

I've gone through a lot of things in my lifetime; Harlow's death being the worst. Years of having a deadbeat father, threats on my life, a stalker, and almost having my business go under in the beginning years.

Not having Clodagh in my life is right up there, too.

But at least I know she's safe, far across the Atlantic Ocean, away from me.

It's been weeks since she last posted anything on social media. I mainly look at pictures of her in New York, taken when she was living with me, trying to convince myself she's still close. It's torture.

I lie awake in the middle of the night as waves of

unease hit me like a storm surge. She's so fucking far away from me now.

But the distance between us keeps her safe.

The bridge behind us, we finally arrive at the casino site after a half-hour drive.

Connor and I have always been hands-on, which is why I'm about to don a hard hat and talk to the foreman and workers of the construction company. Phase 1—the demolition of the old motel—should be complete next week. I want to meet the team to look into the whites of their eyes and know they're telling me the truth.

My driver pulls to a stop, and I get out and am immediately hit with a cacophony of construction sounds.

The cranes, diggers, and half a demolished hotel make the building site an eyesore. But in six months, the Brooklyn skyline will contain a new addition: a sleek hotel and casino that blends aesthetically with its surroundings. I haven't been out here in a few months now.

I wonder if this is where Clodagh wanted to live in Brooklyn. I wonder if it's near the restaurant she went to for her birthday. I'm always fucking wondering.

I look around. Clodagh would like the area. It's an eclectic mix of office blocks, Brooklyn brownstones, cafes, and restaurants.

Something, call it insanity because I'm on a path of self-destruction, has me wandering over to the cafe next to the site. The sign tells me it's been serving traditional Polish cuisine for over fifty years. I barely noticed it on my previous trips here.

My gaze drifts to the window.

Inside, only two tables are occupied. A young couple laughs at one table as the girl feeds the guy. Her long red hair falls into the soup, and she grimaces.

On the tables, old green glass bottles are being used to hold candles, their sides glistening with melting wax. I wonder if the green of the glass is the same shade as Clodagh's eyes.

My chest tightens. Everywhere, there are reminders of her, or maybe I'm actively seeking them out. Clodagh believes all that hokey-pokey shit like astrology. She would probably say this is a sign.

"Do you want to come in, Killian?" comes a voice behind me.

I turn to see pale-blue eyes decorated with wrinkles staring at me.

"I tried calling, but your receptionist wouldn't let me through," Marek Sr. says sadly. "I wanted to say sorry."

"It's ironic that you're apologizing to me," I reply.

"It's necessary. I'm doing it on behalf of my son. I want you to know he wouldn't have done anything serious." He pauses, looking broken, and I feel sorry for the man because I'm a parent too. "He's a decent kid at heart; he just has a short temper. Hopefully, the police caution will make him wise up a bit."

"It's fine," I say curtly, because the man isn't responsible for his son's actions. Just like I wasn't responsible for my father's.

"I'd like to say that I raised him better than that," he says with a heaviness in his voice. "I tried to show him the right way. If you don't set a good example for your kids, what else matters?" He looks at the restaurant. "None of this stuff."

I follow his gaze, seeing my reflection in the glass window. Am I setting a good example for my daughter?

The redhead waves through the window to Marek. He nods in acknowledgment. "She's been coming here since she was a baby with her mom. I'm glad she's with a decent guy."

They look like they're in love. The guy clearly worships her.

I turn to Marek. "This plot of land has been in conflict for a few years now. What were the local folks hoping to get built here?"

"A sports center for the kids and a community center. There's nowhere for them to play sports around here cheaply. Everything costs an arm and a leg these days, huh?"

I'm silent.

"I've made peace with what's happening. Seeing my son fail to control his anger was an awakening of sorts. Perhaps he isn't ready to take over after all." He pauses. "Can we call a truce, Killian?"

I nod. "A truce sounds like a plan."

"Now, will you do me the honor of showing you some authentic Polish cuisine?"

I look over at the site. I'm due to meet the foremen

soon. "Sure. I have twenty minutes."

I watch people come and go as I eat a delicious stew that I can't remember the name of. Who'd have thought shredded cabbage could be so good.

There's a connection with the people who come into the restaurant. Marek knows everyone who walks in, or they know each other.

I fold up my napkin and leave the cash on the table while he's busy entertaining another customer.

He glances at me, his eyes warm and kind, and I put my hand up in thanks.

"Goodbye, Alfred. You'll get your community center."

My words go unheard as I leave. It's for the best since I don't want to see his reaction. Best not to mix emotions with business.

***

"I had a feeling I'd find you here," Connor says.

I glance up at him strolling toward the grave. I knew he was here; I saw him park his car in the chapel lot.

"Do you think she'll ever forgive me?" I ask him.

"Harlow? She'd have never placed the blame on you, Killian. The guy was breaking into houses for years. There's nothing to forgive." He sighs. "But I'm wasting my breath telling you this again."

"Are you here to lecture me about the casino?" I ask in a hollow voice, staring at Harlow's headstone.

"No, that's JP's job, not mine. I'm here because

you look like you live in a cave. You haven't shaved in weeks, and the last time you looked like this was after Harlow died."

"My looks aren't the priority right now."

We remain silent for a moment, pretending to pray because Mom drilled into us that's what you do at a grave.

Connor interrupts the quiet. "I was at The Auld Dog last night, the pub Clodagh worked in."

"What for?"

"Just stopping by." *Bullshit.* "She's moving to London. Starting a whole new life there."

I stay silent, letting his words sink in.

I imagine Clodagh in London creating a new bucket list. Meeting new friends. Meeting new guys.

I'm not sure why the news doesn't sit right with me. Whether she's in Ireland or England makes no difference. I have no claim to her and can't stop her from moving on with her life.

The main thing is that she's happy and safe.

"I figured she'd stay in Ireland," I finally say.

"Clodagh isn't going to live in a bubble for the rest of her life. You know crime rates are higher in London than New York?" Connor says, his voice floating through the silent graveyard. "Most likely, she'll be living in a rough area since rent in London is pricey, and she's in her twenties and doesn't have tons of money. She'll go out, have fun, and the chances are, go home alone on the buses or the subway, perhaps after having a few too many drinks."

"Why the fuck are you telling me all of this?"

"Because I'm trying to figure out what it's going to take for you to get over your issues. Because if you continue to live like this, keeping love at arm's length, what example are you setting for your daughter? Trust no one? Love no one?"

I snort. "That's very poetic for you, Connor."

"Exactly. That's how desperate I am, after weeks, to get through to you. Now, answer the question. What's it gonna take for you to get over your issues?"

His question hangs in the air.

My gaze rests on Harlow's grave, a reminder that I'm doing the right thing. "She's safer away from me."

"Doubtful, based on the spiel I just said. From what Sam and the team told me, she scraped her knee and bruised her wrist. She's an Irish woman; she's tougher than that. Let her decide what's safe for her."

He hands me two pieces of paper, a smile playing on his lips.

"What's this?" I ask.

"Two plane tickets to Dublin. There's a helicopter ready to take you from Dublin to Donegal."

I scan them in disbelief. "Two?"

He smiles. "Teagan said she'll be your wingwoman."

THIRTY-FOUR

Clodagh

Turns out, annoyingly, that Tommy was right. The day Orla had her exam was the last good day of summer.

It's been pissing down ever since. The longest stretch of consecutive rain we've had in five years, and everyone is droning on about it.

And people wonder why thousands of Irish flock to Australia and America every year.

Still, the shite weather has given me the drive I need to focus on my new online small-business course. I managed to blag a sweet discount. It's perfect for folks like me who want to start their own business but lack the knowledge and confidence.

A florist and a plumber are also doing it, and they are just as confused as me on some of the admin stuff. Not gonna lie, it's tough. I thought I'd enjoy the marketing side, but I struggle with it, and don't get me started on tax shit.

One day, I'm determined to give it another shot, but this time, I'm taking it slow so I can really understand each part of running a business.

And today is my last day working at the furniture store. Tomorrow, I fly to London. I've decided to give it a shot. My cousin Michelle lives over there, and I can stay with her until I get a job, and I'll continue my course remotely.

New York seems like a lifetime ago now.

"Clodagh, take this out the front, will you?" Tommy asks me, handing me the finished stool.

"Sure thing." I grab it from him and saunter out of the workshop to the shop.

Mam is pressed against the window, peering out with two women from the village.

"What are you three doing?"

Outside, there's a high-pitched whirring sound. The sound is low, but it's getting significantly louder.

"There's a helicopter. It looks like it's about to land on top of the school. Will it be able to land in the rain?"

"So? It's not like we don't get helicopters occasionally." I roll my eyes and come toward the window. You'd think it was aliens.

A black helicopter hovers. It disappears over the top of the shop.

"Show's over," I say.

Five minutes later, there's shouting outside.

Mam and her friends, who have been chattering for the last hour, run to the window. Out of sheer boredom, I follow.

The street is full of people. There would be nothing unusual about that if this were New York.

But for a Tuesday afternoon in my sleepy village, this is a rare phenomenon. And it's drizzling outside.

"Some gobshite just landed a fucking helicopter," a man in wellies who looks severely pissed off shouts to another guy. "The animals are going nuts."

More people gather. At the far end of the street, I see the helicopter right in the middle of the green. The propellers slow to a halt.

"Who is it?" I ask no one in particular. A trickle of fear runs through me.

And hope.

Killian?

Of course it's not Killian, I huff to myself. Stop dreaming. Hope is a dangerous emotion. Why would he be here? It's morning in New York, and Killian is having breakfast made by his new nanny maid. Or worse, but I can't bear to think about it.

"Is it the army?" someone asks behind me.

My pulse quickens as the propellers come to a complete standstill. The side door cracks open, and a tall figure wearing aviators steps out.

My heart jumps into my fucking throat. My pulse goes from resting to racing in a nanosecond.

He's too far away to see his face clearly, but it's him. I know it's him. Even if he were a hundred miles away, I'd know it was him.

The other side opens, and Teagan steps out, wrapping her coat around her.

"Who the hell is that?" one of Mam's friends asks. Her voice sounds like she's far away, but she's standing beside me.

Boom. Boom. Boom.

My heartbeat is in my ears, like a drumstick bashing against my brain. That's all I can hear.

Mam shrugs. "The president?"

"Don't be silly. It has to be Michael Tierney, the owner of the golf resort."

I watch as Killian stretches his legs outside the helicopter and talks to the pilot. It's like watching a movie. This can't be real. A few people approach him, and he says something to them.

My heart is hammering so badly that I'm going to have a heart attack. What are they doing here?

The guy with Killian points down the street. This way... he's pointing this way.

Oh my fucking God.

This is the part of the movie when someone screams, *run*!

I quickly glance at my dungarees and apron covered in dust and varnish. I imagined this moment so many times in my head. Longed for it. *Prayed* for it.

But now that it's happening, I want to vanish.

He hasn't spotted me yet; I'm hidden behind two farmers. His expression gives nothing away. Not from this far away, anyway.

Teagan pops her gum as they walk down the street and points excitedly to the arts and crafts store.

Any minute now, Killian will see me.

I can't do this; I can't face him in my hometown. I want to flee down the street or hide somewhere.

In fact…

I scuttle over to the side and take cover behind a row of garbage cans next to the furniture store. I'm not good at thinking on my feet when I have to make a fast decision, so this is the best I've got.

"Clodagh?" Mam bleats from the street. "What are you doing?"

"Shush, woman!" I hiss, hunkering down. I just need to wait a few minutes, and they'll pass. "Don't say my name."

"Is she going to the toilet?" her friend asks really, really loudly.

Be quiet, women. I think I *am* going to wet myself.

Mam shakes her head at me and then turns back to her friend. "She's been acting weird since she returned from New York. I don't know what's going on with her."

I squeeze my eyes shut and attempt to slow my racing heartbeat.

A loud voice booms, "Clodagh, what are you doing down there?"

I open my eyes to see Tommy pushing away the bins to reveal me cowering in the corner.

My heart sinks. The bin plan was a big mistake. *Huge.*

When will I see some of this fucking luck of the Irish? It's not even collection day. What's he playing at? Now I'm just squatting down on the ground with my arms hugging my knees like an idiot.

"Clodagh?"

"Killian?" I squawk from my position on the

ground, perched like a weird bird. I don't know why I asked it as a question; maybe because he did.

I stare up at him, frozen in confusion. It's been so long since I heard that low drawl in real life. I had watched interviews with him online as a form of torture a few times. But now the sound of his actual voice knocks the wind out of me.

He extends his hand to pull me up. It takes a minute for my brain to process how to stand. I hope I don't smell like the bins.

He smiles softly. Something that looks like nerves flashes across his face. "If I didn't know better, I'd almost think you were hiding from me."

Teagan rushes toward me and envelops me in a hug. The gesture is a much-needed break from the intensity of seeing Killian.

"Hey, Clodagh!"

"Hey! What a nice surprise. I've missed you," I say into her hair and mean it. If you had asked me on our first day of meeting if I expected to be doing this, I would have laughed in disbelief.

I pull away from Teagan and look between the two of them, my chest tight with confusion and tension. Why didn't she tell me she was coming here?

Killian clears his throat uncomfortably and looks at Teagan. "Sweetheart, can you give us a moment? Then you can talk to Clodagh. Stay close."

She pops a large bubble with her chewing gum. "I'll be over at the crafts store. But hurry up, Dad."

I glare at Mam and her entourage. "Mam, can you

also leave us?"

Her eyes are nearly hanging out of her head. "Aren't you going to introduce me?"

I'm perturbed to observe that she casts Killian a gaze of mild arousal.

"Nope," I say, motioning for him to follow me down the street away from them.

Once we're out of earshot, I turn to him. "Are you here on holiday?"

His lips curl into a soft smile as he holds my gaze for a few seconds. "Of sorts."

I nod, working hard not to let my frozen smile slip. I don't know how to react.

I'm standing at the edge of a cliff. One misstep and I'll become completely undone, pounding my fists on the ground and howling like a madwoman.

"That's nice," I force out, my voice barely creaking past the lump in my throat. "You should drive along the Wild Atlantic Way. It's great to see the sights. Or see it by helicopter. However you're getting around."

He drags his hand through his hair, now darkened from the rain. "I'm going to cut to the chase."

Heart pounding, I stand still and stare at him. "Go ahead."

"I made a mistake. A huge mistake." He looks down at me with those same icy-blue eyes that have haunted my dreams since I left New York. "One I've regretted ever since." Up close, under his eyes looks dark from lack of sleep. "I should never have ended things between us."

"Are you telling me this while swinging by on

your way to the coast or something?" I ask, my voice wavering.

"No. I came here to do this. I came here for you —us. That's why I'm in Ireland." He glances over at Teagan, who appears to have broken a vase. "*Shit.* That's why we're both here."

That's why he's in Ireland?

He steps closer until he's a breath away from me. I never thought I'd see him again now he's here, standing in front of me. His scent hits me, and I want to reach out and take what I want. "I miss you, Clodagh. The house feels so empty without you. My life feels so empty without you. *I* feel empty. I'm asking you to give me another chance." His breath hitches as he pauses. "To forgive me."

I clench my jaw to keep back the tears threatening to escape. *You broke my fucking heart, asshole.* "You were the one who ended us. You don't get to decide when you want to waltz back into my life."

His face falls. He looks flustered. This is a first.

The urge to rush into his waiting arms and melt against his body overwhelms me. But then I remember the expression on his face that day in the office. Cold and detached.

No. My heart won't survive any more breakage.

"What happens when you change your mind again and decide you don't want to fuck the nanny?"

He winces. "It wasn't like that. I thought I was ending it for your own good."

"My own good?" I ask in disbelief.

"Alfred Marek attacked you because of me. You're

safer without me around."

I snort in disbelief. "It was hardly an attack, Killian."

"It could have been worse."

I almost laugh. "Everything could be worse! I fell in a gravel pit when I was ten and broke my leg. It could have been worse then too. The other day, I left my straightener on in Mam's house. That could have been way worse," I say, throwing my hands up in frustration. "You could torment yourself thinking that way about everything."

"I know. I have my own demons that I'm trying to conquer. I'm seeing a therapist. I don't want to make the same mistakes I made in the past."

"What's changed? Why the change of heart?"

"I realized it has to be your decision whether you think we're worth the risk." He gives a sad smile. "And honestly, I'm selfish. I don't want to let you go."

"You hurt me," I whisper.

"I'm sorry." He tries to draw me closer, but I pull out of his reach.

"No." I shake my head. I can't do this again. "It's too late now."

He stares at me, his face clouded in anguish.

"Bullshit. It's not too late. We're both alive."

It's a bit gloomy, but I can't argue with that.

"I'm getting a flight to London tomorrow. I want to start over there."

All the color drains from his face. "Do you want to be with me?"

Yes.

I don't respond.

"I'm in love with you, Clodagh. I'm so in love with you."

I reel at his words, my heart skipping a beat. A spark of hope ignites in my chest, a fleeting feeling that threatens to overwhelm me if I allow it. My mind screams in warning not to trust him again. My heart and head are in a deadly battle, each vying for control over my fragile emotions.

I love you too, Killian Quinn.

"Why me?"

"I've asked myself that question many times."

"Gee, thanks," I say sarcastically.

"At times, you drive me up the wall. You really know how to push my buttons. You have no filter, and you do some outrageous things, and it drives my OCD insane."

I narrow my eyes at him.

"But you're also a beautiful, warm, intelligent woman who makes me laugh. No matter what I'm doing, I can't help but imagine it would be more fun with you. Whether it's sitting on the couch watching a movie or flying over Manhattan in a helicopter. You're always at the back of my mind. I haven't felt this way in so long, and I won't let it go."

A tiny squeak escapes me.

"Clodagh." He takes my hand, and this time, I let him. I haven't felt his touch in so long. "When we first met, you said you thought you were a good role model. Well, you're right. You are the best influence my daughter could have."

Another squeak. My knees are about to give out. I won't remind him that our first meeting was actually with me on my knees with soaps and glass.

Stay strong, woman.

"I don't know if I can trust you again," I finally say.

He nods as if accepting this. As if he expected this. "I can work at winning back your trust. Answer my question. Do you want to be with me?"

Yes.

I want to say yes. I want to shout it.

Fear keeps my mouth shut. I can't say the words.

"Do you want to go to London? Is that truly what you want?"

"Yes," I say. No. Maybe. I don't know. My throat is tight and full of fear. I don't want to open my heart to him only for him to crush it again as he did before.

Fresh tears brim in my eyes. "I have to go, Killian."

He looks so sad as he says, "Your green card to the States has been processed. You can live and work where you want. Look, I'll give you space but don't let this be why you don't come back home."

Home.

Where is home for me now?

I turn away.

"This isn't goodbye, Clodagh. This isn't the end of us. I'll wait."

***

I gaze at the flight information in a daze. The screen changes, and a gate number for my flight appears.

"British Airways flight BA4703 to London is now taking off at gate 16."

"Are you okay, love?" the woman beside me asks, watching me in concern.

"Yeah." I manage a nod and make my way to the departure gate.

THIRTY-FIVE

Clodagh

Two Weeks Later

I tilt my head back toward the sun and close my eyes as the ladies chitchat and set up their mats. It's a gorgeous Saturday morning, and I'm exactly where I should be—teaching yoga for free in the park in Queens.

I can't help but smile.

A new start.

Tomorrow, Orla and I move into our very own apartment in Brooklyn—the dodgy end. Sure, we have no lounge area because it's been converted into a second bedroom. That's the only way we can afford it, but it's still all ours.

A throat clears, a deep voice cutting my daydream.

I snap my eyes to see Killian standing in front of me. My heart practically stops as I take in his handsomeness. A shiver of excitement runs up my spine as our eyes lock. I haven't seen him since that day in Ireland.

"Is there room for one more?"

"How did you know I was back?" I mumble.

He smiles. "I knew the second you landed. I told you I would give you your space. I'm playing the long game. It's the only way I'll win your trust."

I stayed in London for five days before spending a shit ton of money on a last-minute flight to New York. As I stood atop the Shard, the tallest building in Europe, I had a realization. An epiphany.

Sure, you can exchange one exciting city for another; you can surround yourself with cool tourist attractions, never-ending nightlife, appealing job prospects, quirky restaurants...

But you can't take your heart with you. While looking out at the Tower of London, I realized my heart was still in New York. No pretty view could make up for not being near that brownstone, its grumpy owner, or his daughter. Or Orla, of course. I bawled loudly on the viewing deck, and my cousin was very embarrassed.

"Are we starting, Clodagh?" Dominic, one of the footballers, grumbles from his mat.

My cheeks flush as I look around at the guys on their mats, waiting patiently. The women are watching me like a hawk, winking and grinning. One of them has the audacity to wolf-whistle.

I grit my teeth at her in warning.

"Well?" His brow rises expectantly. "Can I join in?"

My pulse soars. "Sure."

His eyes flicker with emotion. "Good. I'd like to buy a block of ten classes. I'll be back every week."

***

Three Weeks Later

We settle onto barstools as the bartender makes our Manhattans. We're celebrating Orla getting to the next set of exams to enter the police force.

I haven't been back to Killian's hotel bar since #soapgate. The first time I clapped eyes on the grumpy billionaire owner. Memories of that day come flooding back. I felt so desperate. Nothing was in my control.

Now I'm in a happier place.

The jazz band plays softly in the corner, creating a quiet backdrop for conversation. I smile thinking about the difference when the band in The Auld Dog plays; you get a sore throat shouting over them.

"What are you smiling about?" Orla asks as the drinks appear in front of us.

"I'm just glad to feel settled finally," I say. I'm starting a new job at a furniture store in Brooklyn.

The pay isn't amazing; in fact, I might have to start a bed-share arrangement to save cash, but it's a start. I'll be back doing a job I love.

"Here's to my best friend Orla getting to the next set of exams to enter the police force," I say, clinking my glass against hers.

Orla's eyes shine with delight.

"So after your exam next Wednesday, what's the next stage?" I ask. "And I still can't believe you're going to become a cop. It sounds better in our accent too."

"Hmm." Orla peeks over my shoulder, then returns her gaze to me. Her expression shifts to guilt.

My heart rate jumps, and I already know, *I just know*, who she's gawking at.

I turn.

He's here.

Alone.

The energy in the room shifts, the same way it felt that first day I set eyes on him.

Heads turn and conversations stop as every eye in the room follows him. Everyone knows who he is. It's like the president has just arrived. He's in a three-piece black suit so sexy he should be auditioning for the next Bond movie.

I clench my glass harder as I face Orla again. "Is this a coincidence, or did you plan this?"

She bites her lip. "Guilty. Anyway, why are you so jittery? The man has been chasing you for weeks now."

"I don't know. I can't help it." Killian gives me belly flips every time I see him. When he winked at me during Saturday's yoga class doing the plow pose, I was so jittery I nearly queefed.

I've seen him a few times lately, but never just the two of us. He's been coming to yoga, and he brings

Teagan with him. The leprechauns seemed to be in control of him again. When I panicked at yoga and said the delivery company let me down at the last minute, he took a day off work to drive to Jersey to pick up materials for me. *Himself.* He drove, *himself.*

"It's time you took him back. You've made him sweat long enough."

"Why?"

"Because if you take him back, I'll get the apartment to myself a few nights a week."

"Gee, thanks," I say sarcastically.

She smiles. "You're welcome. Now, put him out of his misery already. He hates yoga. The scowl on his face after he face-planted during downward-facing dog on Saturday said everything."

I laugh shakily. "You're right; he does hate it. He grunts too much. No one should grunt during yoga."

My body tingles, and I can feel him standing behind me.

"Hey," a low voice murmurs close to my ear.

I swivel on my barstool and find myself staring into an intense pair of blue eyes. The bar and everyone in it fades into nothing. "Hey," I breathe.

"Is this seat taken?"

"You can have mine," Orla chimes in, winking at Killian. Before I can respond, she leaps off the seat.

He smiles at her. "Thanks, Orla."

"I won't wait up," she whispers into my ear before blowing us both a kiss goodbye.

Killian takes a seat on the stool, his eyes sweeping over me from toe to head.

I try not to react even though my heart pounds a million beats a second. "What are you doing here, Killian?" I keep my eyes glued to my drink as I slowly stir it.

"Look at me."

When I look up, he's staring at me. "Please give me the chance to make you happy, to prove myself. Let me love you and show you that I want the best for you." He slips his hands onto both sides of my jawline and draws me closer. "What do I need to do to prove it to you? Do you need me to get on my knees?"

His smirk is so cocky, it pisses me off. "Yes, actually," I deadpan. "That would be a start."

"Okay."

Stunned, I watch as he lowers himself to his knees in front of me. Killian Quinn is literally kneeling before me. If people were staring before, their eyes have fallen out of their heads now.

He looks up at me expectantly, not seeming to care that everyone is watching him. The man has no shame.

"Alright then," I whisper with a giggle, pulling him up to standing height again. "Let's do this on one condition."

"Anything."

I smile. "We burn that manual."

He responds by pulling me in for a kiss so passionate that the entire world around us fades away, and it's just the two of us.

***

Killian

One Week Later

"I love you, Clodagh Kelly, my little thief. My little *heart* thief."

I press my thumb against her clit, with just enough pressure to make her moan, as my other hand caresses her hip.

Her emerald eyes become a little glassy. "Ahhhh. Sir," she says with a breathy laugh. "I'm... I think I'm close."

Her breathing quickens, and her movements become more erratic as she rides my cock. She clenches around me, the climax shattering through her.

"It's mine," I say in a low voice, feeling insanely territorial. Her orgasm will always be mine. "No other guy was meant to have it."

I groan as I come too, hard and fast. I hold her hips tight, ensuring she gets every last drop of me.

She sputters out a laugh before collapsing onto me, her legs still straddling my body. This is the first time she's come while we were having sex. If I were to die now, I'd die a happy man.

I grin up at her as her hands glide over my chest.

"Thank you, Mr. Quinn," she purrs.

"If you really want to thank me, move back in with me," I blurt out.

Shit.

Of course I want it, but I don't want to scare her away so soon. "I'm thirty-six. I'm through playing games. I want you with me."

Her eyes go wide, then she smirks. "Are you trying to get me to clean your bathroom again?"

"Fuck no." I chuckle, trailing my hand down her bare stomach. "You were terrible at it the first time. Mrs. Dalton does a much better job."

Shame she's retiring, though. She's moving to Boston to be with her daughter. From here on out, it's just me and Teagan... and the cleaners from my seven-star hotel.

I gaze into those mesmerizing green eyes of hers and breathe in deeply. "I want you to move in because I love you."

"Okay." She nods, then shakes her head contradictorily. "That's a good reason, but no."

"No?" I jostle her hips. What the hell?

"I love you too, Killian, and I want us to be together forever, but I want to live in Brooklyn with Orla first. Life in New York isn't a *fairy tale*, remember?" She smirks. "In a few years, I'll move in."

"I guess I'll just have to wait." I sigh with a smile on my face. "You're the boss."

EPILOGUE

Clodagh

One Year Later

"Come on, Teagan!" I yell into the wind as she sprints toward the goal. "Killian, are you watching?"

Killian stands beside me, his hands over his eyes and an expression of pure agony. He's such a scaredy-cat sometimes.

I don't know what he's worried about. Since Teagan started playing for the Queens Gaels ladies' team, she's taken no prisoners.

People say Gaelic football is between Aussie Rules and English football. Teagan plays in a full-forward position, which means she's the attacking player going for goals, and she is a *machine*. She quit ballet a few months back, deciding Gaelic football was more her thing.

Killian takes a deep breath. "It got a bit rough out there. I wanted to run onto the pitch and drag her off."

I roll my eyes playfully. "I don't know what you're worried about; the opposing team is terrified of her."

Teagan and I still haven't broached the topic of her having a boyfriend on the guys' team, but I don't think Killian is ready for that yet.

"Five minutes until penalties," I say, wrapping my arms around his waist. "Then you can relax."

He nods. "How about a drink at Marek's restaurant afterward to calm my nerves?"

I smile. It's the first time Teagan's team is playing at the new Brooklyn community center that Killian built.

"That sounds great. Although I'm not staying out too late. I have to get up early in the morning."

"Your boss must be a real tyrant," he teases.

"Nah, not a five o'clock kind of tyrant." I'm now my own boss and have been pushing myself out of bed at six o'clock every morning.

I'm renting a tiny studio from Uncle Sean's friend Paddy, who I think might be in the Irish mob, but he offered me a good deal on the place. It's so small that you couldn't swing a cat in it, but it's only twenty minutes by bike from Orla's and my apartment in Brooklyn. I wish I'd never told Granny Deirdre, who messages me daily about cyclists killed in the city.

The orders have been steady lately, and I recently got a more significant order from a chain of furniture stores. I finished my online business course. There were even a few tears with some of the modules, but I did it. I didn't get any special recognition—no graduation hat or fancy certificate

—but I feel better equipped to take baby steps in the business world. Now I'm like Scrooge, tracking every penny and monitoring where it goes.

Killian is mentoring me with the business side of things, and even Teagan is helping out for a few hours on Saturday. However, Killian insists on making her work for minimum wage so she can learn the value of money. To make up for it, I take her out for burgers afterward.

"Why don't we just have one beer and then get some takeout from L'Oignon du Monde?" Killian suggests.

"That sounds like a great plan," I reply with a smile.

What a perfect night. A low-key local bar followed by a fancy romantic Central Park dinner.

My gaze flickers up to Killian, who presses his lips against my forehead. We've been going from strength to strength, albeit with a few arguments, because when opposites attract, what else do you expect?

I still think he's grumpy, and he thinks I'm a "live wire." Sounds like old-man talk to me.

Right now, we have a great balance. I stay over at the Fifth Avenue townhouse three nights a week, which means Orla can have her hedge fund guy over (he grew on her). He was nice enough to explain the concept of hedge funds to me; it sounds like an incredibly dull job.

I wave to Liam, who is a few rows down. He has a baby now with Sheila. He moved on quickly, and I'm happy for him.

Teagan has the ball again and takes off toward the goal, dodging defenders left and right. She's on fire today.

"Gooooaaal!" I scream as Teagan sends the ball sailing into the net.

Another Year Later

"I have one thing on my bucket list that I want to fulfill," Killian tells me as we stroll hand in hand through Central Park.

I glance at him skeptically. "You don't have a bucket list."

"I do now."

In two days, Killian, Teagan, and I fly to Ireland to travel the Wild Atlantic Way. We'll end up in Donegal. I've been working crazy hours to get the stock orders out so I can relax on my trip.

He pulls me closer, and I glide my hands over his chest. Unfortunately it's covered in a hoodie. I love the way he feels. I could spend all night exploring his body with my fingertips. It's my favorite pastime.

I think back to our conversations this past week about what we'll do in Ireland. "I'm not kissing the Blarney Stone. I'll watch you do it, but don't make me do it. I heard a rumor that people pee over it."

He chuckles. "My item is more substantial than kissing the Blarney Stone."

He pauses, then lowers himself to one knee, right in the middle of Central Park.

My jaw drops with him.

My eyes go wide, and my heart starts pounding. "What are you... are you...?"

He smiles up at me. Those eyes of his still have the power to send delicious shivers through me. "I wanted to do this now so we can tell your mum and gran back in Ireland. If you say yes, that is."

Holy fucking potatoes. He's got a ring. A mix of excitement and nerves rush through my veins.

I glance around, flustered. A few people seem vaguely interested, but this is New York, so no one seems too shocked by Killian's grand gesture.

"Clodagh, Kelly. Is tú mo grá."

I love you, in Irish. I silently pray he doesn't try to say more because I haven't spoken it since school and only remember the rude words now.

"You and Teagan are my whole world. You own my heart. All I want is to spend the rest of my days with you both and give Teagan lots of siblings. It doesn't matter where we end up as long as we're together."

"Yes, I will marry you!" I practically scream, throwing my arms around his neck and squeezing him tightly. "Oh, Clodagh Quinn, that sounds lovely!"

He laughs below me as he says, "You didn't let me ask my question yet. Will you marry me?"

"Yes!" I yell, resisting the urge to whoop.

Looks like I got my slice of the Big Apple. *And* I got seven-star orgasms.

THE END

ACKNOWLEDGEMENT

A great big shout out to Adi – thank you so much. You've been such an amazing supporter and a sounding board for my ideas. This book really wouldn't be the same without your help. This book is dedicated to you.

Thank you to the lovely TL Swan, who has written so many funny, engaging books and been a fantastic mentor to independent authors. Your generosity in sharing your knowledge and experience is a testament to your character. I can't thank you enough for the hours of laughter your books have given me, and for the way you encourage other authors in their own journeys.

To my beta readers, Adi, Caroline, Sara, Britt and Suzie, thank you for your constructive feedback that made Clodagh and Killian's story so much better.

Thank you to Heather, my content editor. Clodagh and Killian's story is so much stronger because of you.

Thank you to Cate Hogan for your invaluable

feedback and to Stacey and Kari, my talented cover designers, for creating such beautiful covers.

Thanks to Jenny for your thorough copy editing and flexibility and Britt and Sarah for your fabulous meticulous proofreads.

And last but not least, I owe a huge thank you to my readers. Your support means the world to me and it keeps me motivated to write more stories. Thanks for joining me on this journey!

Rosa x

ABOUT ROSA

I'm Rosa, a contemporary romance author based in the UK. My stories revolve around strong and sassy heroines, who are paired with alpha heroes, creating a blend of steamy and humorous moments.

My characters are far from perfect; they have genuine flaws and insecurities that make them relatable and human.

I love incorporating certain tropes into my work, such as billionaire alphas, age gap romances, workplace romances, enemies-to-lovers, and grumpy sunshine characters.

Join my newsletter for updates and bonus content at www.rosalucasauthor.com

ALSO BY ROSA

Have you met the grumpy London misters yet? Each one in the series is a standalone, dual-point-of-view romantic comedy with heat, banter and a happy ending.

The London Mister Series

Taming Mr. Walker

Resisting Mr. Kane

Fighting Mr. Knight

63980875R00245